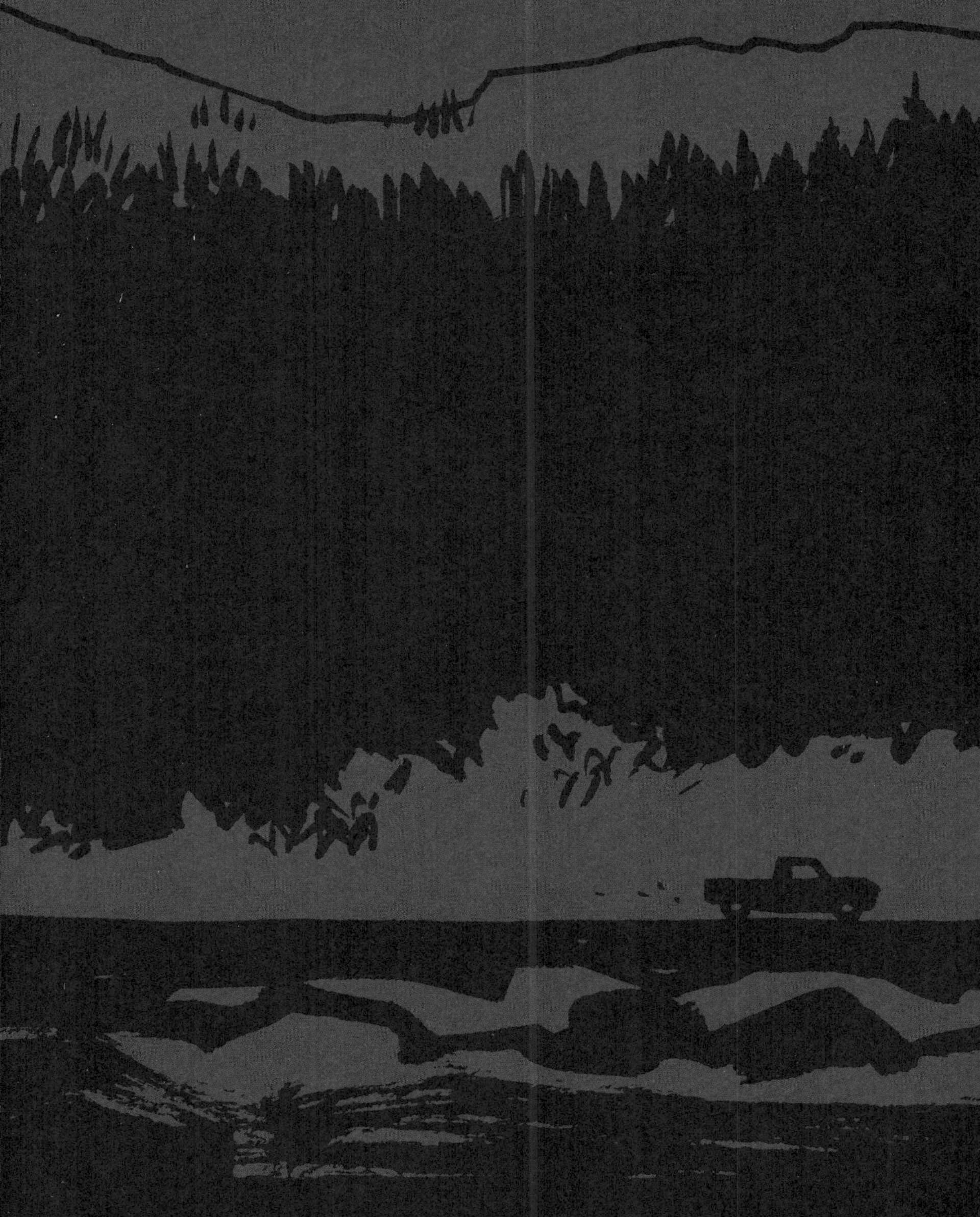

RECKLESS

IMAGE COMICS, INC.
Todd McFarlane – President
Jim Valentino – Vice President
Marc Silvestri – Chief Executive Officer
Erik Larsen – Chief Financial Officer
Robert Kirkman – Chief Operating Officer

Eric Stephenson – Publisher / Chief Creative Officer
Shanna Matuszak – Editorial Coordinator
Marla Eizik – Talent Liaison

Nicole Lapalme – Controller
Leanna Counter – Accounting Analyst
Sue Korpela – Accounting & HR Manager

Jeff Boison – Director of Sales & Publishing Planning
Dirk Wood – Director of International Sales & Licensing
Alex Cox – Director of Direct Market & Specialty Sales
Chloe Ramos-Peterson – Book Market & Library Sales Manager
Emilio Bautista – Digital Sales Coordinator

Kat Salazar – Director of PR & Marketing
Drew Fitzgerald – Marketing Content Associate

Heather Doornink – Production Director
Drew Gill – Art Director
Hilary DiLoreto – Print Manager
Tricia Ramos – Traffic Manager
Erika Schnatz – Senior Production Artist
Ryan Brewer – Production Artist
Deanna Phelps – Production Artist
IMAGECOMICS.COM

RECKLESS

First printing. December 2020.

Printed in Canada.

For international rights, contact: ag@fullbleedrights.com.

ISBN: 978-1-5343-1851-9.

 Publication design by Sean Phillips

RECKLESS

by Ed Brubaker
and Sean Phillips

colors by Jacob Phillips

This Thing I Heard

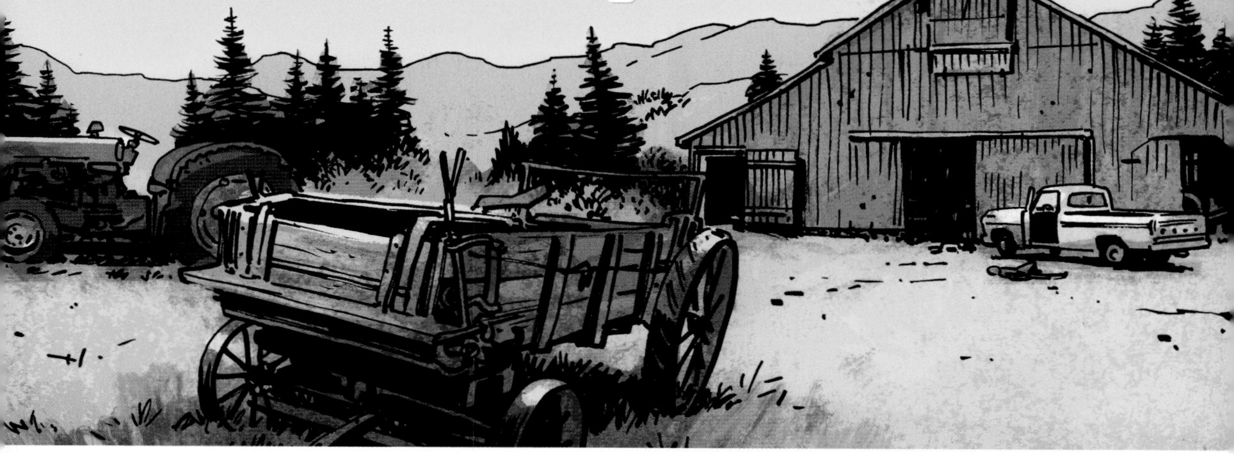

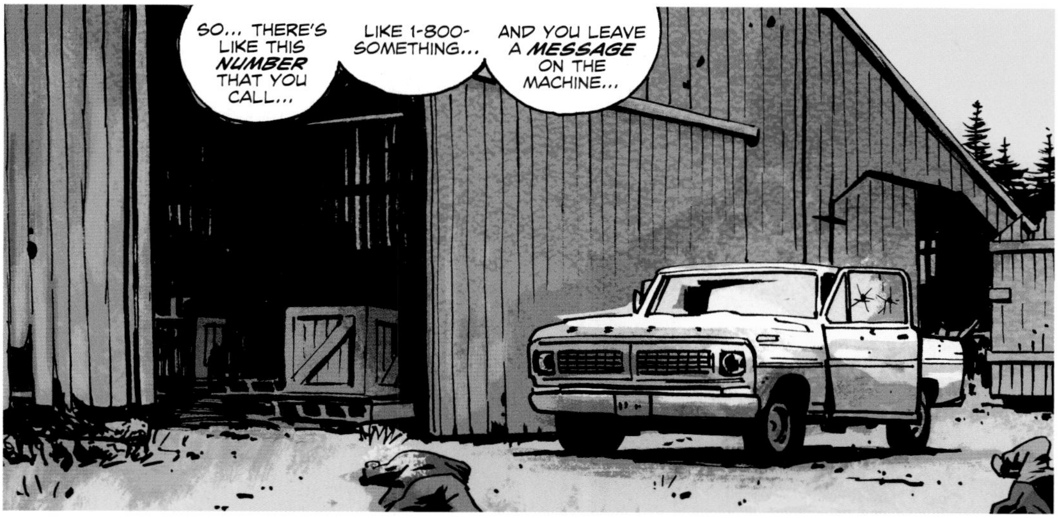

SO... THERE'S LIKE THIS *NUMBER* THAT YOU CALL...
LIKE 1-800-SOMETHING...
AND YOU LEAVE A *MESSAGE* ON THE MACHINE...

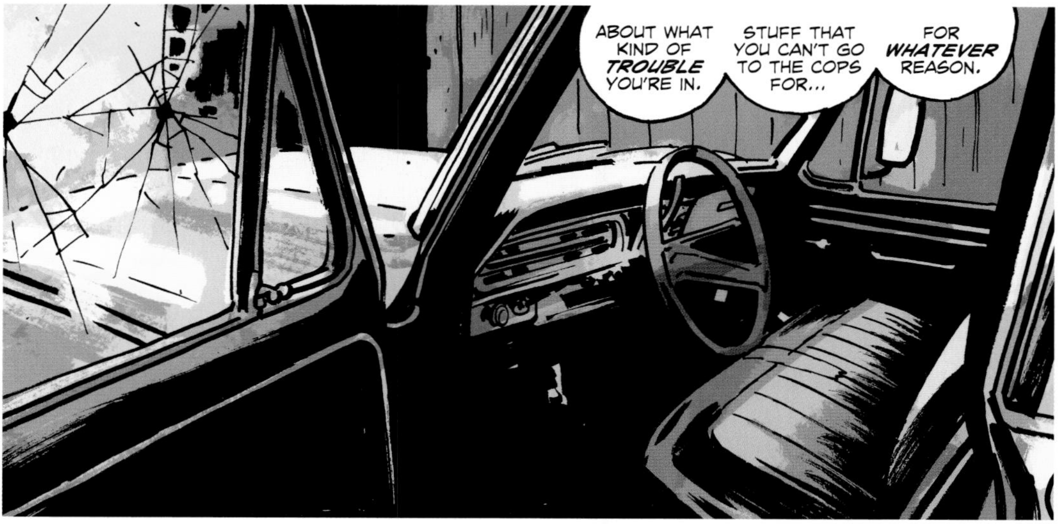

ABOUT WHAT KIND OF *TROUBLE* YOU'RE IN.
STUFF THAT YOU CAN'T GO TO THE COPS FOR...
FOR *WHATEVER* REASON.

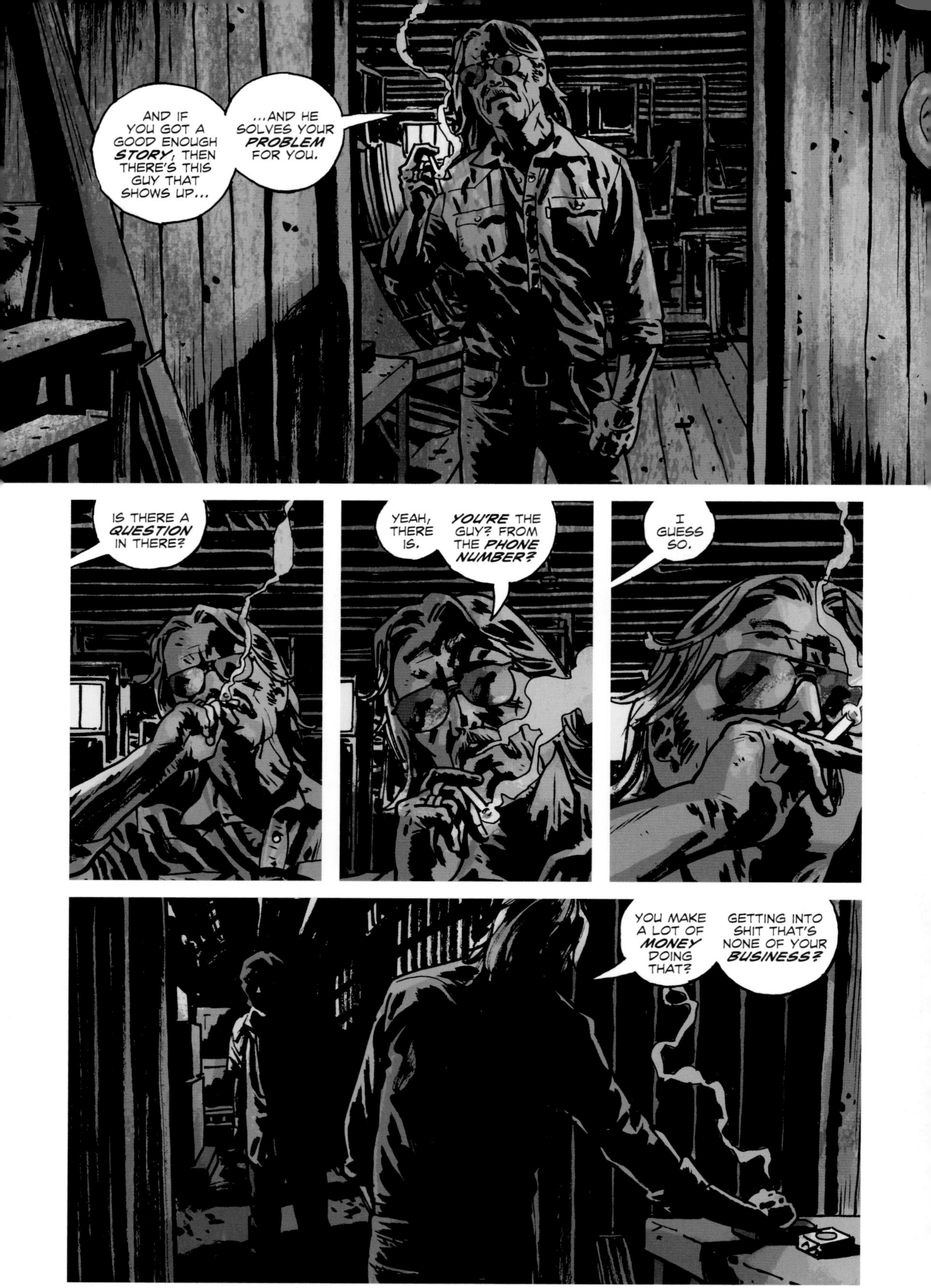
AND IF YOU GOT A GOOD ENOUGH STORY, THEN THERE'S THIS GUY THAT SHOWS UP...
...AND HE SOLVES YOUR PROBLEM FOR YOU.
IS THERE A QUESTION IN THERE?
YEAH, THERE IS.
YOU'RE THE GUY? FROM THE PHONE NUMBER?
I GUESS SO.
YOU MAKE A LOT OF MONEY DOING THAT?
GETTING INTO SHIT THAT'S NONE OF YOUR BUSINESS?

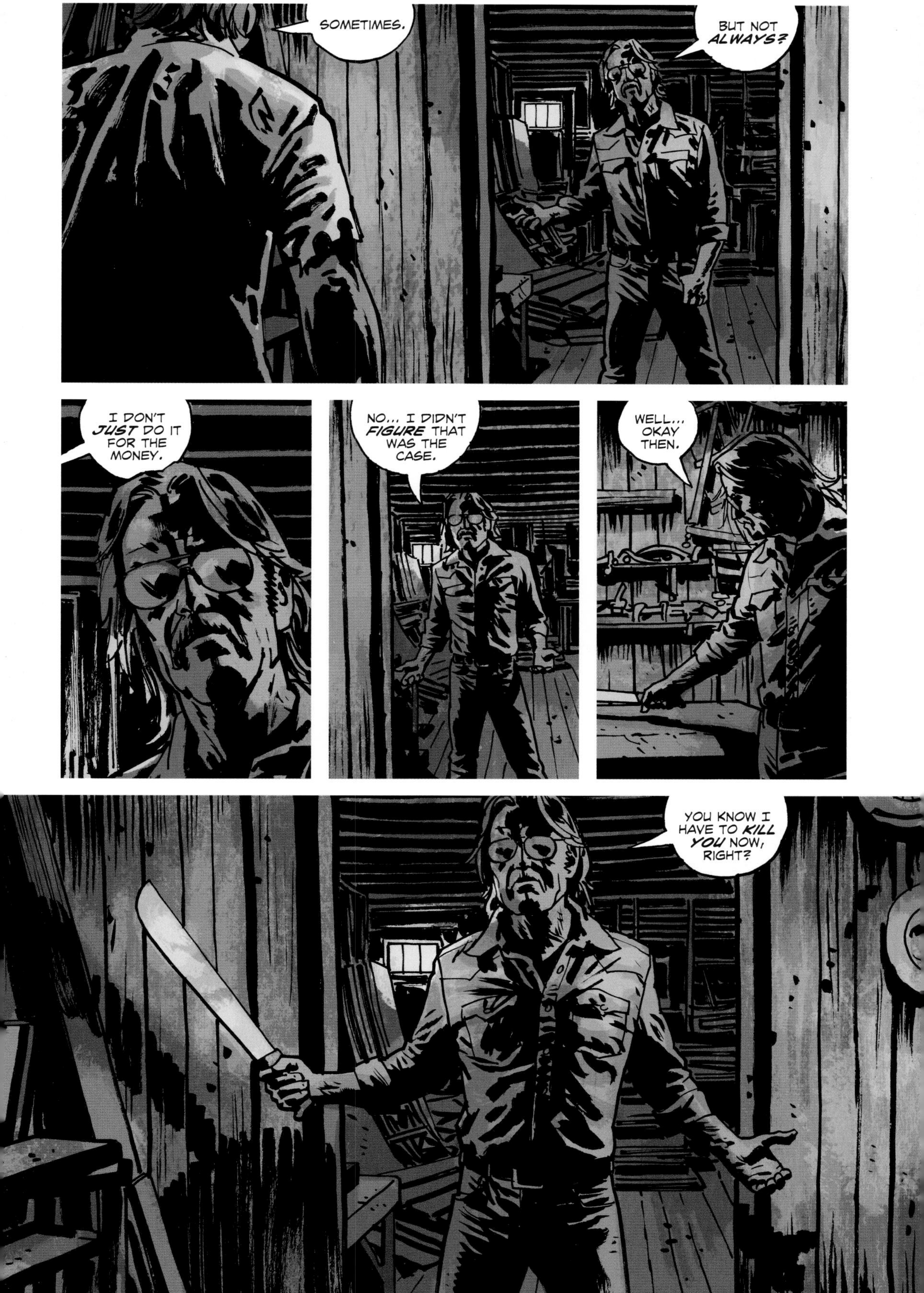
SOMETIMES.
BUT NOT ALWAYS?
I DON'T JUST DO IT FOR THE MONEY.
NO... I DIDN'T FIGURE THAT WAS THE CASE.
WELL... OKAY THEN.
YOU KNOW I HAVE TO KILL YOU NOW, RIGHT?

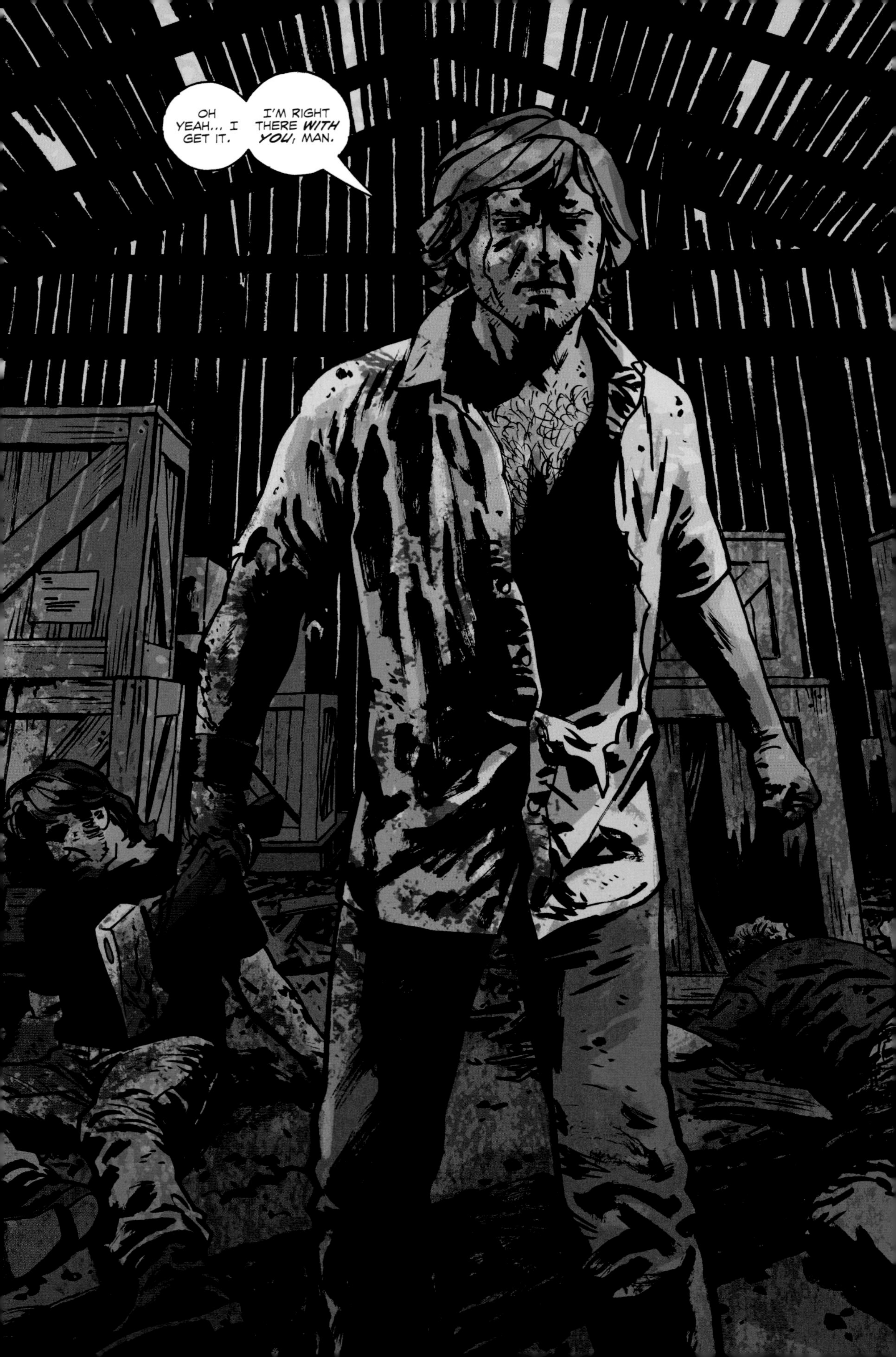
OH YEAH... I GET IT.
I'M RIGHT THERE *WITH YOU*, MAN.

I Wouldn't Really Call it Work

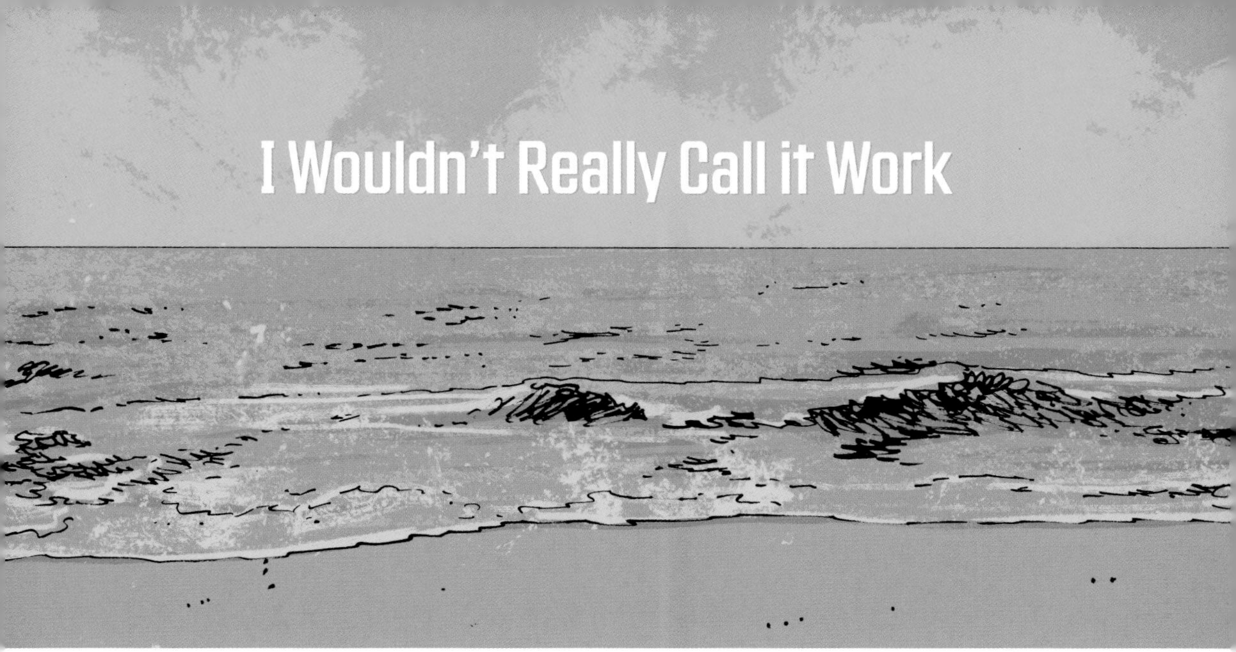

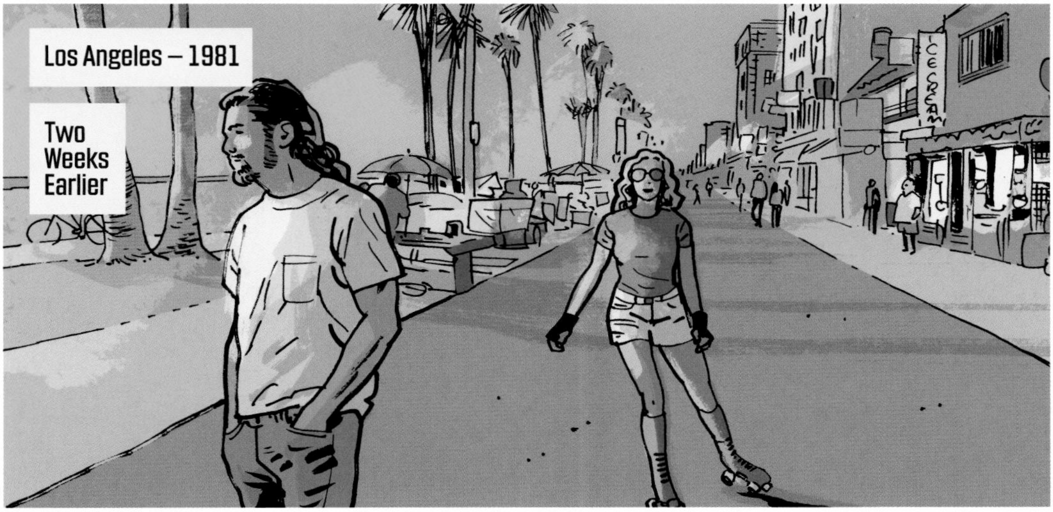
Los Angeles – 1981
Two Weeks Earlier
ICE CREAM

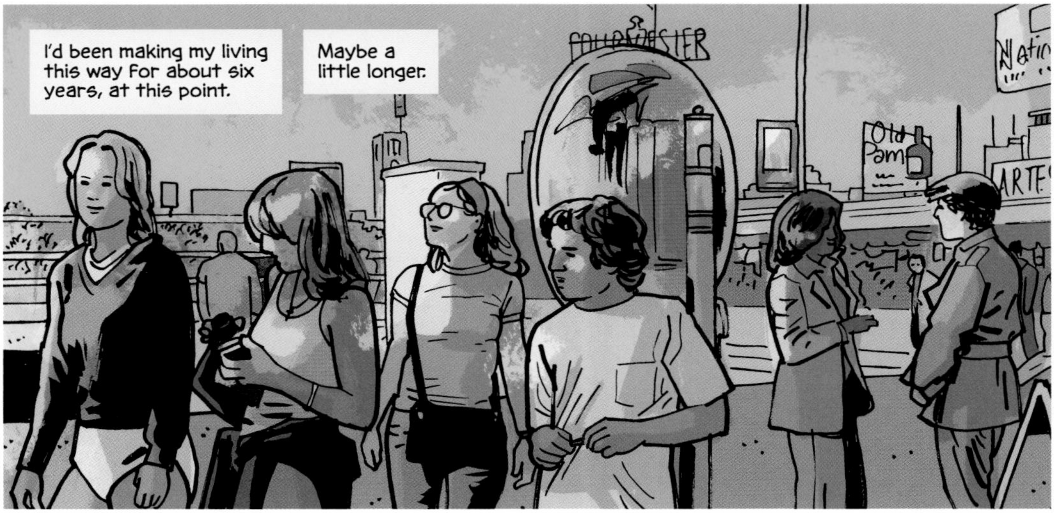
I'd been making my living this way for about six years, at this point.
Maybe a little longer.

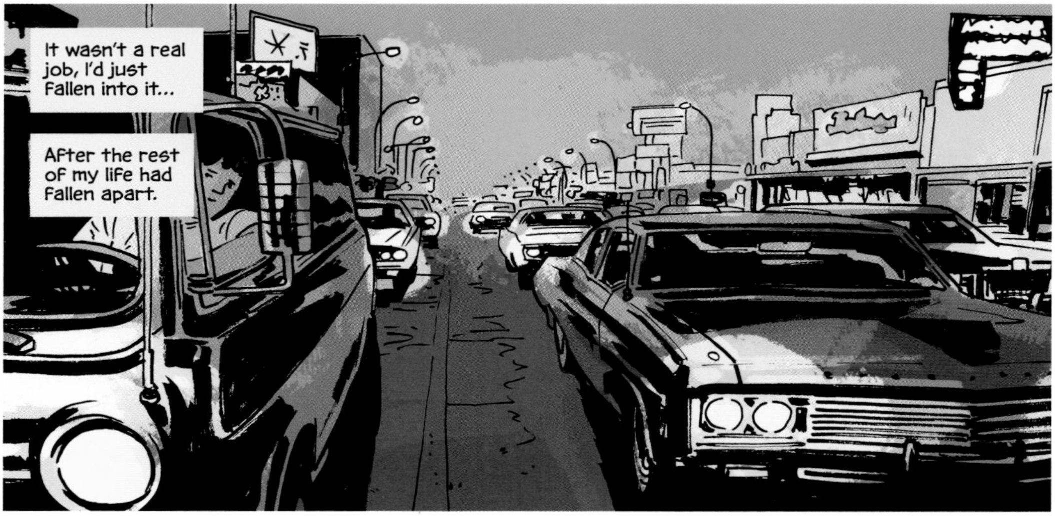
It wasn't a real job, I'd just fallen into it...
After the rest of my life had fallen apart.

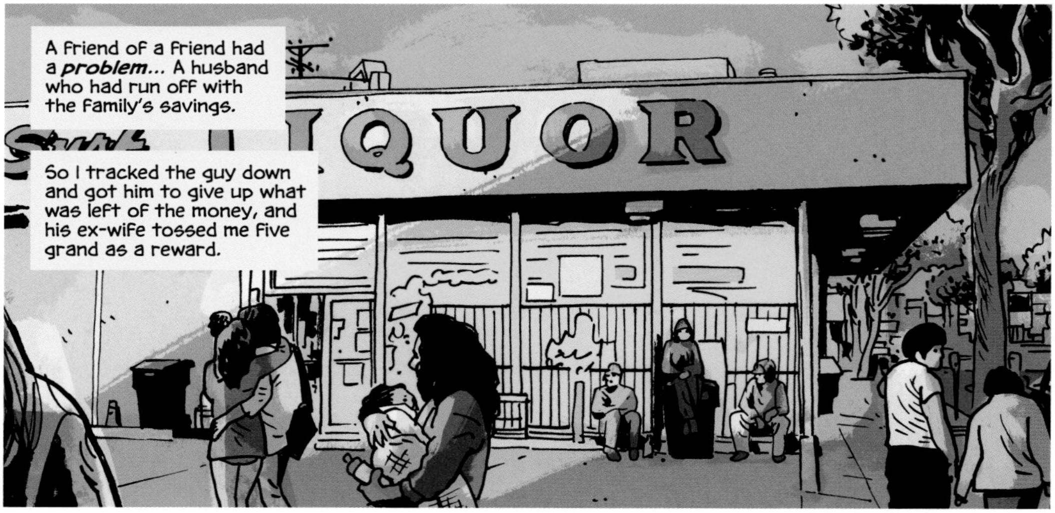
A friend of a friend had a ***problem***... A husband who had run off with the family's savings.
So I tracked the guy down and got him to give up what was left of the money, and his ex-wife tossed me five grand as a reward.

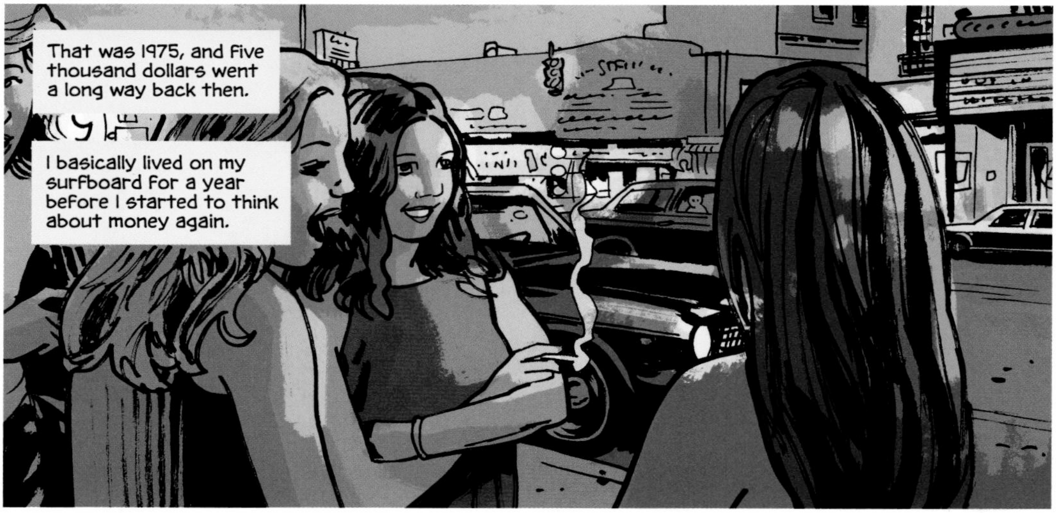
That was 1975, and five thousand dollars went a long way back then.
I basically lived on my surfboard for a year before I started to think about money again.

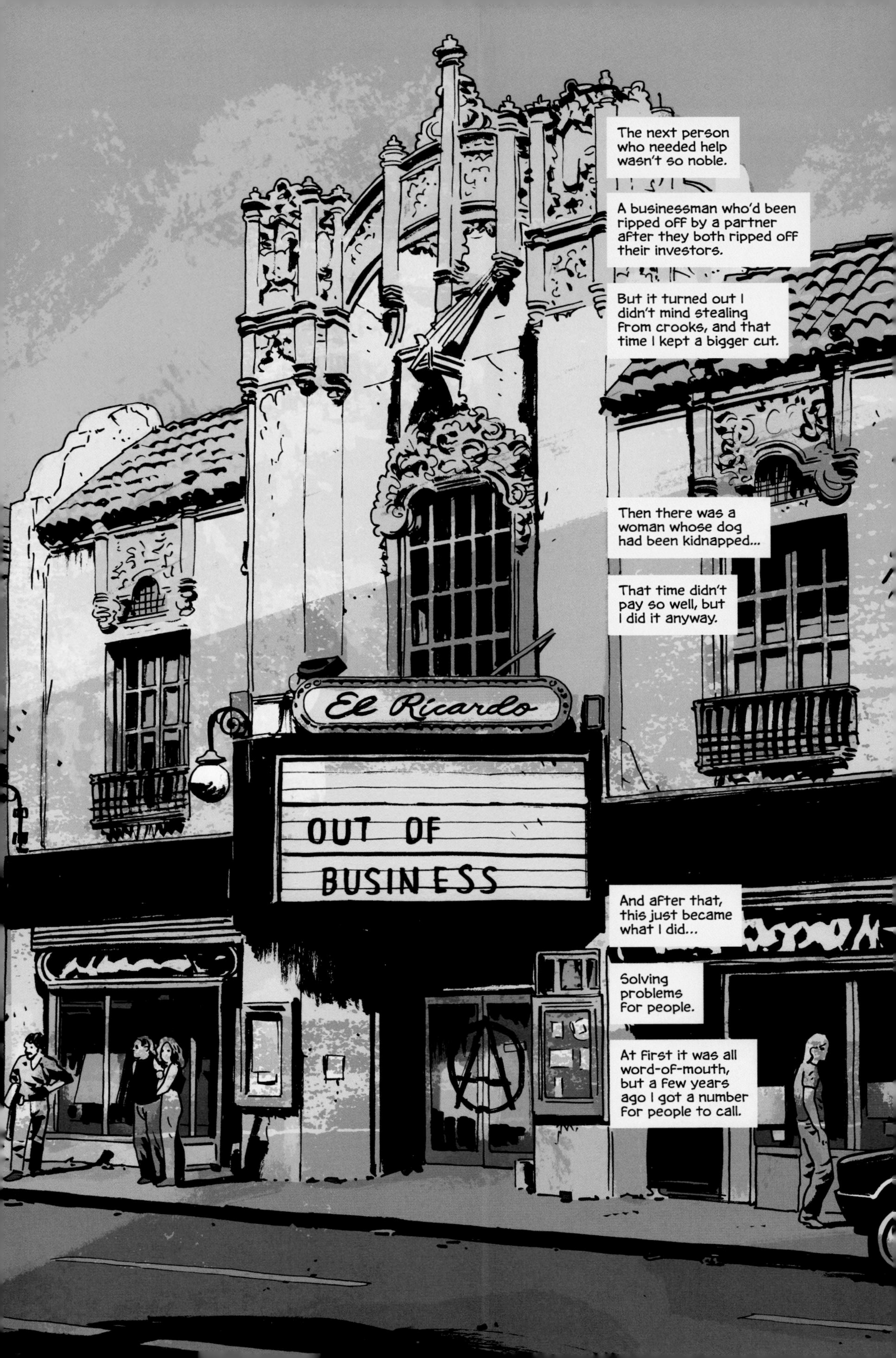
The next person who needed help wasn't so noble.
A businessman who'd been ripped off by a partner after they both ripped off their investors.
But it turned out I didn't mind stealing from crooks, and that time I kept a bigger cut.
Then there was a woman whose dog had been kidnapped...
That time didn't pay so well, but I did it anyway.
El Ricardo
OUT OF BUSINESS
And after that, this just became what I did...
Solving problems for people.
At first it was all word-of-mouth, but a few years ago I got a number for people to call.

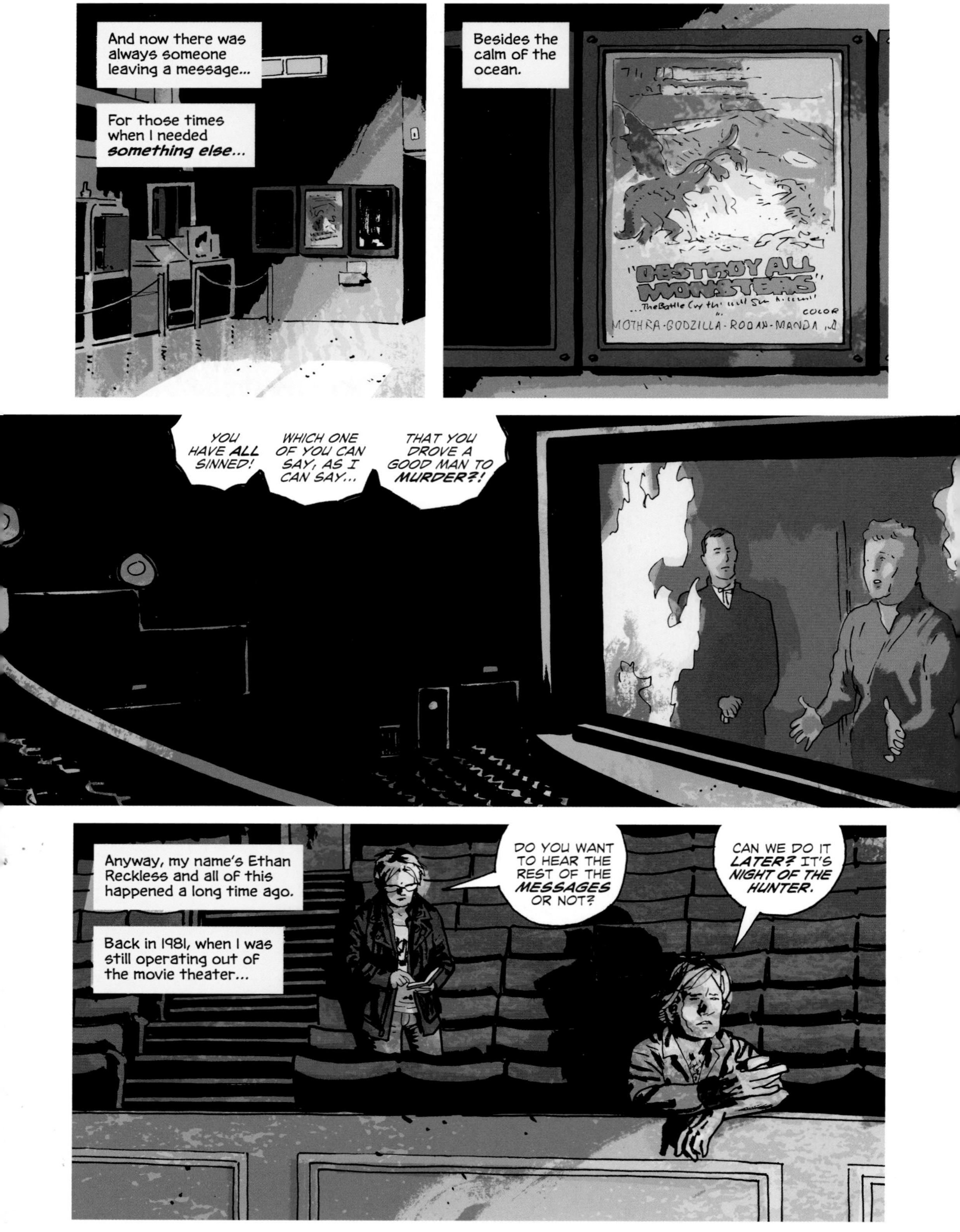
And now there was always someone leaving a message...
For those times when I needed ***something else...***
Besides the calm of the ocean.
"DESTROY ALL MONSTERS"
COLOR
MOTHRA-GODZILLA-RODAN-MANDA
YOU HAVE ***ALL*** SINNED!
WHICH ONE OF YOU CAN SAY, AS I CAN SAY...
THAT YOU DROVE A GOOD MAN TO ***MURDER?!***
Anyway, my name's Ethan Reckless and all of this happened a long time ago.
Back in 1981, when I was still operating out of the movie theater...
DO YOU WANT TO HEAR THE REST OF THE ***MESSAGES*** OR NOT?
CAN WE DO IT ***LATER?*** IT'S ***NIGHT OF THE HUNTER.***

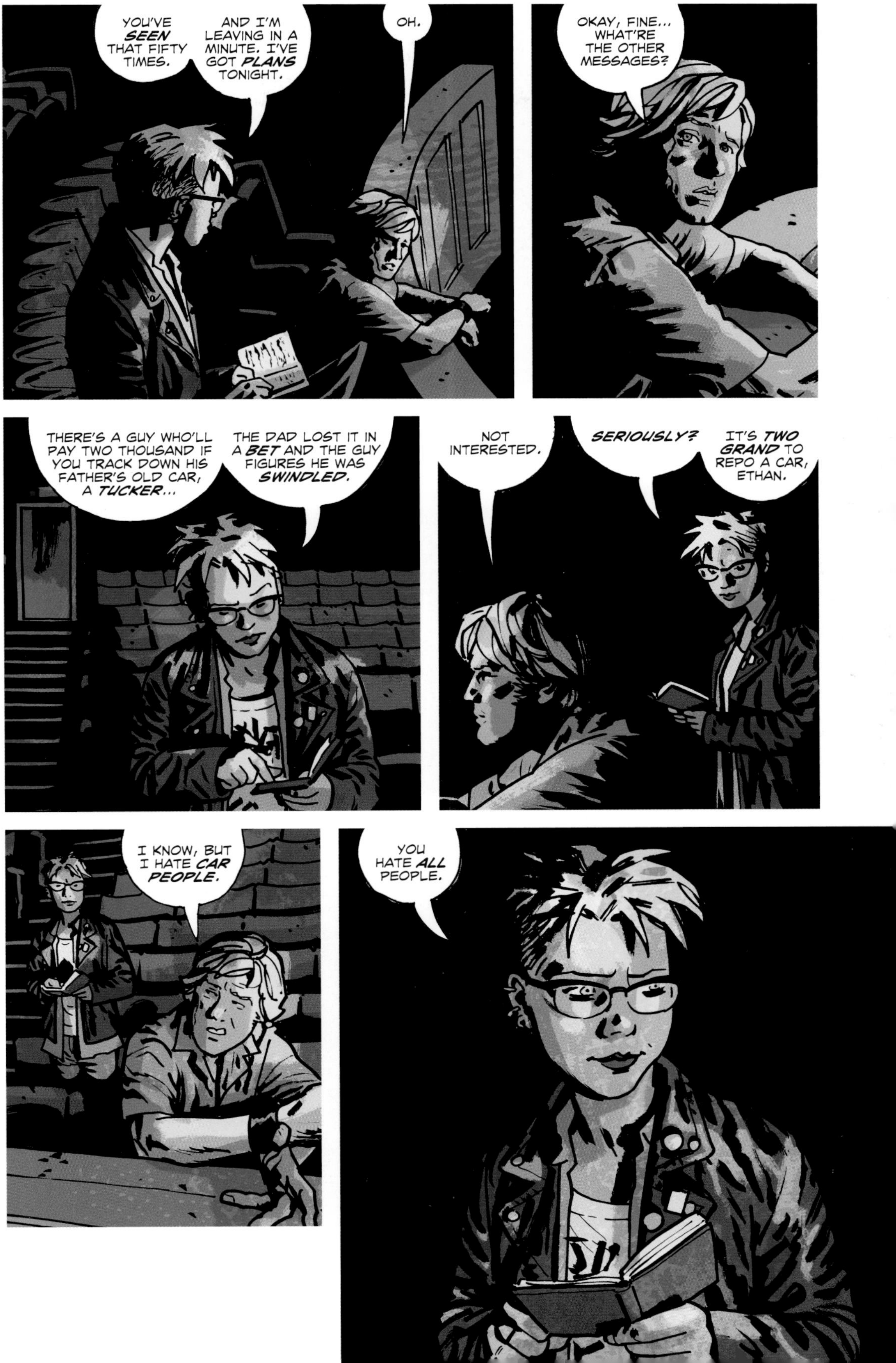
YOU'VE SEEN THAT FIFTY TIMES.
AND I'M LEAVING IN A MINUTE. I'VE GOT PLANS TONIGHT.
OH.
OKAY, FINE... WHAT'RE THE OTHER MESSAGES?
THERE'S A GUY WHO'LL PAY TWO THOUSAND IF YOU TRACK DOWN HIS FATHER'S OLD CAR, A TUCKER...
THE DAD LOST IT IN A BET AND THE GUY FIGURES HE WAS SWINDLED.
NOT INTERESTED.
SERIOUSLY?
IT'S TWO GRAND TO REPO A CAR, ETHAN.
I KNOW, BUT I HATE CAR PEOPLE.
YOU HATE ALL PEOPLE.

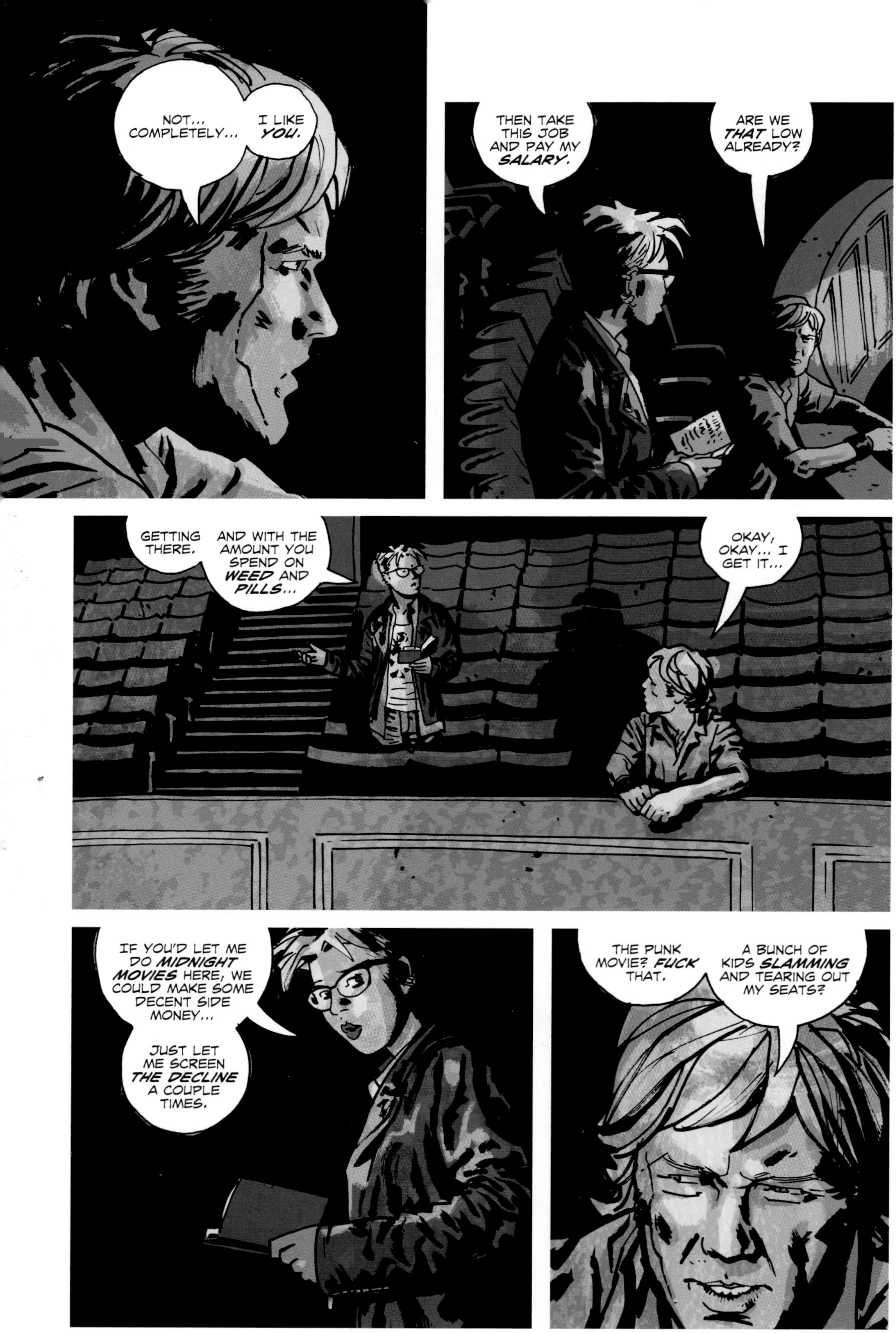
NOT... COMPLETELY...
I LIKE YOU.
THEN TAKE THIS JOB AND PAY MY SALARY.
ARE WE THAT LOW ALREADY?
GETTING THERE.
AND WITH THE AMOUNT YOU SPEND ON WEED AND PILLS...
OKAY, OKAY... I GET IT...
IF YOU'D LET ME DO MIDNIGHT MOVIES HERE, WE COULD MAKE SOME DECENT SIDE MONEY...
JUST LET ME SCREEN THE DECLINE A COUPLE TIMES.
THE PUNK MOVIE? FUCK THAT.
A BUNCH OF KIDS SLAMMING AND TEARING OUT MY SEATS?

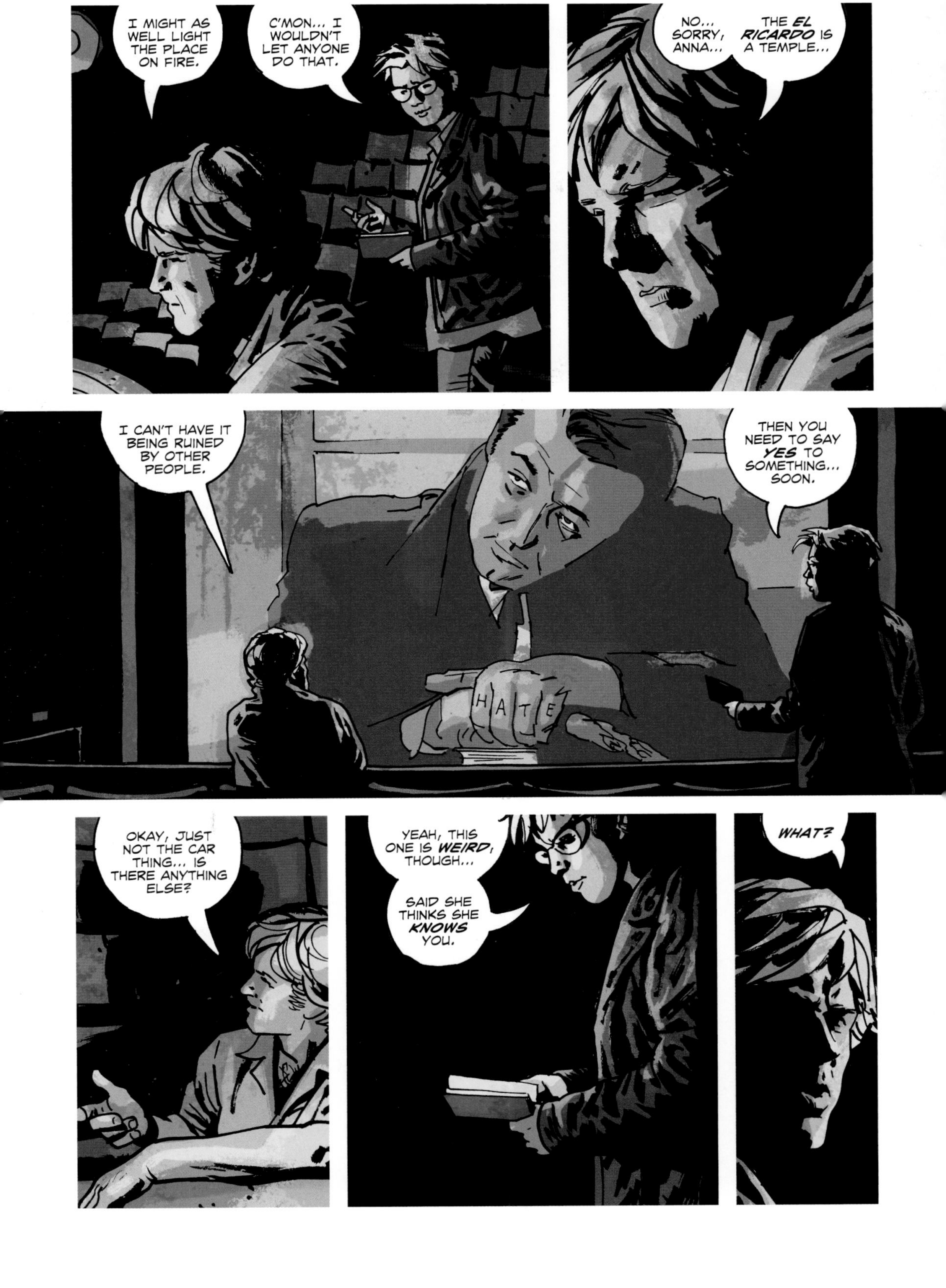
I MIGHT AS WELL LIGHT THE PLACE ON FIRE.
C'MON... I WOULDN'T LET ANYONE DO THAT.
NO... SORRY, ANNA...
THE *EL RICARDO* IS A TEMPLE...
I CAN'T HAVE IT BEING RUINED BY OTHER PEOPLE.
THEN YOU NEED TO SAY *YES* TO SOMETHING... SOON.
HATE
OKAY, JUST NOT THE CAR THING... IS THERE ANYTHING ELSE?
YEAH, THIS ONE IS *WEIRD*, THOUGH...
SAID SHE THINKS SHE *KNOWS* YOU.
WHAT?

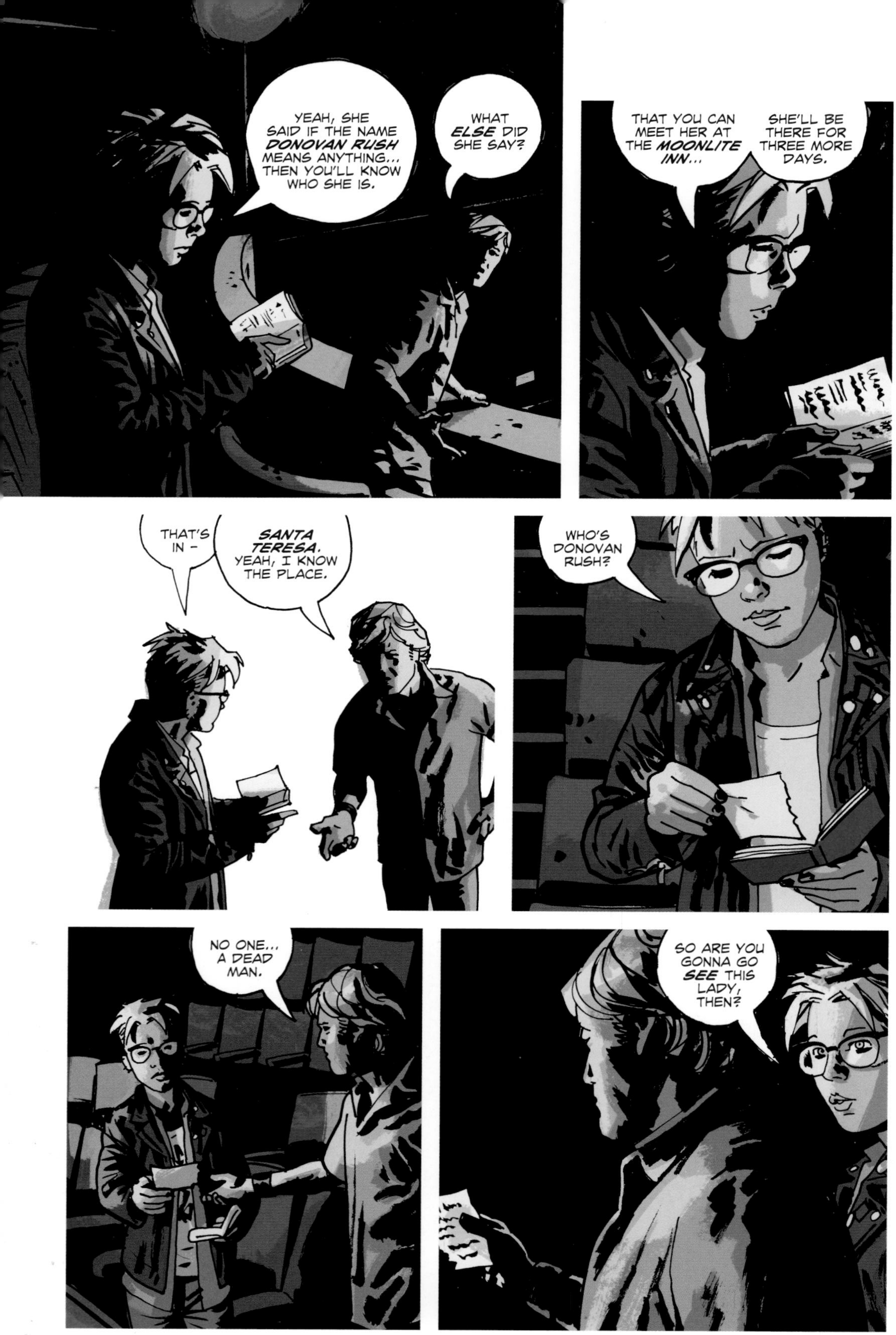

YEAH, SHE SAID IF THE NAME DONOVAN RUSH MEANS ANYTHING... THEN YOU'LL KNOW WHO SHE IS.
WHAT ELSE DID SHE SAY?
THAT YOU CAN MEET HER AT THE MOONLITE INN...
SHE'LL BE THERE FOR THREE MORE DAYS.
THAT'S IN –
SANTA TERESA. YEAH, I KNOW THE PLACE.
WHO'S DONOVAN RUSH?
NO ONE... A DEAD MAN.
SO ARE YOU GONNA GO SEE THIS LADY, THEN?

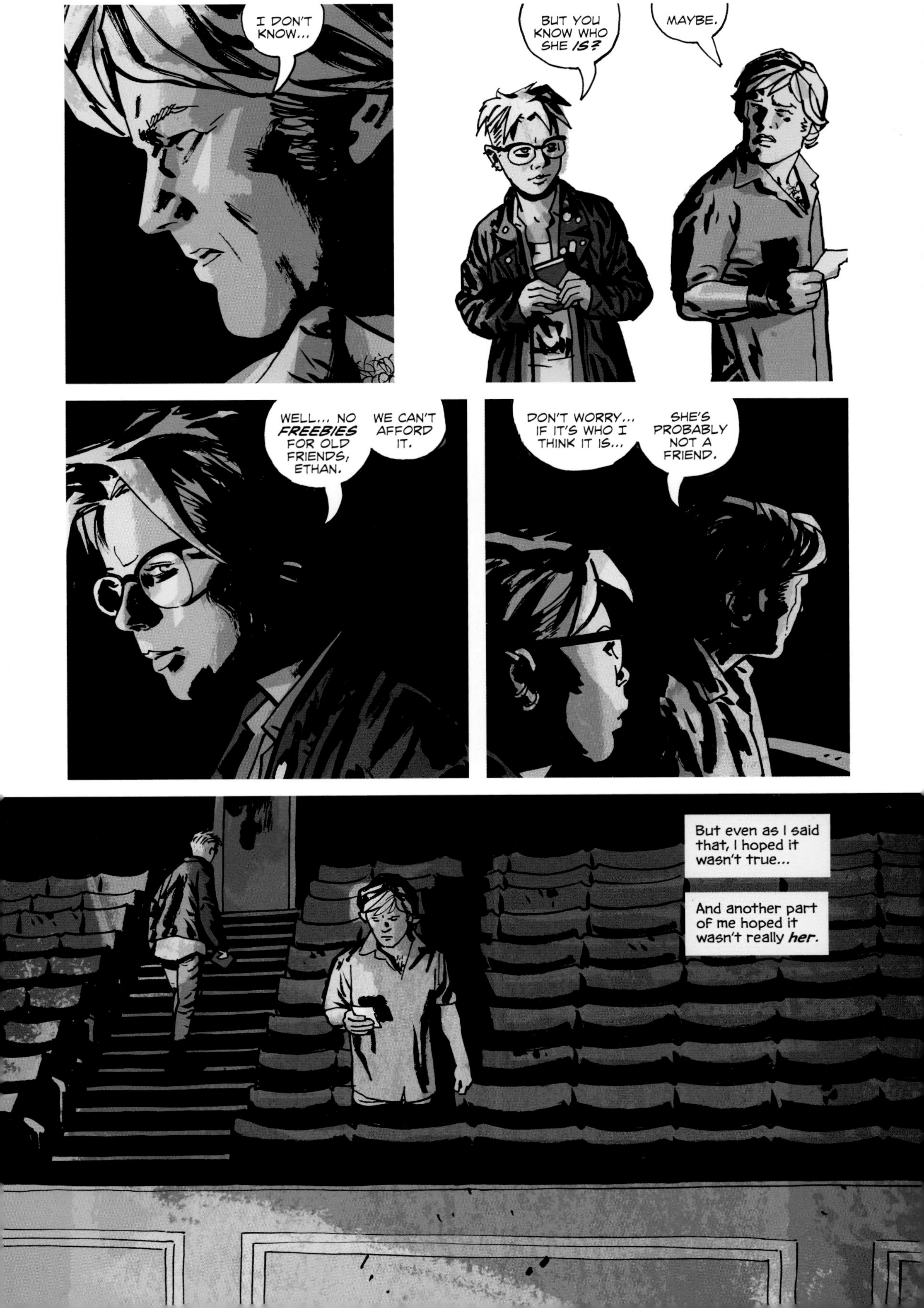
I DON'T KNOW...
BUT YOU KNOW WHO SHE *IS?*
MAYBE.
WELL... NO ***FREEBIES*** FOR OLD FRIENDS, ETHAN.
WE CAN'T AFFORD IT.
DON'T WORRY... IF IT'S WHO I THINK IT IS...
SHE'S PROBABLY NOT A FRIEND.
But even as I said that, I hoped it wasn't true...
And another part of me hoped it wasn't really ***her***.

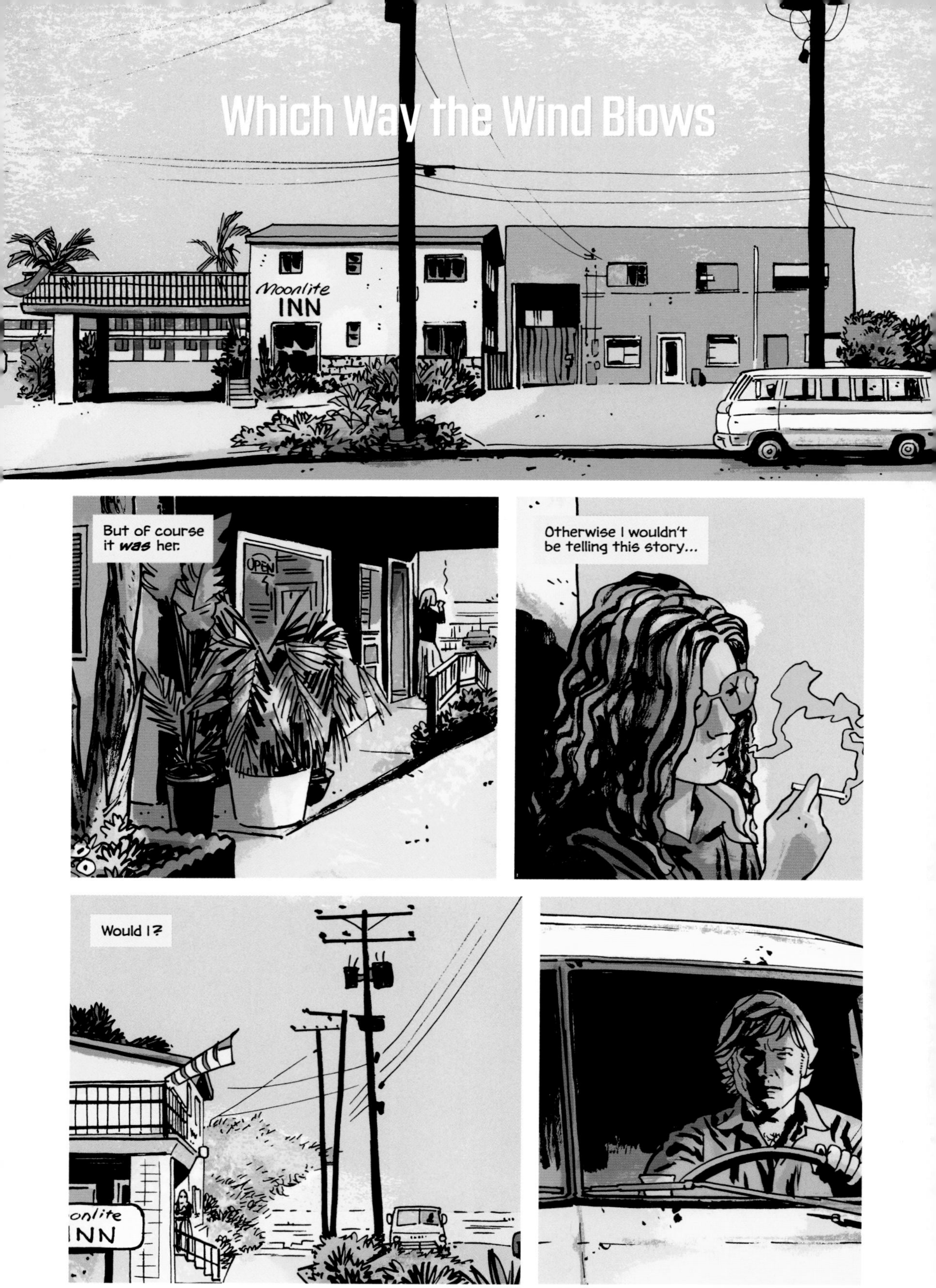
Which Way the Wind Blows
Moonlite INN
But of course it *was* her.
OPEN
Otherwise I wouldn't be telling this story...
Would I?
onlite INN

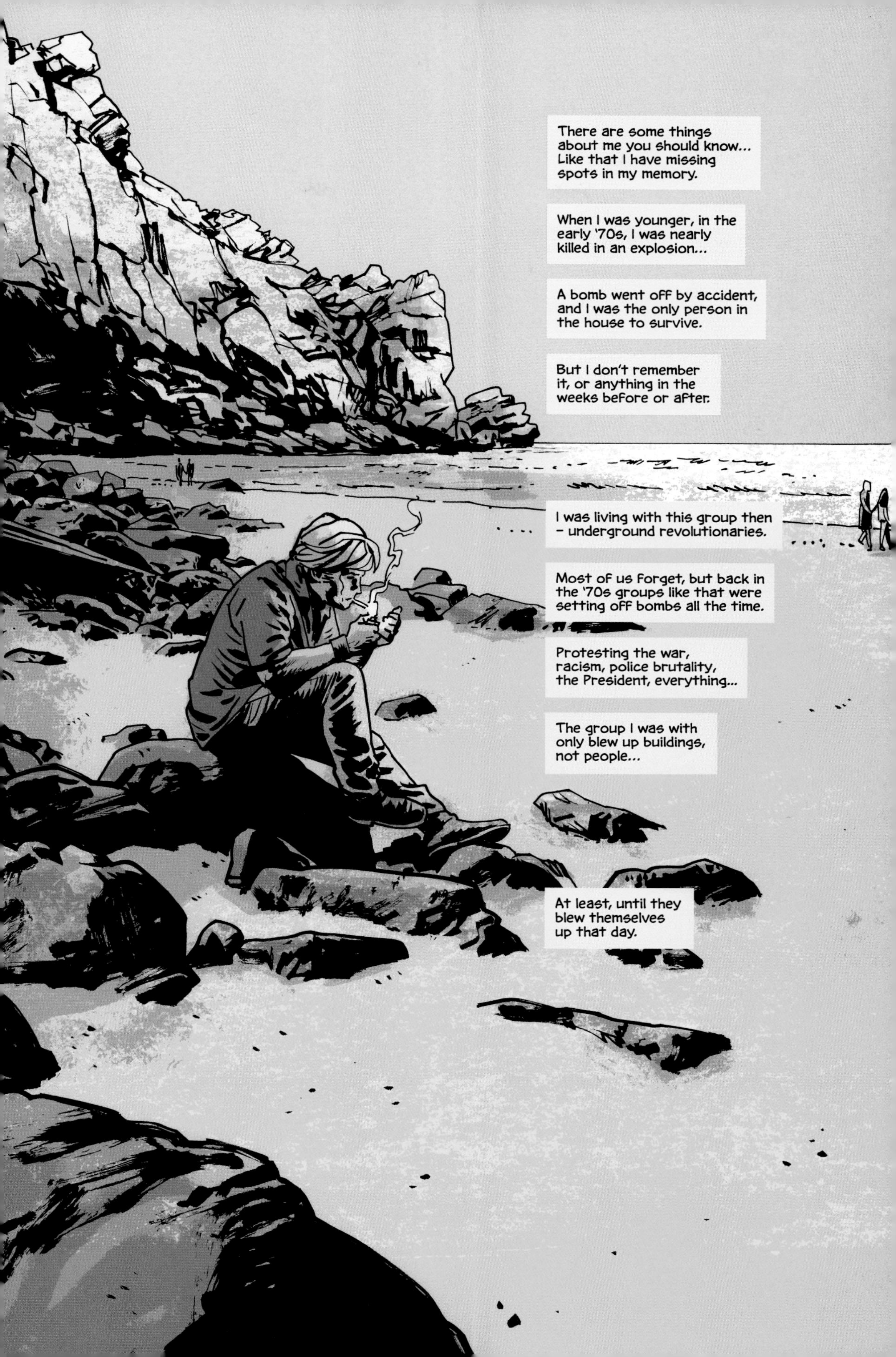
There are some things about me you should know... Like that I have missing spots in my memory.
When I was younger, in the early '70s, I was nearly killed in an explosion...
A bomb went off by accident, and I was the only person in the house to survive.
But I don't remember it, or anything in the weeks before or after.
I was living with this group then - underground revolutionaries.
Most of us forget, but back in the '70s groups like that were setting off bombs all the time.
Protesting the war, racism, police brutality, the President, everything...
The group I was with only blew up buildings, not people...
At least, until they blew themselves up that day.

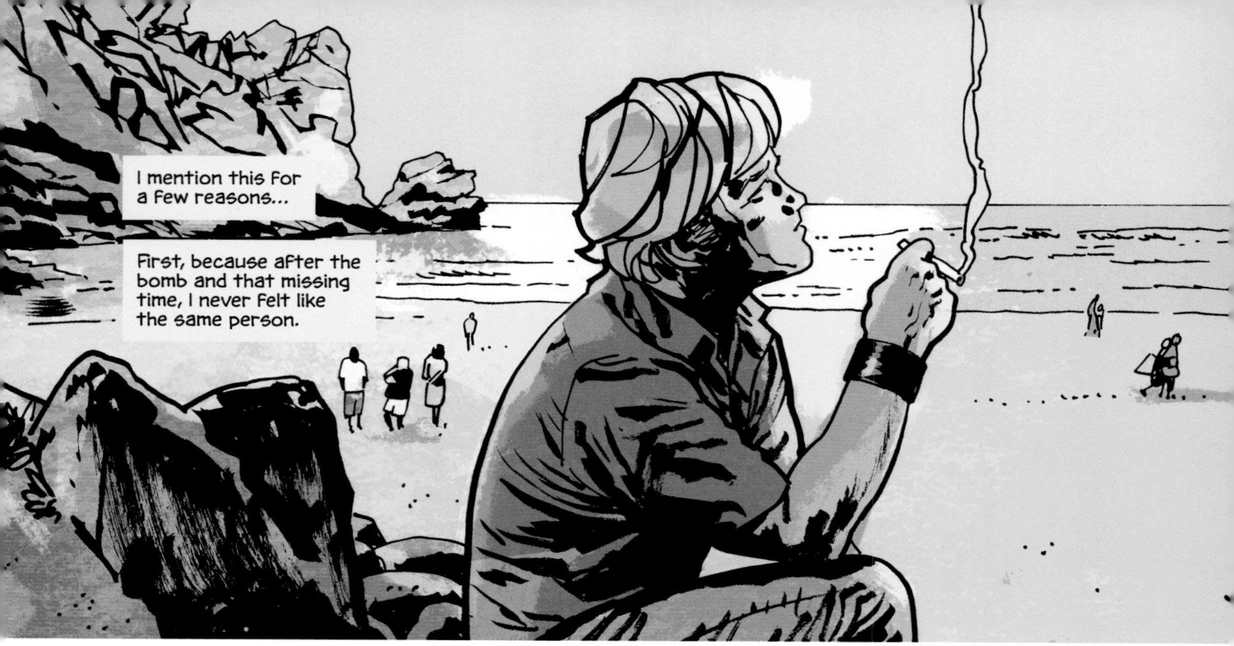
I mention this for a few reasons...
First, because after the bomb and that missing time, I never felt like the same person.

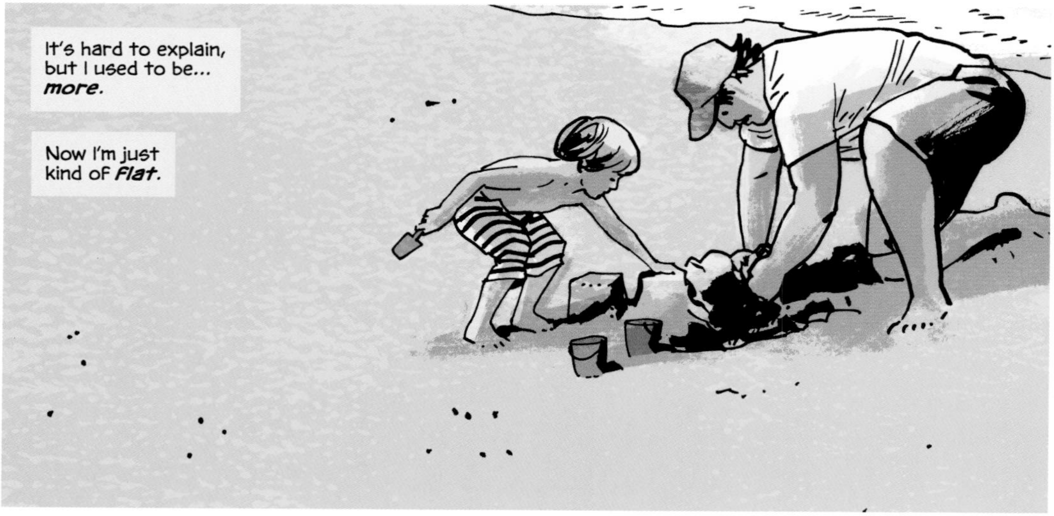
It's hard to explain, but I used to be... *more.*
Now I'm just kind of *flat*.

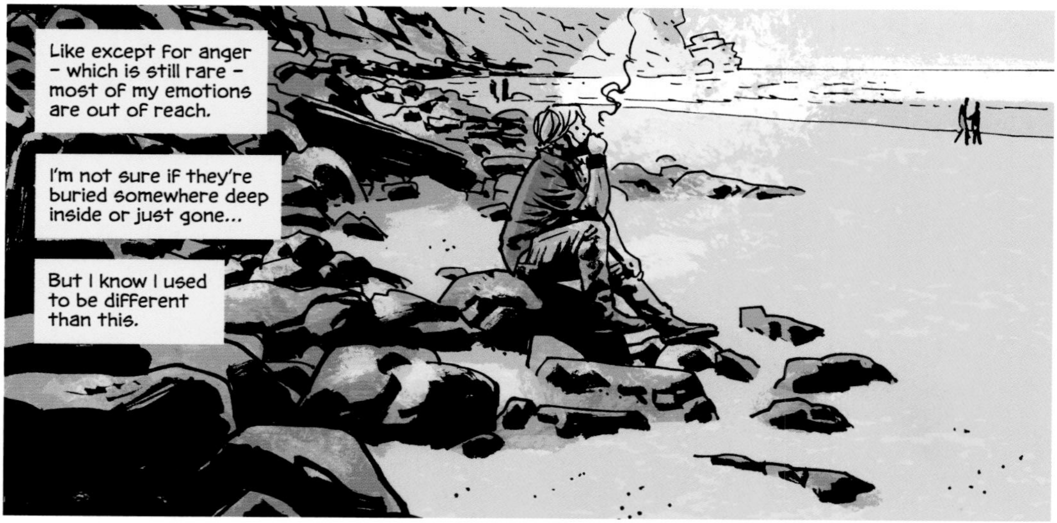
Like except for anger – which is still rare – most of my emotions are out of reach.
I'm not sure if they're buried somewhere deep inside or just gone...
But I know I used to be different than this.

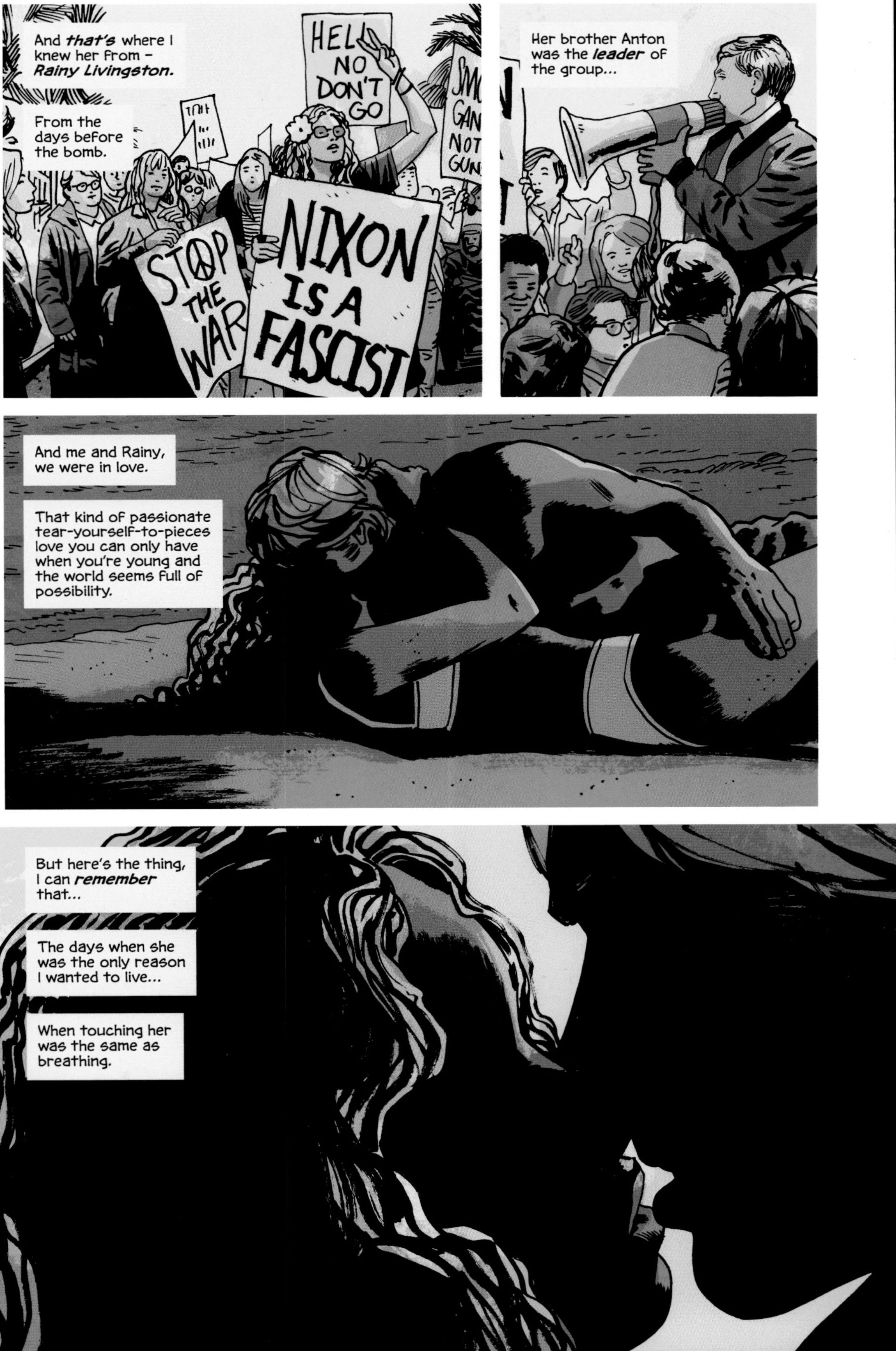

And *that's* where I knew her from – *Rainy Livingston.*
From the days before the bomb.
NO DON'T GO
STOP THE WAR
NIXON IS A FASCIST
Her brother Anton was the *leader* of the group...
And me and Rainy, we were in love.
That kind of passionate tear-yourself-to-pieces love you can only have when you're young and the world seems full of possibility.
But here's the thing, I can *remember* that...
The days when she was the only reason I wanted to live...
When touching her was the same as breathing.

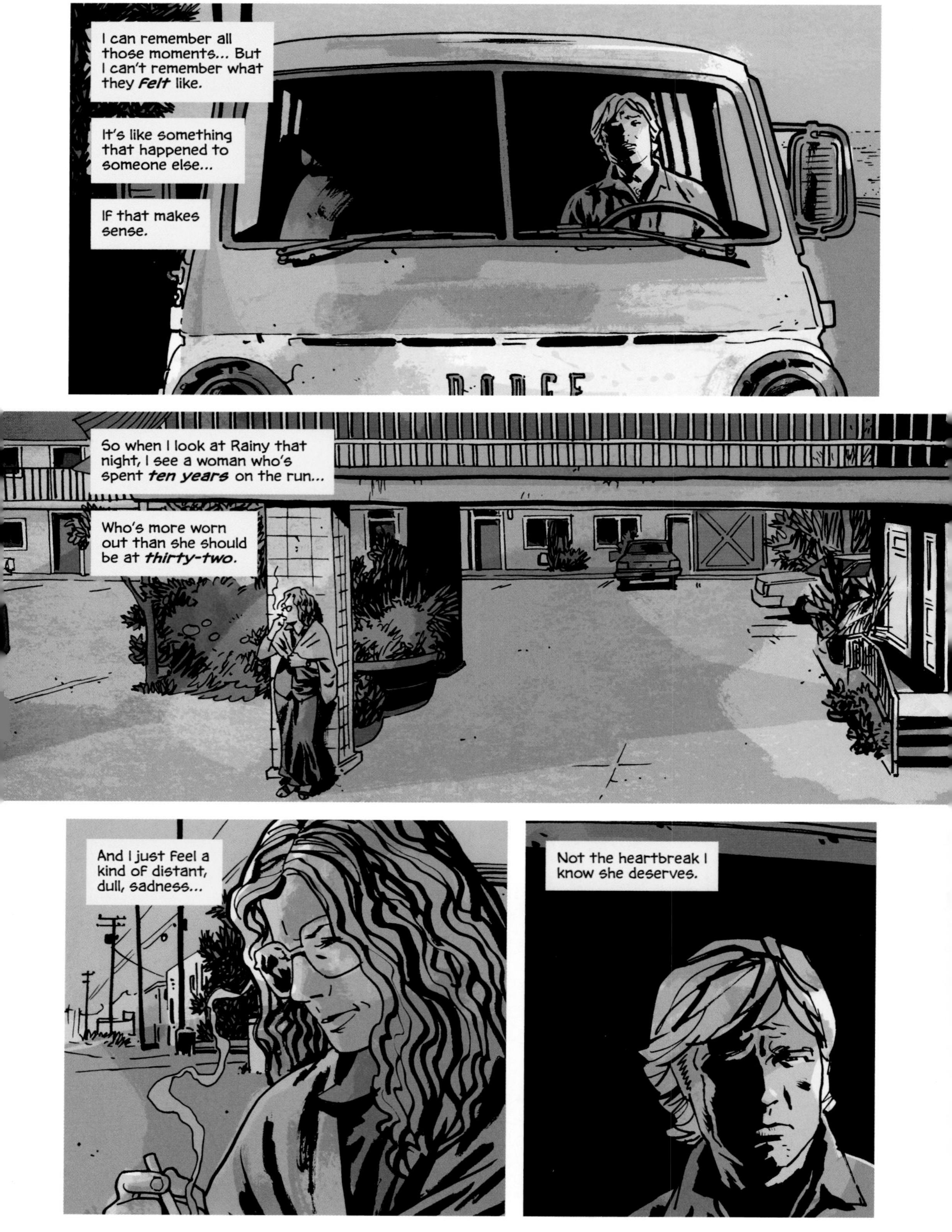
I can remember all those moments... But I can't remember what they *felt* like.
It's like something that happened to someone else...
If that makes sense.
So when I look at Rainy that night, I see a woman who's spent *ten years* on the run...
Who's more worn out than she should be at *thirty-two.*
And I just feel a kind of distant, dull, sadness...
Not the heartbreak I know she deserves.

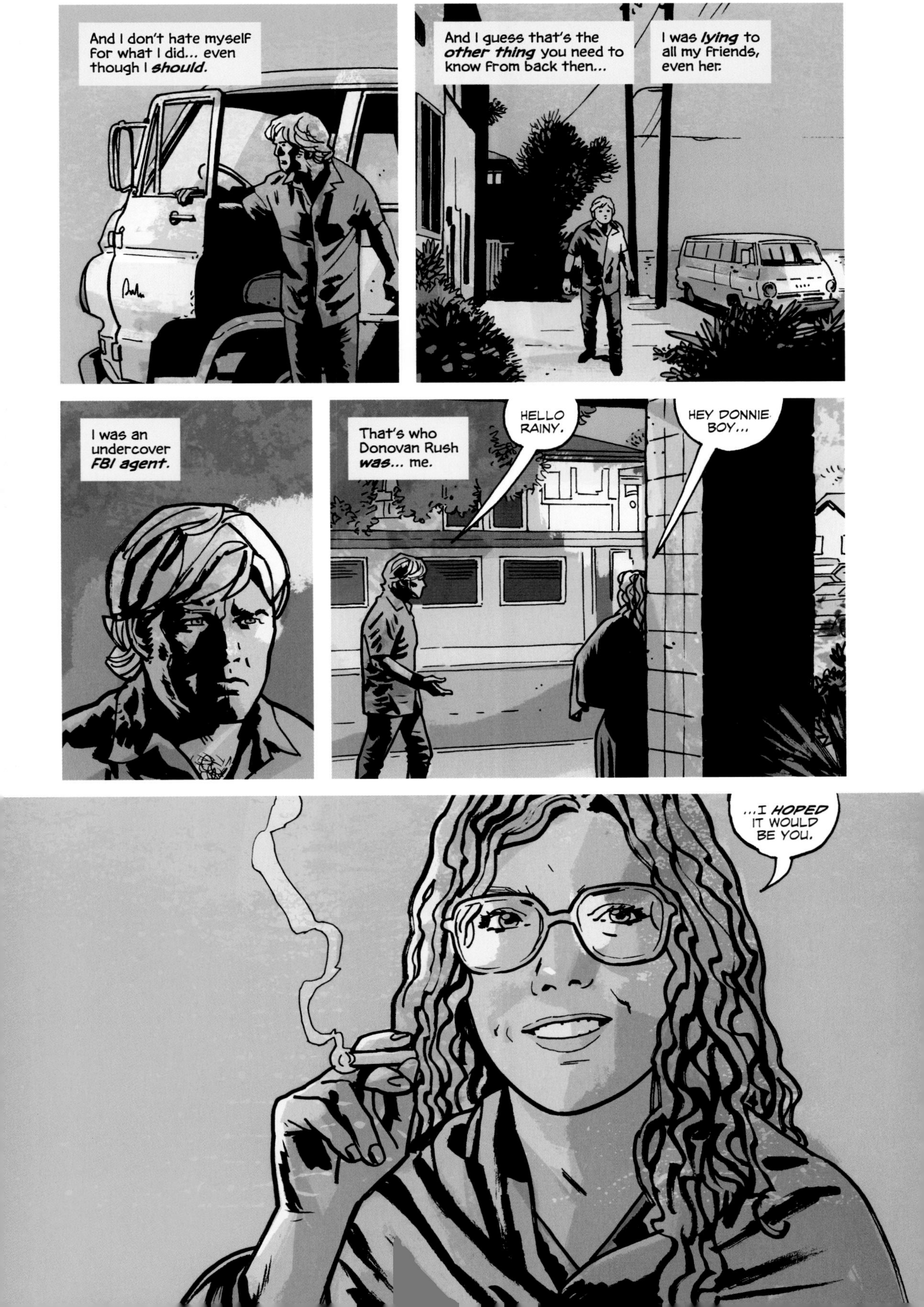
And I don't hate myself for what I did... even though I should.
And I guess that's the other thing you need to know from back then...
I was lying to all my friends, even her.
I was an undercover FBI agent.
That's who Donovan Rush was... me.
HELLO RAINY.
HEY DONNIE BOY...
...I HOPED IT WOULD BE YOU.

The Underground Woman

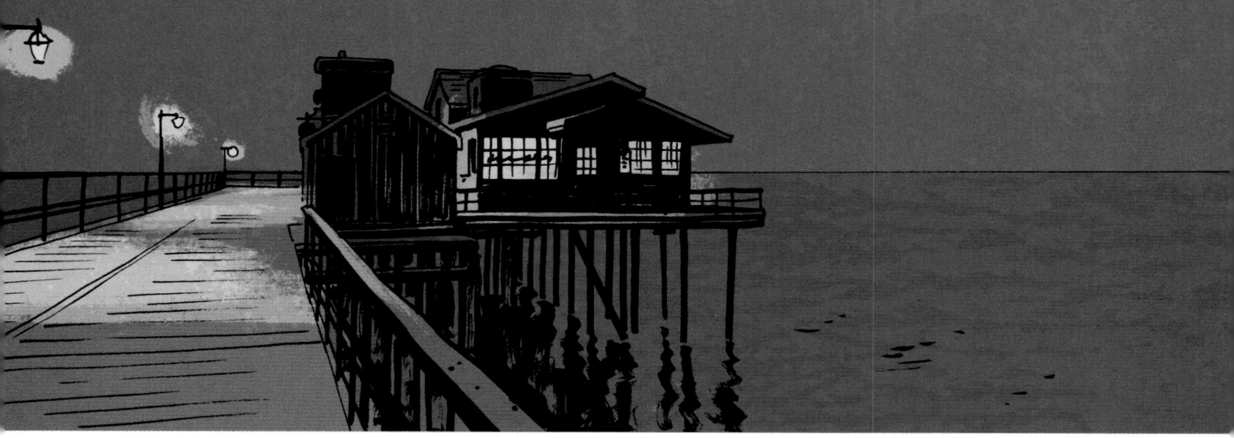

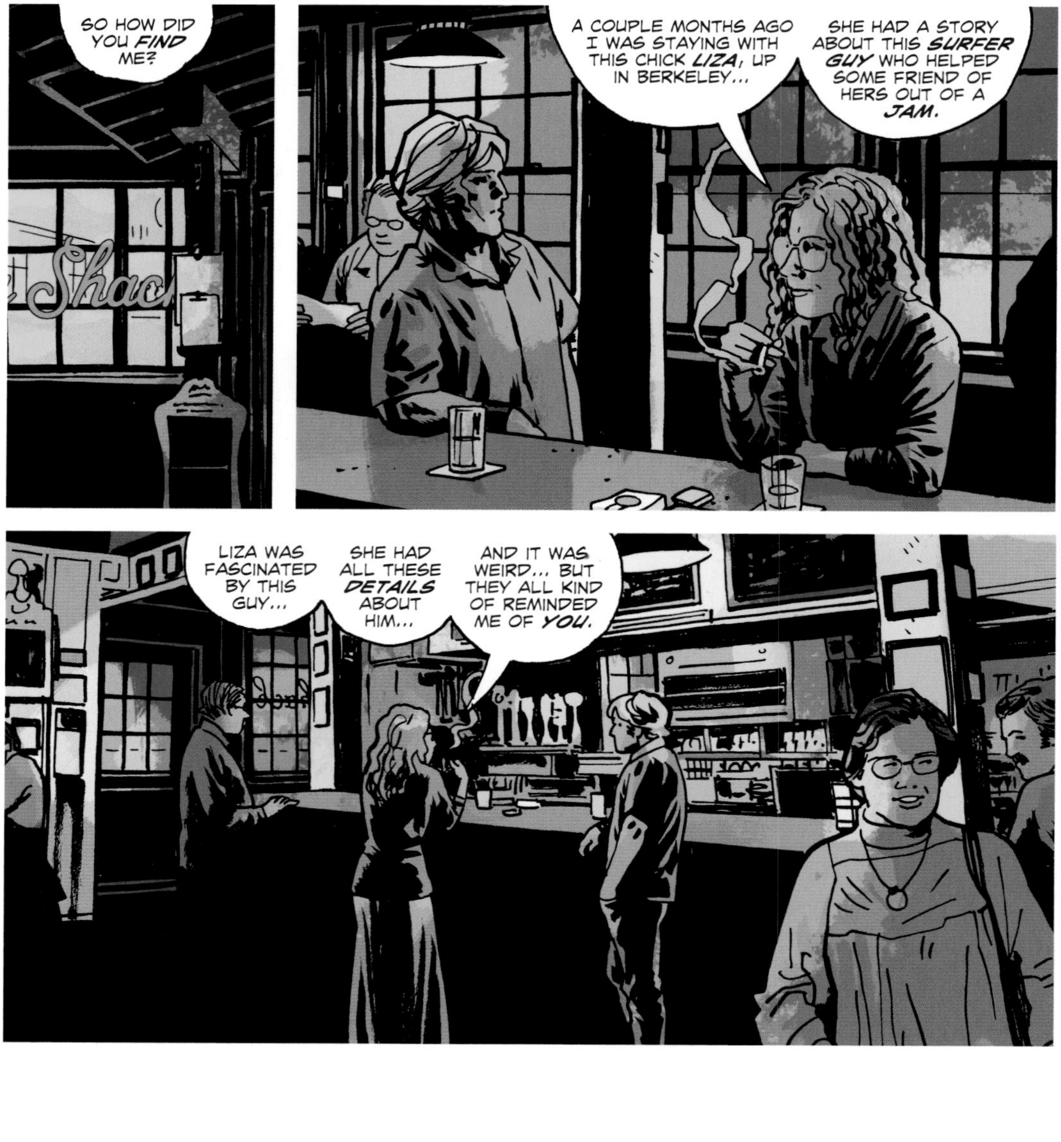

SO HOW DID YOU *FIND* ME?
A COUPLE MONTHS AGO I WAS STAYING WITH THIS CHICK *LIZA*, UP IN BERKELEY...
SHE HAD A STORY ABOUT THIS *SURFER GUY* WHO HELPED SOME FRIEND OF HERS OUT OF A *JAM.*
LIZA WAS FASCINATED BY THIS GUY...
SHE HAD ALL THESE *DETAILS* ABOUT HIM...
AND IT WAS WEIRD... BUT THEY ALL KIND OF REMINDED ME OF *YOU.*

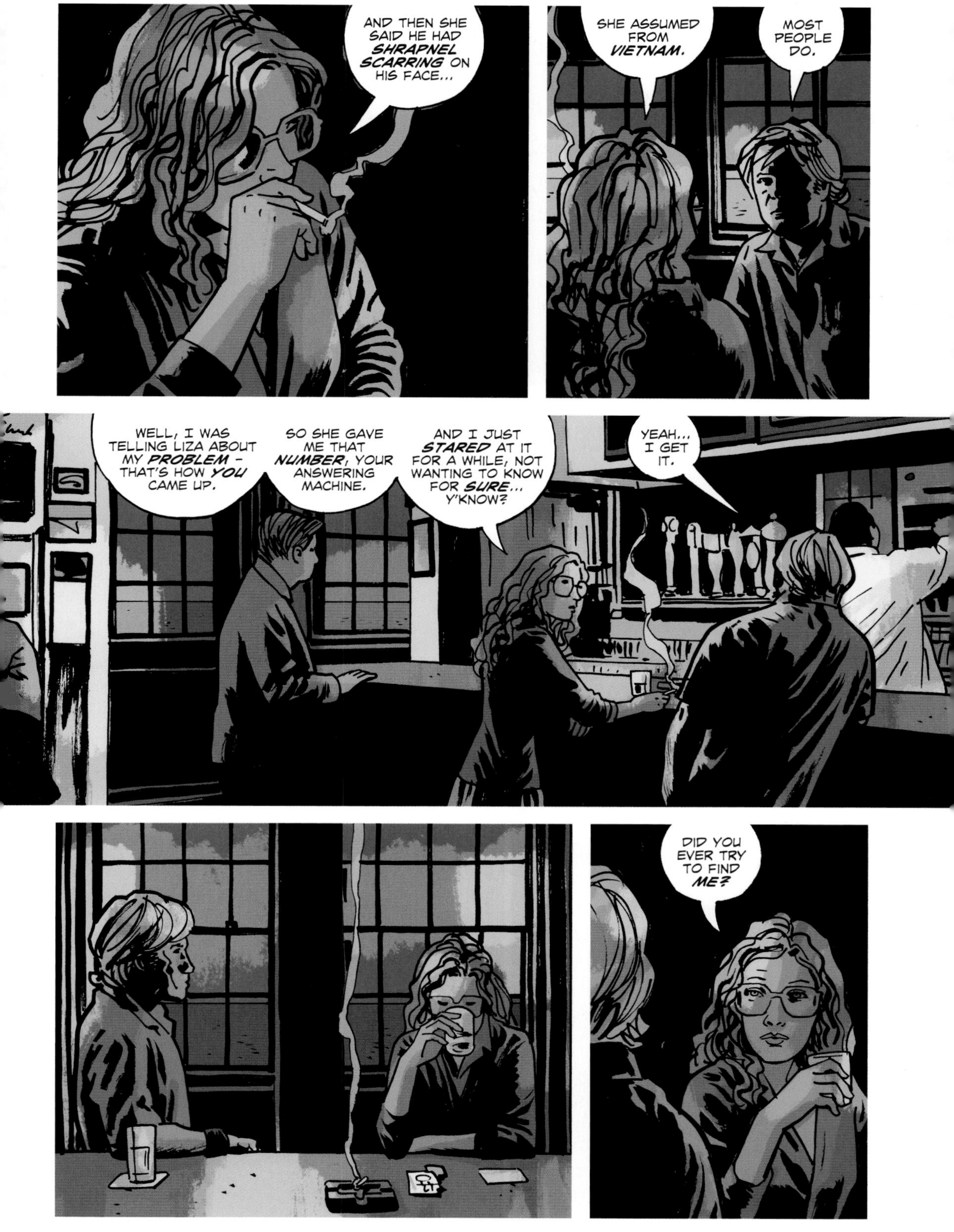
AND THEN SHE SAID HE HAD SHRAPNEL SCARRING ON HIS FACE...
SHE ASSUMED FROM VIETNAM.
MOST PEOPLE DO.
WELL, I WAS TELLING LIZA ABOUT MY PROBLEM -- THAT'S HOW YOU CAME UP.
SO SHE GAVE ME THAT NUMBER, YOUR ANSWERING MACHINE.
AND I JUST STARED AT IT FOR A WHILE, NOT WANTING TO KNOW FOR SURE... Y'KNOW?
YEAH... I GET IT.
DID YOU EVER TRY TO FIND ME?

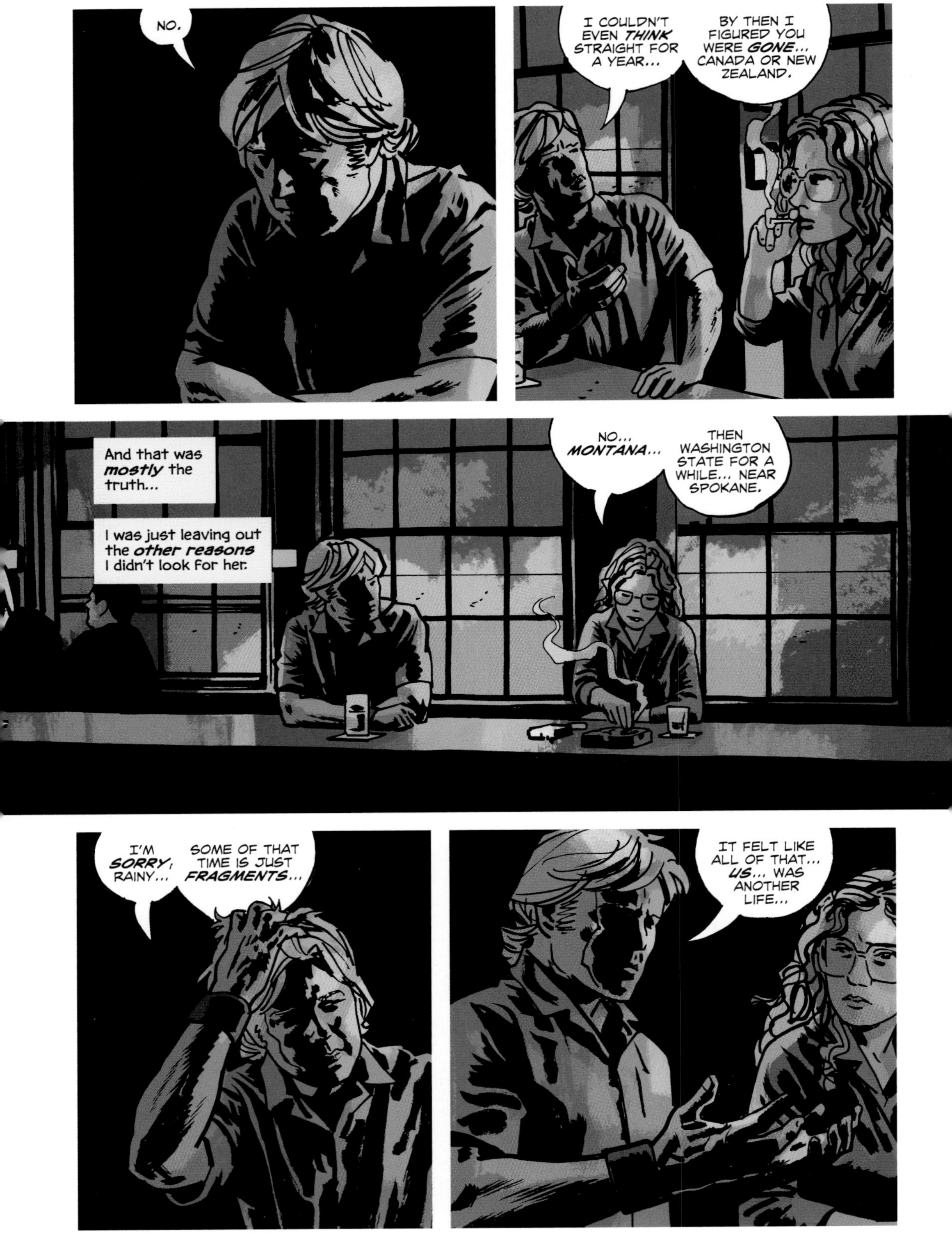
NO.
I COULDN'T EVEN THINK STRAIGHT FOR A YEAR...
BY THEN I FIGURED YOU WERE GONE... CANADA OR NEW ZEALAND.
And that was mostly the truth...
I was just leaving out the other reasons I didn't look for her.
NO... MONTANA...
THEN WASHINGTON STATE FOR A WHILE... NEAR SPOKANE.
I'M SORRY, RAINY...
SOME OF THAT TIME IS JUST FRAGMENTS...
IT FELT LIKE ALL OF THAT... US... WAS ANOTHER LIFE...

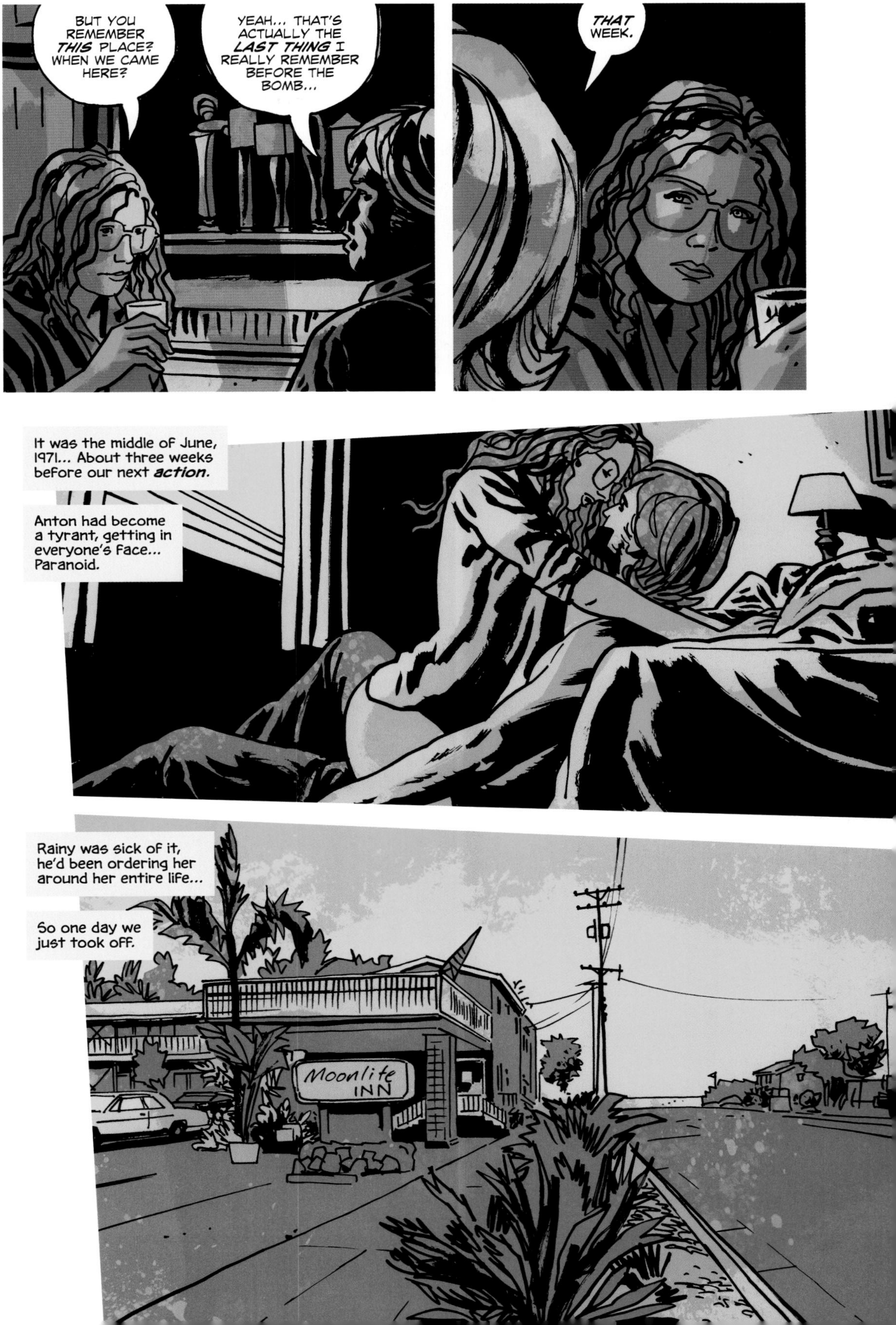

BUT YOU REMEMBER THIS PLACE? WHEN WE CAME HERE?
YEAH... THAT'S ACTUALLY THE LAST THING I REALLY REMEMBER BEFORE THE BOMB...
THAT WEEK.
It was the middle of June, 1971... About three weeks before our next action.
Anton had become a tyrant, getting in everyone's face... Paranoid.
Rainy was sick of it, he'd been ordering her around her entire life...
So one day we just took off.
Moonlite INN

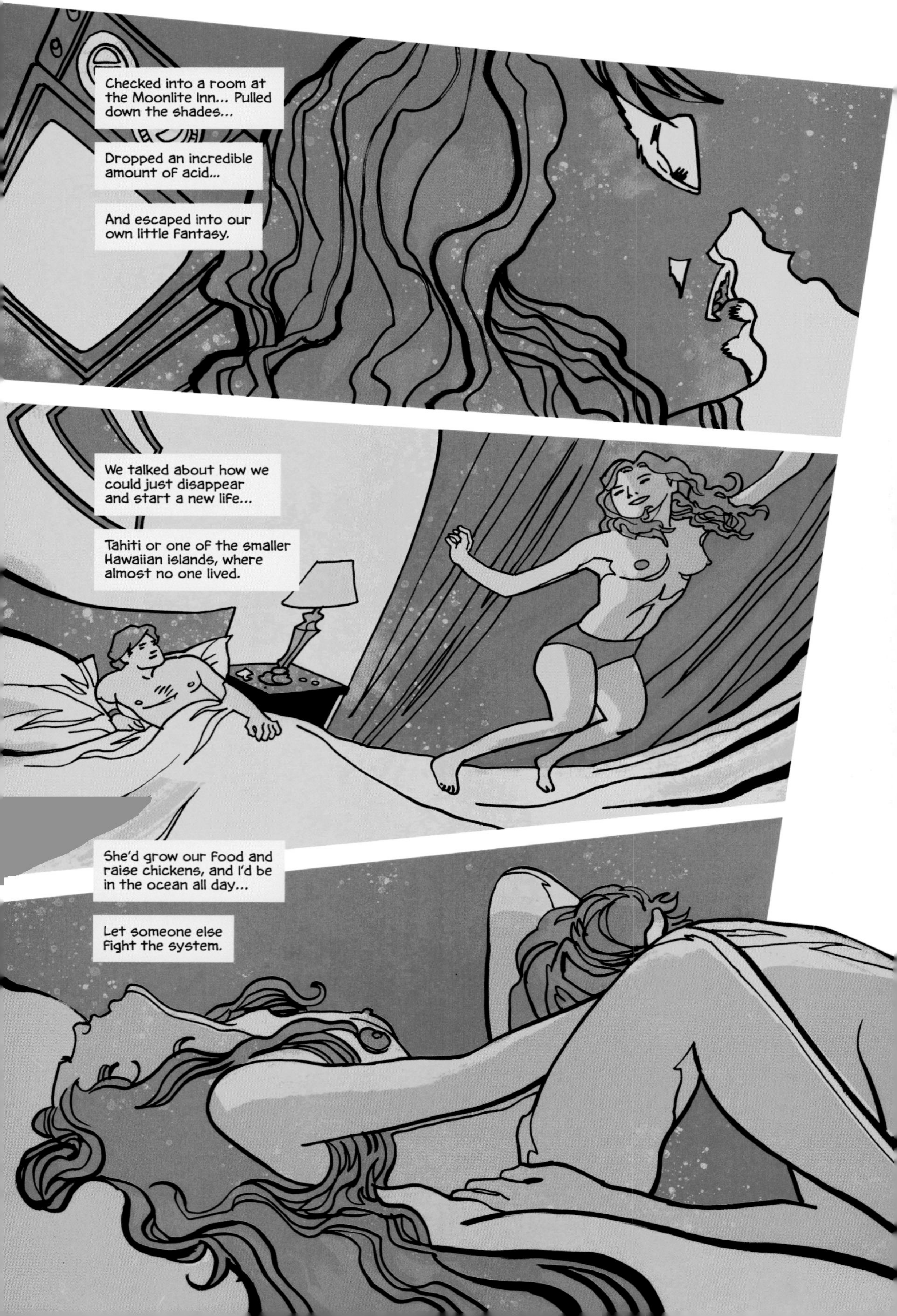
Checked into a room at the Moonlite Inn... Pulled down the shades...
Dropped an incredible amount of acid...
And escaped into our own little fantasy.
We talked about how we could just disappear and start a new life...
Tahiti or one of the smaller Hawaiian islands, where almost no one lived.
She'd grow our food and raise chickens, and I'd be in the ocean all day...
Let someone else fight the system.

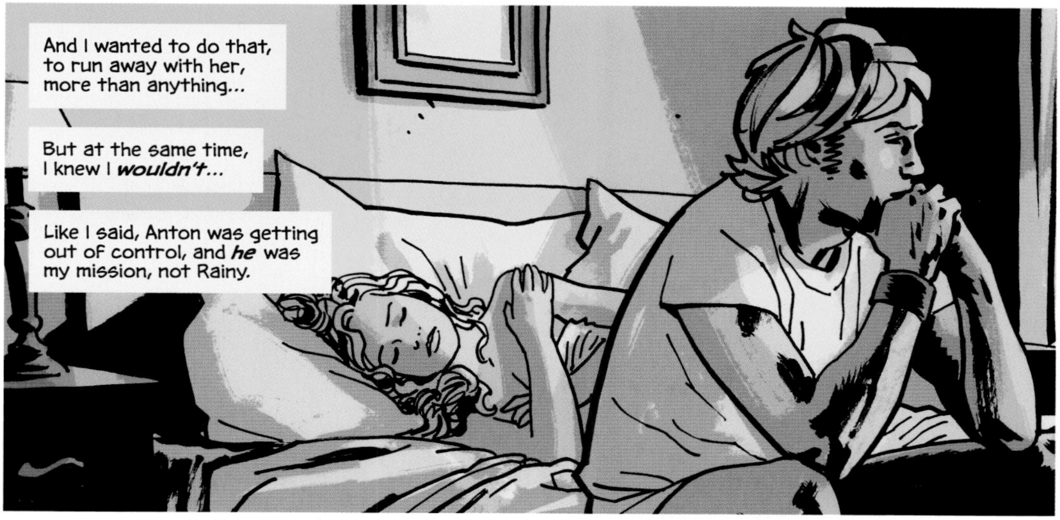
And I wanted to do that, to run away with her, more than anything...
But at the same time, I knew I *wouldn't*...
Like I said, Anton was getting out of control, and *he* was my mission, not Rainy.

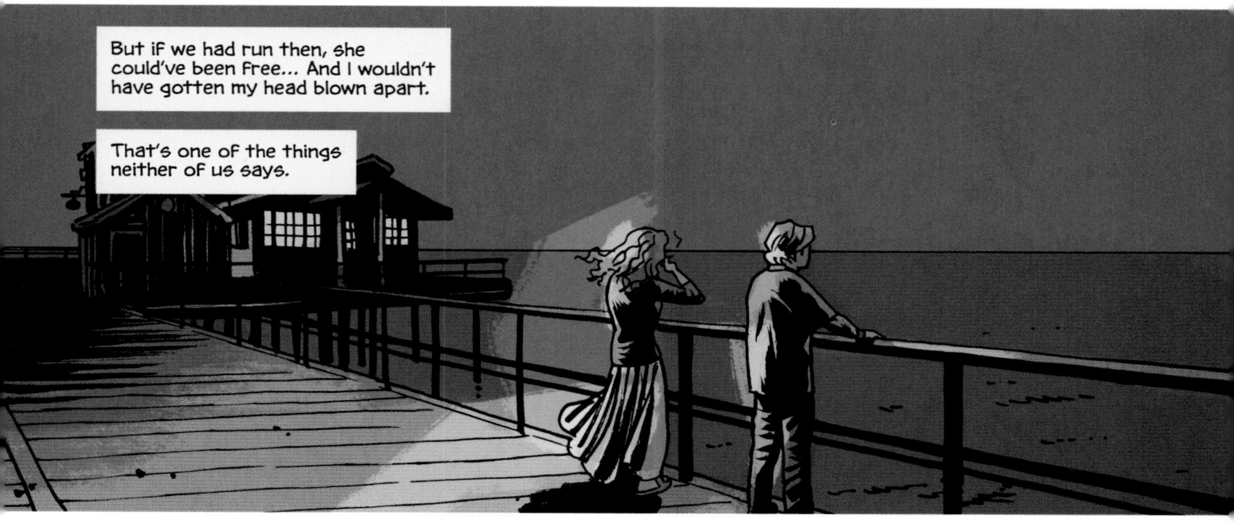
But if we had run then, she could've been free... And I wouldn't have gotten my head blown apart.
That's one of the things neither of us says.

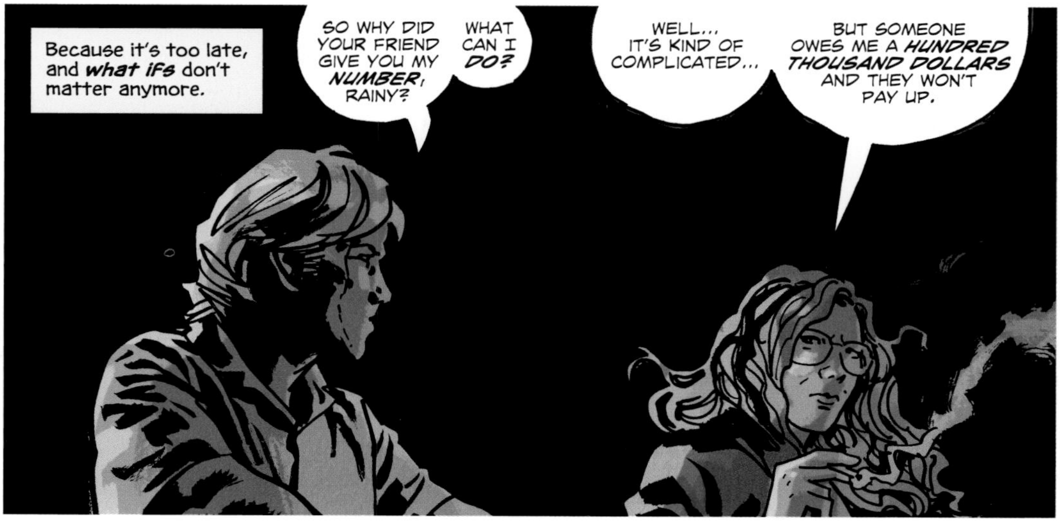
Because it's too late, and *what ifs* don't matter anymore.
SO WHY DID YOUR FRIEND GIVE YOU MY *NUMBER*, RAINY?
WHAT CAN I *DO?*
WELL... IT'S KIND OF COMPLICATED...
BUT SOMEONE OWES ME A *HUNDRED THOUSAND DOLLARS* AND THEY WON'T PAY UP.

SOUNDS SIMPLE ENOUGH.

WHAT'S THE *COMPLICATED* PART?

IT'S MY *SHARE* FROM A BANK ROBBERY.

AH.

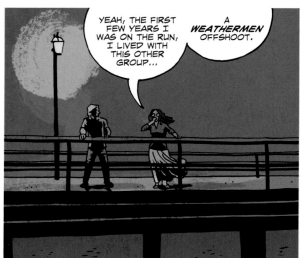

YEAH, THE FIRST FEW YEARS I WAS ON THE RUN, I LIVED WITH THIS OTHER GROUP...

A *WEATHERMEN* OFFSHOOT.

WE ROBBED A *BANK* IN KANSAS CITY IN '74, BUT IT WENT BAD.

TWO COPS GOT SHOT... ONE OF THEM DIED.

WE SPLIT UP AFTER THAT, WENT DEEP UNDERGROUND.

THE PLAN WAS TO LEAVE THE MONEY *HIDDEN* FOR A FEW YEARS, 'TIL ALL THE HEAT BLEW OVER...

EXCEPT WHEN I CALLED MY *CONTACT*, HE TOLD ME IT WAS ALL *GONE*.

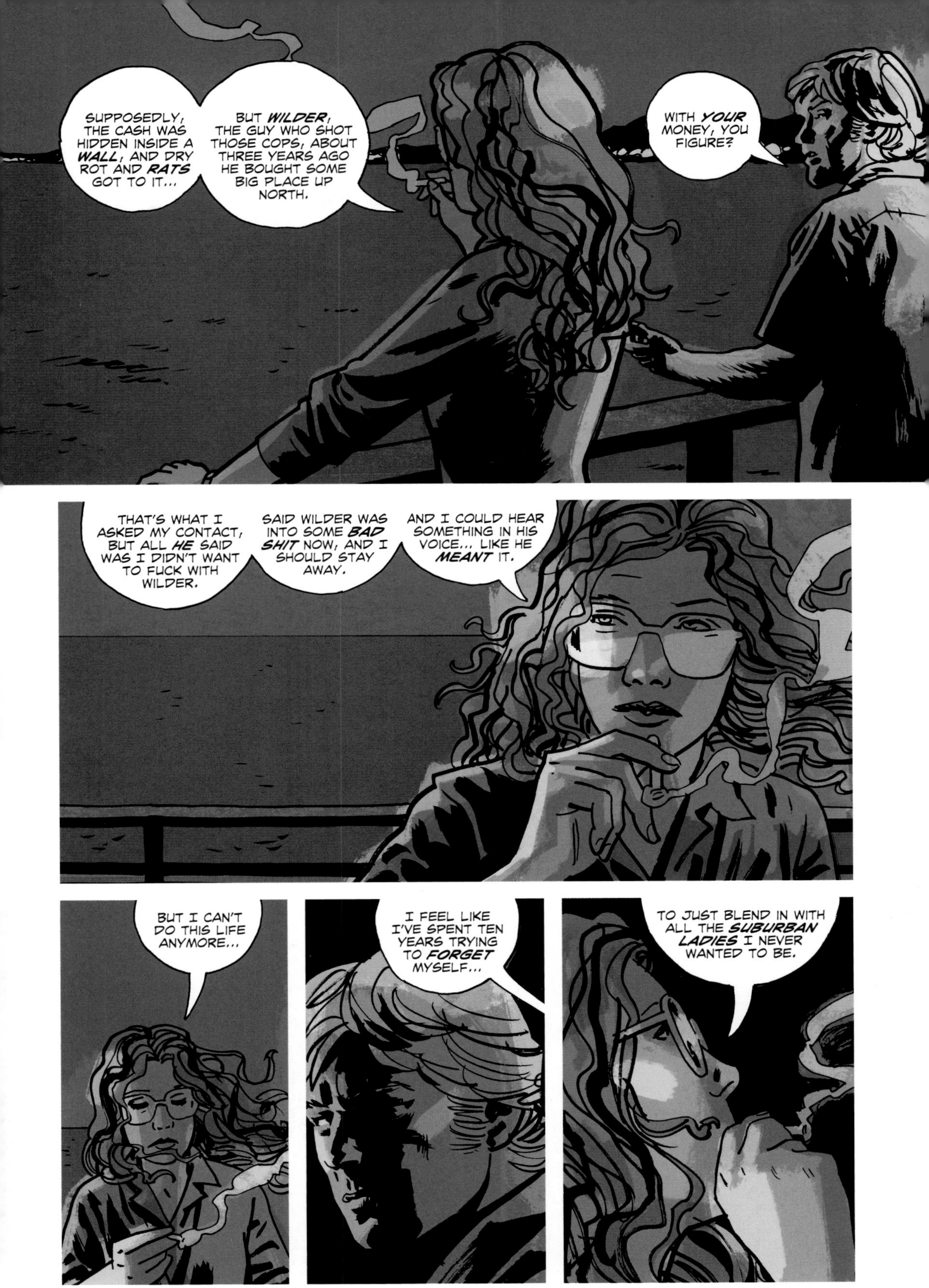
SUPPOSEDLY, THE CASH WAS HIDDEN INSIDE A WALL, AND DRY ROT AND RATS GOT TO IT...
BUT WILDER, THE GUY WHO SHOT THOSE COPS, ABOUT THREE YEARS AGO HE BOUGHT SOME BIG PLACE UP NORTH.
WITH YOUR MONEY, YOU FIGURE?
THAT'S WHAT I ASKED MY CONTACT, BUT ALL HE SAID WAS I DIDN'T WANT TO FUCK WITH WILDER.
SAID WILDER WAS INTO SOME BAD SHIT NOW, AND I SHOULD STAY AWAY.
AND I COULD HEAR SOMETHING IN HIS VOICE... LIKE HE MEANT IT.
BUT I CAN'T DO THIS LIFE ANYMORE...
I FEEL LIKE I'VE SPENT TEN YEARS TRYING TO FORGET MYSELF...
TO JUST BLEND IN WITH ALL THE SUBURBAN LADIES I NEVER WANTED TO BE.

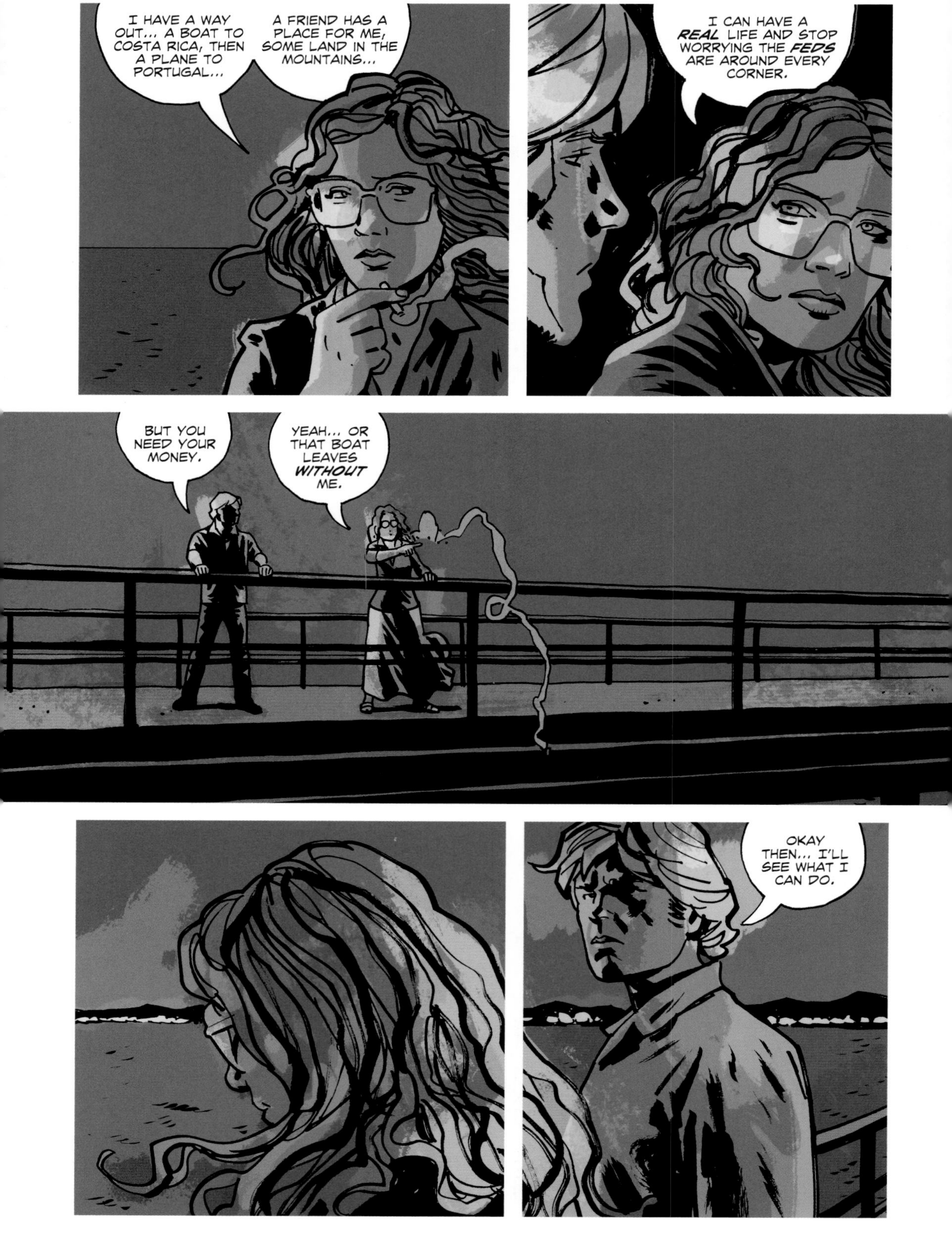
I HAVE A WAY OUT... A BOAT TO COSTA RICA, THEN A PLANE TO PORTUGAL...
A FRIEND HAS A PLACE FOR ME, SOME LAND IN THE MOUNTAINS...
I CAN HAVE A *REAL* LIFE AND STOP WORRYING THE *FEDS* ARE AROUND EVERY CORNER.
BUT YOU NEED YOUR MONEY.
YEAH... OR THAT BOAT LEAVES *WITHOUT* ME.
OKAY THEN... I'LL SEE WHAT I CAN DO.

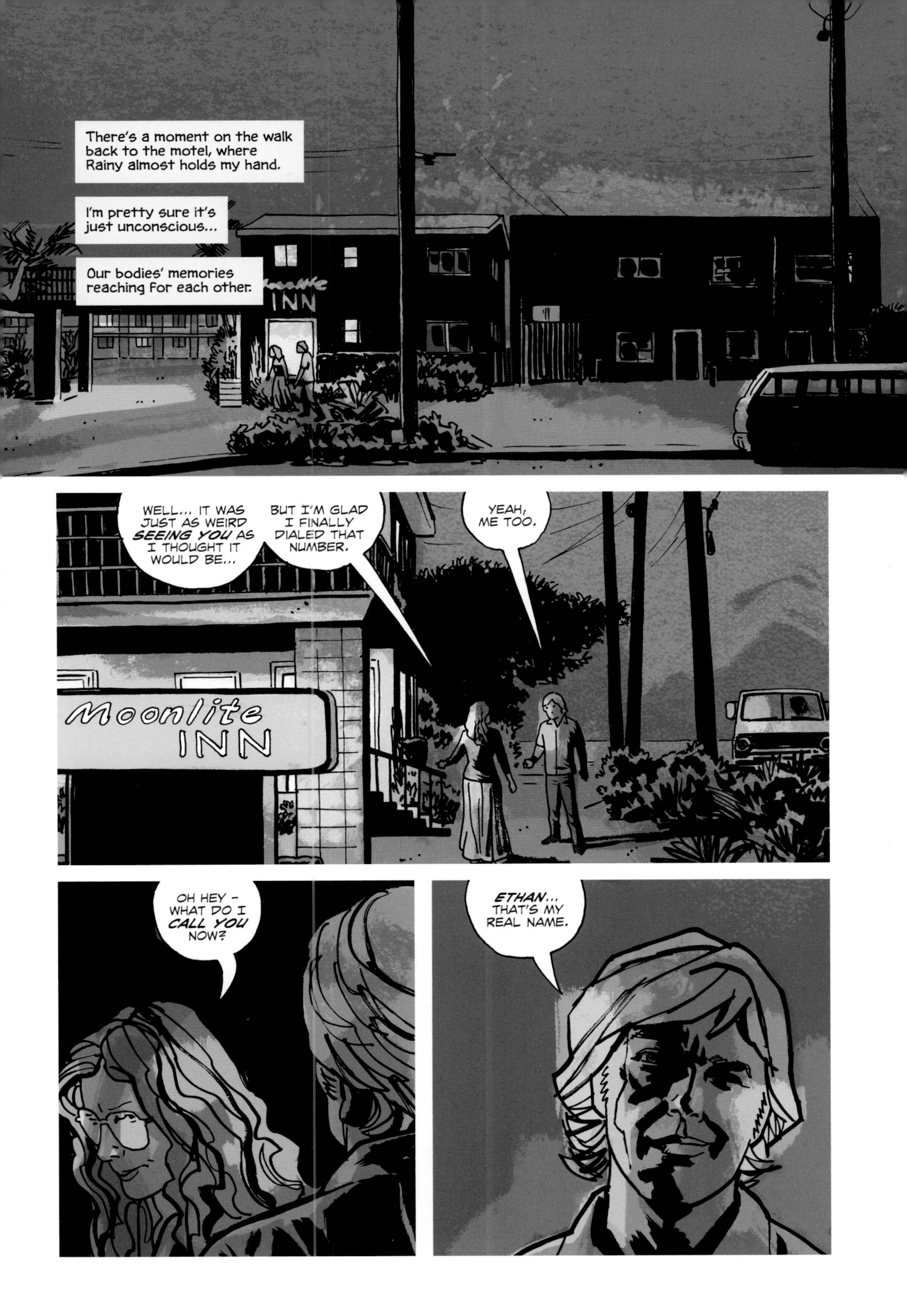
There's a moment on the walk back to the motel, where Rainy almost holds my hand.
I'm pretty sure it's just unconscious...
Our bodies' memories reaching for each other.
INN
WELL... IT WAS JUST AS WEIRD SEEING YOU AS I THOUGHT IT WOULD BE...
BUT I'M GLAD I FINALLY DIALED THAT NUMBER.
YEAH, ME TOO.
Moonlite INN
OH HEY - WHAT DO I CALL YOU NOW?
ETHAN... THAT'S MY REAL NAME.

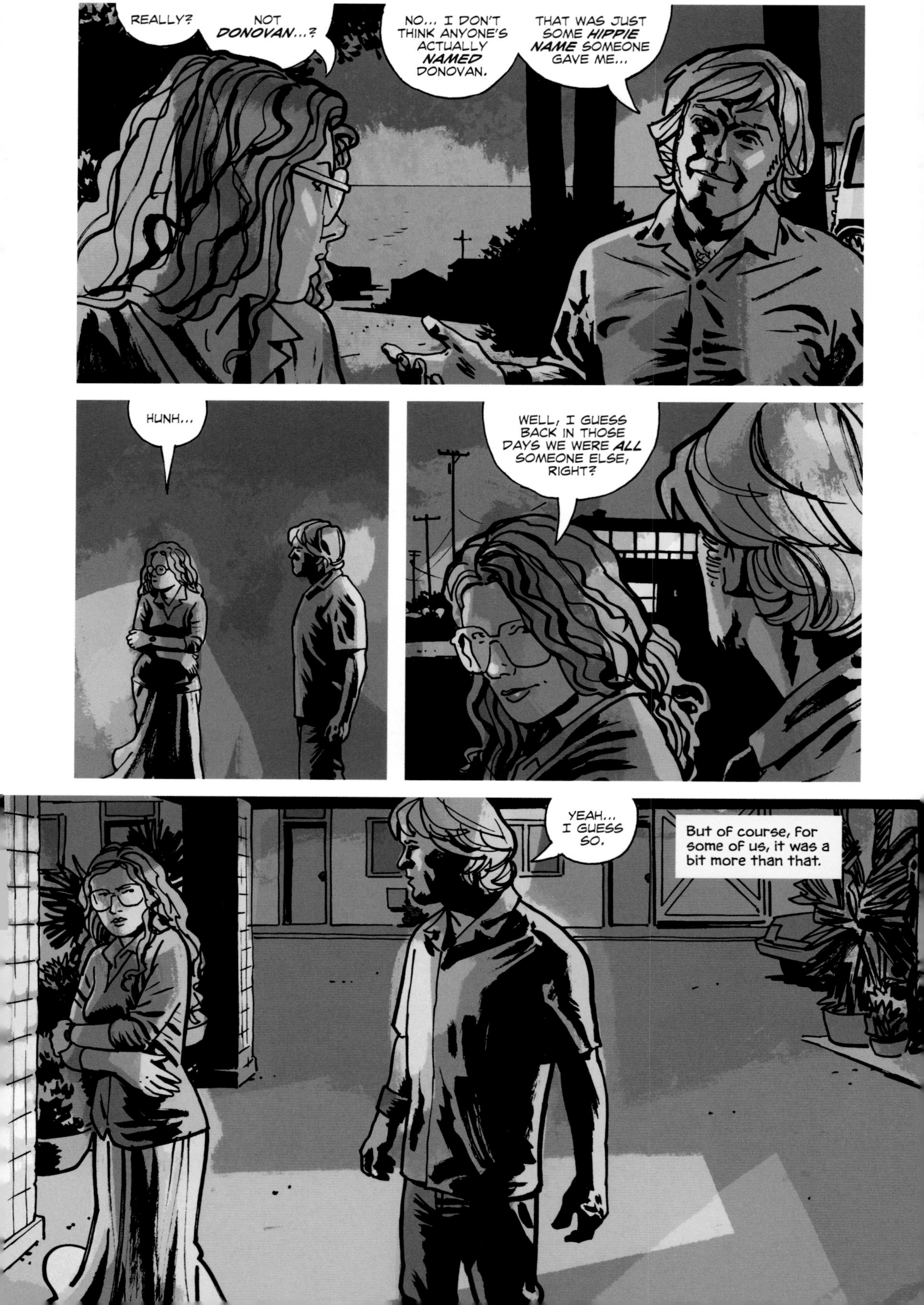
REALLY?
NOT DONOVAN...?
NO... I DON'T THINK ANYONE'S ACTUALLY NAMED DONOVAN.
THAT WAS JUST SOME HIPPIE NAME SOMEONE GAVE ME...
HUNH...
WELL, I GUESS BACK IN THOSE DAYS WE WERE ALL SOMEONE ELSE, RIGHT?
YEAH... I GUESS SO.
But of course, for some of us, it was a bit more than that.

The Fortunate Son

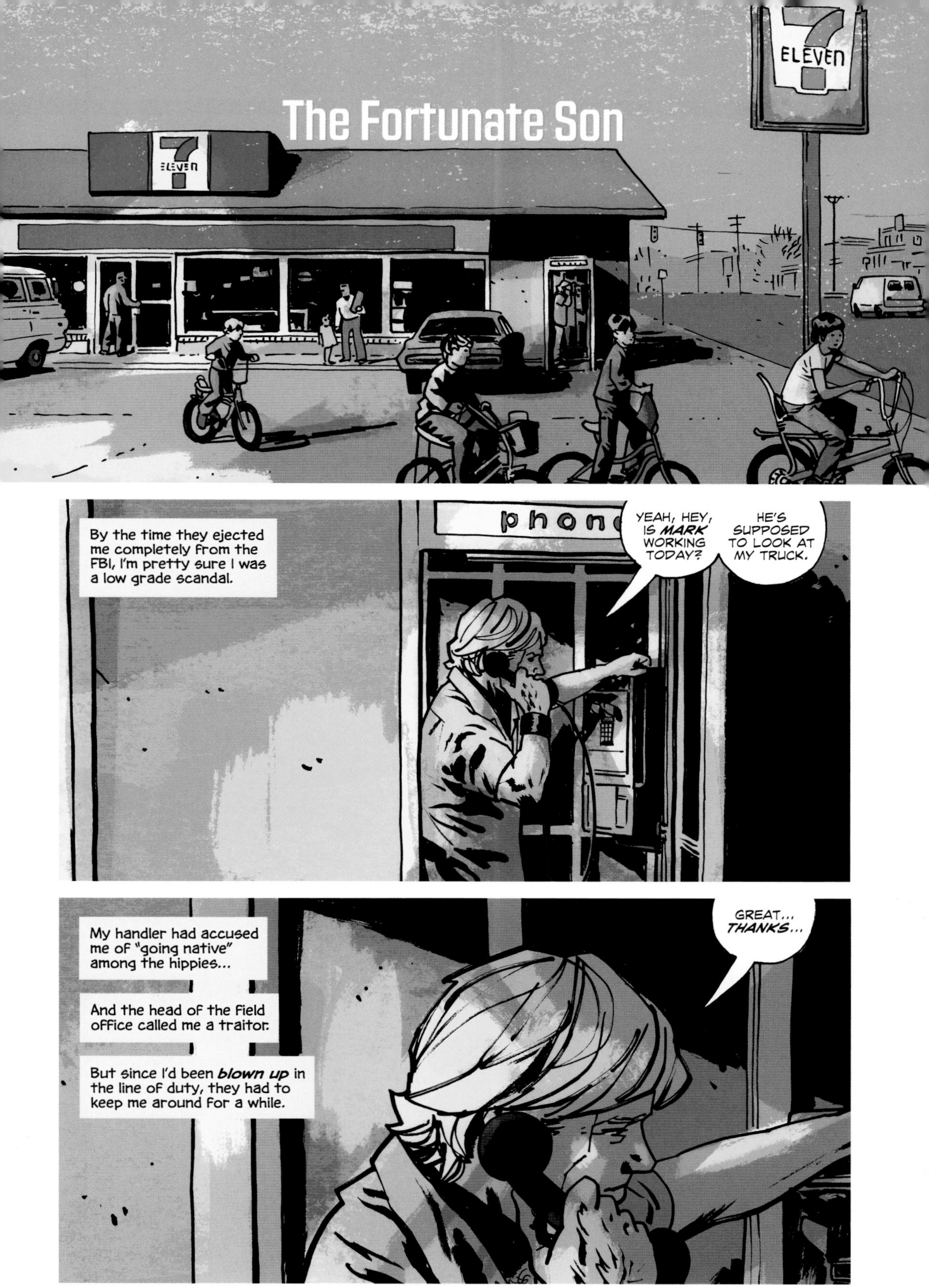
7 ELEVEN
7 ELEVEN
phone
By the time they ejected me completely from the FBI, I'm pretty sure I was a low grade scandal.
YEAH, HEY, IS **MARK** WORKING TODAY?
HE'S SUPPOSED TO LOOK AT MY TRUCK.
My handler had accused me of "going native" among the hippies...
And the head of the field office called me a traitor.
But since I'd been ***blown up*** in the line of duty, they had to keep me around for a while.
GREAT... ***THANKS***...

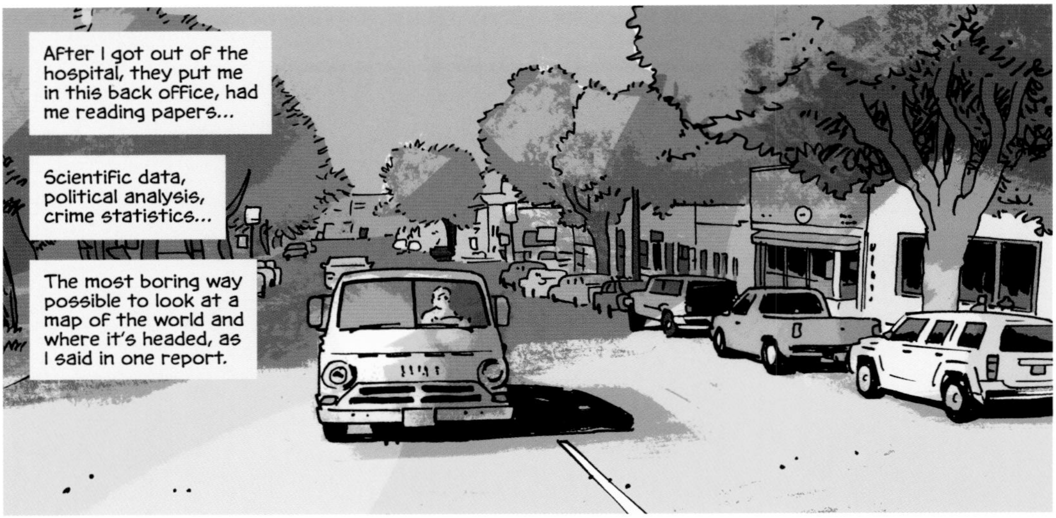
After I got out of the hospital, they put me in this back office, had me reading papers...
Scientific data, political analysis, crime statistics...
The most boring way possible to look at a map of the world and where it's headed, as I said in one report.

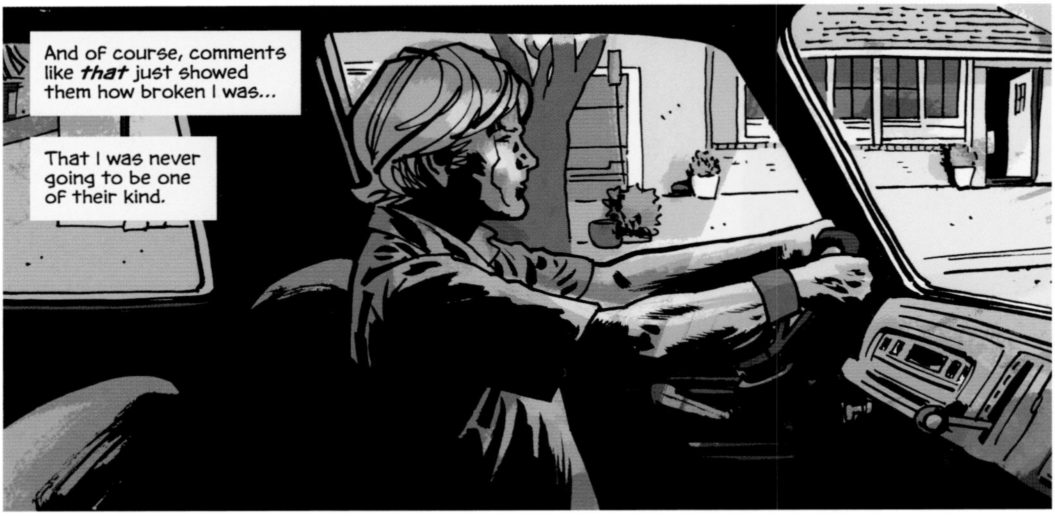
And of course, comments like *that* just showed them how broken I was...
That I was never going to be one of their kind.

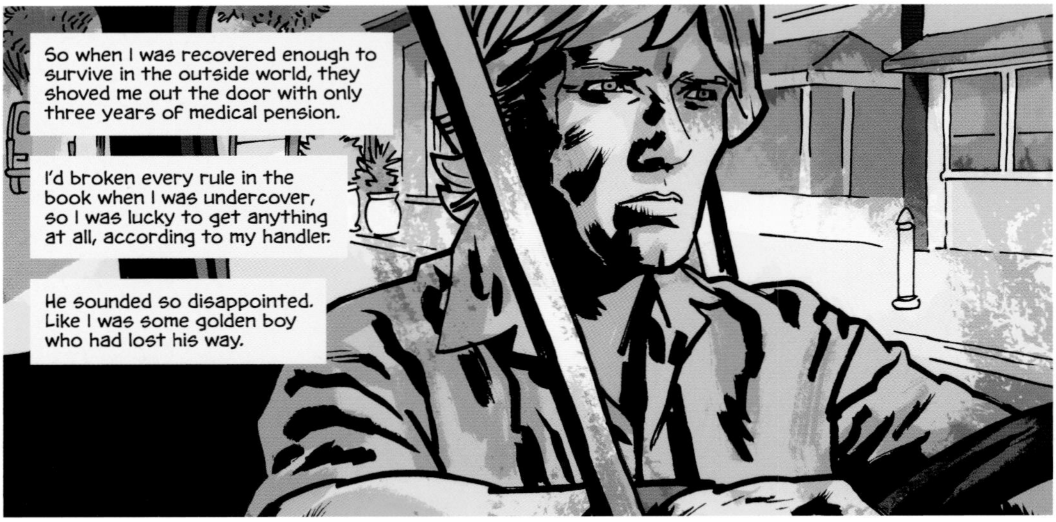
So when I was recovered enough to survive in the outside world, they shoved me out the door with only three years of medical pension.
I'd broken every rule in the book when I was undercover, so I was lucky to get anything at all, according to my handler.
He sounded so disappointed. Like I was some golden boy who had lost his way.

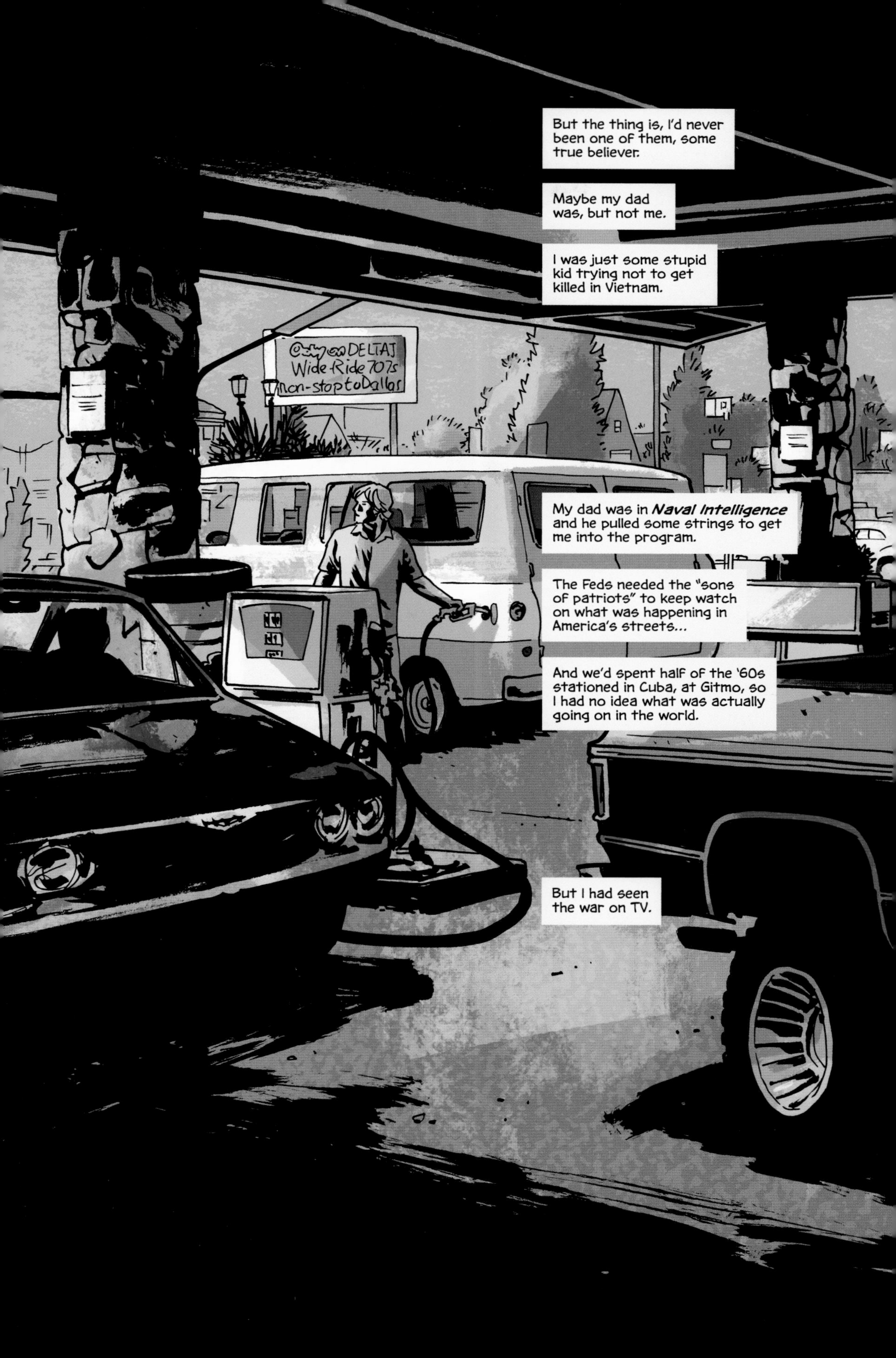
DELTA
Wide-Ride 707s
non-stop to Dallas
But the thing is, I'd never been one of them, some true believer.
Maybe my dad was, but not me.
I was just some stupid kid trying not to get killed in Vietnam.
My dad was in ***Naval Intelligence*** and he pulled some strings to get me into the program.
The Feds needed the "sons of patriots" to keep watch on what was happening in America's streets...
And we'd spent half of the '60s stationed in Cuba, at Gitmo, so I had no idea what was actually going on in the world.
But I had seen the war on TV.

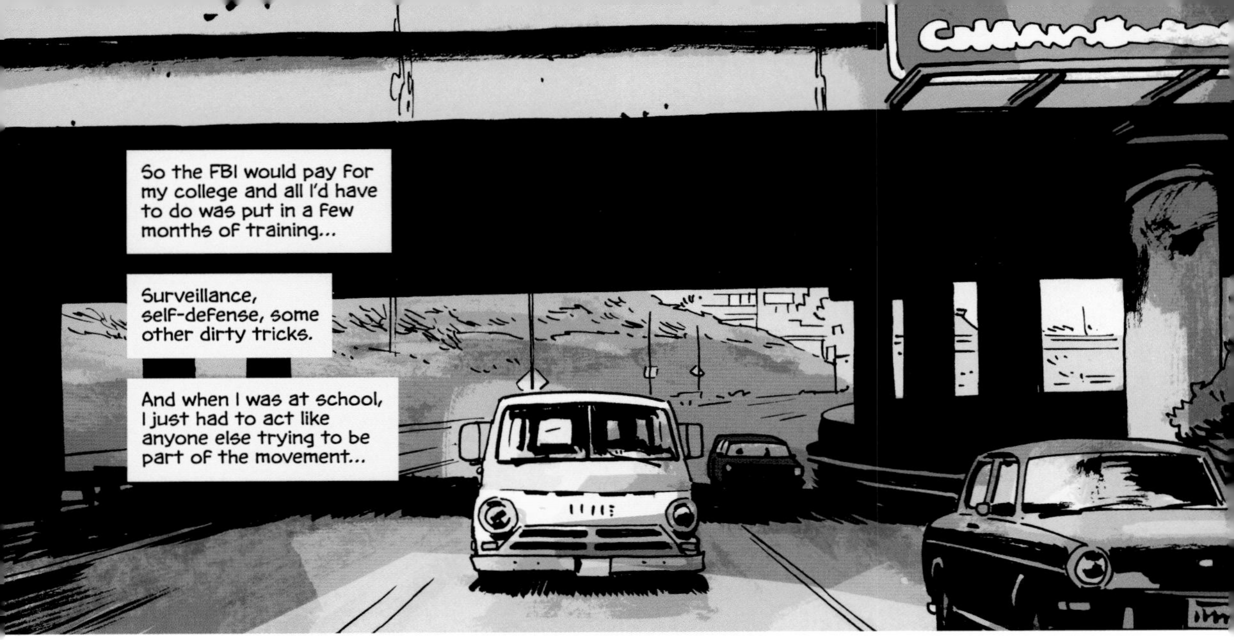
So the FBI would pay for my college and all I'd have to do was put in a few months of training...
Surveillance, self-defense, some other dirty tricks.
And when I was at school, I just had to act like anyone else trying to be part of the movement...

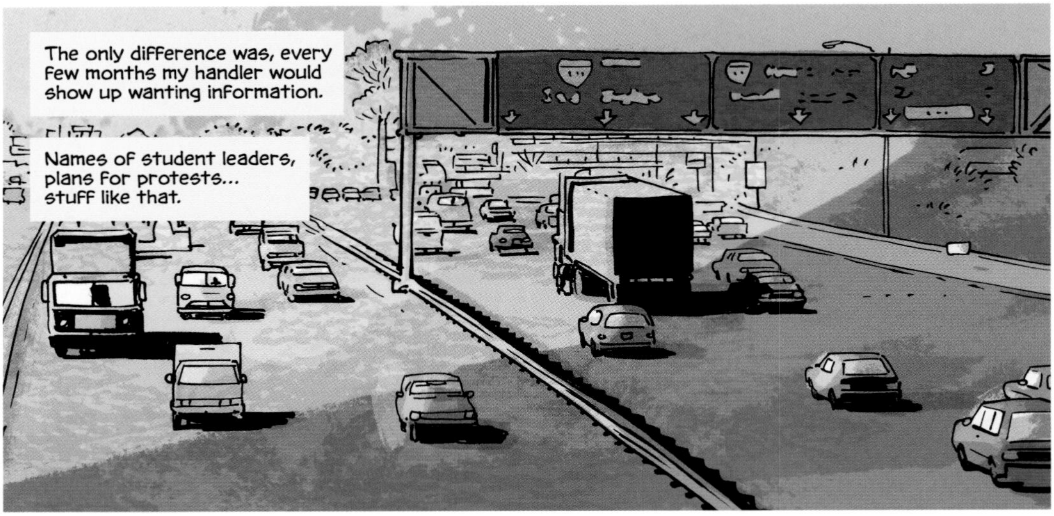
The only difference was, every few months my handler would show up wanting information.
Names of student leaders, plans for protests... stuff like that.

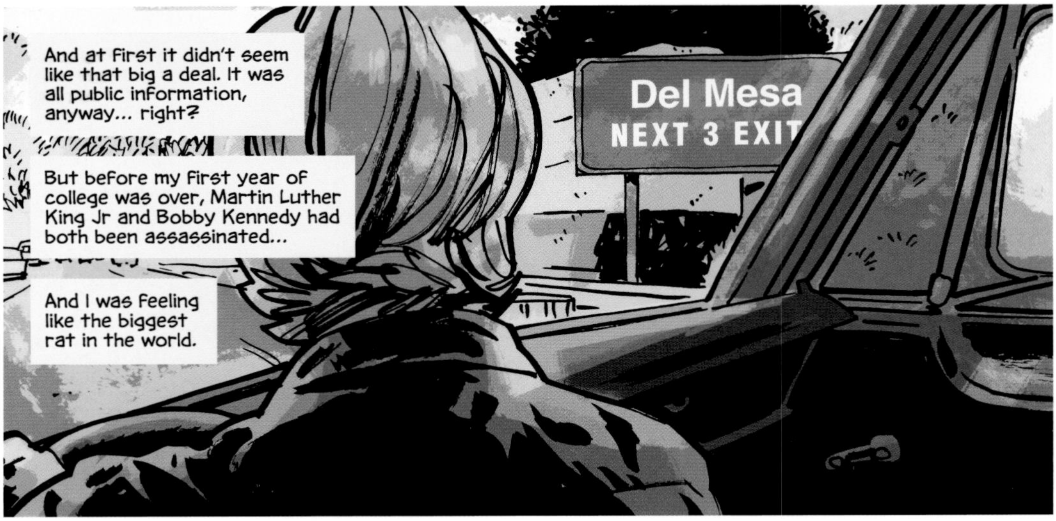
And at first it didn't seem like that big a deal. It was all public information, anyway... right?
Del Mesa
NEXT 3 EXIT
But before my first year of college was over, Martin Luther King Jr and Bobby Kennedy had both been assassinated...
And I was feeling like the biggest rat in the world.

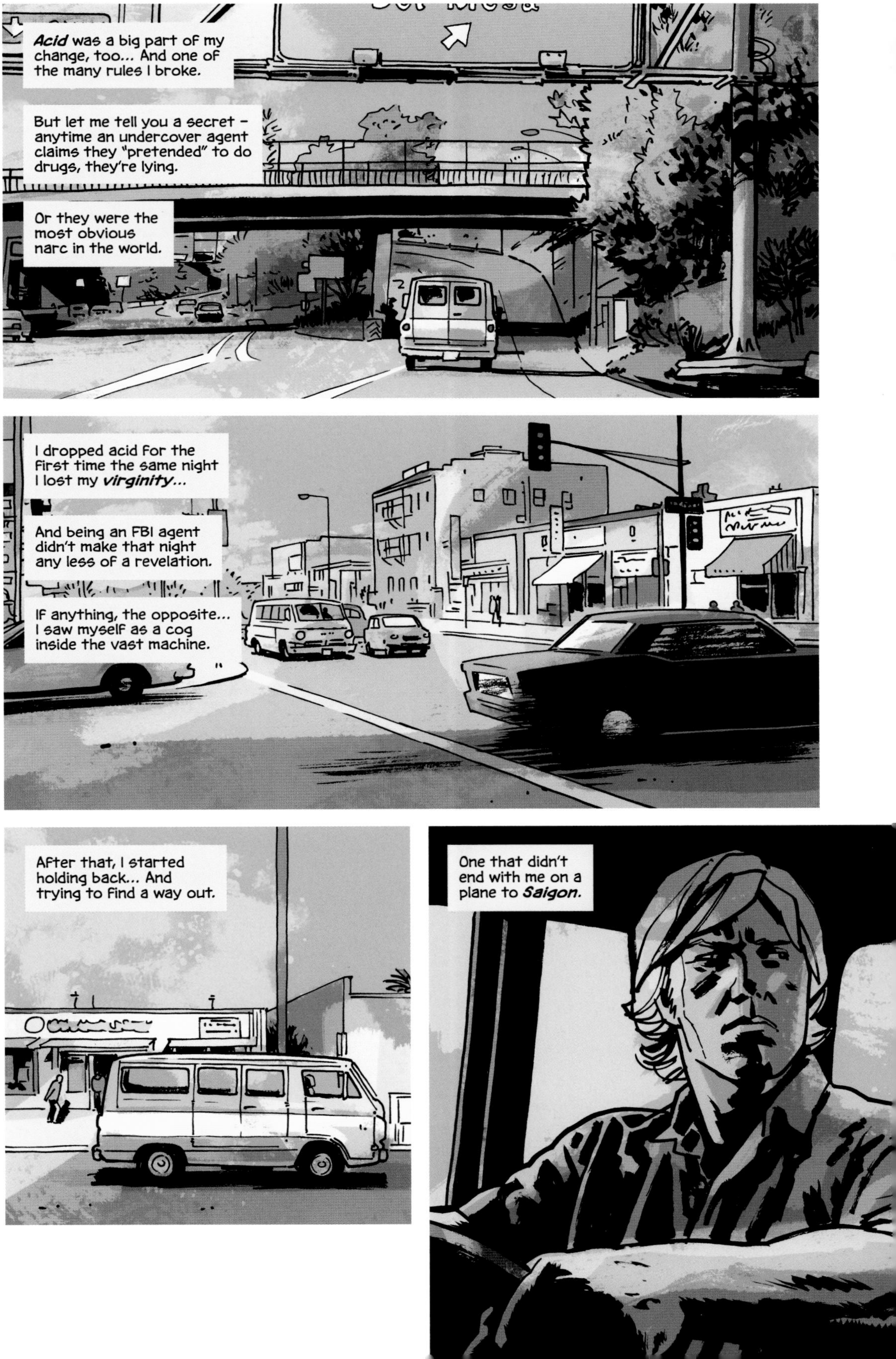
Acid was a big part of my change, too... And one of the many rules I broke.
But let me tell you a secret – anytime an undercover agent claims they "pretended" to do drugs, they're lying.
Or they were the most obvious narc in the world.
I dropped acid for the first time the same night I lost my *virginity*...
And being an FBI agent didn't make that night any less of a revelation.
If anything, the opposite... I saw myself as a cog inside the vast machine.
After that, I started holding back... And trying to find a way out.
One that didn't end with me on a plane to *Saigon*.

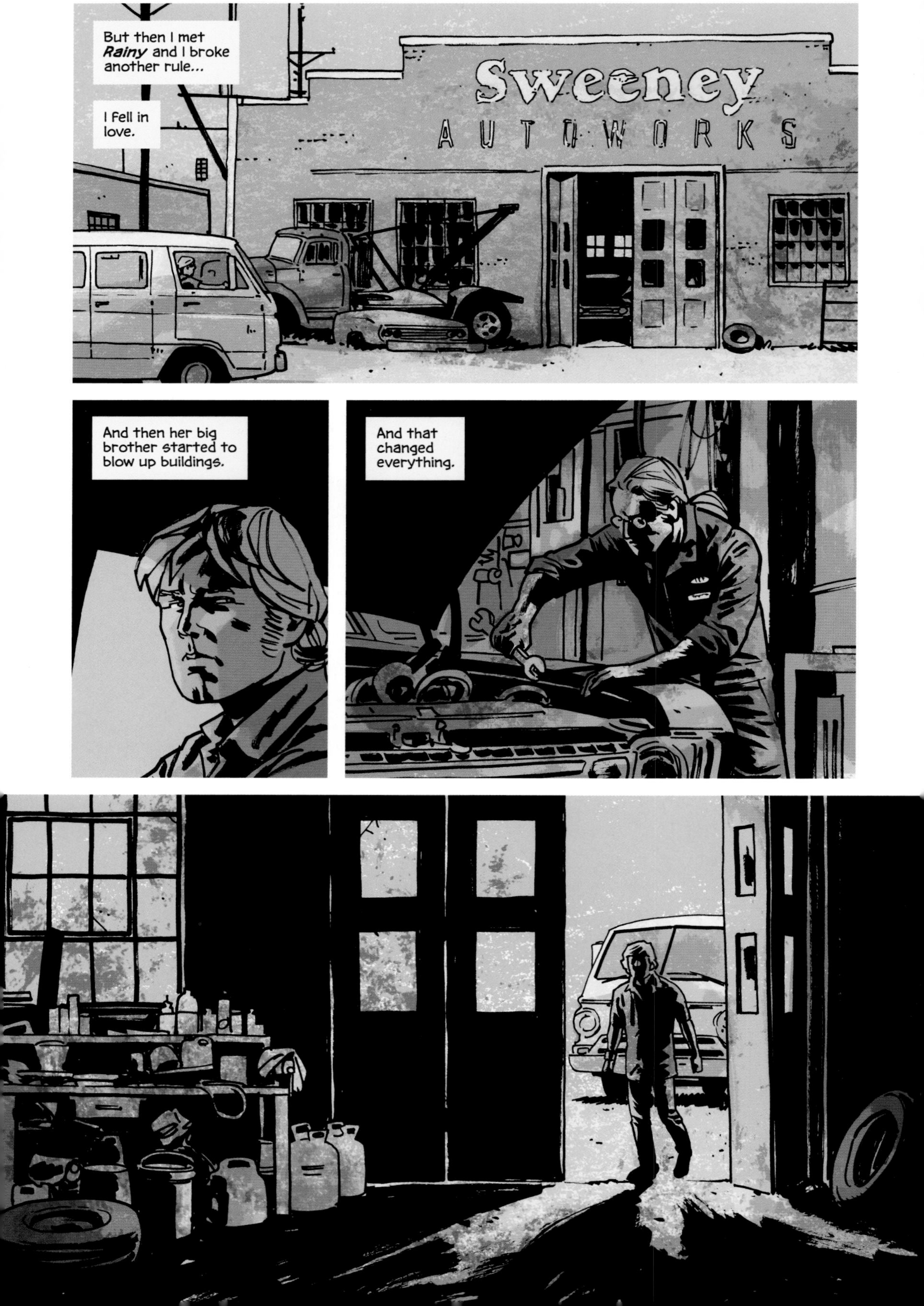
But then I met *Rainy* and I broke another rule...
I fell in love.
Sweeney
AUTOWORKS
And then her big brother started to blow up buildings.
And that changed everything.

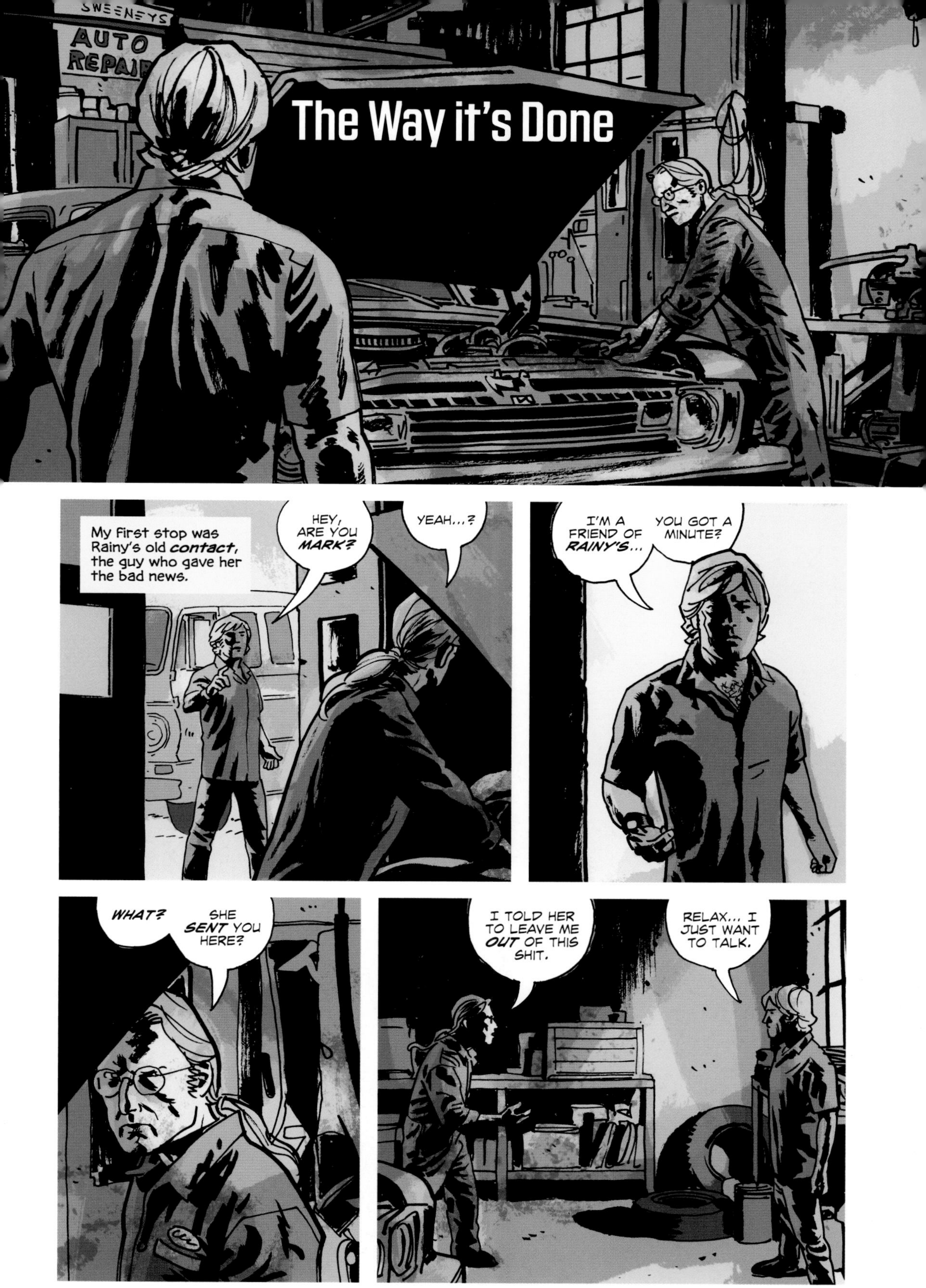
SWEENEYS
AUTO
The Way it's Done
My first stop was Rainy's old *contact*, the guy who gave her the bad news.
HEY, ARE YOU *MARK?*
YEAH...?
I'M A FRIEND OF *RAINY'S*...
YOU GOT A MINUTE?
WHAT?
SHE *SENT* YOU HERE?
I TOLD HER TO LEAVE ME *OUT* OF THIS SHIT.
RELAX... I JUST WANT TO TALK.

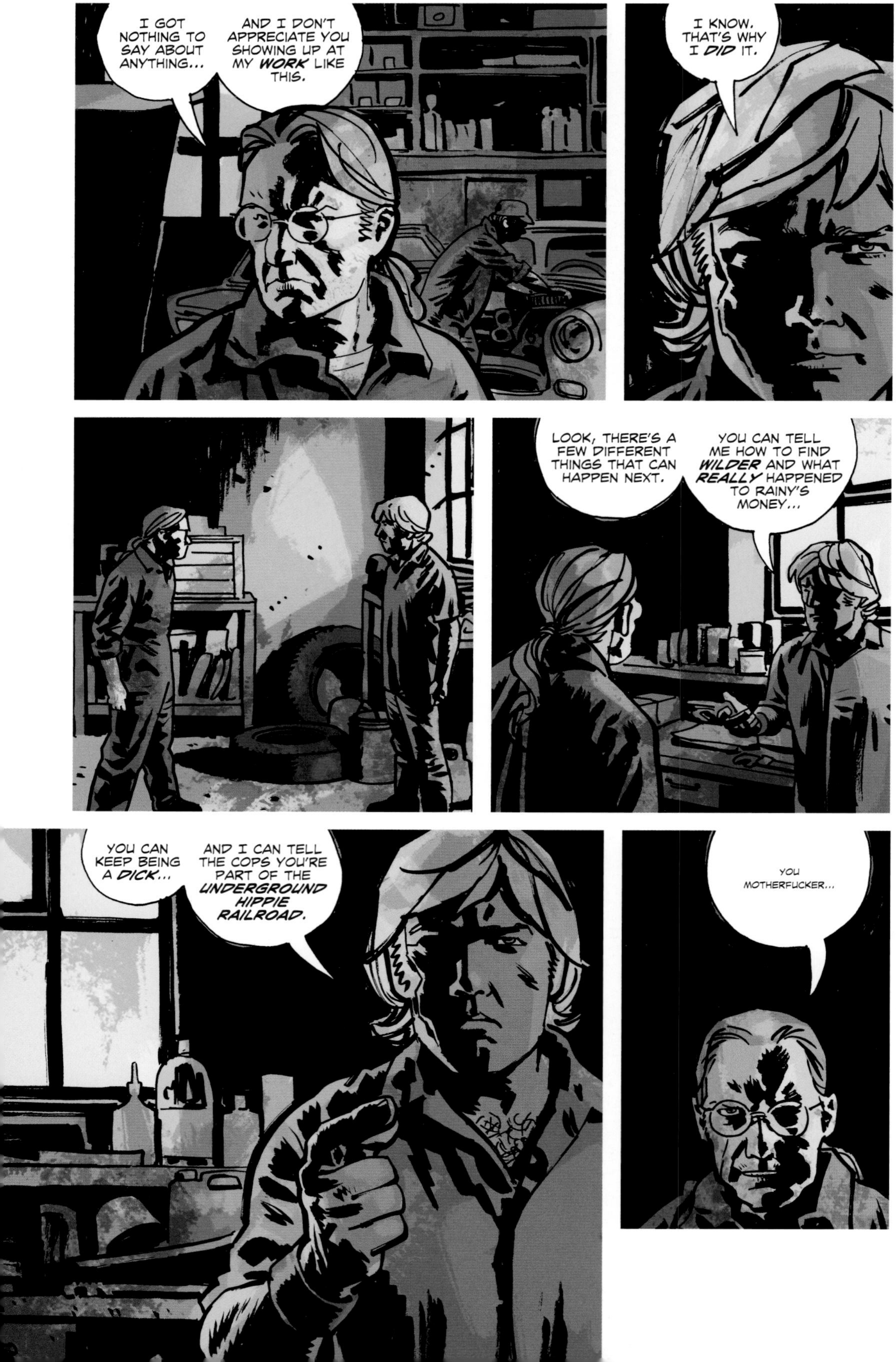
I GOT NOTHING TO SAY ABOUT ANYTHING...
AND I DON'T APPRECIATE YOU SHOWING UP AT MY *WORK* LIKE THIS.
I KNOW. THAT'S WHY I *DID* IT.
LOOK, THERE'S A FEW DIFFERENT THINGS THAT CAN HAPPEN NEXT.
YOU CAN TELL ME HOW TO FIND *WILDER* AND WHAT *REALLY* HAPPENED TO RAINY'S MONEY...
YOU CAN KEEP BEING A *DICK*...
AND I CAN TELL THE COPS YOU'RE PART OF THE *UNDERGROUND HIPPIE RAILROAD.*
YOU MOTHERFUCKER...

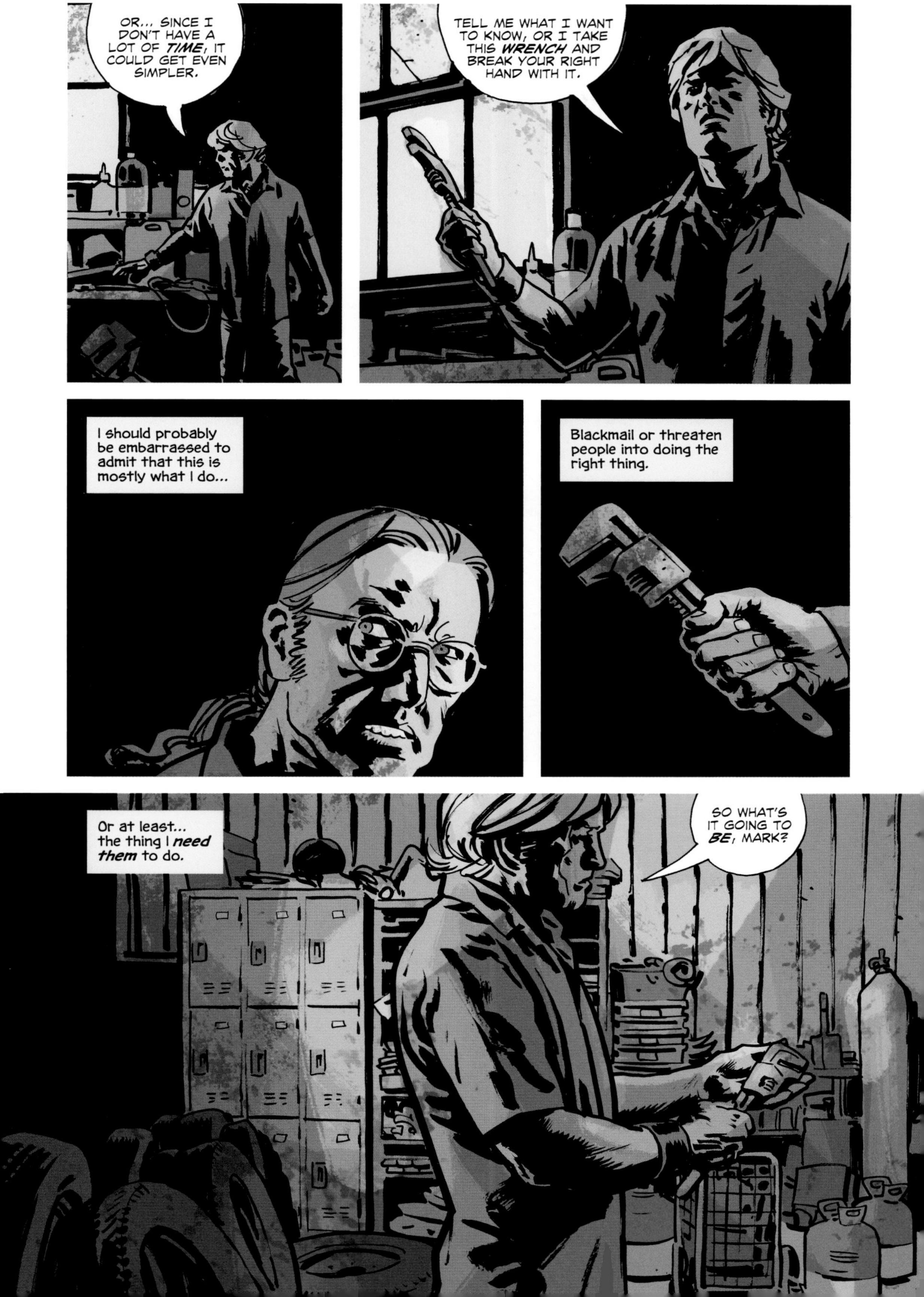
OR... SINCE I DON'T HAVE A LOT OF *TIME*, IT COULD GET EVEN SIMPLER.
TELL ME WHAT I WANT TO KNOW, OR I TAKE THIS *WRENCH* AND BREAK YOUR RIGHT HAND WITH IT.
I should probably be embarrassed to admit that this is mostly what I do...
Blackmail or threaten people into doing the right thing.
Or at least... the thing I *need them* to do.
SO WHAT'S IT GOING TO *BE*, MARK?

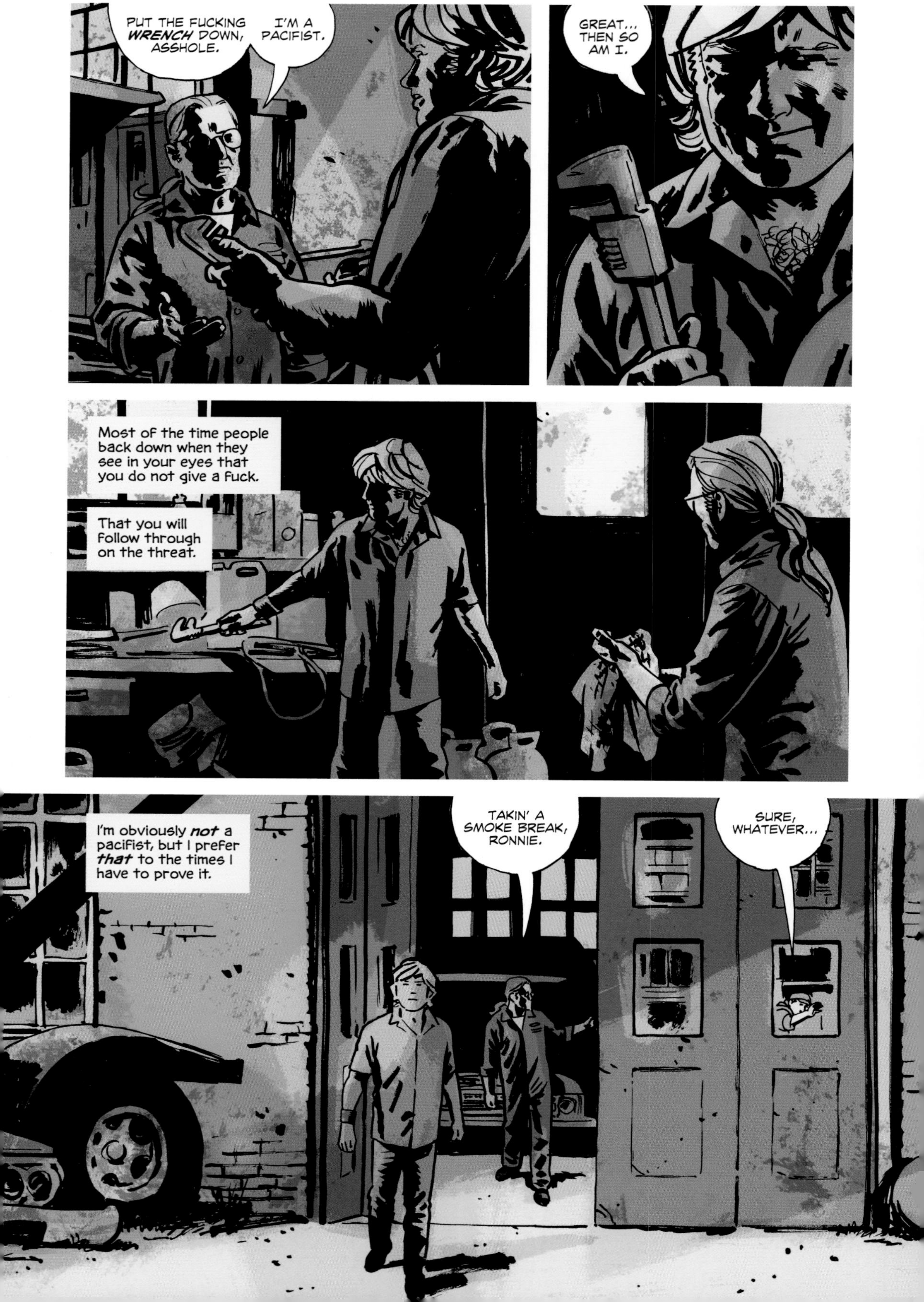
PUT THE FUCKING *WRENCH* DOWN, ASSHOLE.
I'M A PACIFIST.
GREAT... THEN SO AM I.
Most of the time people back down when they see in your eyes that you do not give a fuck.
That you will follow through on the threat.
I'm obviously *not* a pacifist, but I prefer *that* to the times I have to prove it.
TAKIN' A SMOKE BREAK, RONNIE.
SURE, WHATEVER...

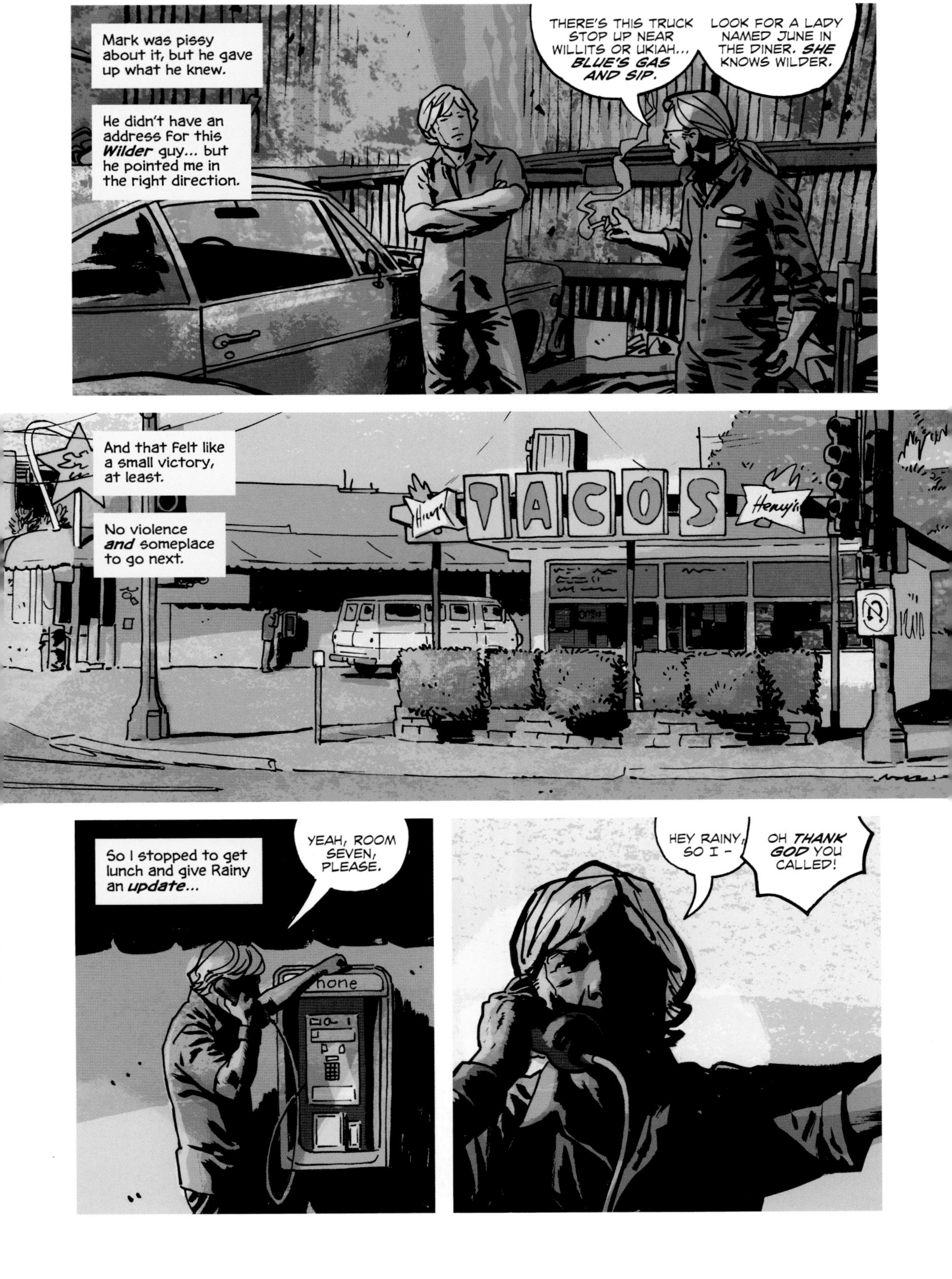

Mark was pissy about it, but he gave up what he knew.
He didn't have an address for this *Wilder* guy... but he pointed me in the right direction.
THERE'S THIS TRUCK STOP UP NEAR WILLITS OR UKIAH... *BLUE'S GAS AND SIP.*
LOOK FOR A LADY NAMED JUNE IN THE DINER. *SHE* KNOWS WILDER.
And that felt like a small victory, at least.
No violence *and* someplace to go next.
TACOS
Henry's
So I stopped to get lunch and give Rainy an *update*...
YEAH, ROOM SEVEN, PLEASE.
HEY RAINY, SO I -
OH *THANK GOD* YOU CALLED!

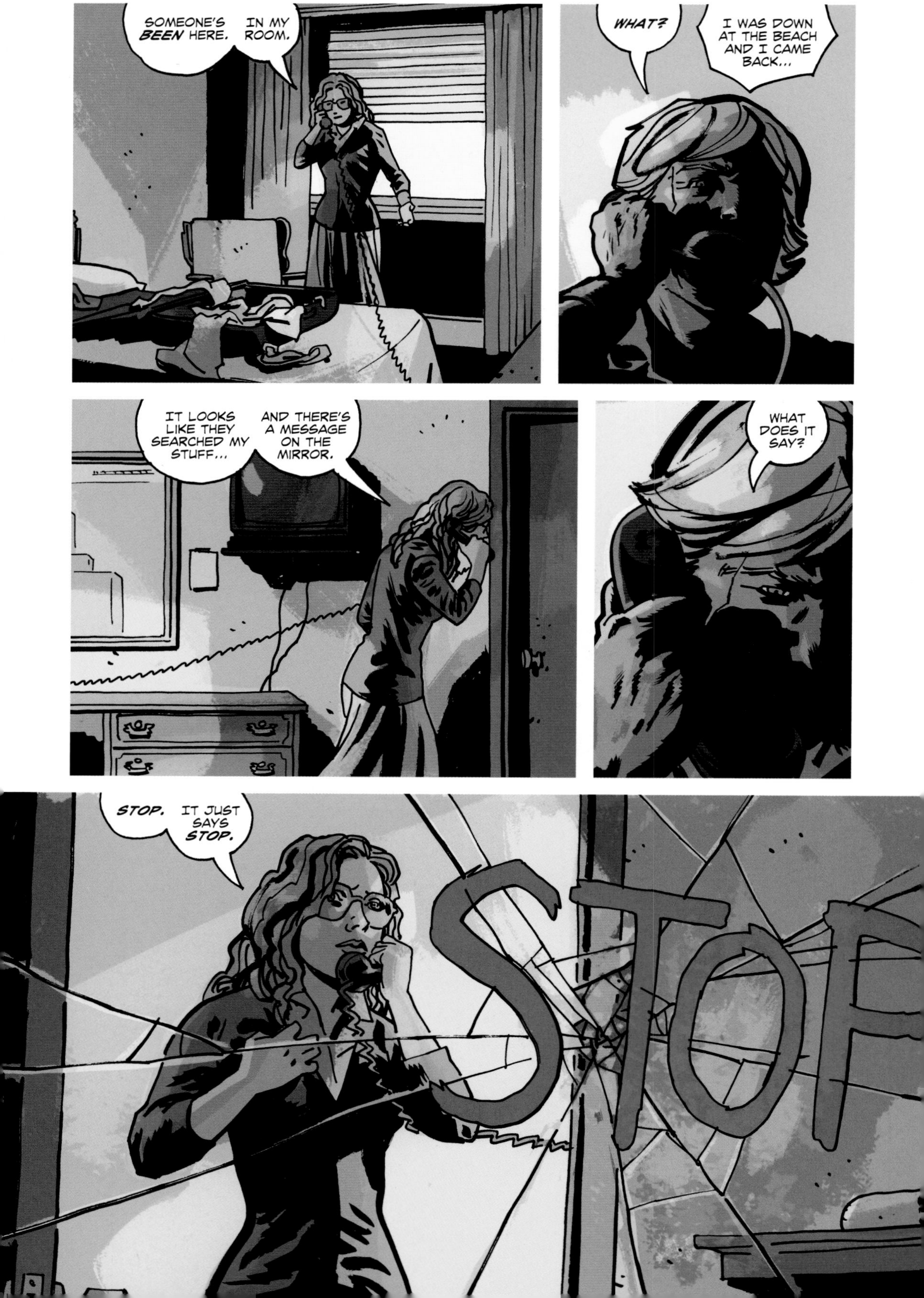
SOMEONE'S *BEEN* HERE.
IN MY ROOM.
WHAT?
I WAS DOWN AT THE BEACH AND I CAME BACK...
IT LOOKS LIKE THEY SEARCHED MY STUFF...
AND THERE'S A MESSAGE ON THE MIRROR.
WHAT DOES IT SAY?
STOP. IT JUST SAYS *STOP.*
STOP

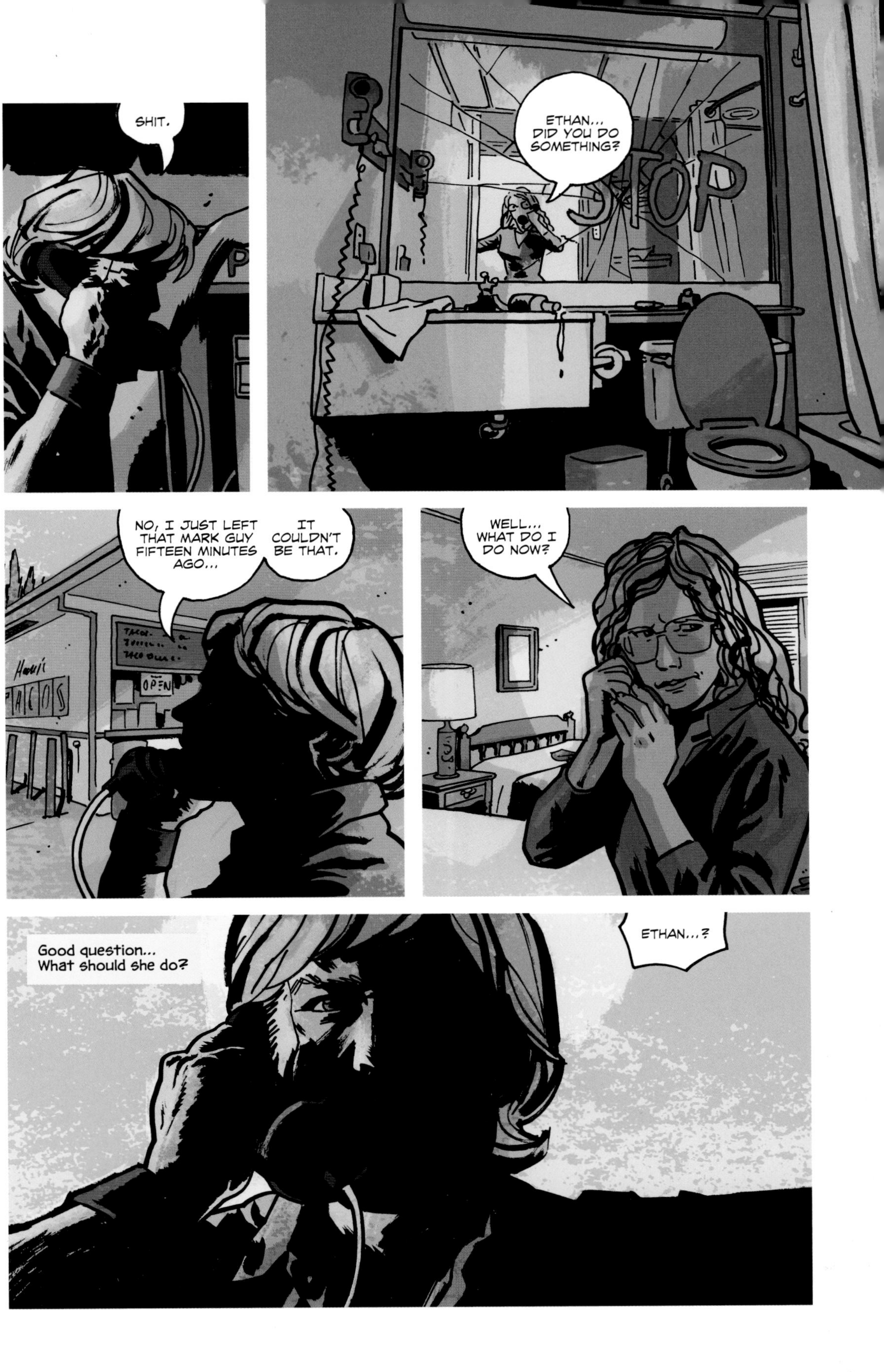
SHIT.
ETHAN... DID YOU DO SOMETHING?
STOP
NO, I JUST LEFT THAT MARK GUY FIFTEEN MINUTES AGO...
IT COULDN'T BE THAT.
OPEN
WELL... WHAT DO I DO NOW?
Good question... What should she do?
ETHAN...?

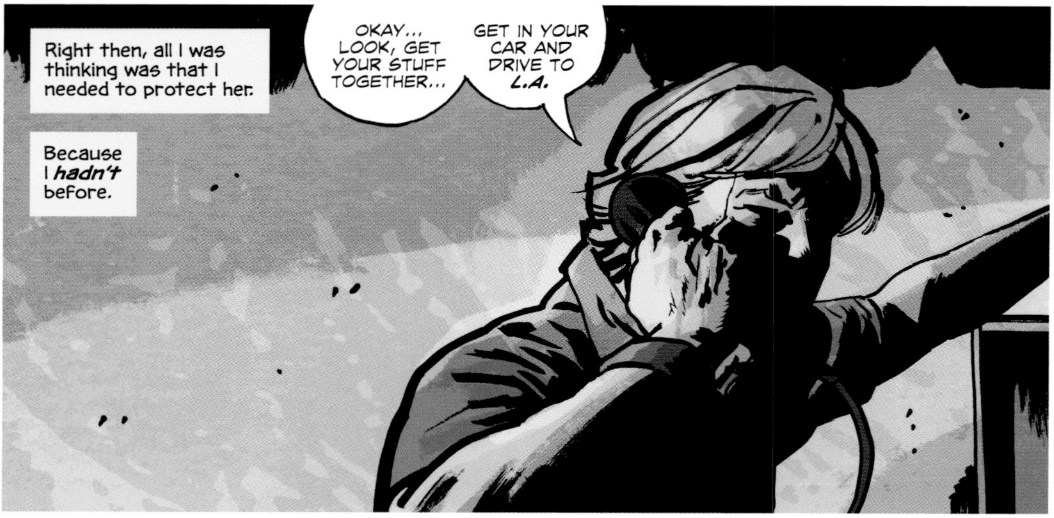

Right then, all I was thinking was that I needed to protect her.
Because I *hadn't* before.
OKAY... LOOK, GET YOUR STUFF TOGETHER...
GET IN YOUR CAR AND DRIVE TO *L.A.*

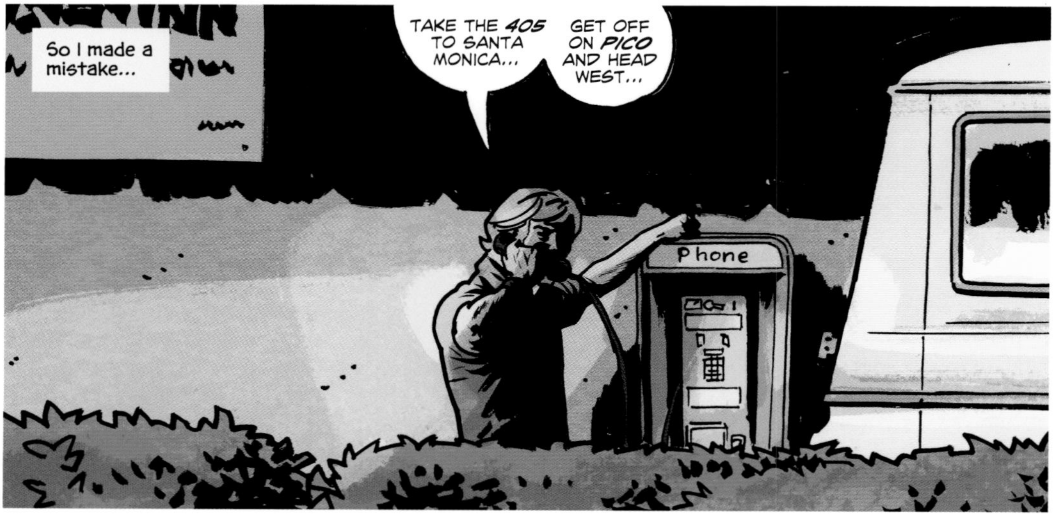

So I made a mistake...
TAKE THE *405* TO SANTA MONICA...
GET OFF ON *PICO* AND HEAD WEST...
Phone

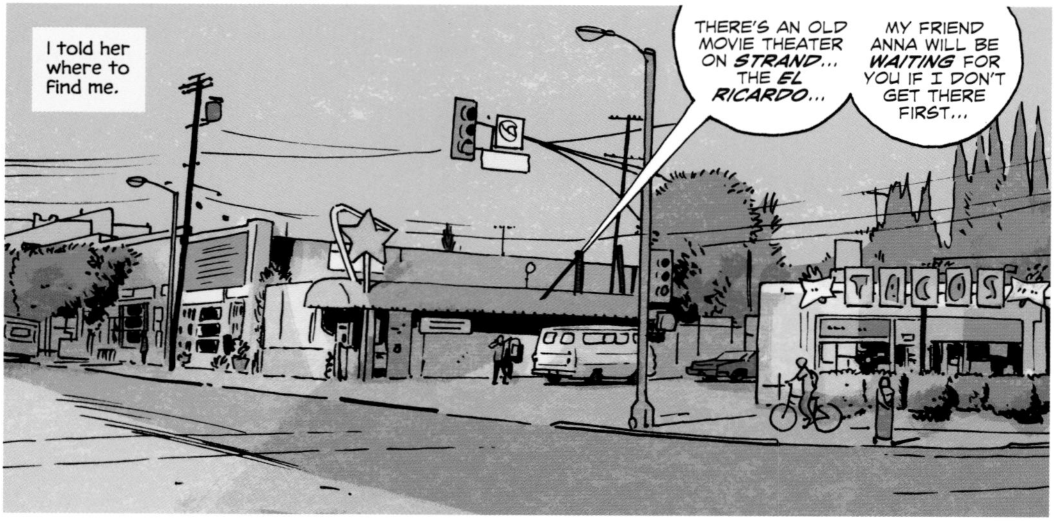

I told her where to find me.
THERE'S AN OLD MOVIE THEATER ON *STRAND*... THE *EL RICARDO*...
MY FRIEND ANNA WILL BE *WAITING* FOR YOU IF I DON'T GET THERE FIRST...
TACOS

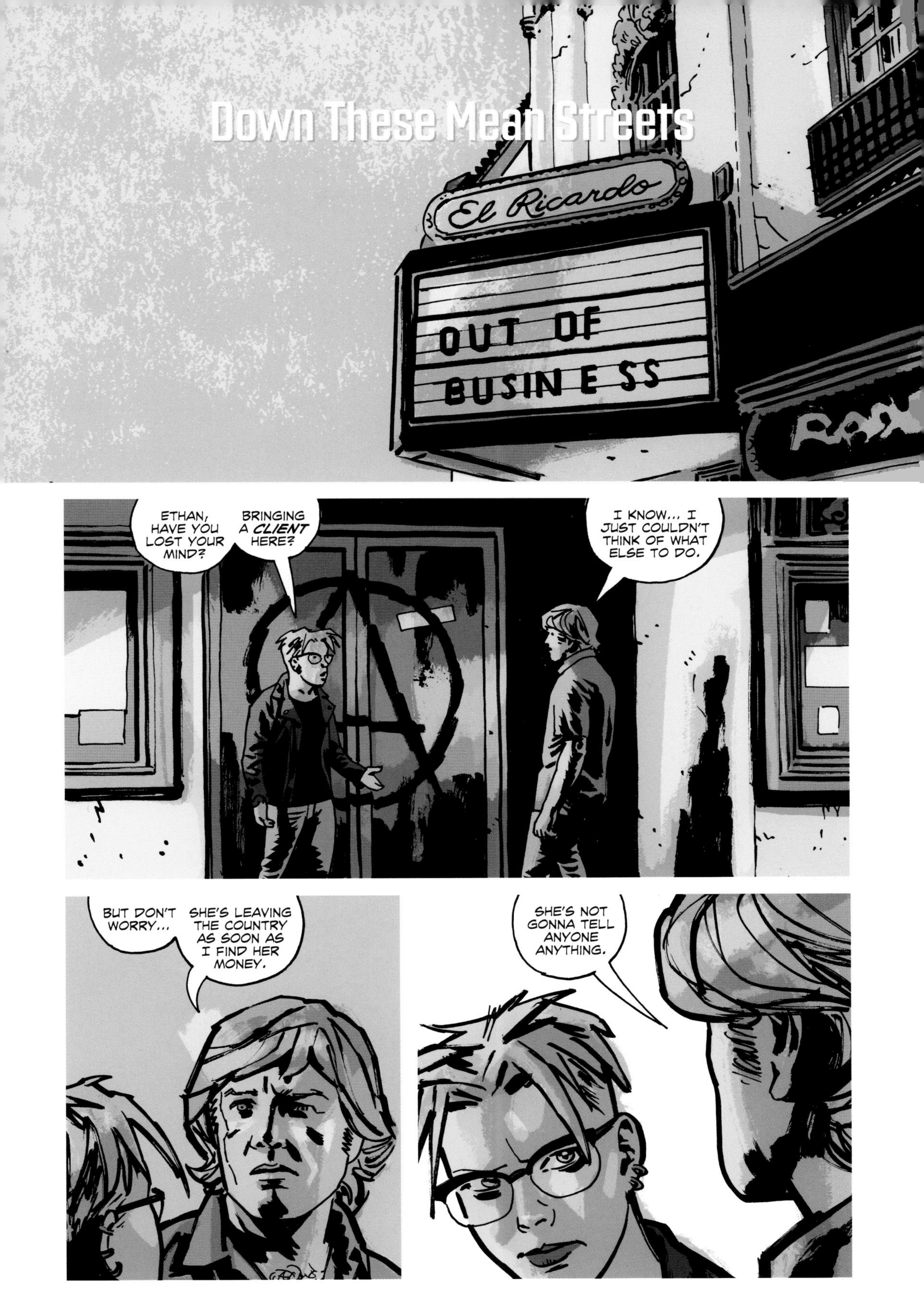
Down These Mean Streets
El Ricardo
OUT OF BUSINESS
ETHAN, HAVE YOU LOST YOUR MIND?
BRINGING A *CLIENT* HERE?
I KNOW... I JUST COULDN'T THINK OF WHAT ELSE TO DO.
BUT DON'T WORRY...
SHE'S LEAVING THE COUNTRY AS SOON AS I FIND HER MONEY.
SHE'S NOT GONNA TELL ANYONE ANYTHING.

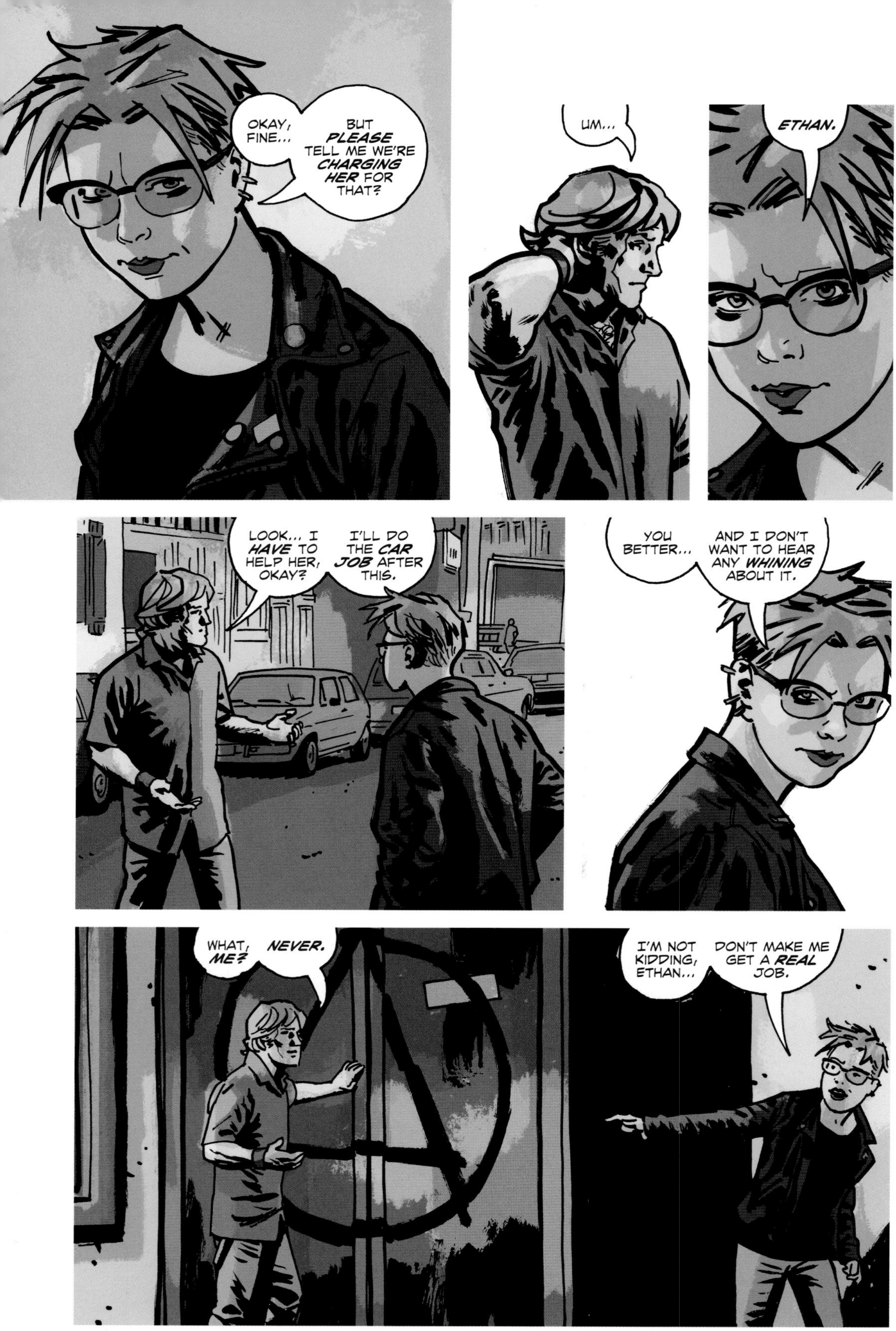

OKAY, FINE...
BUT PLEASE TELL ME WE'RE CHARGING HER FOR THAT?
UM...
ETHAN.
LOOK... I HAVE TO HELP HER, OKAY?
I'LL DO THE CAR JOB AFTER THIS.
YOU BETTER...
AND I DON'T WANT TO HEAR ANY WHINING ABOUT IT.
WHAT, ME?
NEVER.
I'M NOT KIDDING, ETHAN...
DON'T MAKE ME GET A REAL JOB.

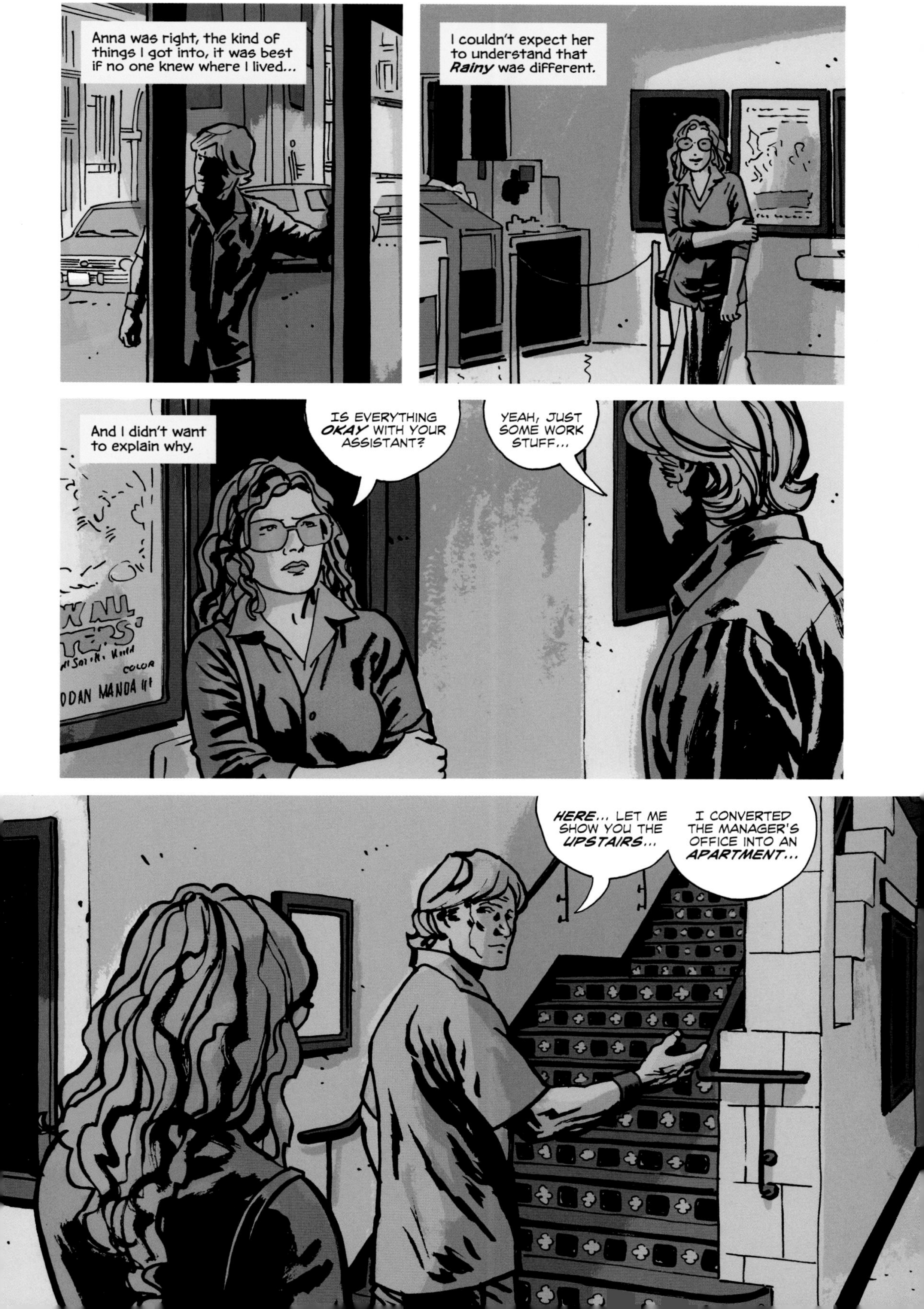
Anna was right, the kind of things I got into, it was best if no one knew where I lived...
I couldn't expect her to understand that *Rainy* was different.
And I didn't want to explain why.
IS EVERYTHING *OKAY* WITH YOUR ASSISTANT?
YEAH, JUST SOME WORK STUFF...
HERE... LET ME SHOW YOU THE *UPSTAIRS*...
I CONVERTED THE MANAGER'S OFFICE INTO AN *APARTMENT*...

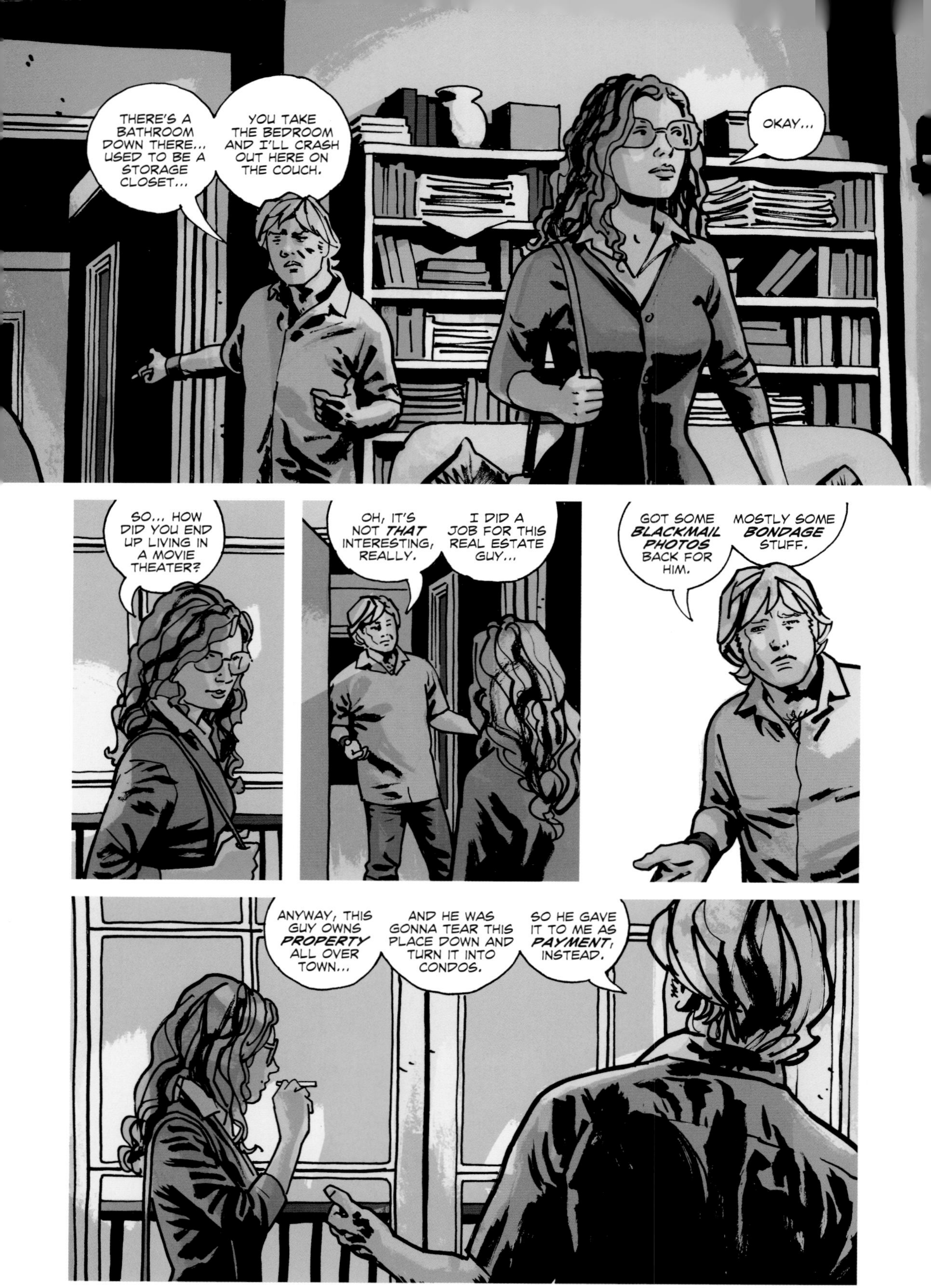
THERE'S A BATHROOM DOWN THERE... USED TO BE A STORAGE CLOSET...
YOU TAKE THE BEDROOM AND I'LL CRASH OUT HERE ON THE COUCH.
OKAY...
SO... HOW DID YOU END UP LIVING IN A MOVIE THEATER?
OH, IT'S NOT *THAT* INTERESTING, REALLY.
I DID A JOB FOR THIS REAL ESTATE GUY...
GOT SOME *BLACKMAIL PHOTOS* BACK FOR HIM.
MOSTLY SOME *BONDAGE* STUFF.
ANYWAY, THIS GUY OWNS *PROPERTY* ALL OVER TOWN...
AND HE WAS GONNA TEAR THIS PLACE DOWN AND TURN IT INTO CONDOS.
SO HE GAVE IT TO ME AS *PAYMENT*, INSTEAD.

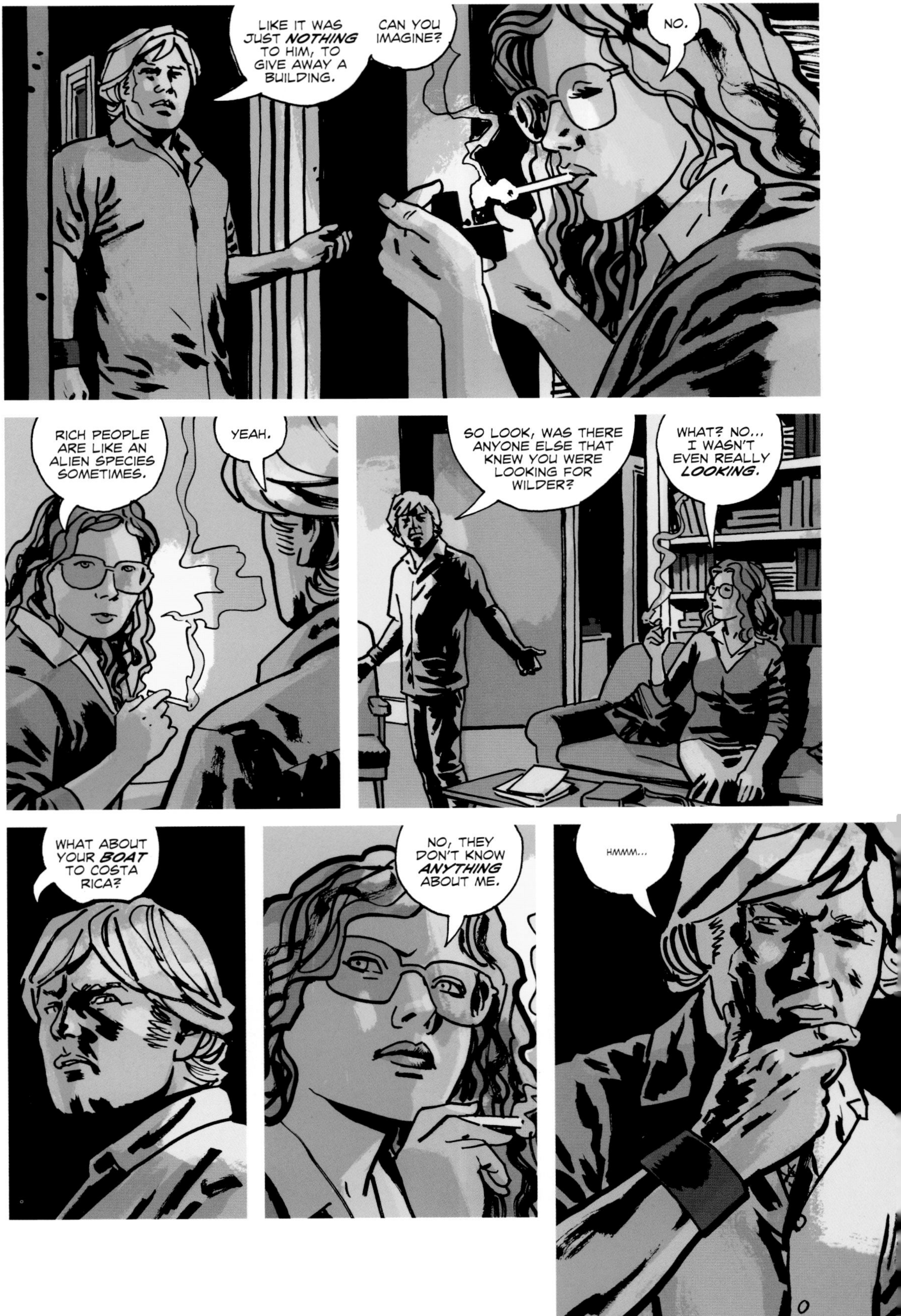
LIKE IT WAS JUST *NOTHING* TO HIM, TO GIVE AWAY A BUILDING.
CAN YOU IMAGINE?
NO.
RICH PEOPLE ARE LIKE AN ALIEN SPECIES SOMETIMES.
YEAH.
SO LOOK, WAS THERE ANYONE ELSE THAT KNEW YOU WERE LOOKING FOR WILDER?
WHAT? NO... I WASN'T EVEN REALLY *LOOKING.*
WHAT ABOUT YOUR *BOAT* TO COSTA RICA?
NO, THEY DON'T KNOW *ANYTHING* ABOUT ME.
HMMM...

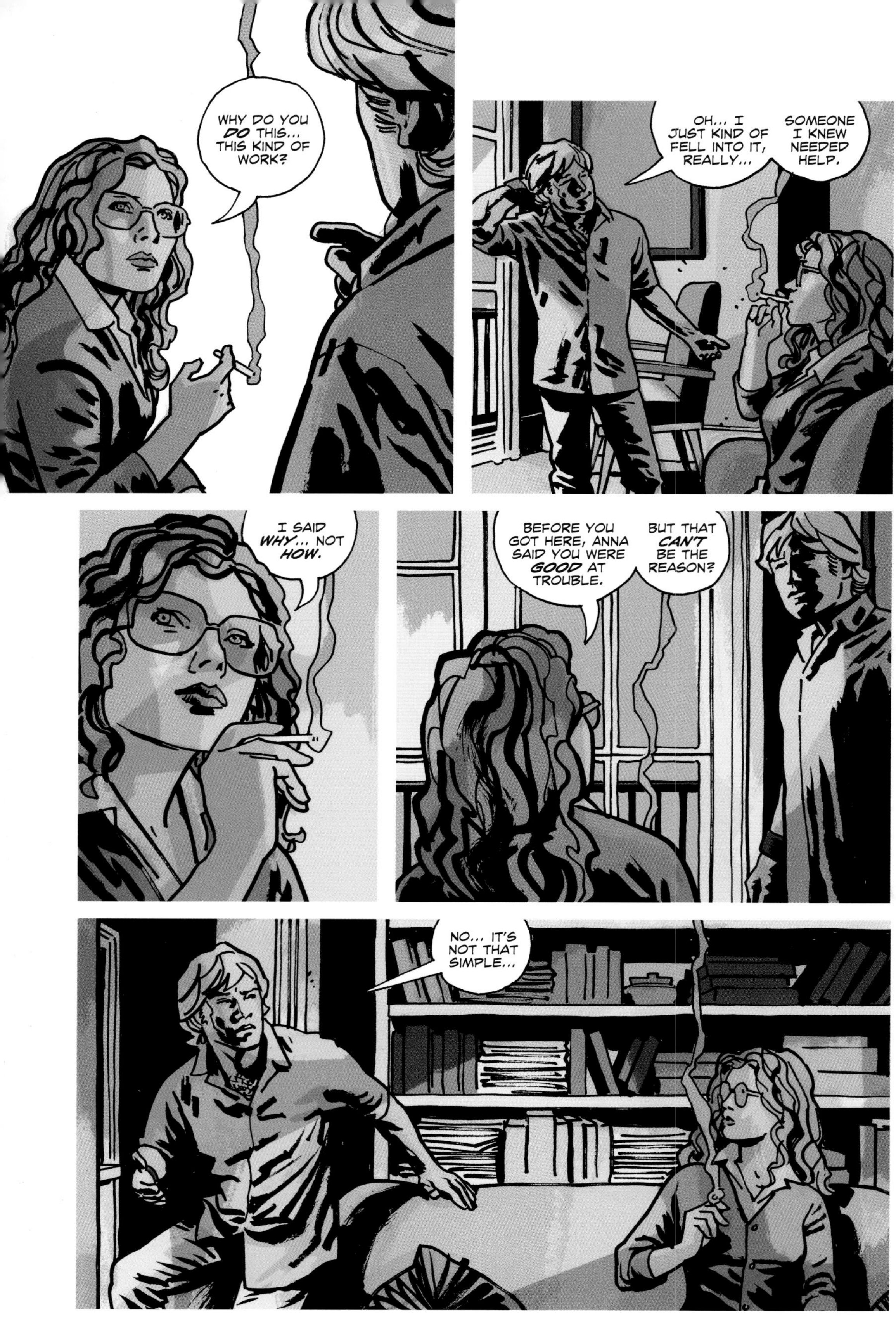
WHY DO YOU *DO* THIS... THIS KIND OF WORK?
OH... I JUST KIND OF FELL INTO IT, REALLY...
SOMEONE I KNEW NEEDED HELP.
I SAID *WHY*... NOT *HOW*.
BEFORE YOU GOT HERE, ANNA SAID YOU WERE *GOOD* AT TROUBLE.
BUT THAT *CAN'T* BE THE REASON?
NO... IT'S NOT THAT SIMPLE...

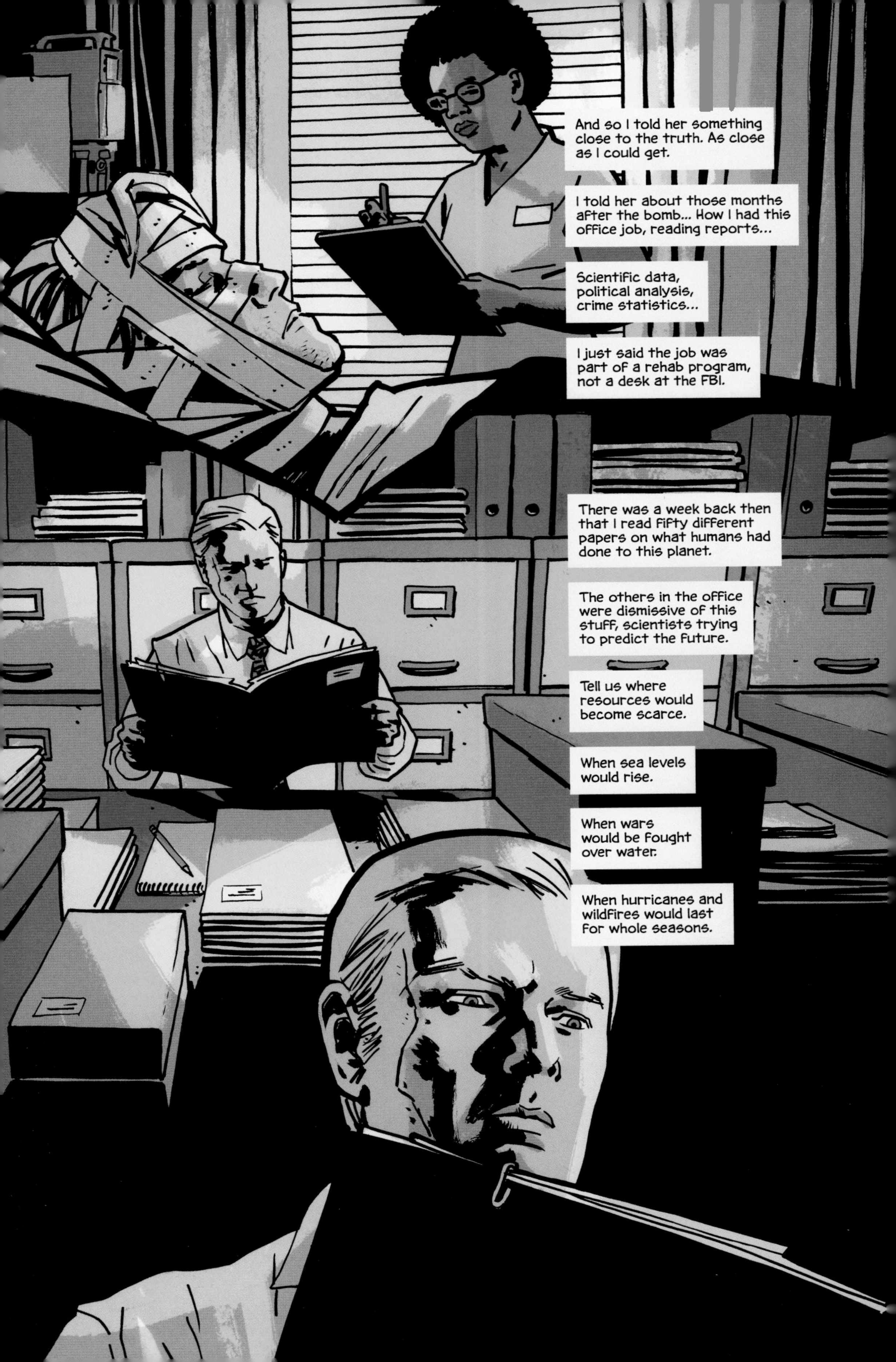
And so I told her something close to the truth. As close as I could get.
I told her about those months after the bomb... How I had this office job, reading reports...
Scientific data, political analysis, crime statistics...
I just said the job was part of a rehab program, not a desk at the FBI.
There was a week back then that I read fifty different papers on what humans had done to this planet.
The others in the office were dismissive of this stuff, scientists trying to predict the future.
Tell us where resources would become scarce.
When sea levels would rise.
When wars would be fought over water.
When hurricanes and wildfires would last for whole seasons.

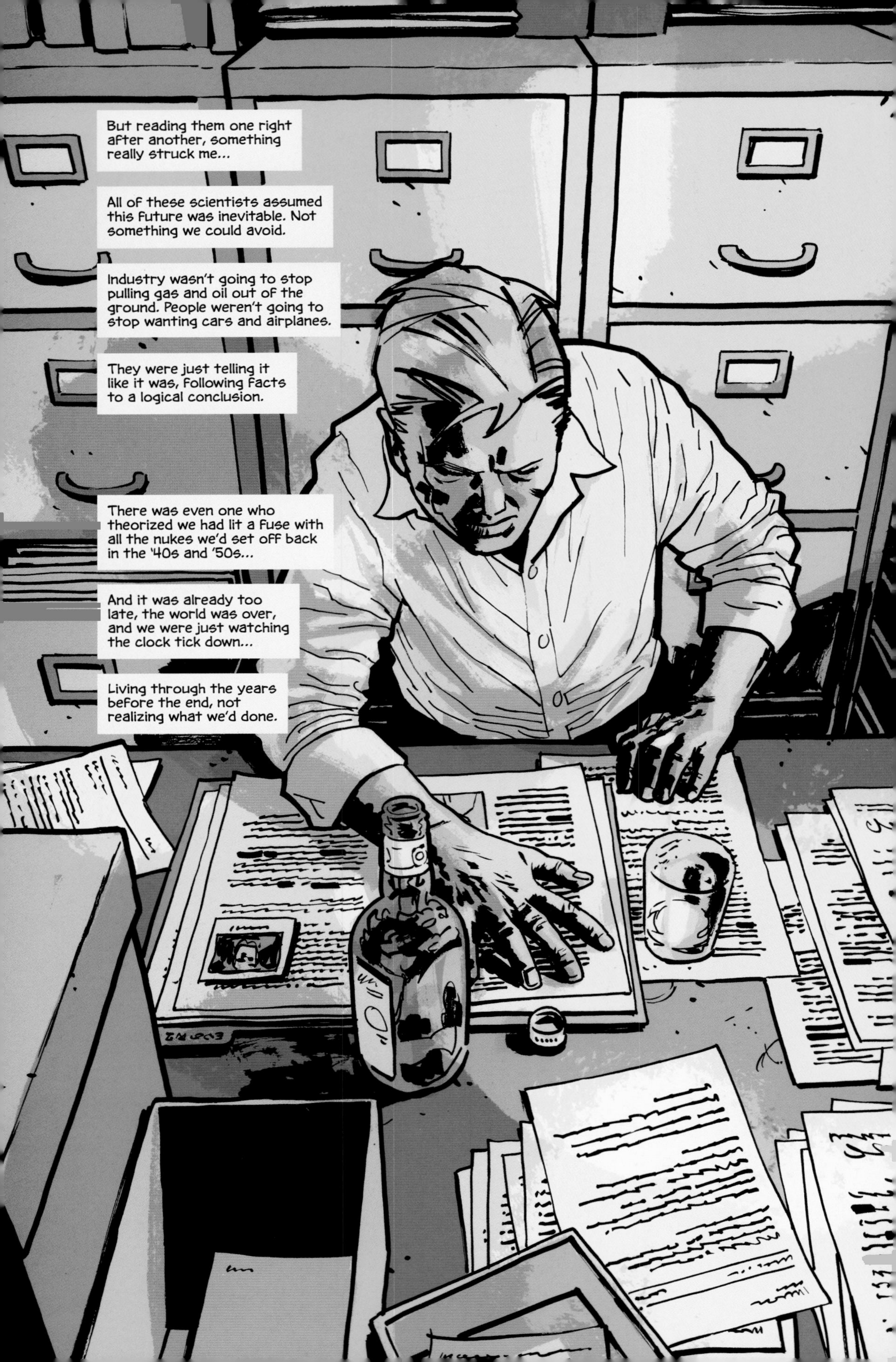
But reading them one right after another, something really struck me...
All of these scientists assumed this future was inevitable. Not something we could avoid.
Industry wasn't going to stop pulling gas and oil out of the ground. People weren't going to stop wanting cars and airplanes.
They were just telling it like it was, following facts to a logical conclusion.
There was even one who theorized we had lit a fuse with all the nukes we'd set off back in the '40s and '50s...
And it was already too late, the world was over, and we were just watching the clock tick down...
Living through the years before the end, not realizing what we'd done.

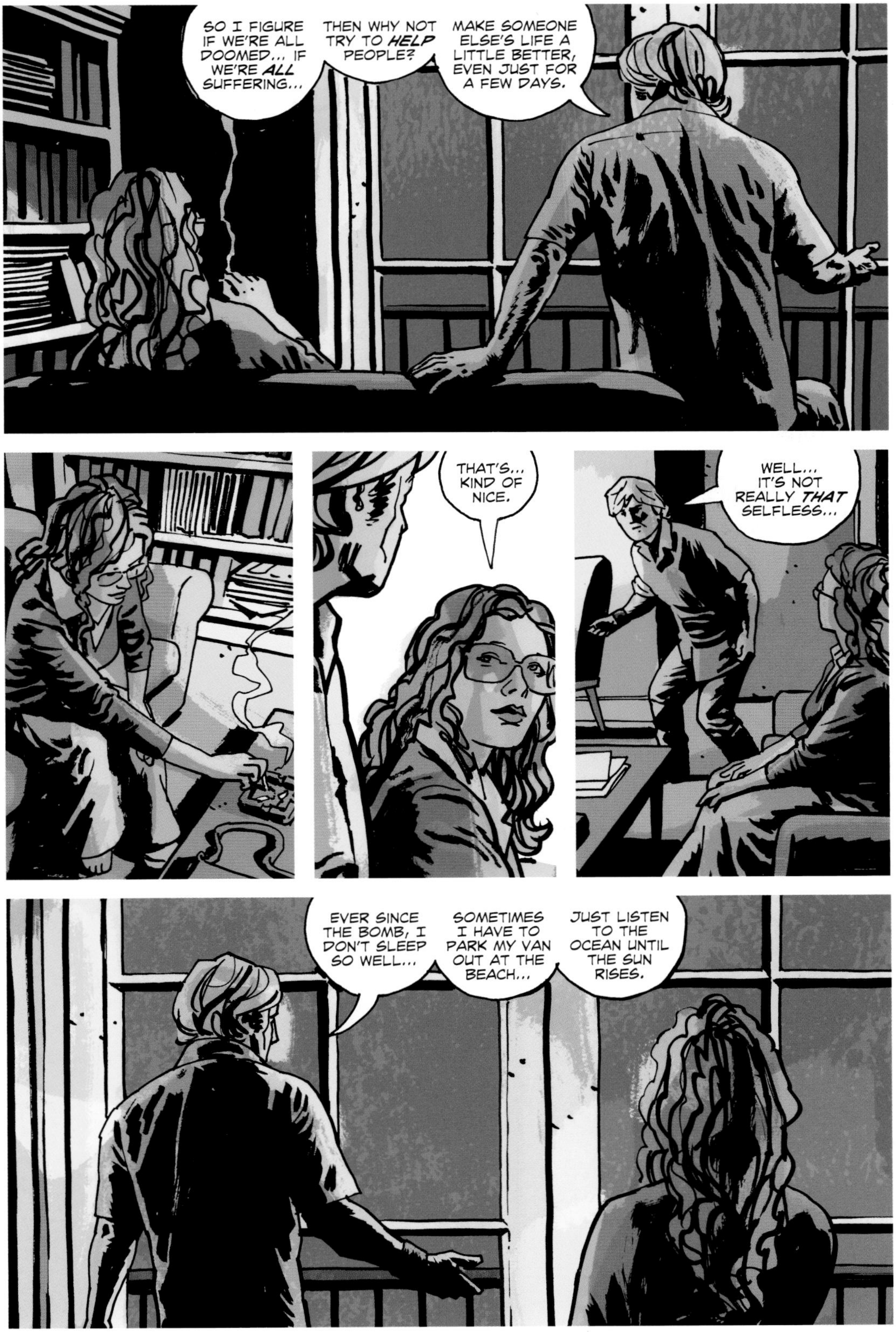
SO I FIGURE IF WE'RE ALL DOOMED... IF WE'RE *ALL* SUFFERING...
THEN WHY NOT TRY TO *HELP* PEOPLE?
MAKE SOMEONE ELSE'S LIFE A LITTLE BETTER, EVEN JUST FOR A FEW DAYS.
THAT'S... KIND OF NICE.
WELL... IT'S NOT REALLY *THAT* SELFLESS...
EVER SINCE THE BOMB, I DON'T SLEEP SO WELL...
SOMETIMES I HAVE TO PARK MY VAN OUT AT THE BEACH...
JUST LISTEN TO THE OCEAN UNTIL THE SUN RISES.

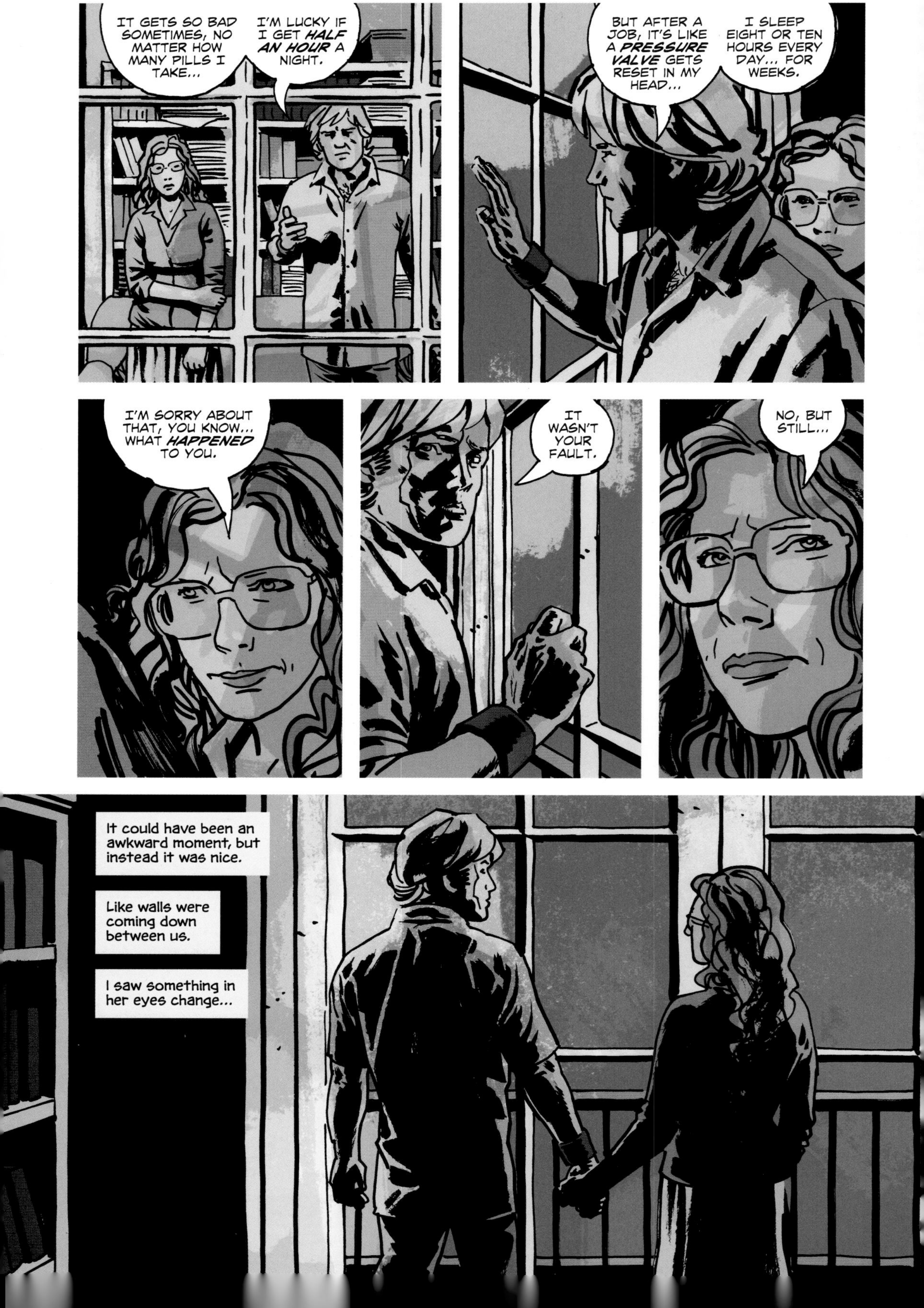
IT GETS SO BAD SOMETIMES, NO MATTER HOW MANY PILLS I TAKE...
I'M LUCKY IF I GET *HALF AN HOUR* A NIGHT.
BUT AFTER A JOB, IT'S LIKE A *PRESSURE VALVE* GETS RESET IN MY HEAD...
I SLEEP EIGHT OR TEN HOURS EVERY DAY... FOR WEEKS.
I'M SORRY ABOUT THAT, YOU KNOW... WHAT *HAPPENED* TO YOU.
IT WASN'T YOUR FAULT.
NO, BUT STILL...
It could have been an awkward moment, but instead it was nice.
Like walls were coming down between us.
I saw something in her eyes change...

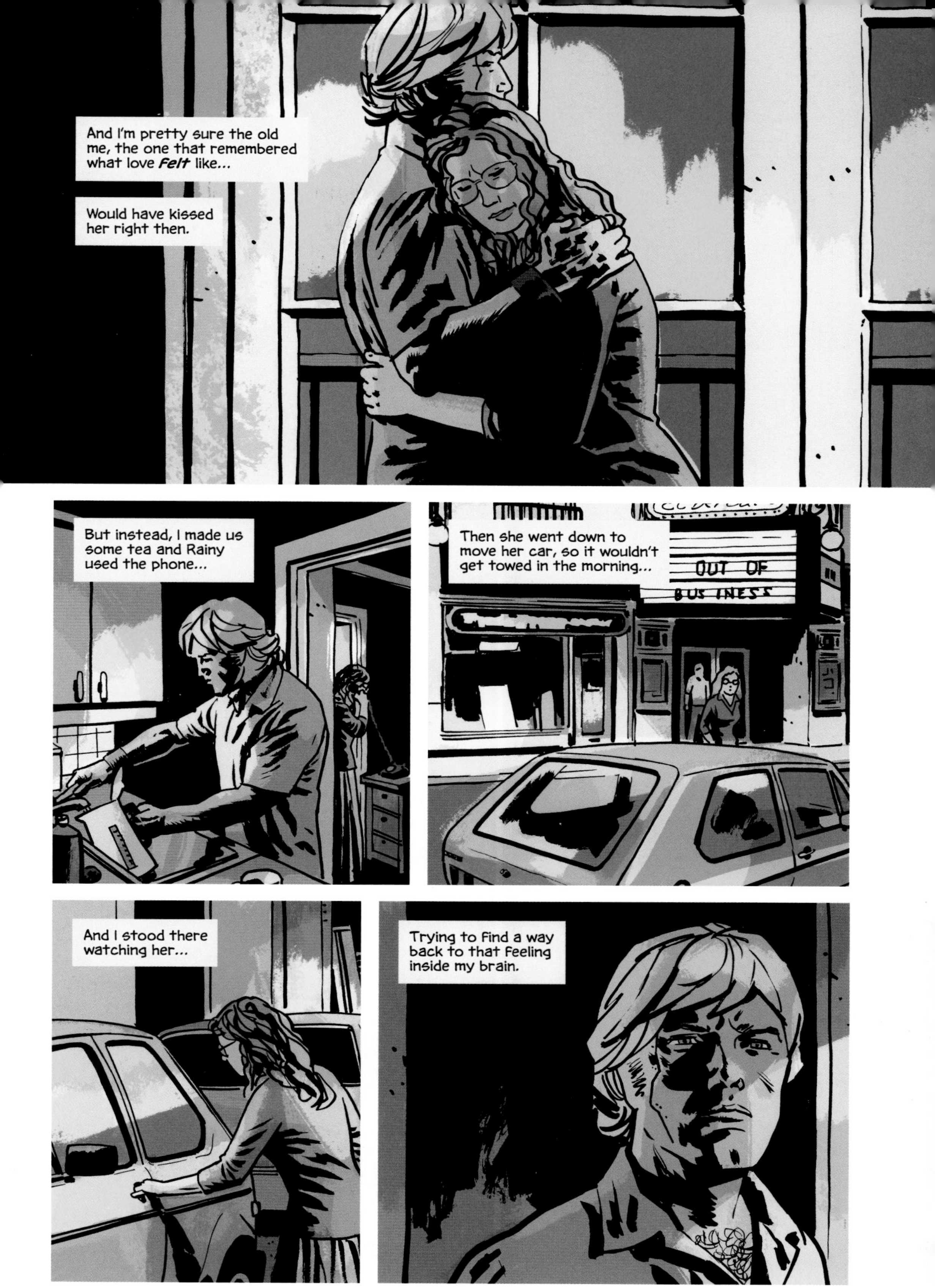
And I'm pretty sure the old me, the one that remembered what love *Felt* like...
Would have kissed her right then.
But instead, I made us some tea and Rainy used the phone...
Then she went down to move her car, so it wouldn't get towed in the morning...
OUT OF
BUSINESS
And I stood there watching her...
Trying to find a way back to that feeling inside my brain.

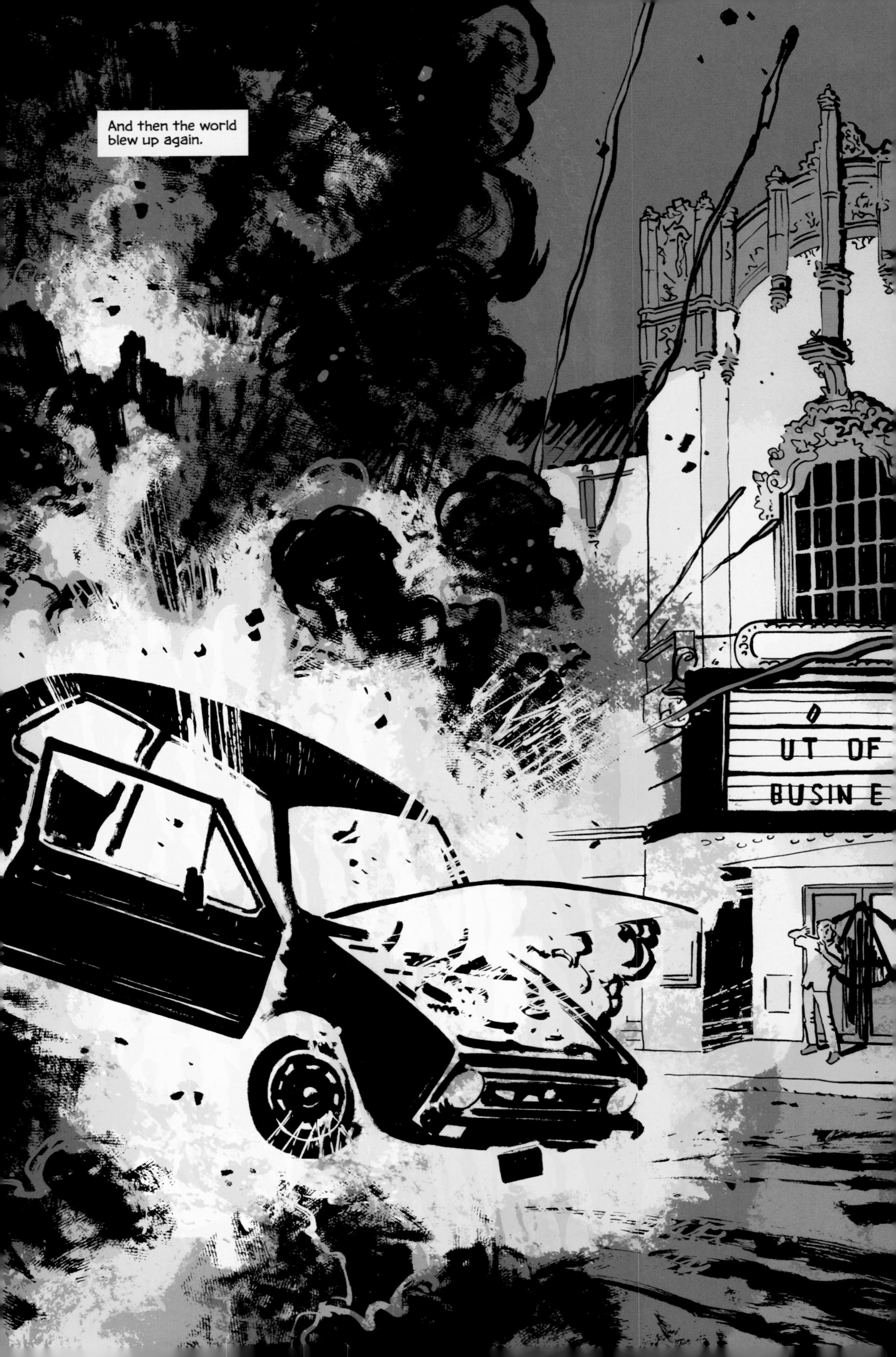
And then the world blew up again.
UT OF
BUSIN E

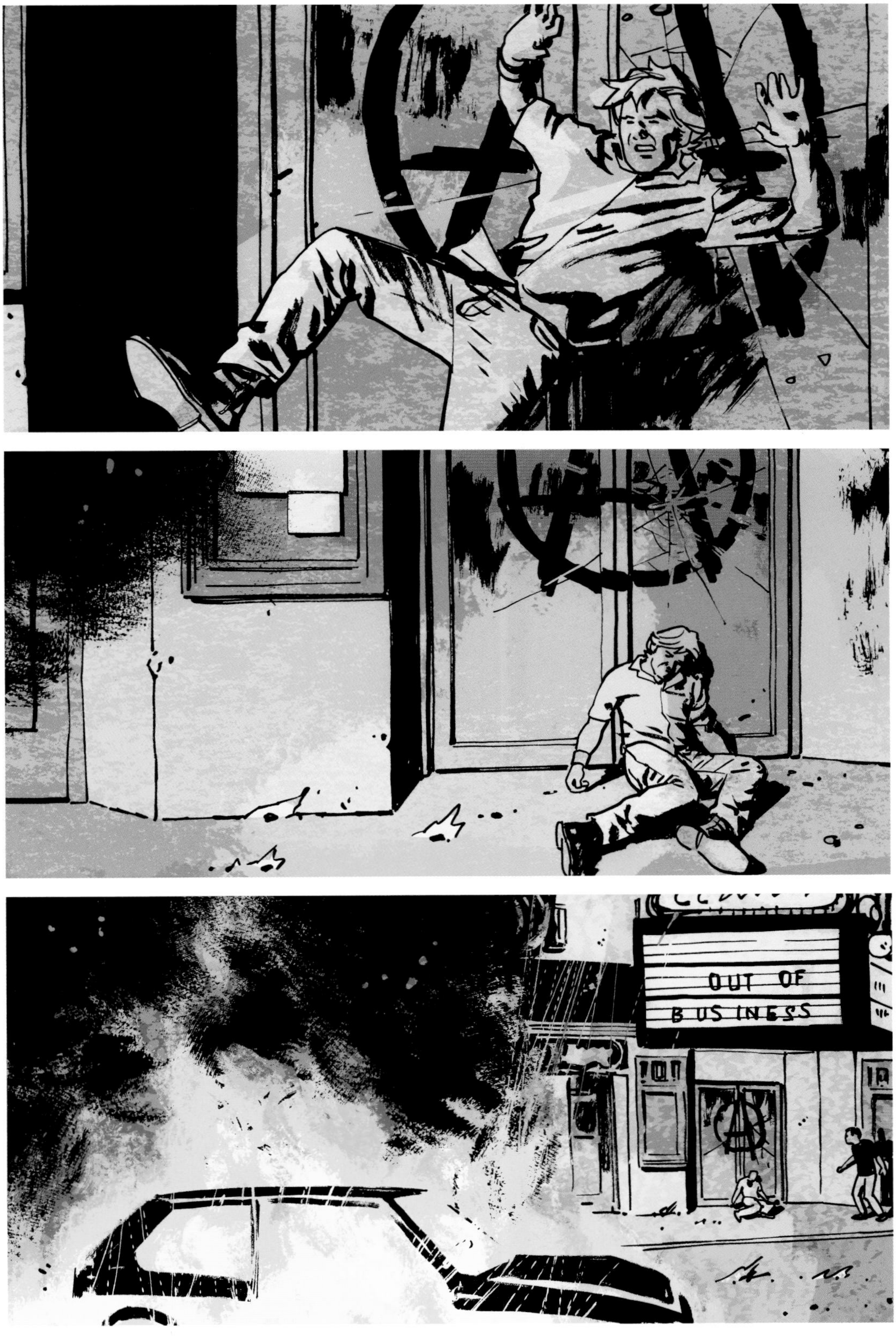
OUT OF
BUSINESS

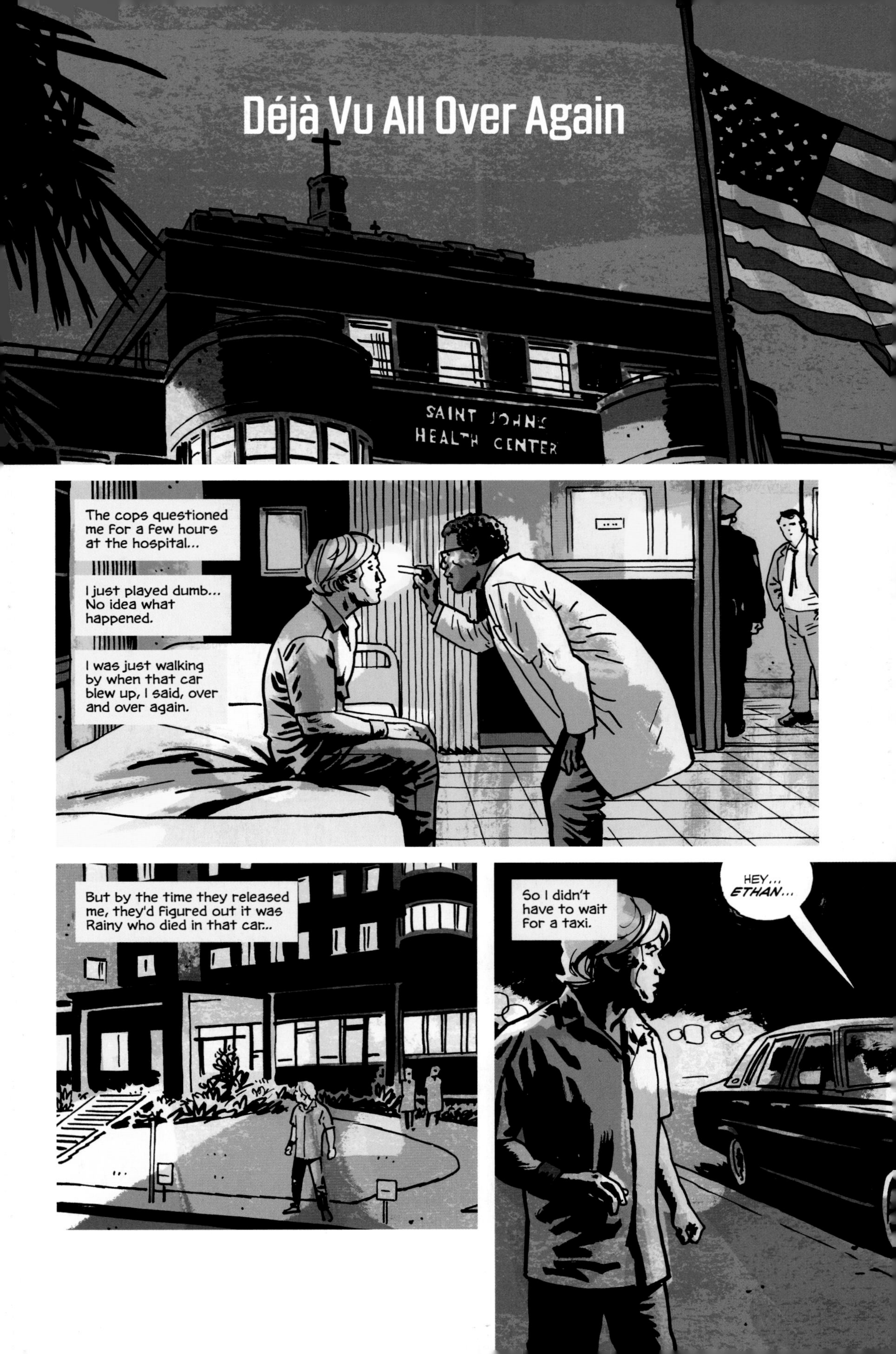
Déjà Vu All Over Again
SAINT JOHNS
HEALTH CENTER
The cops questioned me for a few hours at the hospital...
I just played dumb... No idea what happened.
I was just walking by when that car blew up, I said, over and over again.
But by the time they released me, they'd figured out it was Rainy who died in that car...
...
So I didn't have to wait for a taxi.
HEY... ETHAN...

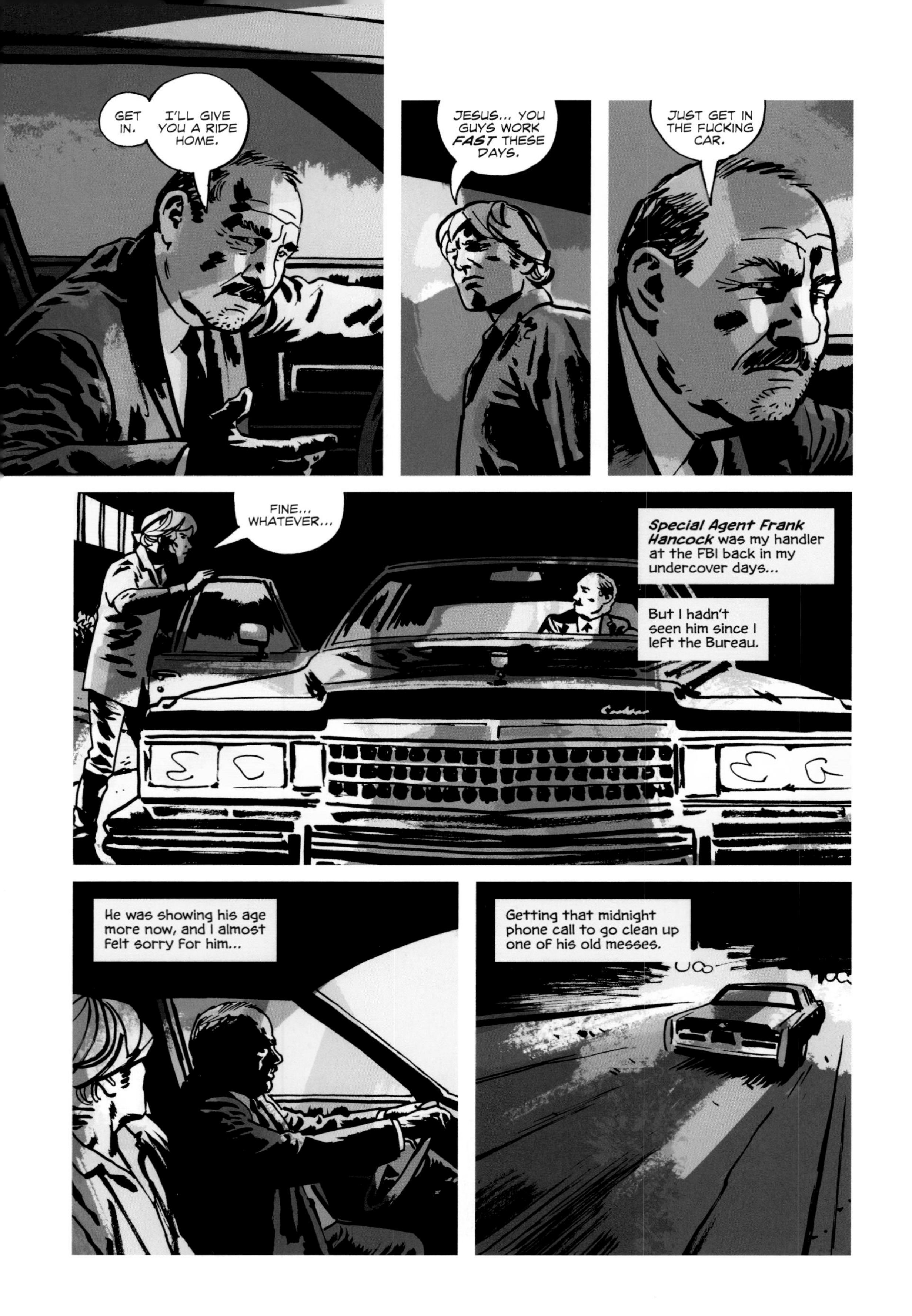
GET IN.
I'LL GIVE YOU A RIDE HOME.
JESUS... YOU GUYS WORK *FAST* THESE DAYS.
JUST GET IN THE FUCKING CAR.
FINE... WHATEVER...
Special Agent Frank Hancock was my handler at the FBI back in my undercover days...
But I hadn't seen him since I left the Bureau.
He was showing his age more now, and I almost felt sorry for him...
Getting that midnight phone call to go clean up one of his old messes.

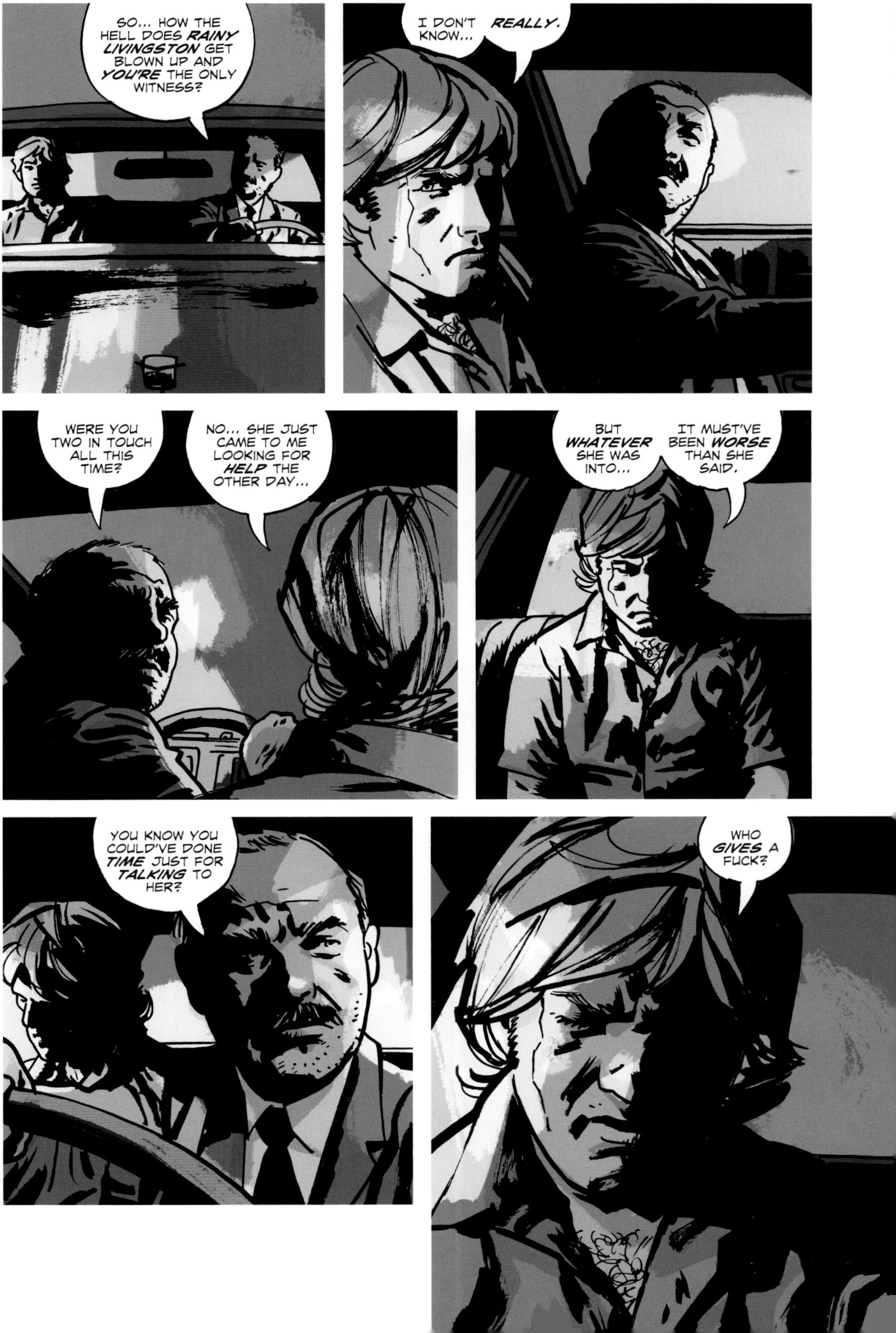
SO... HOW THE HELL DOES RAINY LIVINGSTON GET BLOWN UP AND YOU'RE THE ONLY WITNESS?
I DON'T KNOW...
REALLY.
WERE YOU TWO IN TOUCH ALL THIS TIME?
NO... SHE JUST CAME TO ME LOOKING FOR HELP THE OTHER DAY...
BUT WHATEVER SHE WAS INTO...
IT MUST'VE BEEN WORSE THAN SHE SAID.
YOU KNOW YOU COULD'VE DONE TIME JUST FOR TALKING TO HER?
WHO GIVES A FUCK?

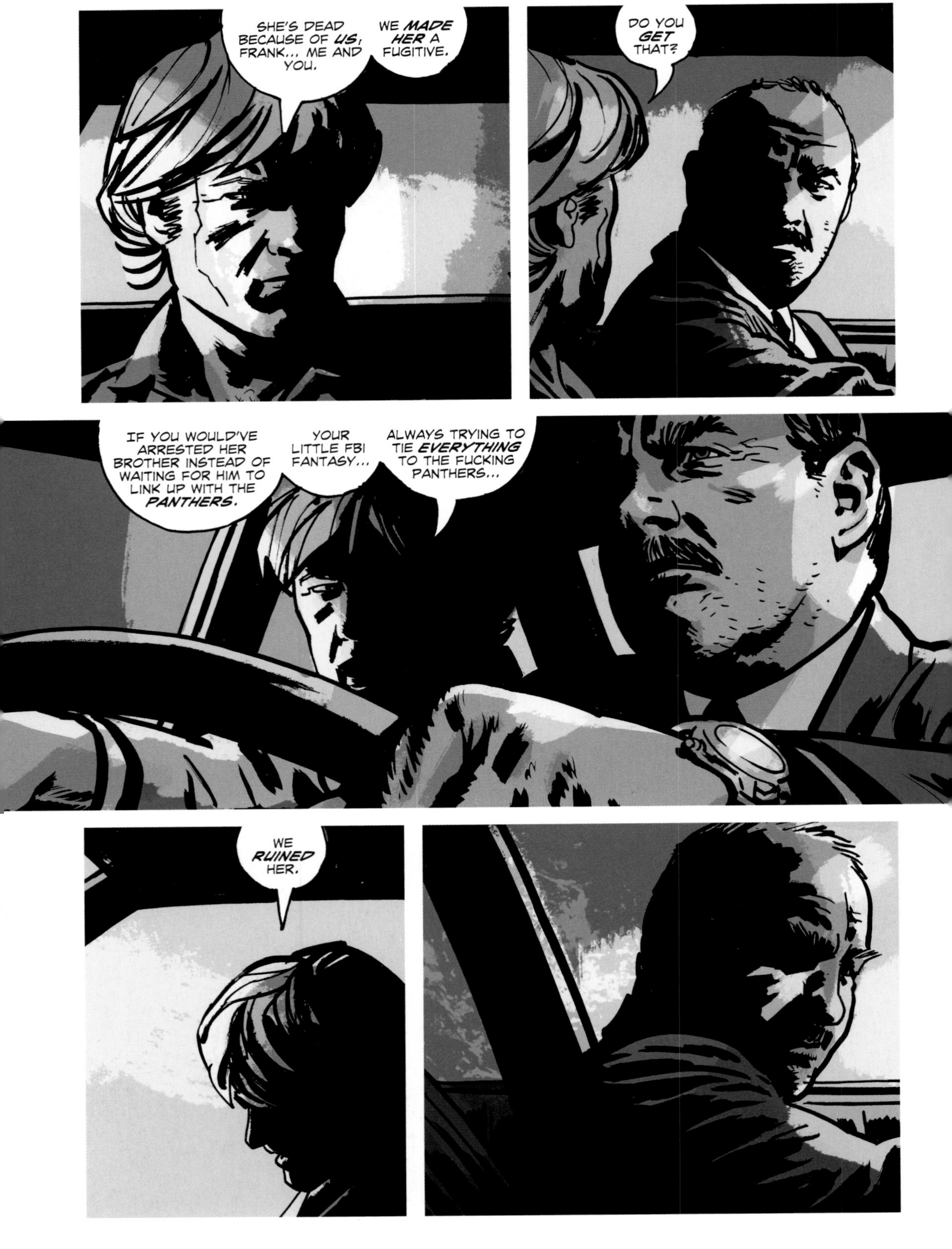
SHE'S DEAD BECAUSE OF US, FRANK... ME AND YOU.
WE MADE HER A FUGITIVE.
DO YOU GET THAT?
IF YOU WOULD'VE ARRESTED HER BROTHER INSTEAD OF WAITING FOR HIM TO LINK UP WITH THE PANTHERS.
YOUR LITTLE FBI FANTASY...
ALWAYS TRYING TO TIE EVERYTHING TO THE FUCKING PANTHERS...
WE RUINED HER.

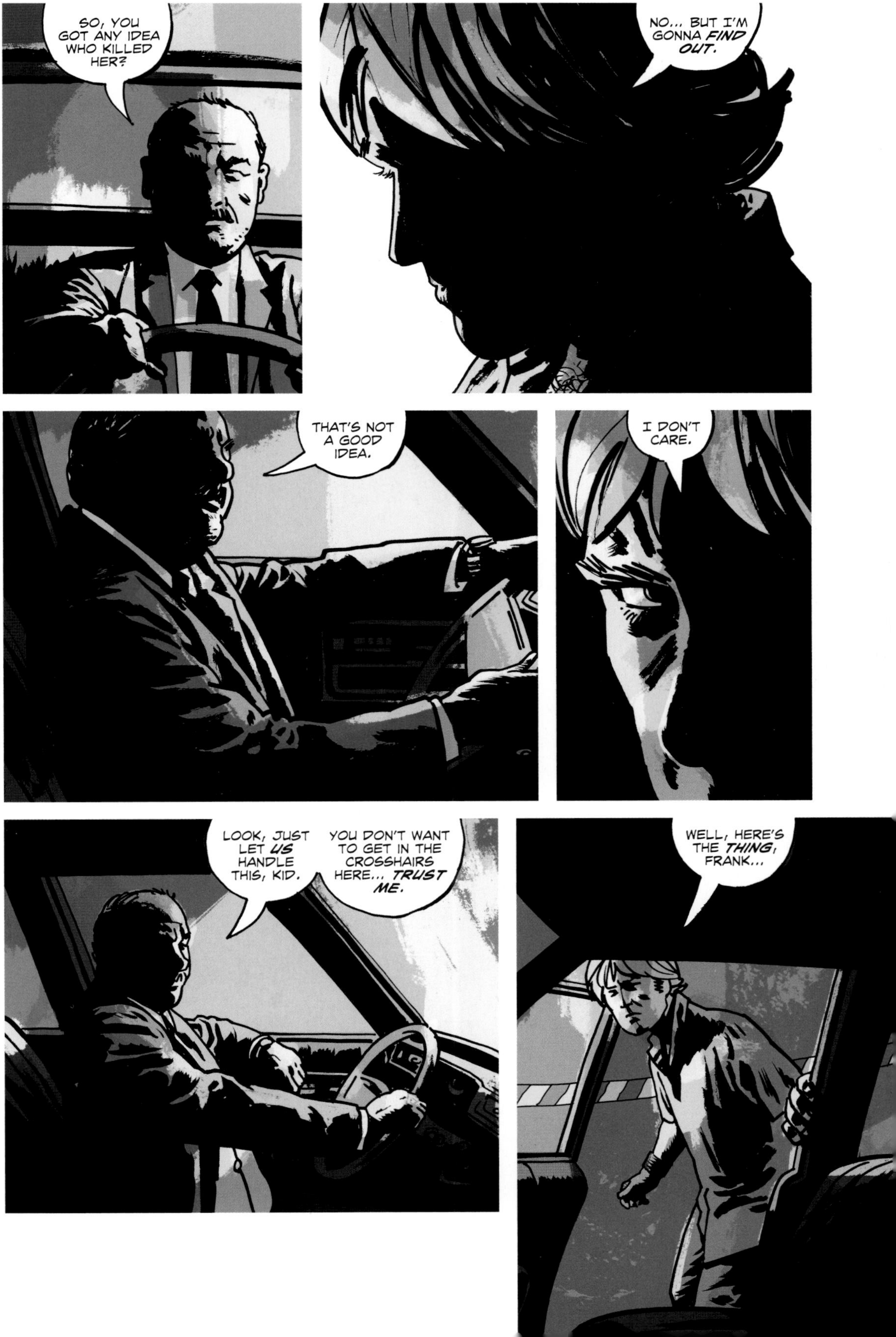
SO, YOU GOT ANY IDEA WHO KILLED HER?
NO... BUT I'M GONNA *FIND OUT*.
THAT'S NOT A GOOD IDEA.
I DON'T CARE.
LOOK, JUST LET *US* HANDLE THIS, KID.
YOU DON'T WANT TO GET IN THE CROSSHAIRS HERE... *TRUST ME*.
WELL, HERE'S THE *THING*, FRANK...

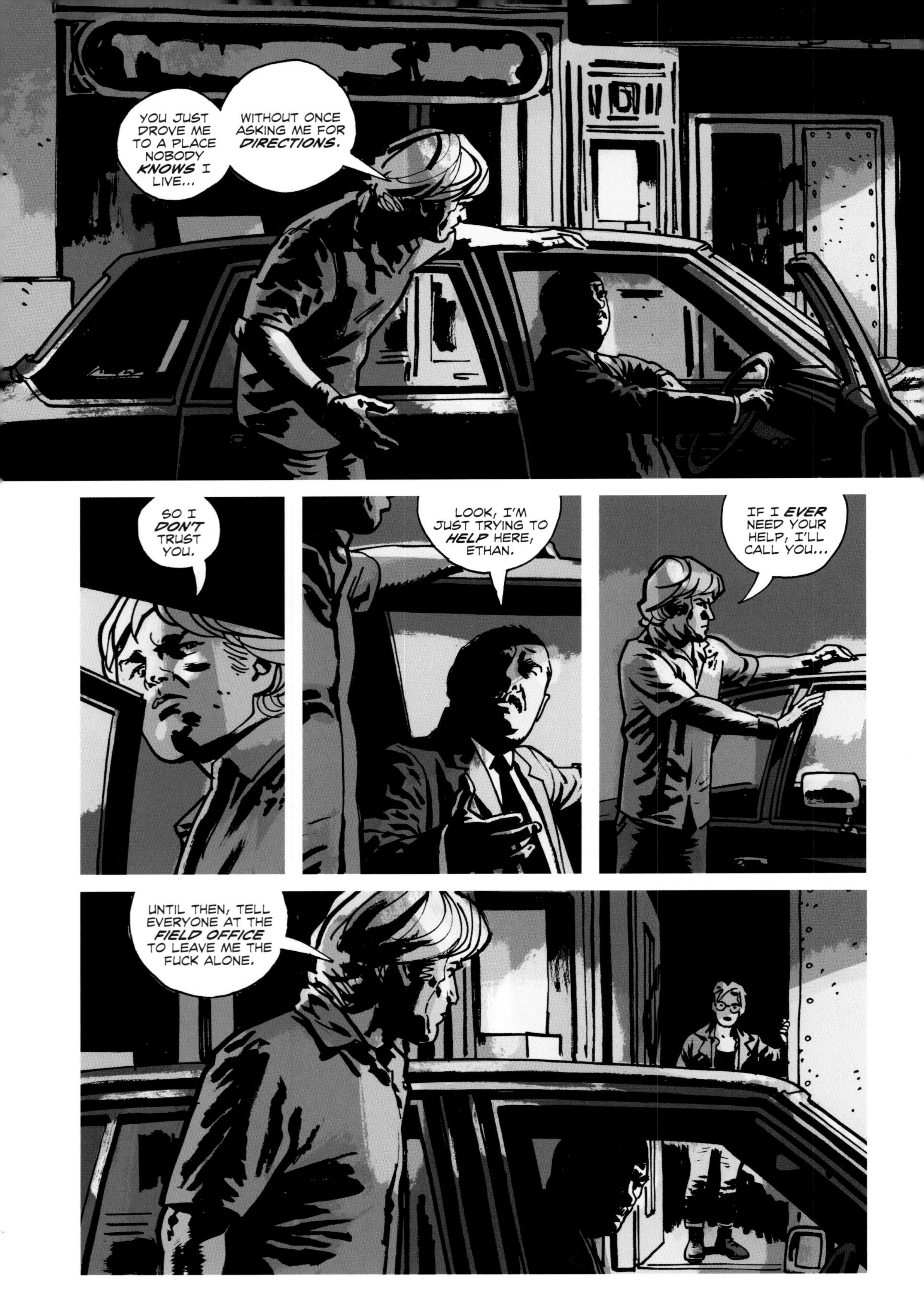
YOU JUST DROVE ME TO A PLACE NOBODY KNOWS I LIVE...
WITHOUT ONCE ASKING ME FOR DIRECTIONS.
SO I DON'T TRUST YOU.
LOOK, I'M JUST TRYING TO HELP HERE, ETHAN.
IF I EVER NEED YOUR HELP, I'LL CALL YOU...
UNTIL THEN, TELL EVERYONE AT THE FIELD OFFICE TO LEAVE ME THE FUCK ALONE.

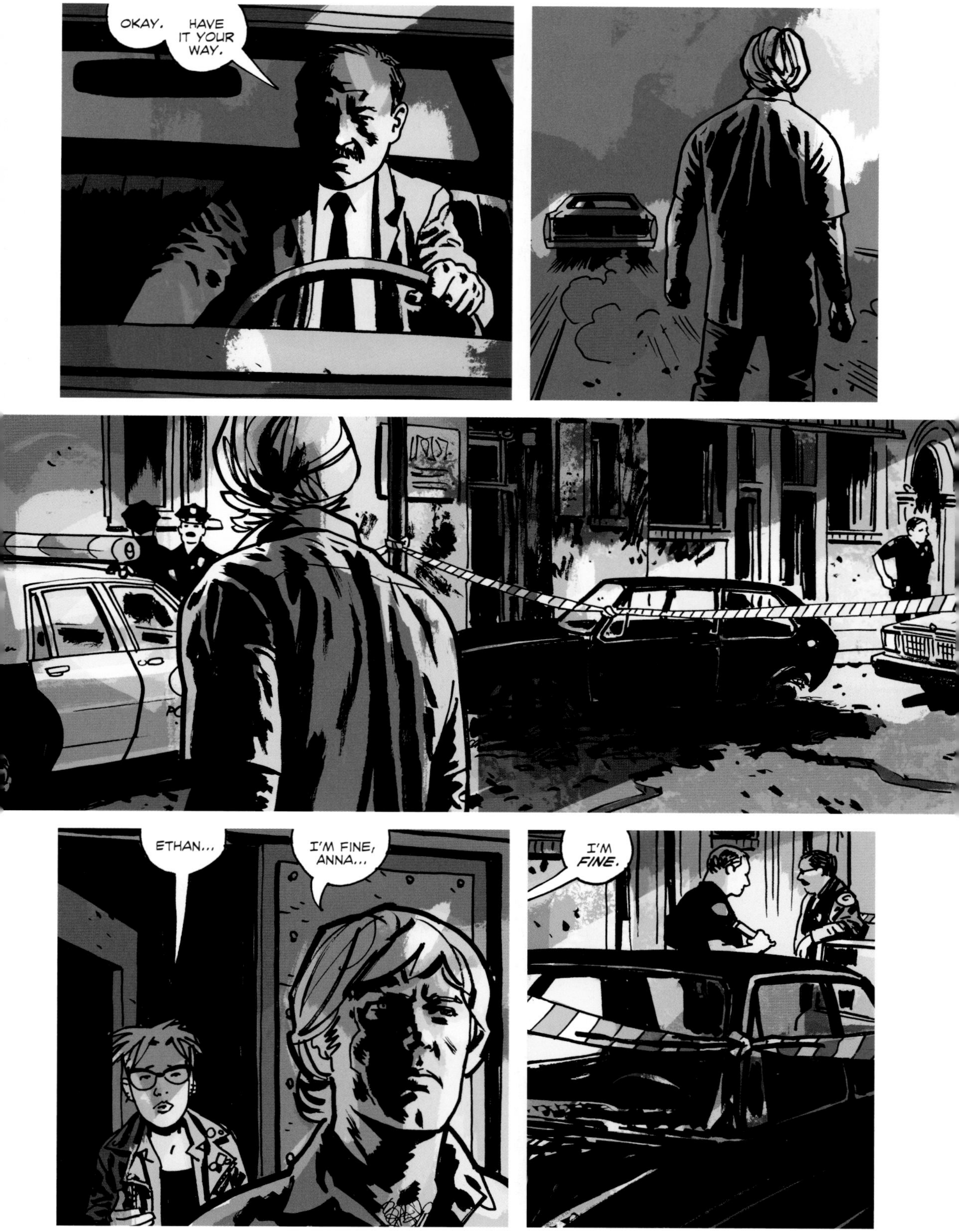
OKAY. HAVE IT YOUR WAY.
ETHAN...
I'M FINE, ANNA...
I'M *FINE*.

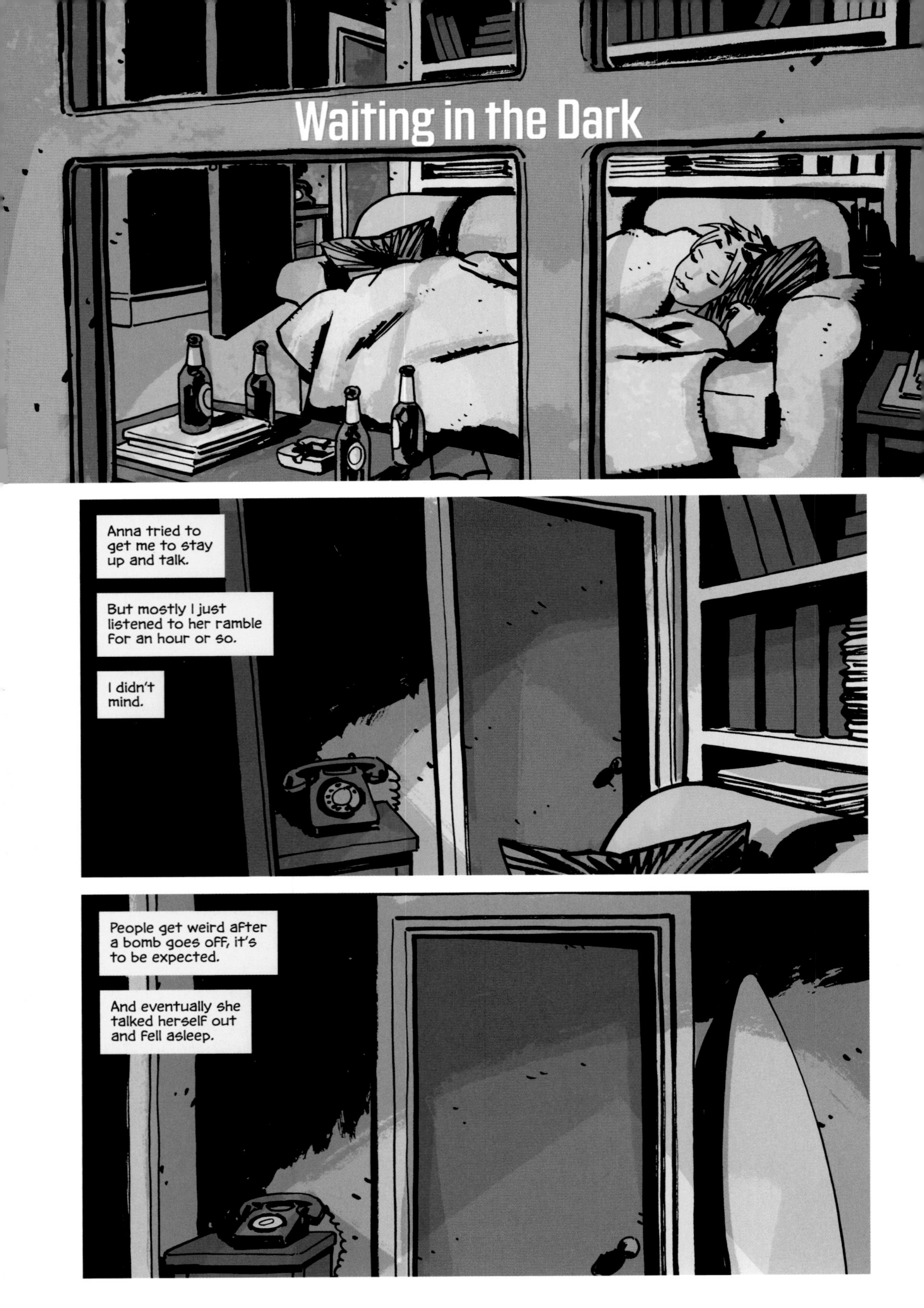
Waiting in the Dark
Anna tried to get me to stay up and talk.
But mostly I just listened to her ramble for an hour or so.
I didn't mind.
People get weird after a bomb goes off, it's to be expected.
And eventually she talked herself out and fell asleep.

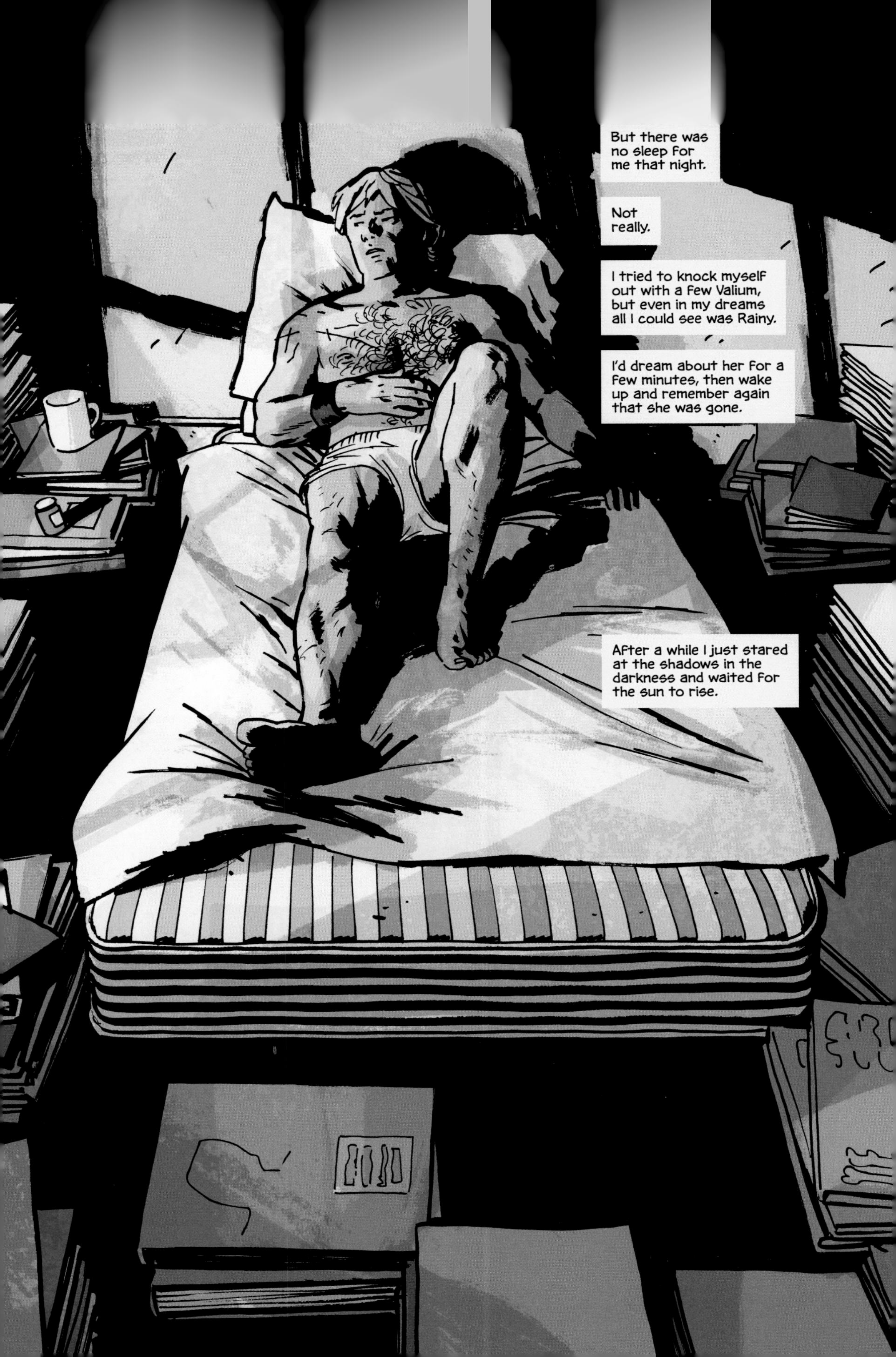
But there was no sleep for me that night.
Not really.
I tried to knock myself out with a few Valium, but even in my dreams all I could see was Rainy.
I'd dream about her for a few minutes, then wake up and remember again that she was gone.
After a while I just stared at the shadows in the darkness and waited for the sun to rise.

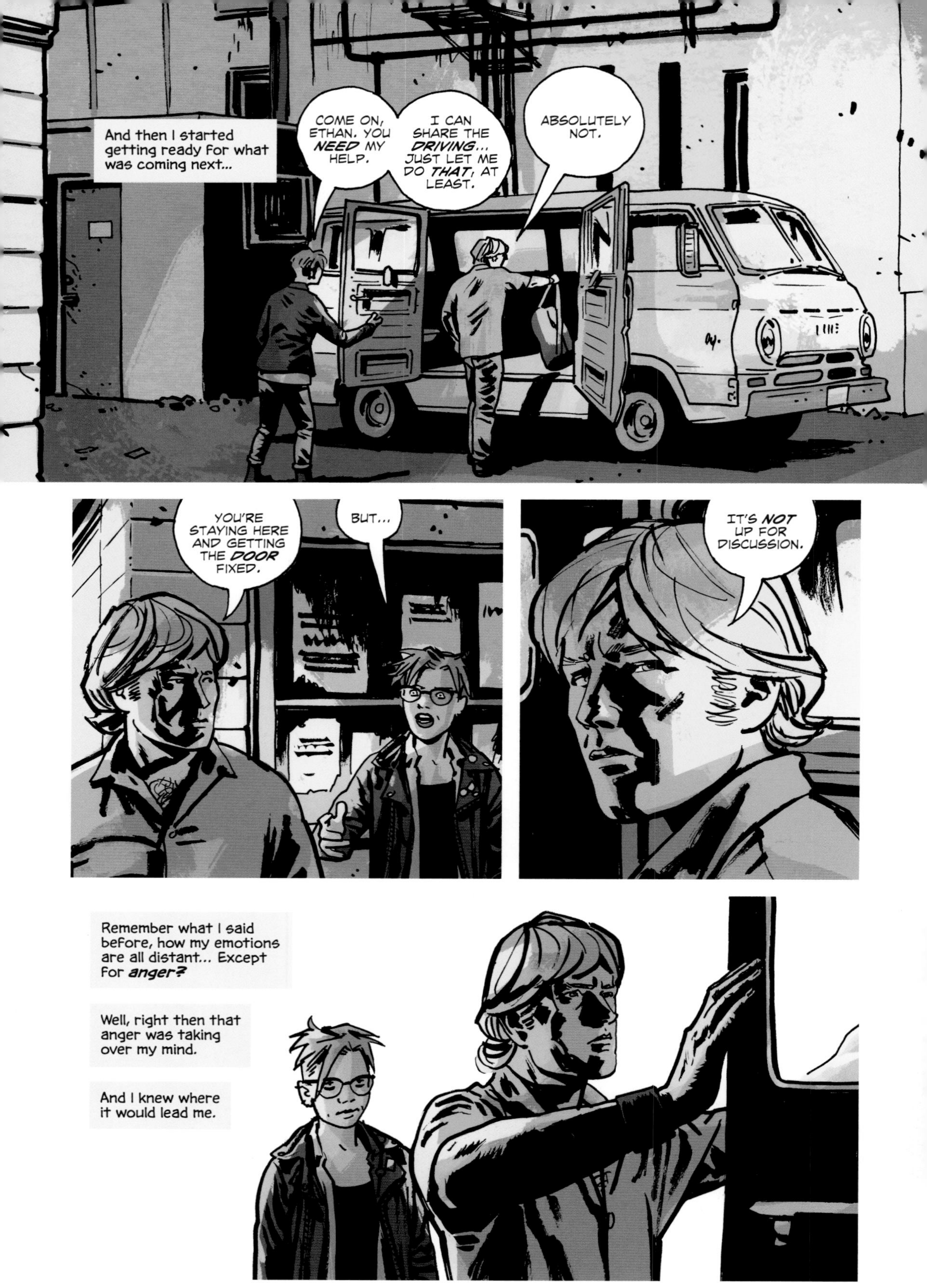

And then I started getting ready for what was coming next...
COME ON, ETHAN. YOU *NEED* MY HELP.
I CAN SHARE THE *DRIVING*... JUST LET ME DO *THAT*, AT LEAST.
ABSOLUTELY NOT.
YOU'RE STAYING HERE AND GETTING THE *DOOR* FIXED.
BUT...
IT'S *NOT* UP FOR DISCUSSION.
Remember what I said before, how my emotions are all distant... Except for *anger?*
Well, right then that anger was taking over my mind.
And I knew where it would lead me.

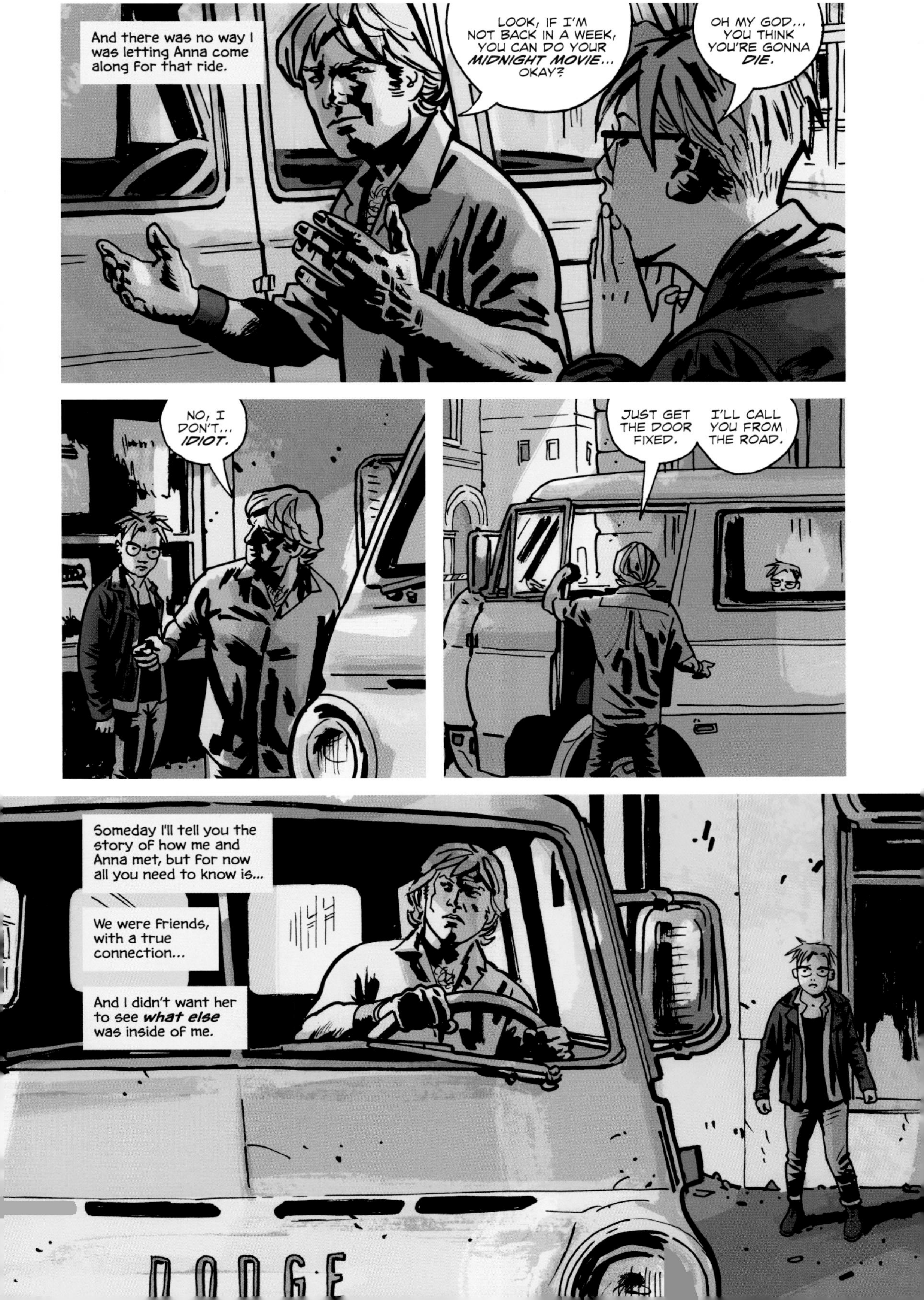

And there was no way I was letting Anna come along for that ride.
LOOK, IF I'M NOT BACK IN A WEEK, YOU CAN DO YOUR *MIDNIGHT MOVIE*... OKAY?
OH MY GOD... YOU THINK YOU'RE GONNA *DIE*.
NO, I DON'T... *IDIOT*.
JUST GET THE DOOR FIXED.
I'LL CALL YOU FROM THE ROAD.
Someday I'll tell you the story of how me and Anna met, but for now all you need to know is...
We were friends, with a true connection...
And I didn't want her to see ***what else*** was inside of me.
DODGE

The Next Few Days

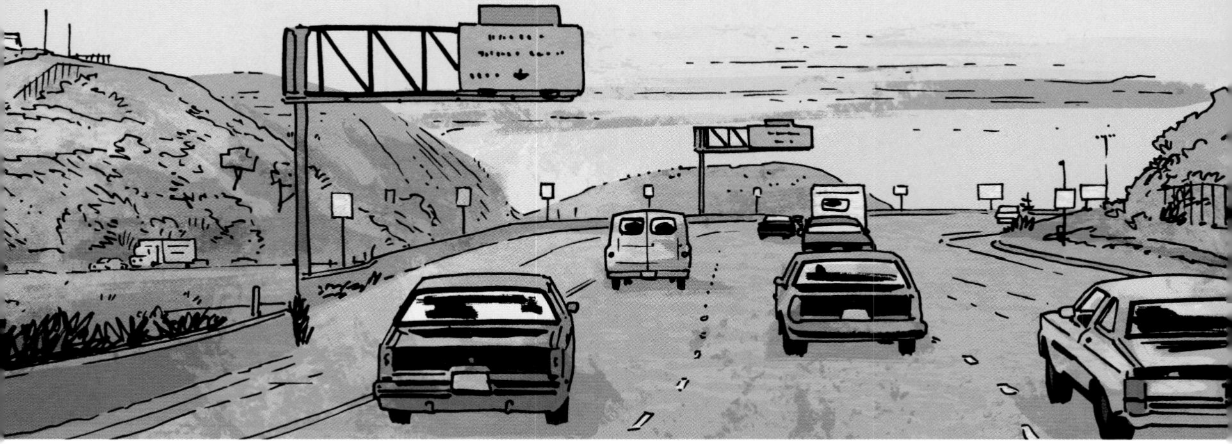

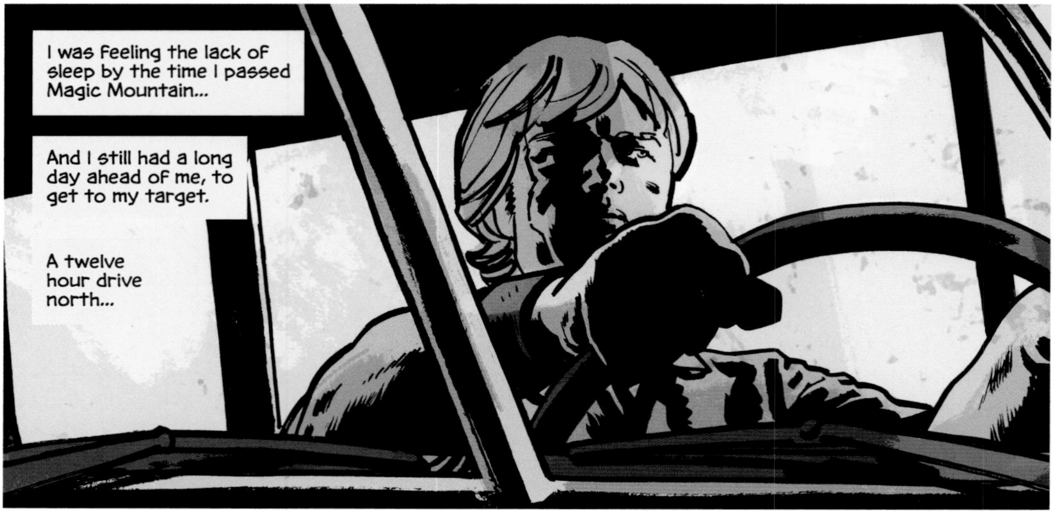
I was feeling the lack of sleep by the time I passed Magic Mountain...
And I still had a long day ahead of me, to get to my target.
A twelve hour drive north...

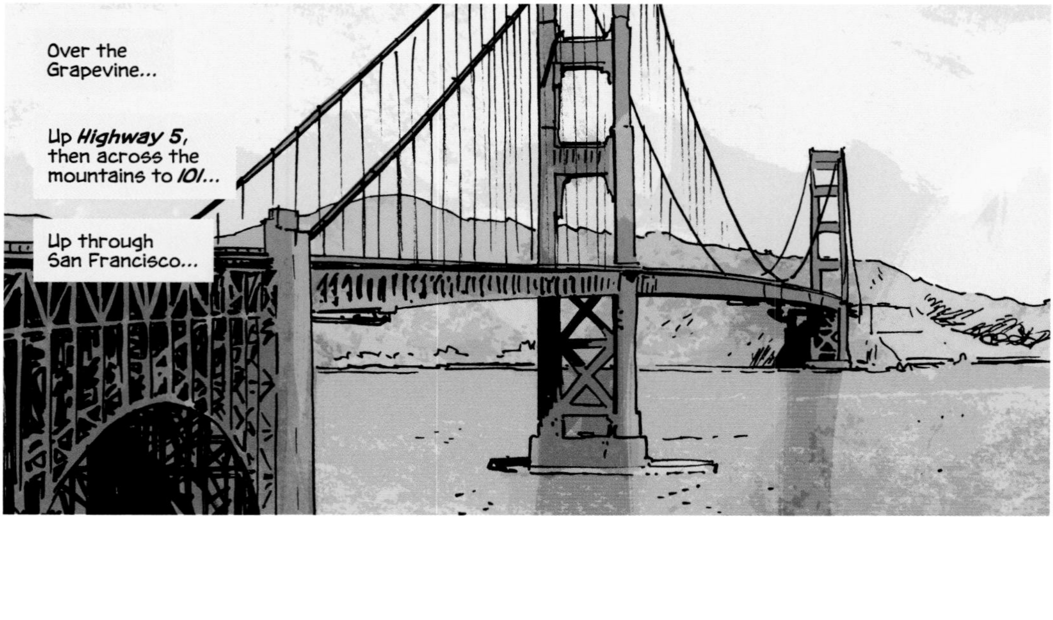
Over the Grapevine...
Up *Highway 5*, then across the mountains to *101*...
Up through San Francisco...

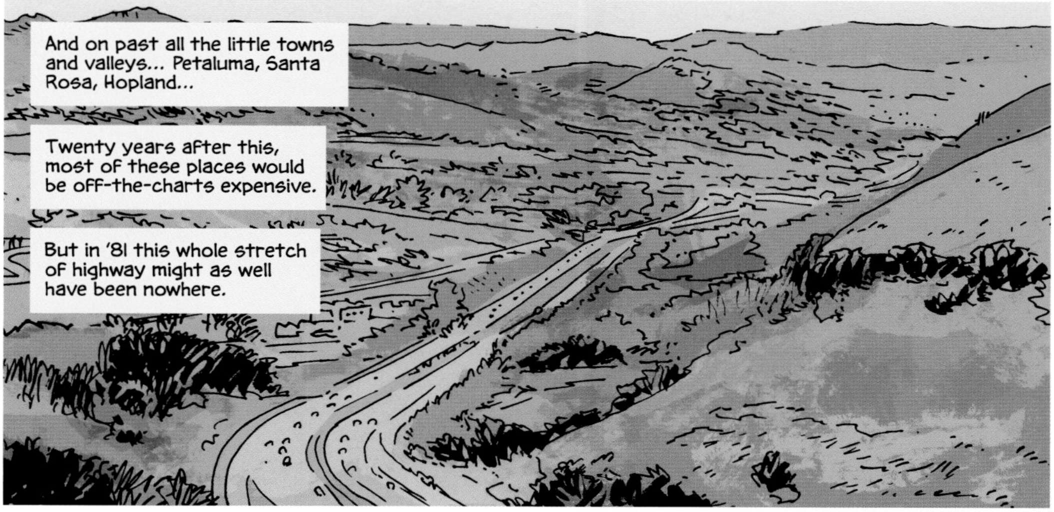
And on past all the little towns and valleys... Petaluma, Santa Rosa, Hopland...
Twenty years after this, most of these places would be off-the-charts expensive.
But in '81 this whole stretch of highway might as well have been nowhere.

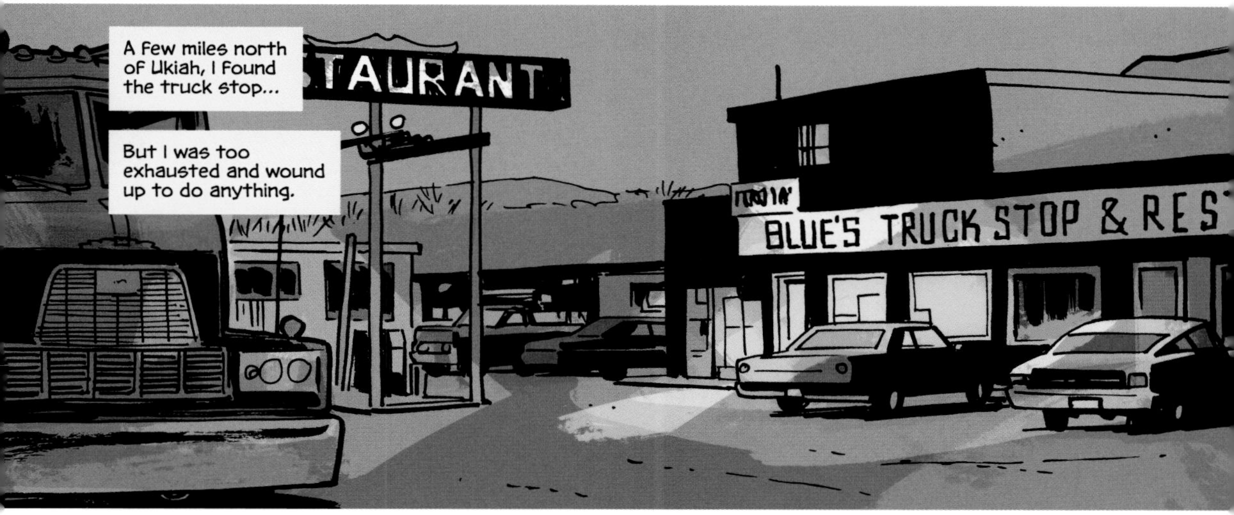
A few miles north of Ukiah, I found the truck stop...
But I was too exhausted and wound up to do anything.
STAURANT
BLUE'S TRUCK STOP & RES

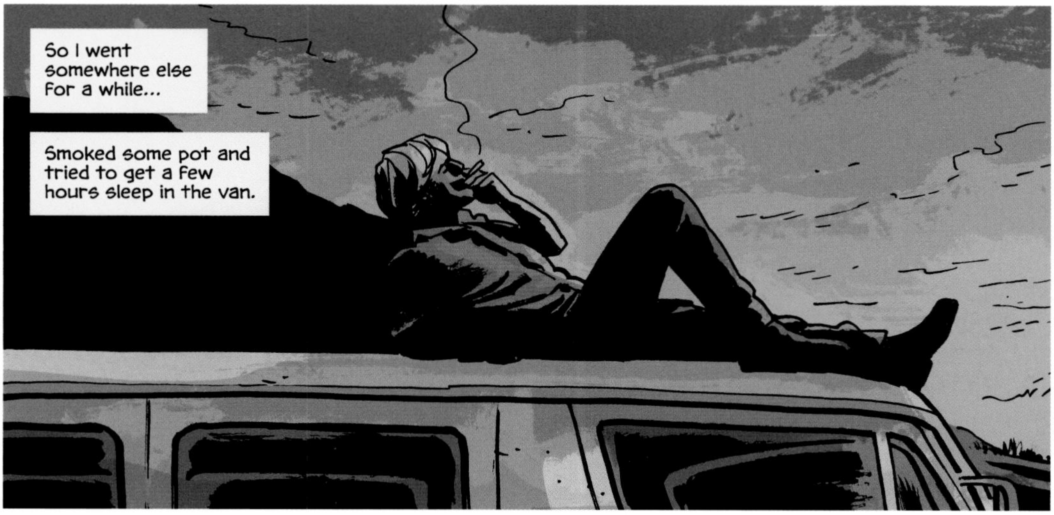
So I went somewhere else for a while...
Smoked some pot and tried to get a few hours sleep in the van.

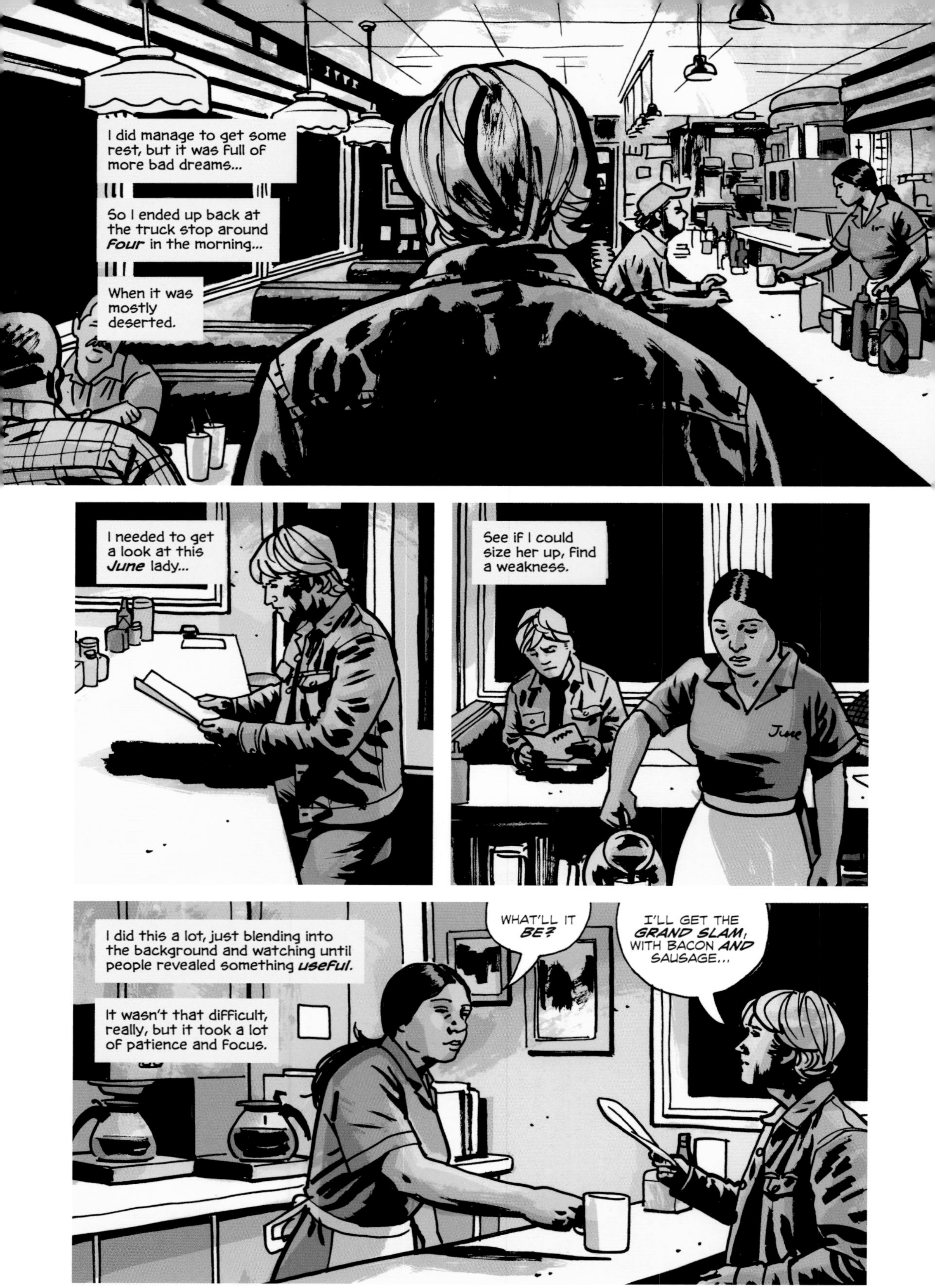
I did manage to get some rest, but it was full of more bad dreams...
So I ended up back at the truck stop around *four* in the morning...
When it was mostly deserted.
I needed to get a look at this *June* lady...
See if I could size her up, find a weakness.
June
I did this a lot, just blending into the background and watching until people revealed something *useful*.
It wasn't that difficult, really, but it took a lot of patience and focus.
WHAT'LL IT *BE?*
I'LL GET THE *GRAND SLAM*, WITH BACON *AND* SAUSAGE...

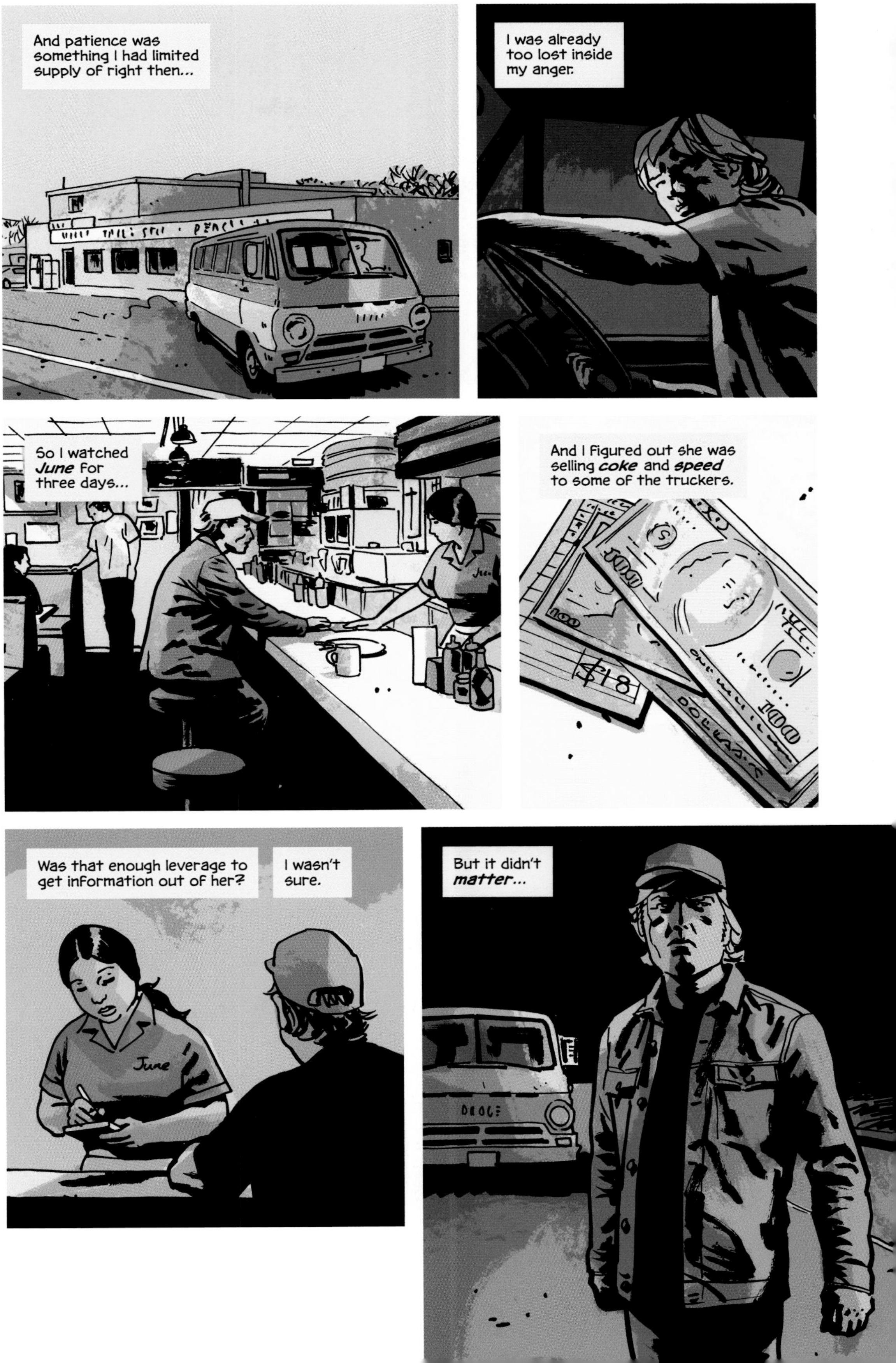
And patience was something I had limited supply of right then...
I was already too lost inside my anger.
So I watched *June* for three days...
And I figured out she was selling ***coke*** and ***speed*** to some of the truckers.
Was that enough leverage to get information out of her?
I wasn't sure.
But it didn't ***matter...***

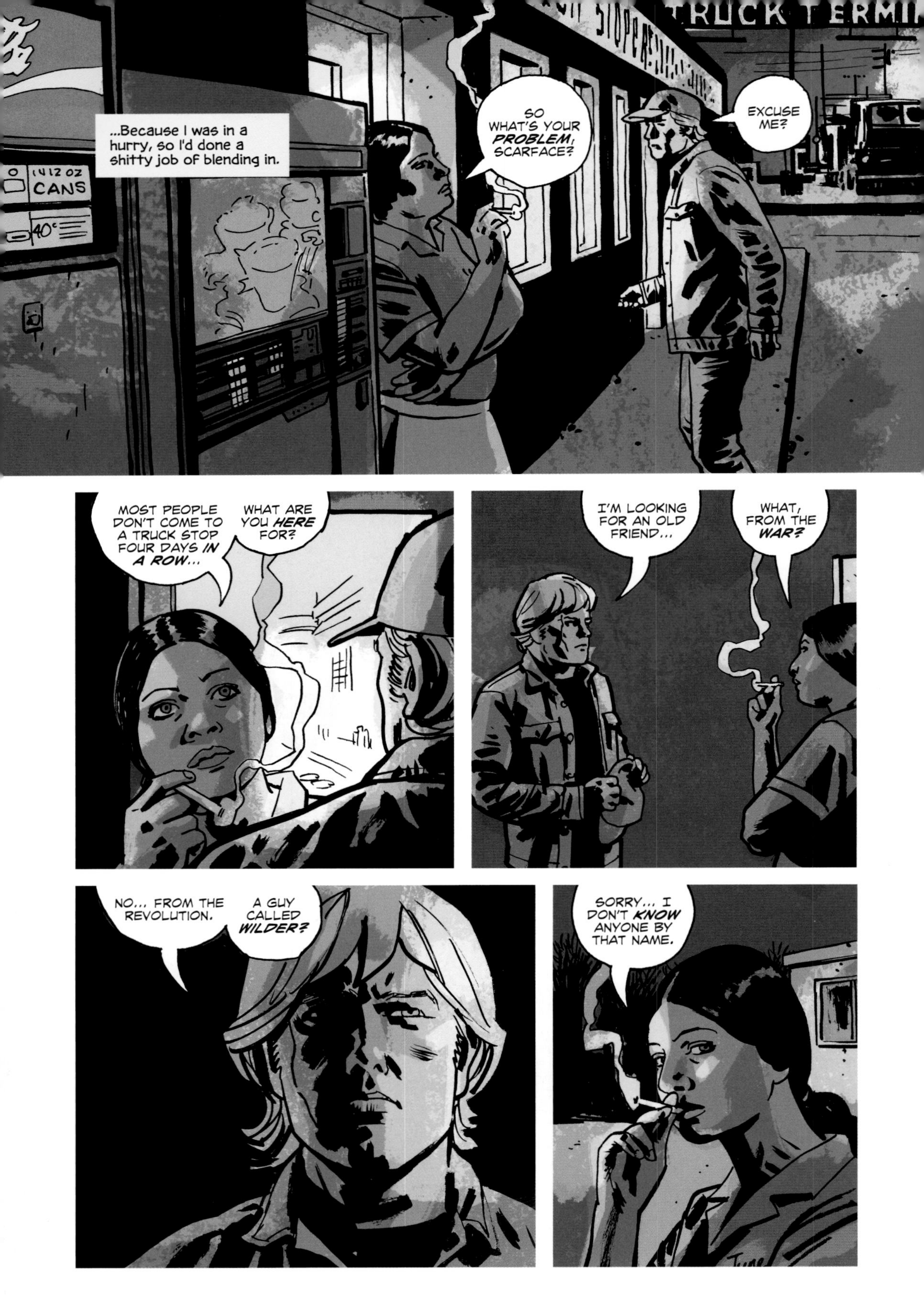
...Because I was in a hurry, so I'd done a shitty job of blending in.
SO WHAT'S YOUR PROBLEM, SCARFACE?
EXCUSE ME?
MOST PEOPLE DON'T COME TO A TRUCK STOP FOUR DAYS IN A ROW...
WHAT ARE YOU HERE FOR?
I'M LOOKING FOR AN OLD FRIEND...
WHAT, FROM THE WAR?
NO... FROM THE REVOLUTION.
A GUY CALLED WILDER?
SORRY... I DON'T KNOW ANYONE BY THAT NAME.

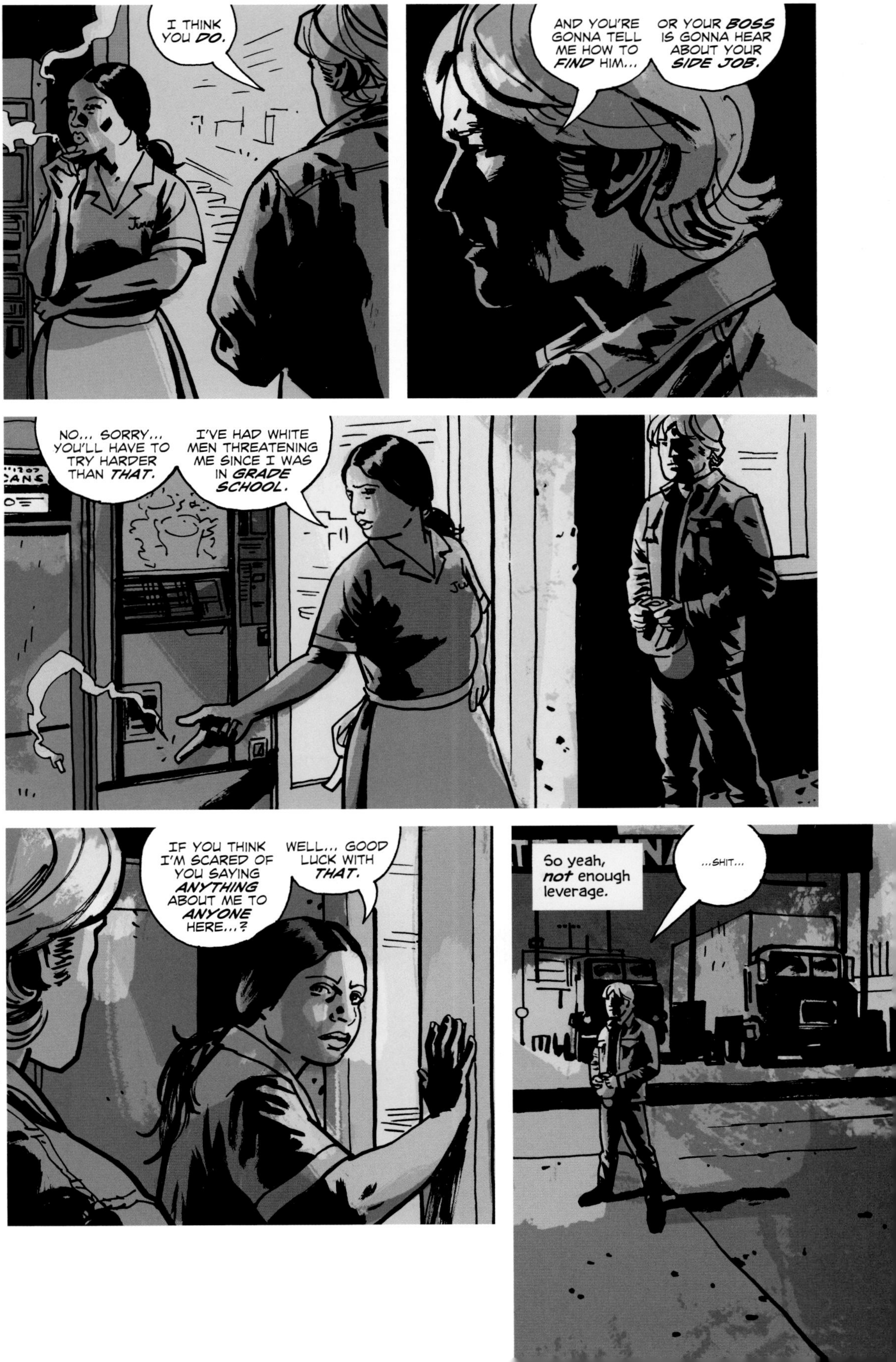

I THINK YOU *DO.*
AND YOU'RE GONNA TELL ME HOW TO *FIND* HIM...
OR YOUR *BOSS* IS GONNA HEAR ABOUT YOUR *SIDE JOB.*
NO... SORRY... YOU'LL HAVE TO TRY HARDER THAN *THAT.*
I'VE HAD WHITE MEN THREATENING ME SINCE I WAS IN *GRADE SCHOOL.*
IF YOU THINK I'M SCARED OF YOU SAYING *ANYTHING* ABOUT ME TO *ANYONE* HERE...?
WELL... GOOD LUCK WITH *THAT.*
So yeah, **not** enough leverage.
...SHIT...

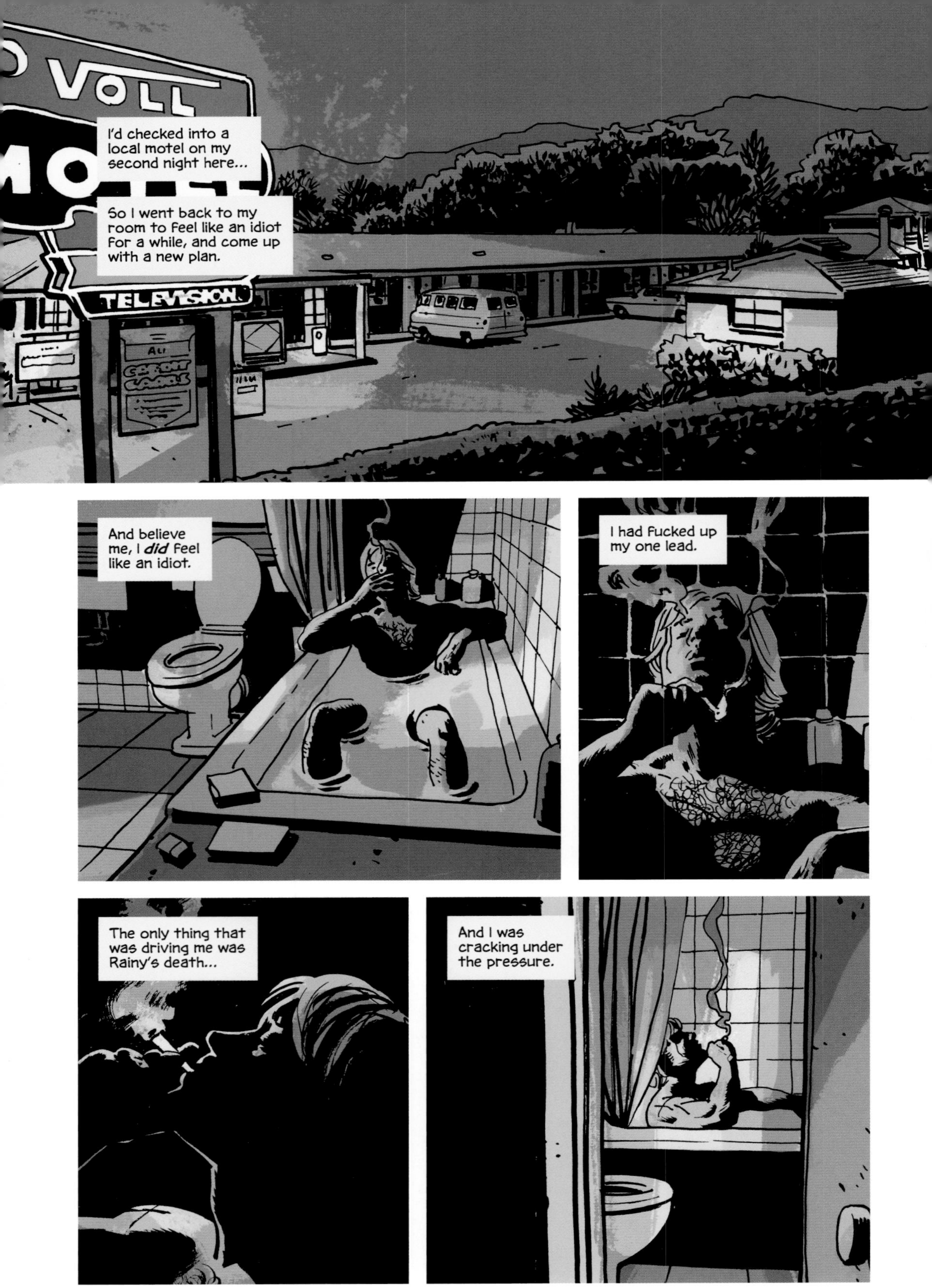

VOLL
TELEVISION
I'd checked into a local motel on my second night here...
So I went back to my room to feel like an idiot for a while, and come up with a new plan.
And believe me, I *did* feel like an idiot.
I had fucked up my one lead.
The only thing that was driving me was Rainy's death...
And I was cracking under the pressure.

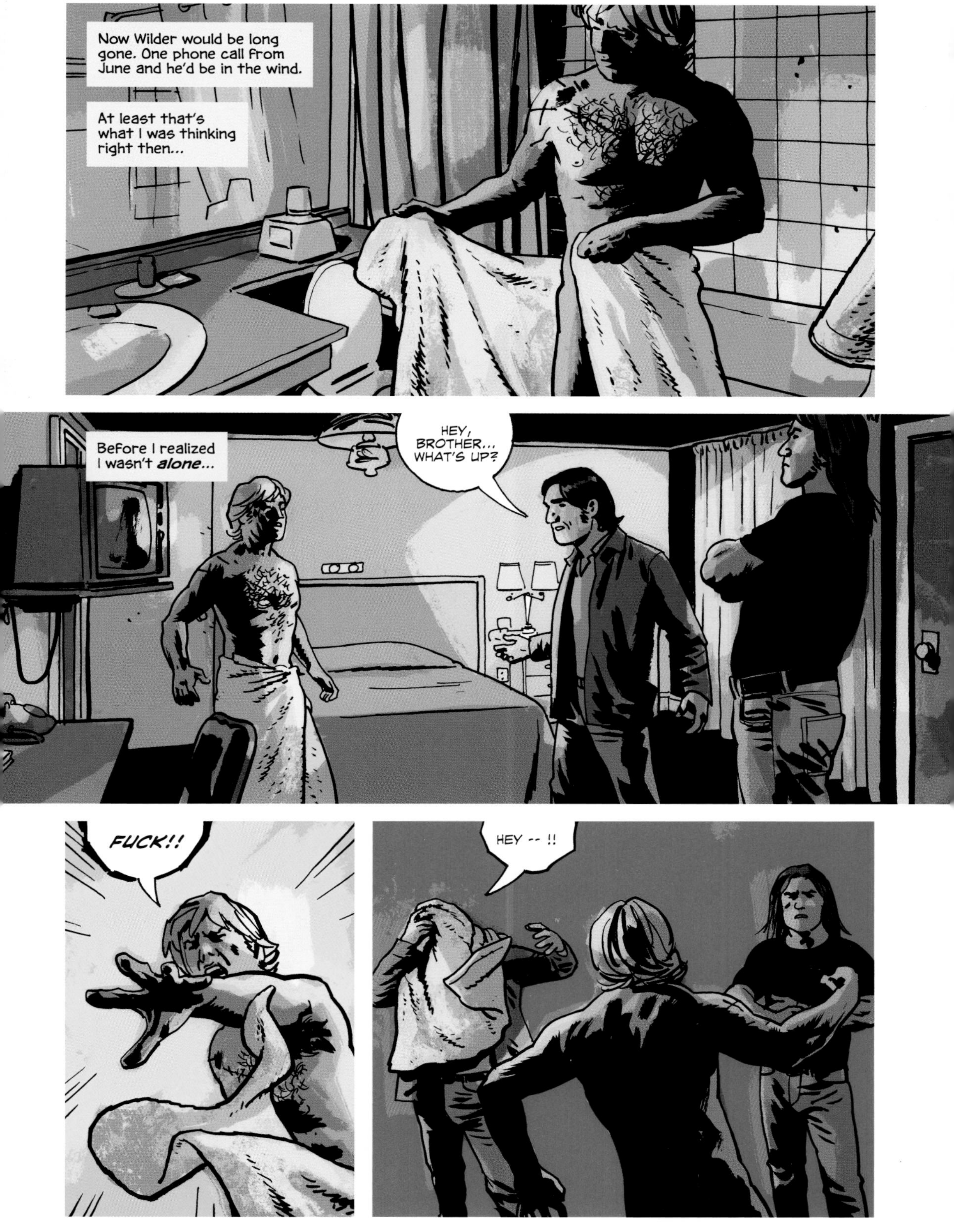
Now Wilder would be long gone. One phone call from June and he'd be in the wind.
At least that's what I was thinking right then...
Before I realized I wasn't *alone*...
HEY, BROTHER... WHAT'S UP?
FUCK!!
HEY -- !!

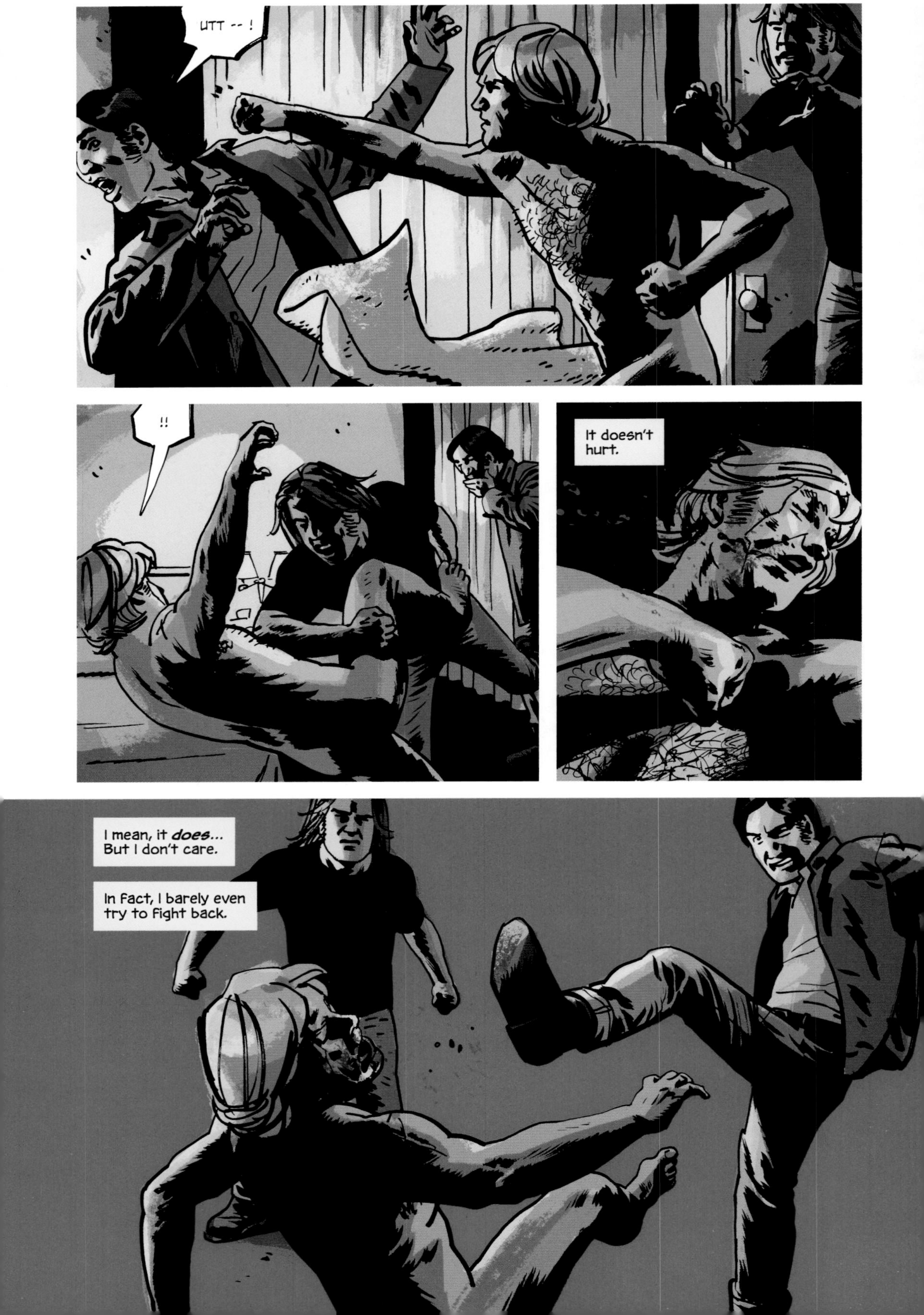
UTT -- !
!!
It doesn't hurt.
I mean, it *does*... But I don't care.
In fact, I barely even try to fight back.

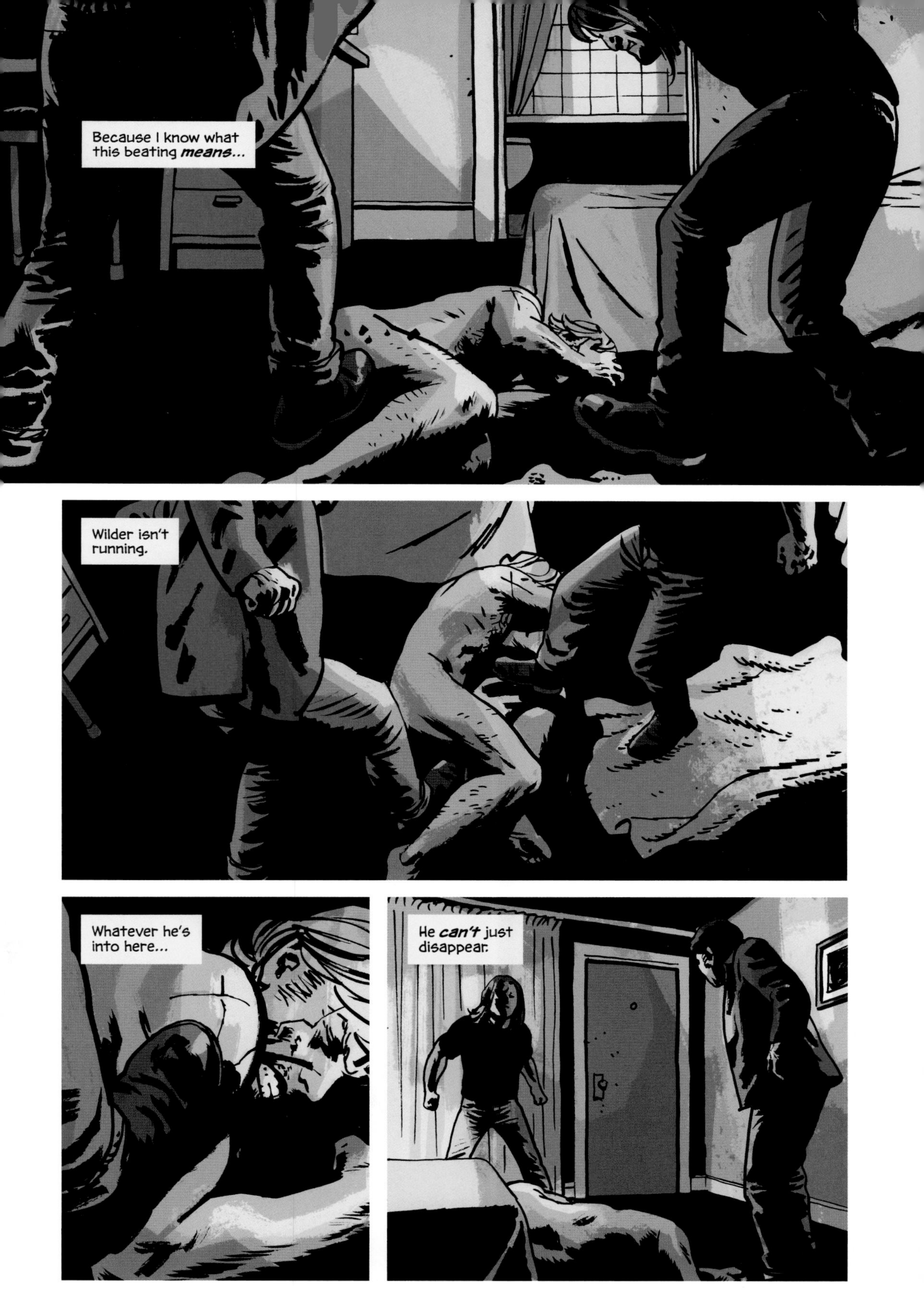
Because I know what this beating *means*...
Wilder isn't running.
Whatever he's into here...
He *can't* just disappear.

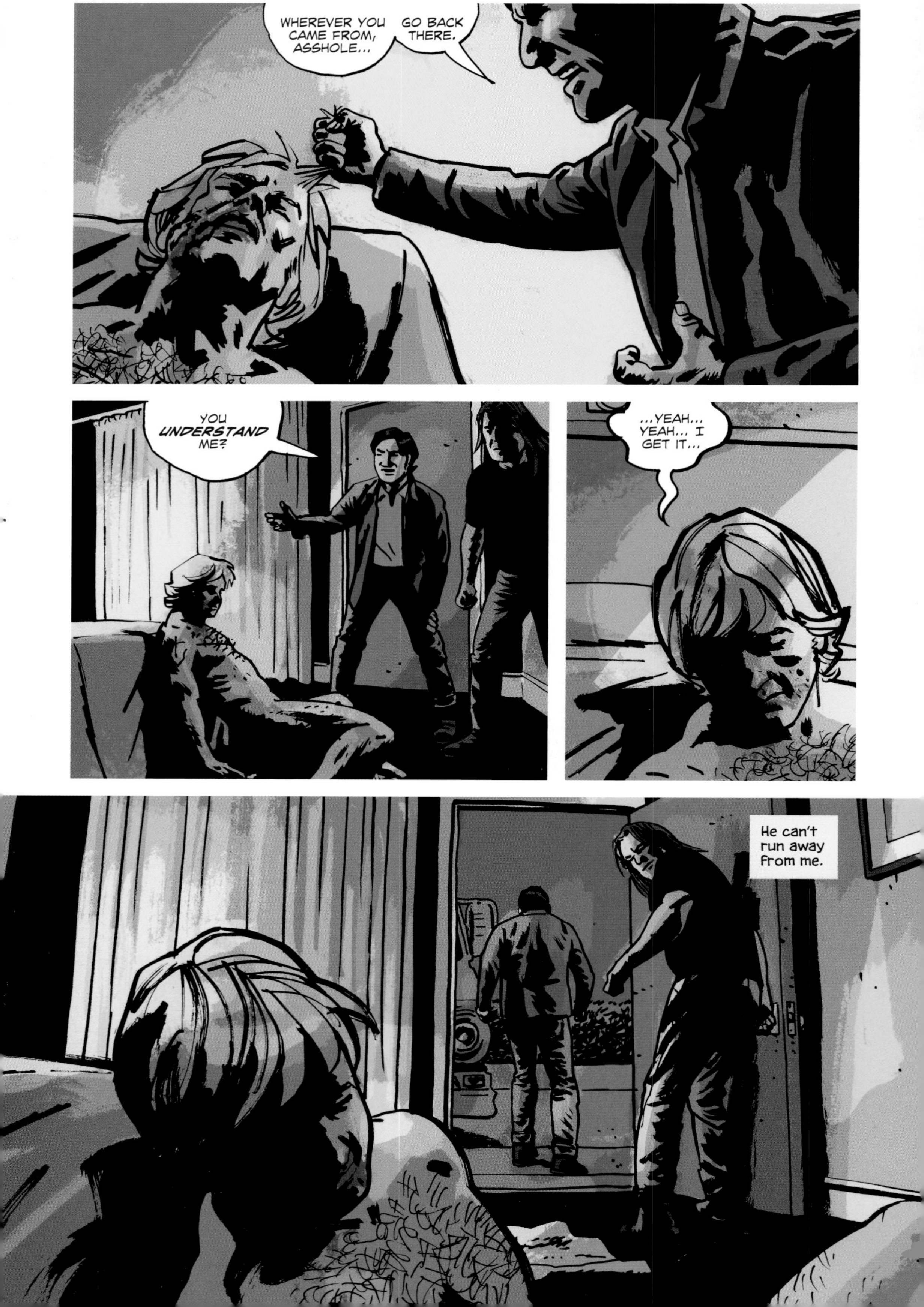
WHEREVER YOU CAME FROM, ASSHOLE...
GO BACK THERE.
YOU UNDERSTAND ME?
...YEAH... YEAH... I GET IT...
He can't run away from me.

How to Not Waste Second Chances

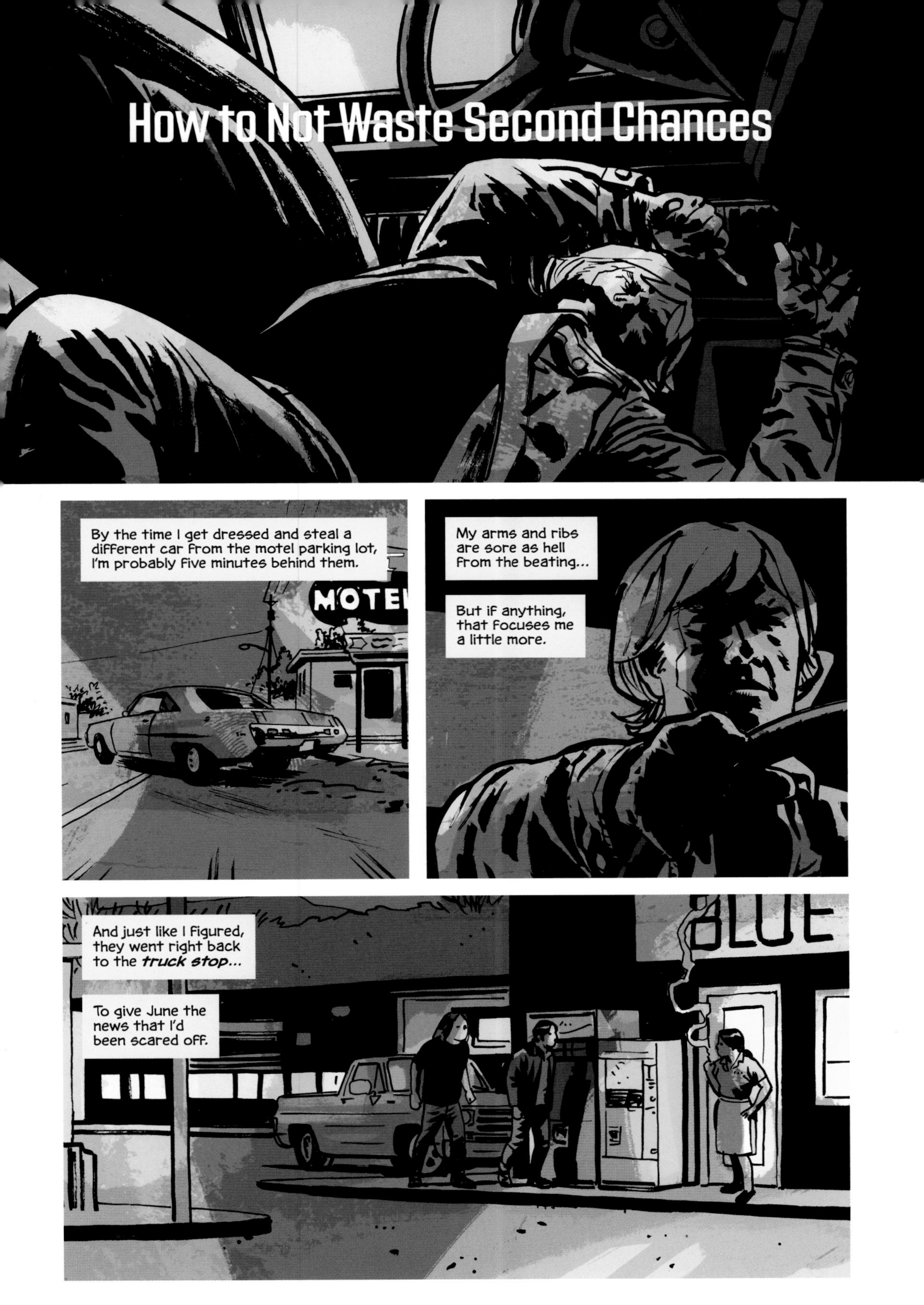

By the time I get dressed and steal a different car from the motel parking lot, I'm probably five minutes behind them.
MOTEL
My arms and ribs are sore as hell from the beating...
But if anything, that focuses me a little more.
And just like I figured, they went right back to the *truck stop*...
To give June the news that I'd been scared off.
BLUE

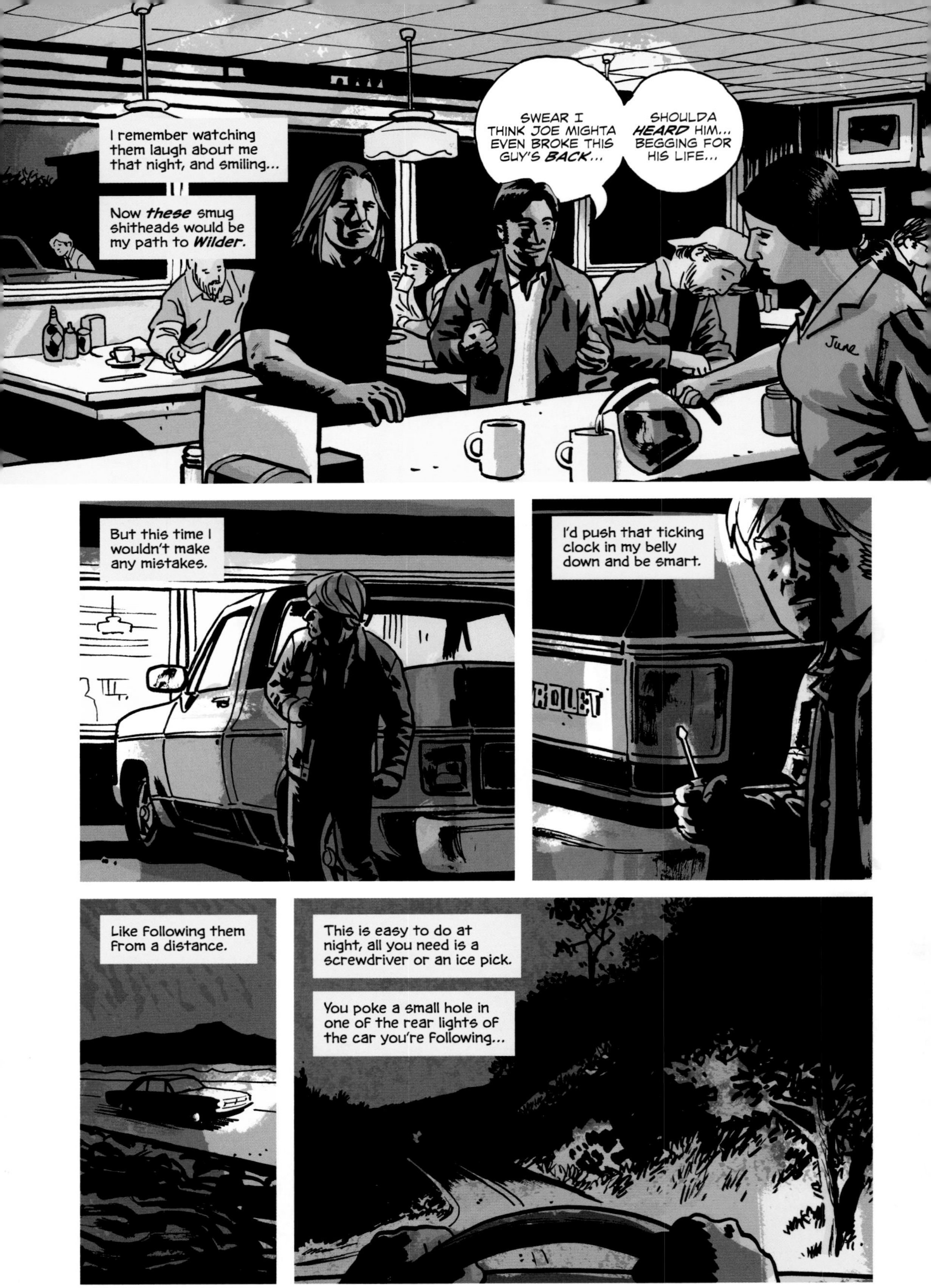

I remember watching them laugh about me that night, and smiling...
Now *these* smug shitheads would be my path to *Wilder*.
SWEAR I THINK JOE MIGHTA EVEN BROKE THIS GUY'S *BACK*...
SHOULDA *HEARD* HIM... BEGGING FOR HIS LIFE...
June
But this time I wouldn't make any mistakes.
I'd push that ticking clock in my belly down and be smart.
Like following them from a distance.
This is easy to do at night, all you need is a screwdriver or an ice pick.
You poke a small hole in one of the rear lights of the car you're following...

And they stand out in the darkness, one taillight *much brighter* than the other... Even from far behind.

It's an old FBI trick.

So where do I follow these guys?

They head east along the river for about an hour...

On a windy mountain road I don't enjoy much, especially at night.

And we end up in *Eel Valley*, which used to be an *Indian Res*, but half the land had been sold off to ranchers fifty years ago.

So now it was one of those places where rich landowners were surrounded by abject poverty...

And the only reason anyone ever came here was because of the casino.

WELCOME TO

EEL VALLEY

ברוכים הוא ברוך דזה

קזינו ספוובוקה

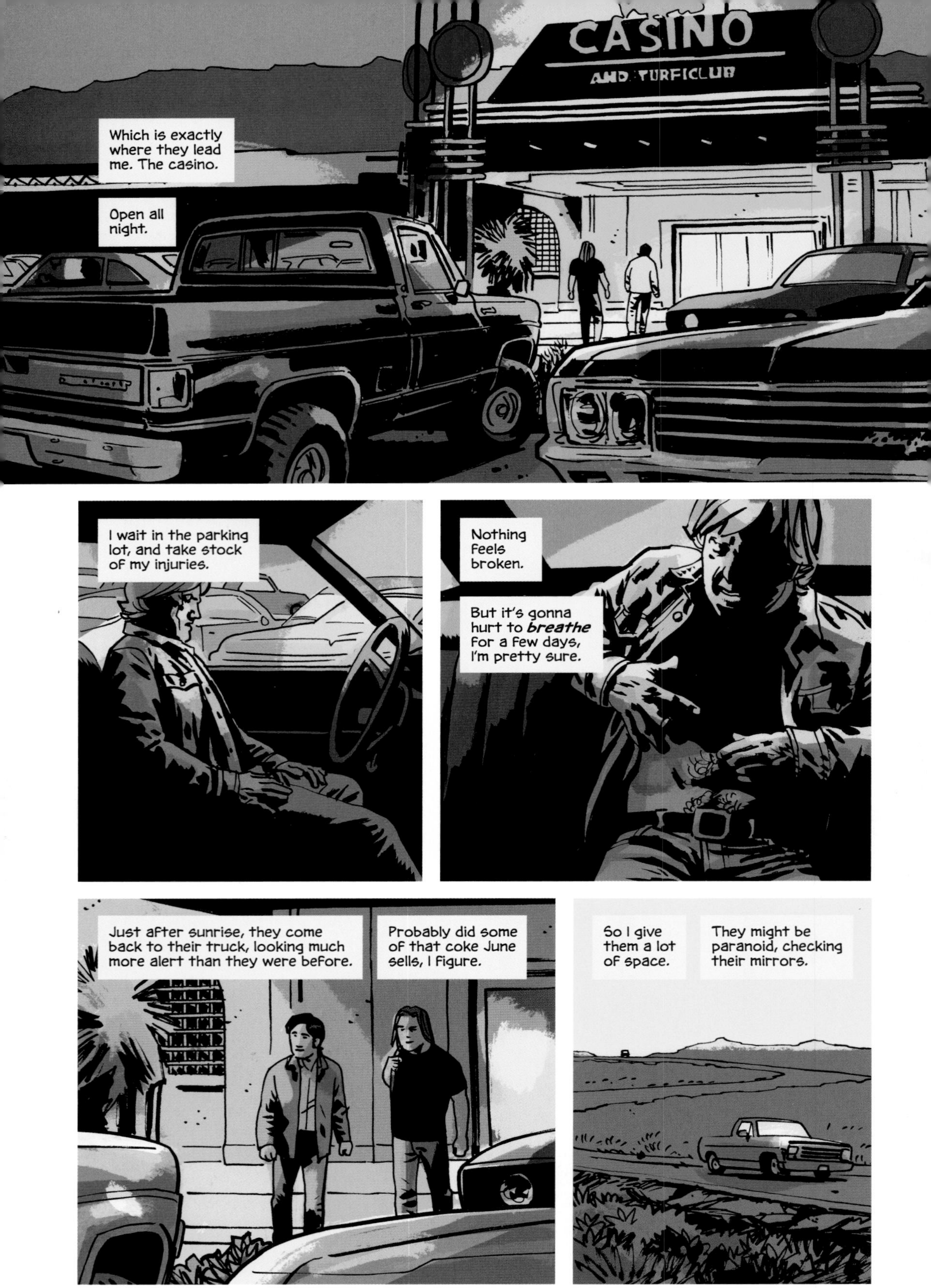
CASINO
AND TURFICLUB
Which is exactly where they lead me. The casino.
Open all night.
I wait in the parking lot, and take stock of my injuries.
Nothing feels broken.
But it's gonna hurt to *breathe* for a few days, I'm pretty sure.
Just after sunrise, they come back to their truck, looking much more alert than they were before.
Probably did some of that coke June sells, I figure.
So I give them a lot of space.
They might be paranoid, checking their mirrors.

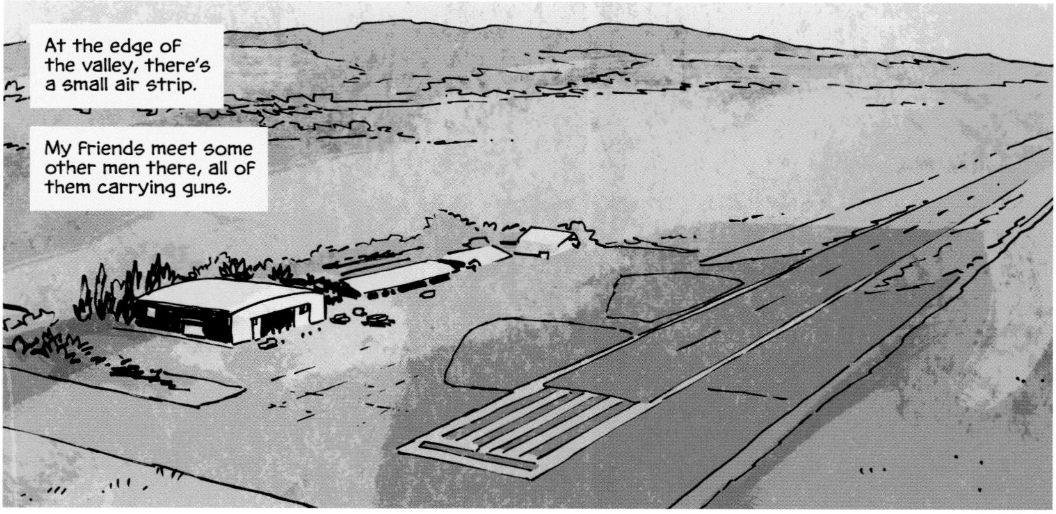
At the edge of the valley, there's a small air strip.
My friends meet some other men there, all of them carrying guns.

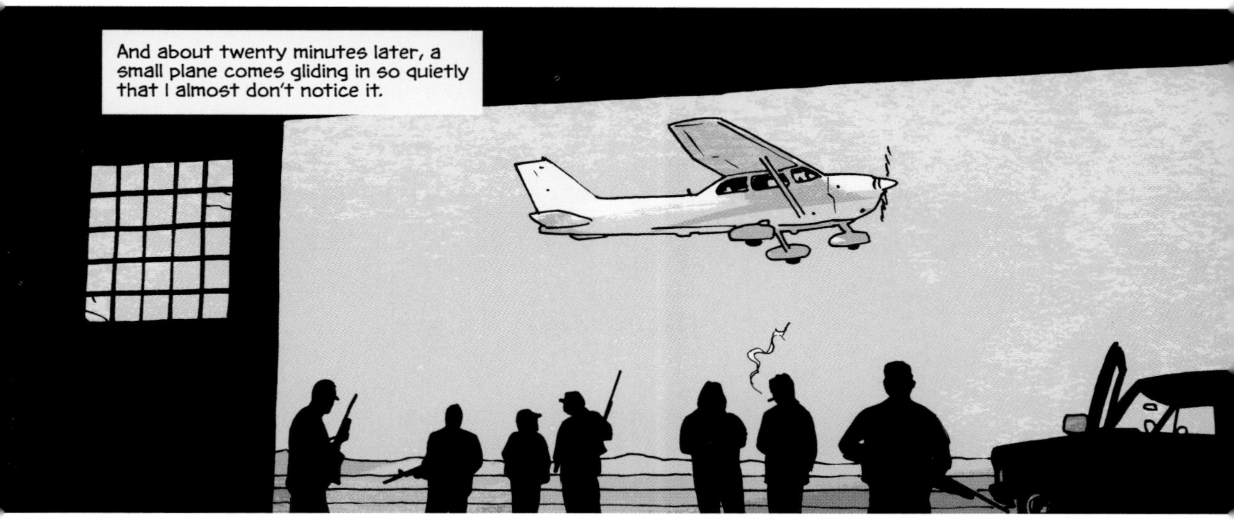
And about twenty minutes later, a small plane comes gliding in so quietly that I almost don't notice it.

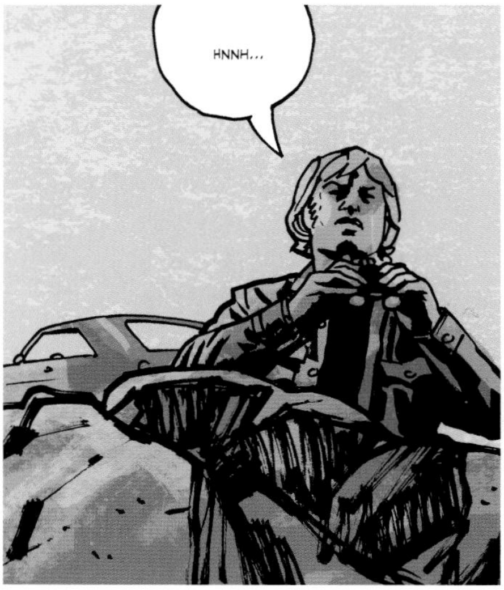
HNNH...

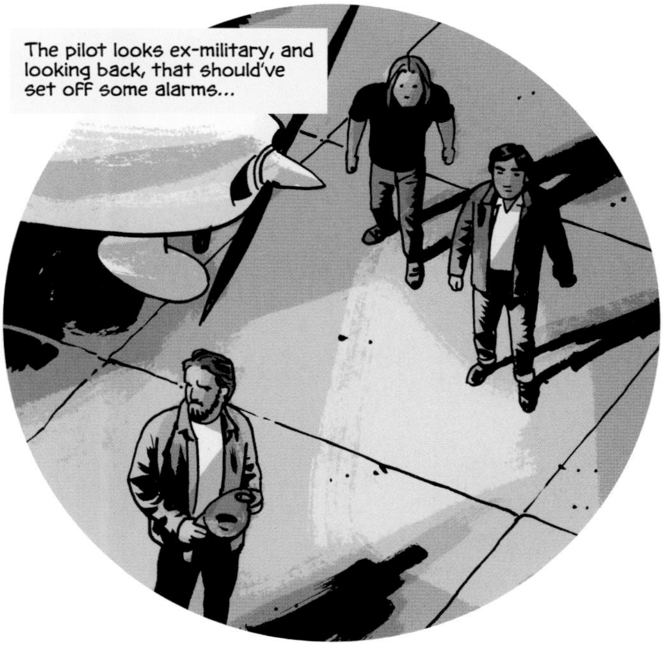
The pilot looks ex-military, and looking back, that should've set off some alarms...

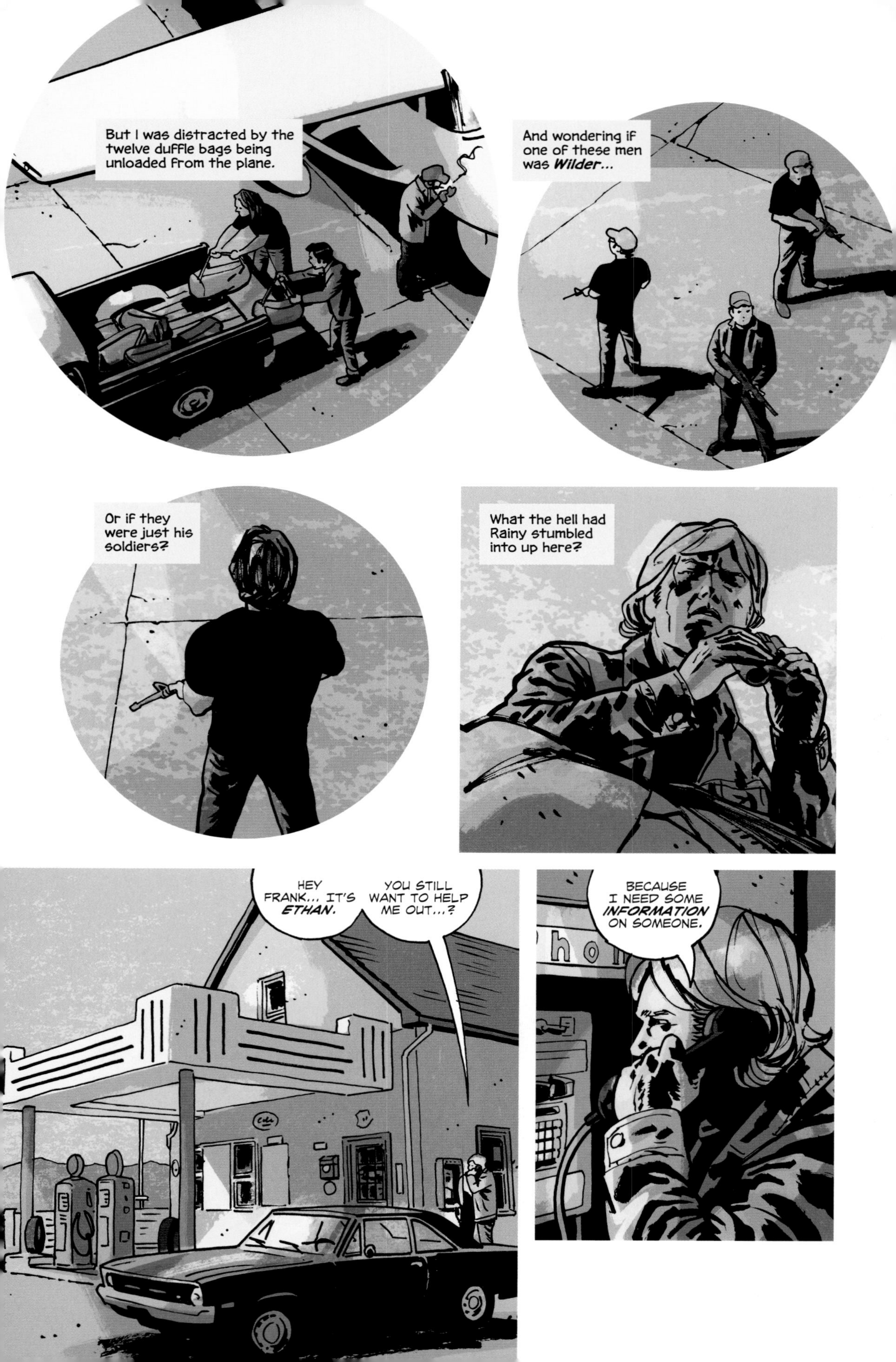
But I was distracted by the twelve duffle bags being unloaded from the plane.
And wondering if one of these men was *Wilder*...
Or if they were just his soldiers?
What the hell had Rainy stumbled into up here?
HEY FRANK... IT'S *ETHAN.*
YOU STILL WANT TO HELP ME OUT...?
BECAUSE I NEED SOME *INFORMATION* ON SOMEONE.

The Art of War

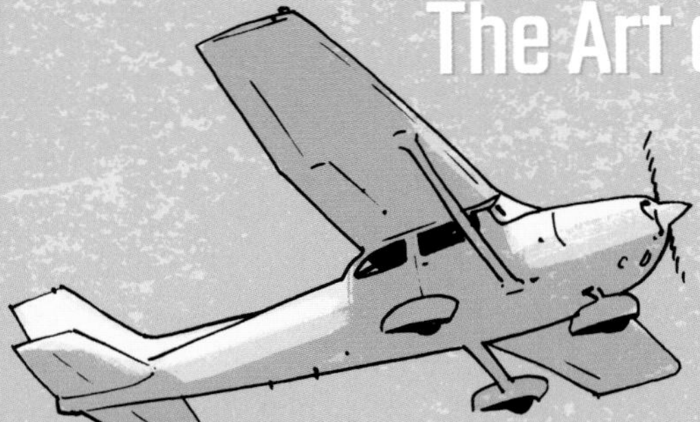

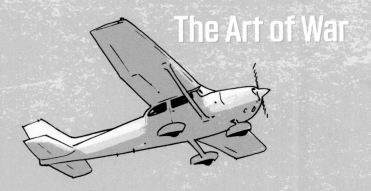

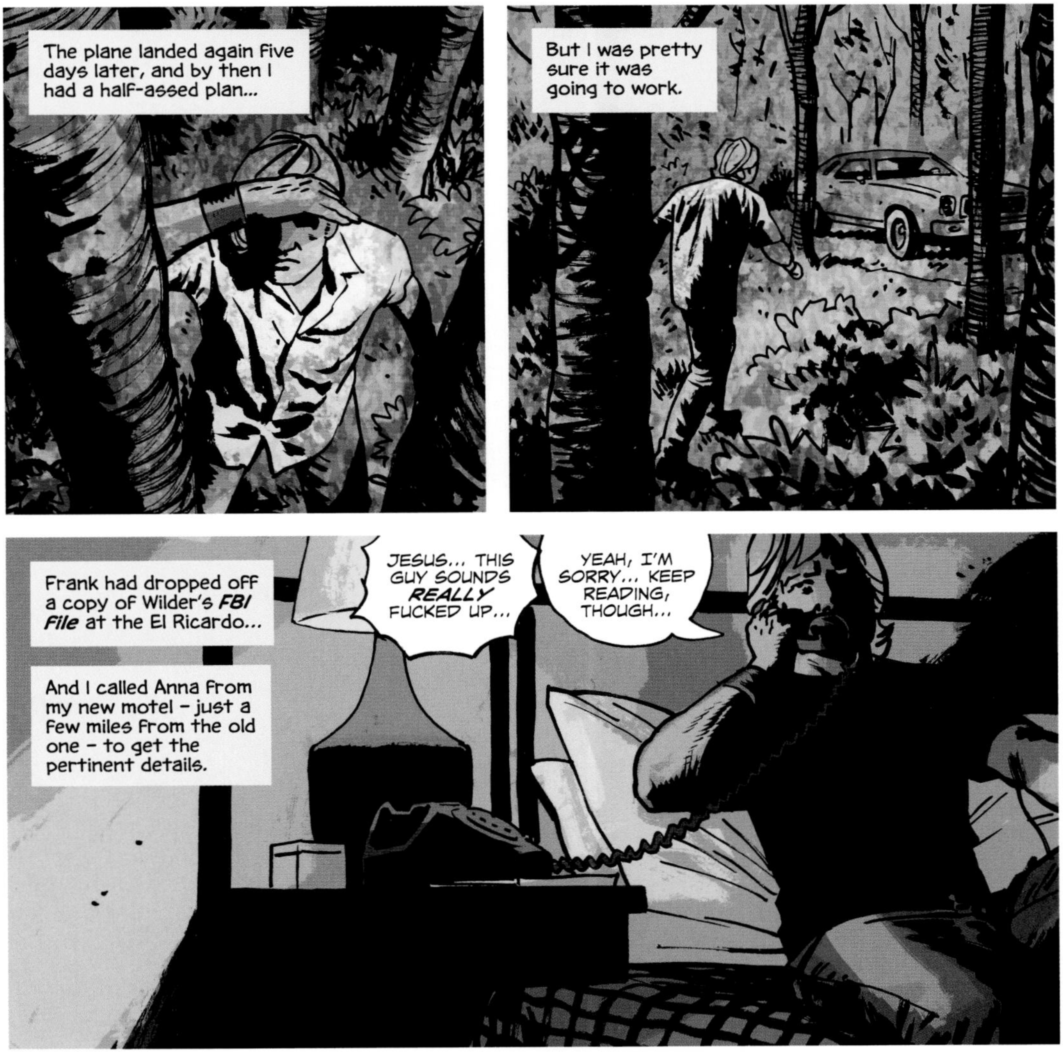
The plane landed again five days later, and by then I had a half-assed plan...
But I was pretty sure it was going to work.
Frank had dropped off a copy of Wilder's *FBI File* at the El Ricardo...
And I called Anna from my new motel – just a few miles from the old one – to get the pertinent details.
JESUS... THIS GUY SOUNDS *REALLY* FUCKED UP...
YEAH, I'M SORRY... KEEP READING, THOUGH...

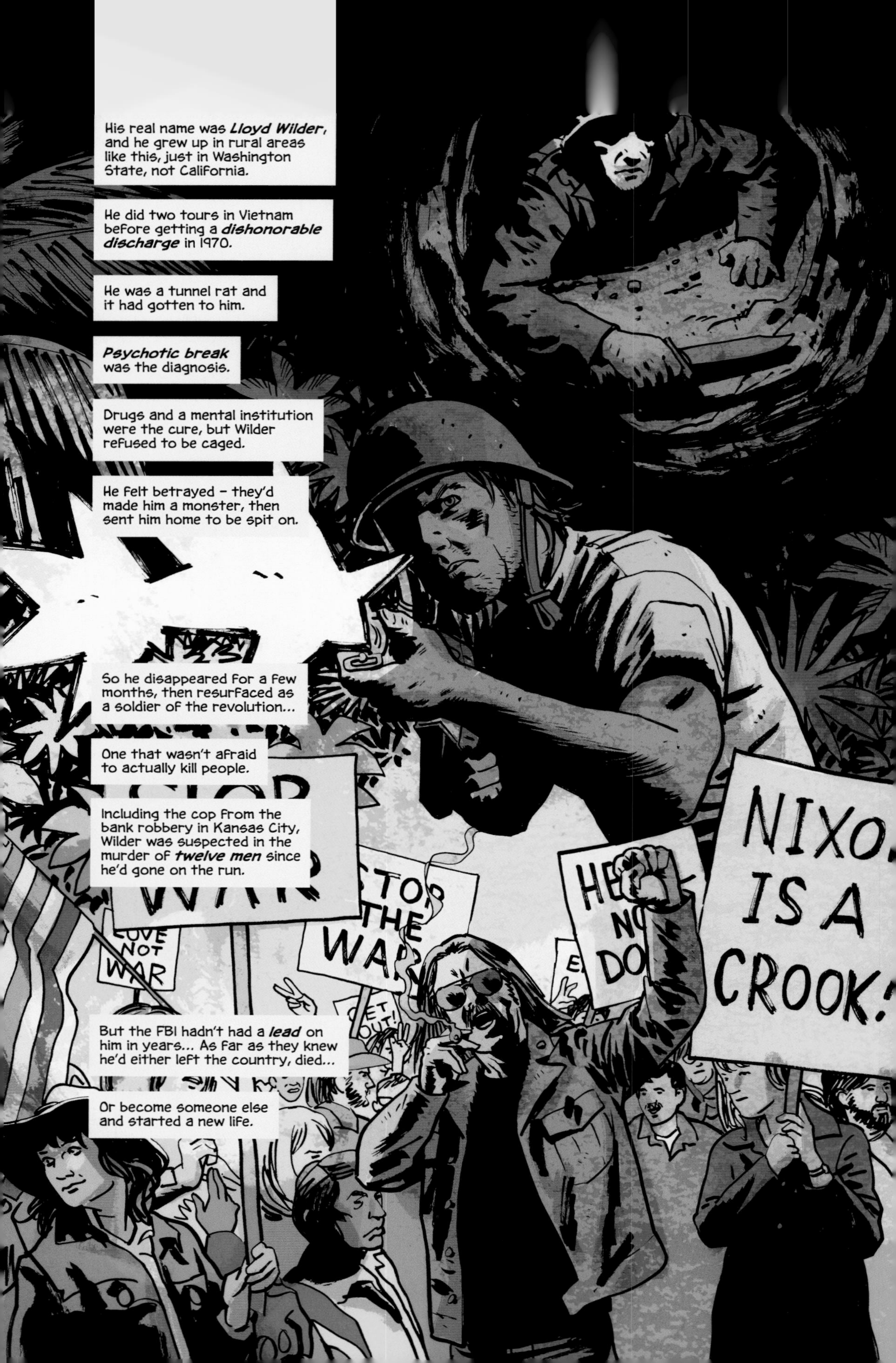

His real name was *Lloyd Wilder*, and he grew up in rural areas like this, just in Washington State, not California.
He did two tours in Vietnam before getting a *dishonorable discharge* in 1970.
He was a tunnel rat and it had gotten to him.
Psychotic break was the diagnosis.
Drugs and a mental institution were the cure, but Wilder refused to be caged.
He felt betrayed – they'd made him a monster, then sent him home to be spit on.
So he disappeared for a few months, then resurfaced as a soldier of the revolution...
One that wasn't afraid to actually kill people.
Including the cop from the bank robbery in Kansas City, Wilder was suspected in the murder of *twelve men* since he'd gone on the run.
NIXO IS A CROOK!
STOP THE WAR
LOVE NOT WAR
But the FBI hadn't had a *lead* on him in years... As far as they knew he'd either left the country, died...
Or become someone else and started a new life.

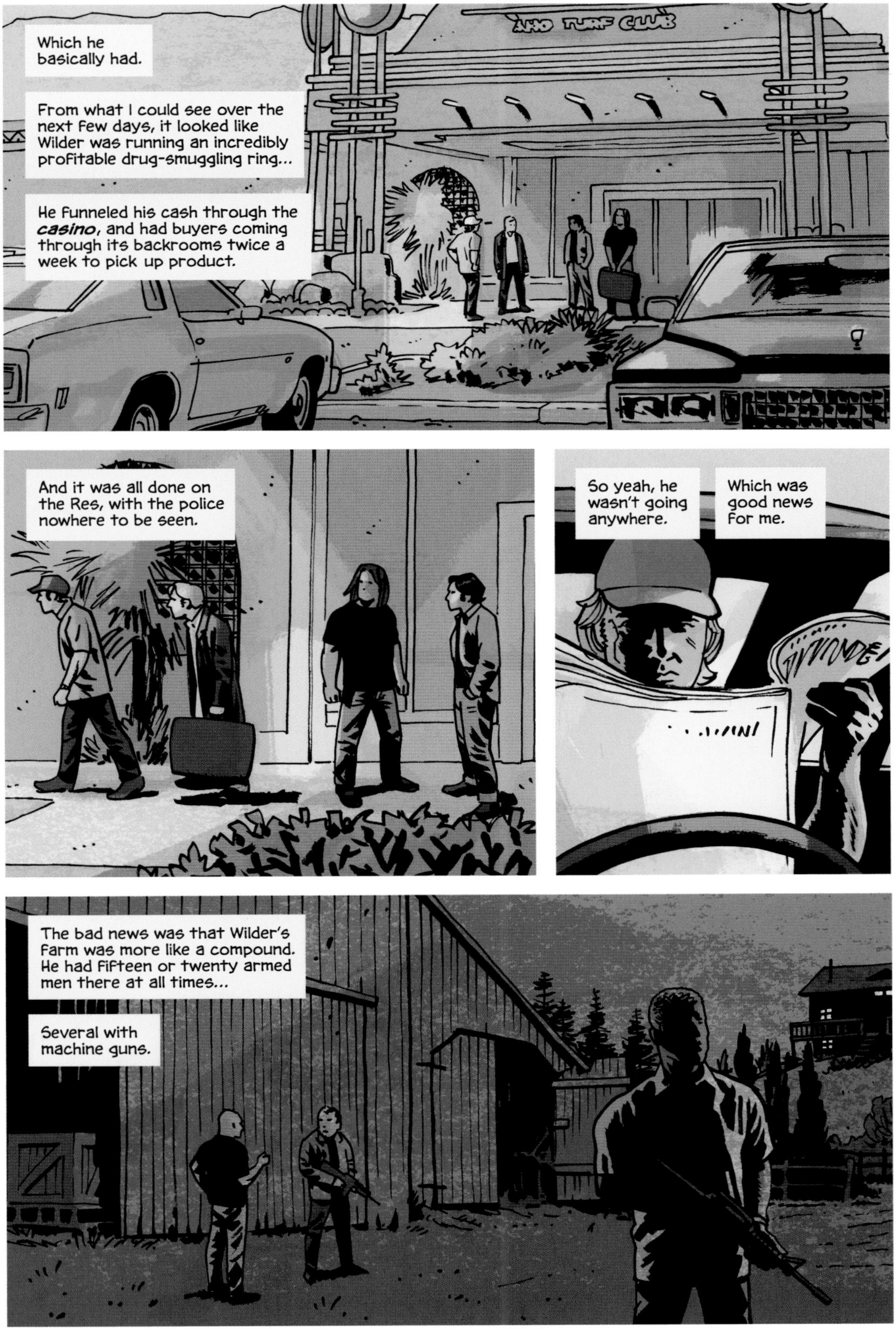
Which he basically had.
From what I could see over the next few days, it looked like Wilder was running an incredibly profitable drug-smuggling ring...
He funneled his cash through the *casino*, and had buyers coming through its backrooms twice a week to pick up product.
And it was all done on the Res, with the police nowhere to be seen.
So yeah, he wasn't going anywhere.
Which was good news for me.
The bad news was that Wilder's farm was more like a compound. He had fifteen or twenty armed men there at all times...
Several with machine guns.

And the man himself rarely left the main house...

It took me hours of waiting before I finally spotted him.

He looked like nothing to me... Unimpressive.

Not worth whatever trouble was coming next.

And yet my eyes were trying to light him on Fire with the hate I felt right then.

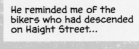
He reminded me of the bikers who had descended on Haight Street...

Wolves in hippie clothing.

The idea of someone like that killing Rainy Filled me with rage.

REDHAWK AIRFIELD NO TRESPAS

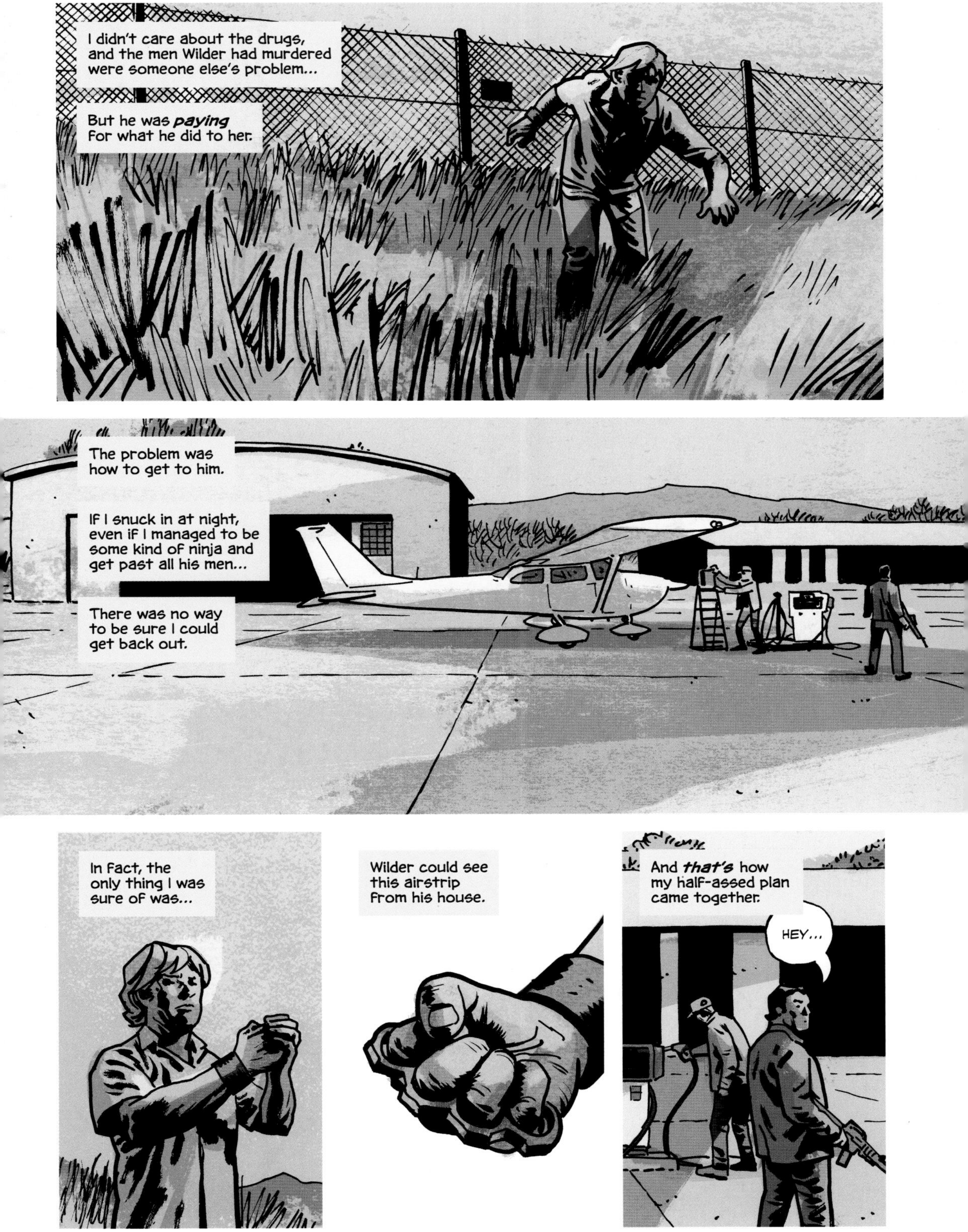
I didn't care about the drugs, and the men Wilder had murdered were someone else's problem...
But he was *paying* for what he did to her.
The problem was how to get to him.
If I snuck in at night, even if I managed to be some kind of ninja and get past all his men...
There was no way to be sure I could get back out.
In fact, the only thing I was sure of was...
Wilder could see this airstrip from his house.
And *that's* how my half-assed plan came together.
HEY...

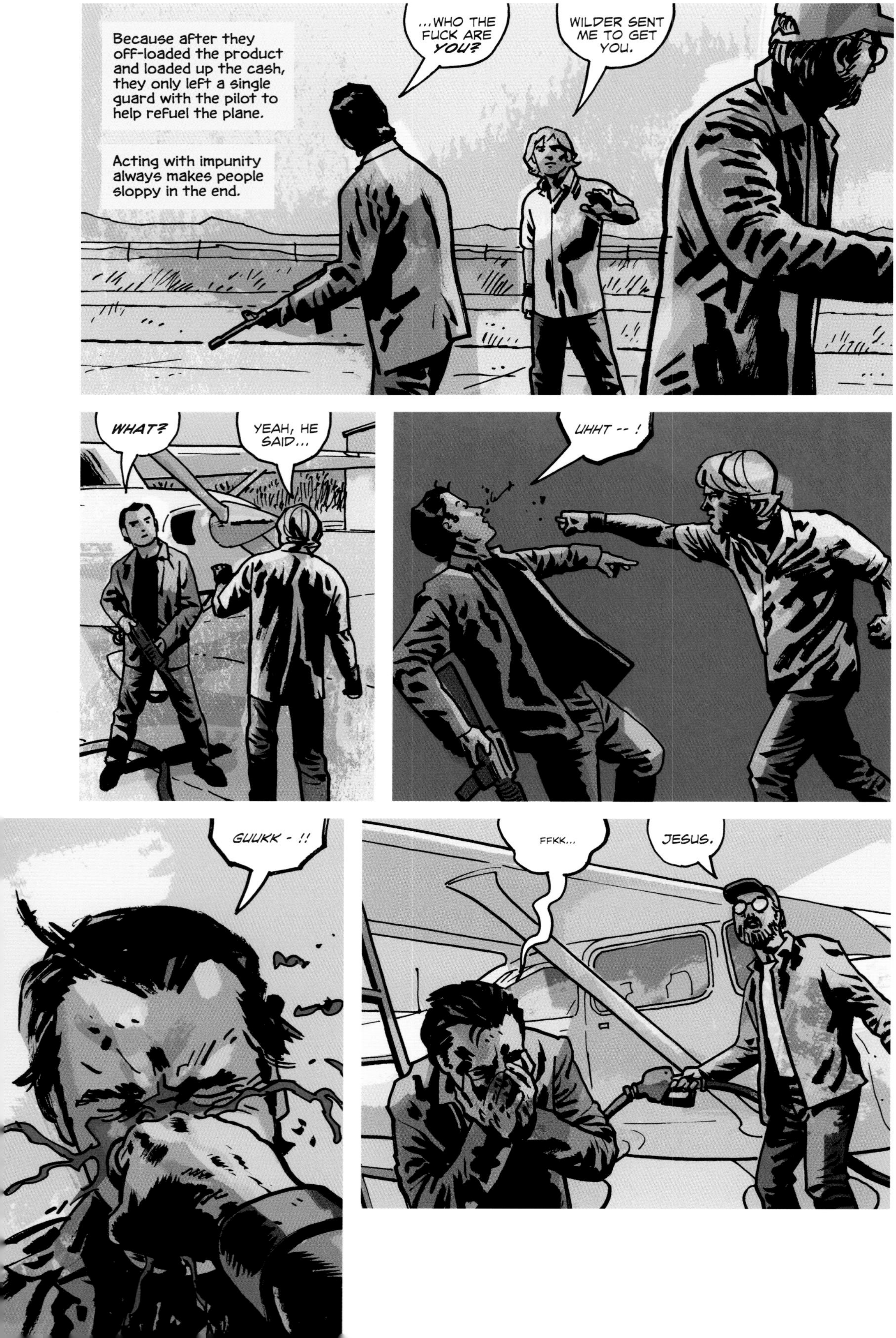
Because after they off-loaded the product and loaded up the cash, they only left a single guard with the pilot to help refuel the plane.
Acting with impunity always makes people sloppy in the end.
...WHO THE FUCK ARE *YOU?*
WILDER SENT ME TO GET YOU.
WHAT?
YEAH, HE SAID...
UHHT -- !
GUUKK - !!
FFKK...
JESUS.

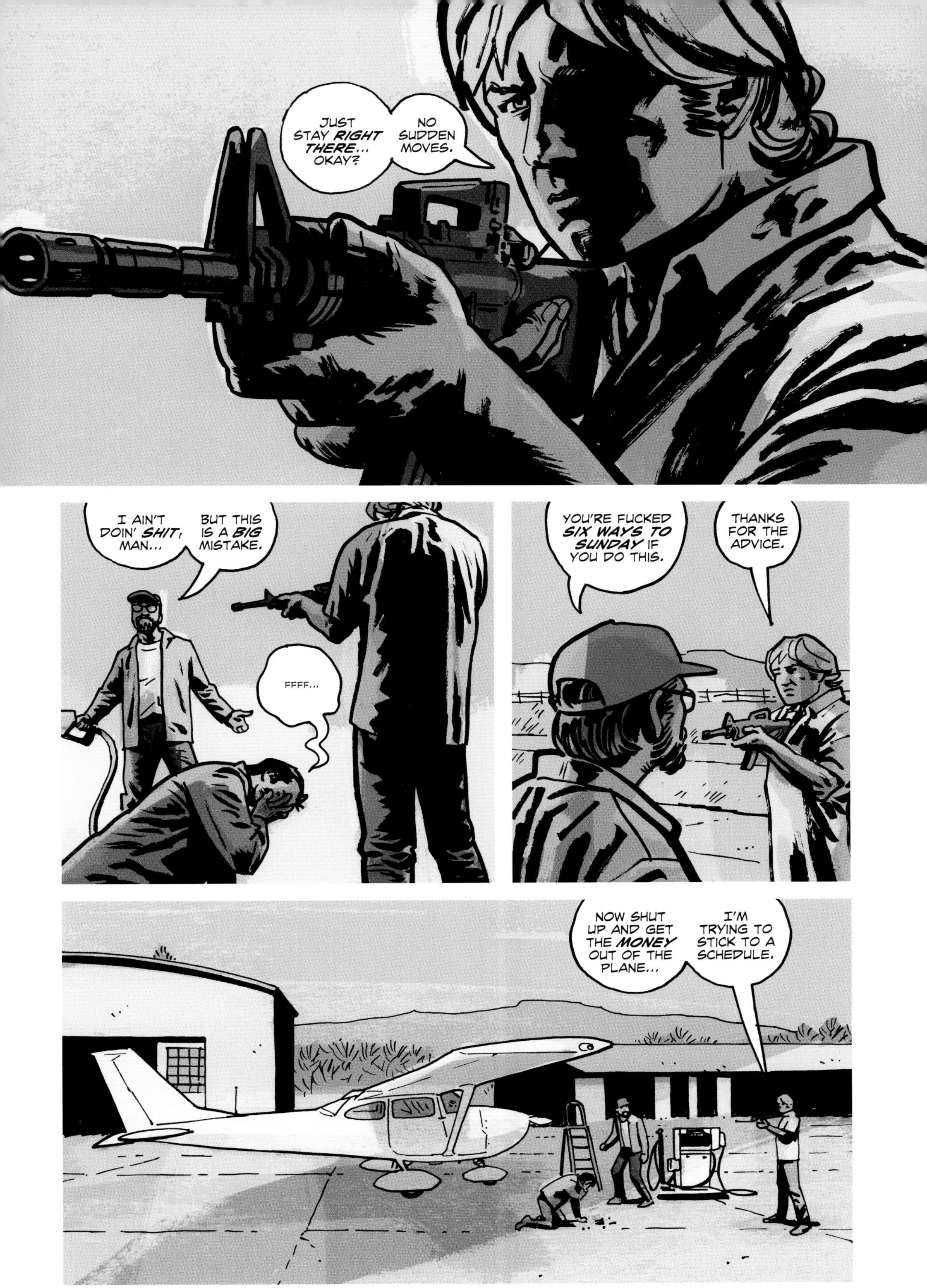
JUST STAY RIGHT THERE... OKAY?
NO SUDDEN MOVES.
I AIN'T DOIN' SHIT, MAN...
BUT THIS IS A BIG MISTAKE.
FFFF...
YOU'RE FUCKED SIX WAYS TO SUNDAY IF YOU DO THIS.
THANKS FOR THE ADVICE.
...
...
NOW SHUT UP AND GET THE MONEY OUT OF THE PLANE...
I'M TRYING TO STICK TO A SCHEDULE.

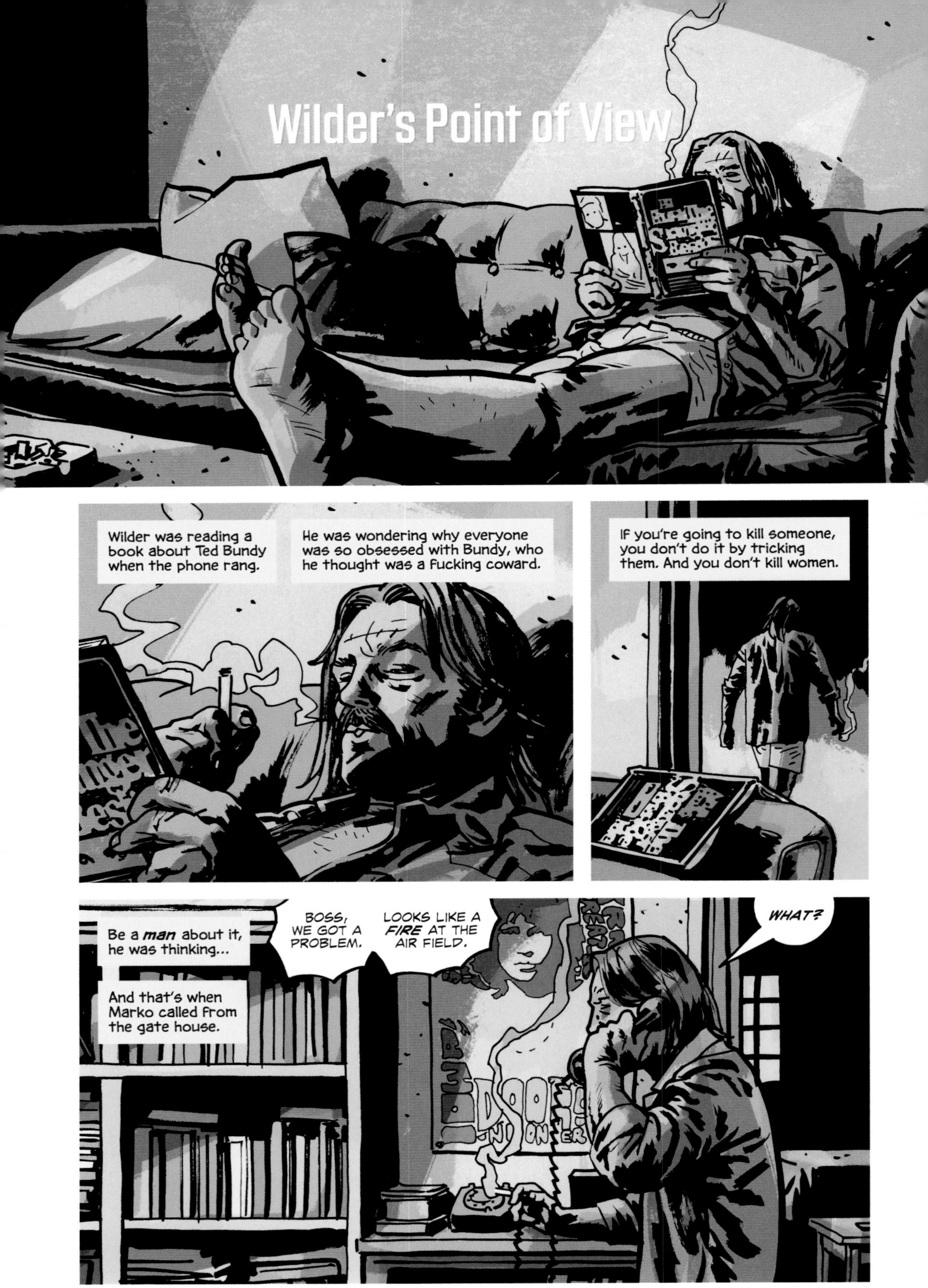
Wilder's Point of View
Wilder was reading a book about Ted Bundy when the phone rang.
He was wondering why everyone was so obsessed with Bundy, who he thought was a fucking coward.
If you're going to kill someone, you don't do it by tricking them. And you don't kill women.
Be a *man* about it, he was thinking...
And that's when Marko called from the gate house.
BOSS, WE GOT A PROBLEM.
LOOKS LIKE A *FIRE* AT THE AIR FIELD.
WHAT?

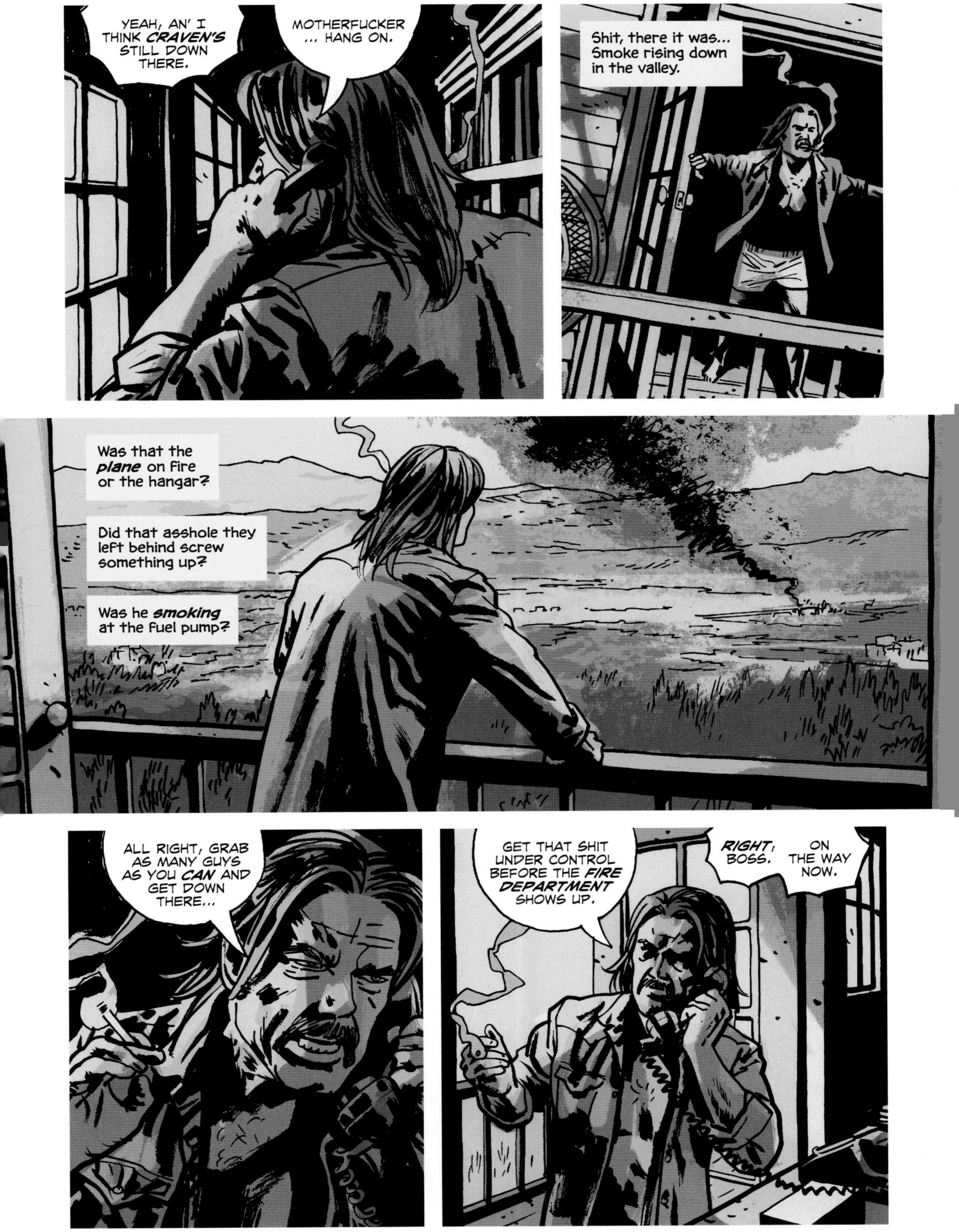
YEAH, AN' I THINK CRAVEN'S STILL DOWN THERE.
MOTHERFUCKER ... HANG ON.
Shit, there it was... Smoke rising down in the valley.
Was that the plane on fire or the hangar?
Did that asshole they left behind screw something up?
Was he smoking at the fuel pump?
ALL RIGHT, GRAB AS MANY GUYS AS YOU CAN AND GET DOWN THERE...
GET THAT SHIT UNDER CONTROL BEFORE THE FIRE DEPARTMENT SHOWS UP.
RIGHT, BOSS.
ON THE WAY NOW.

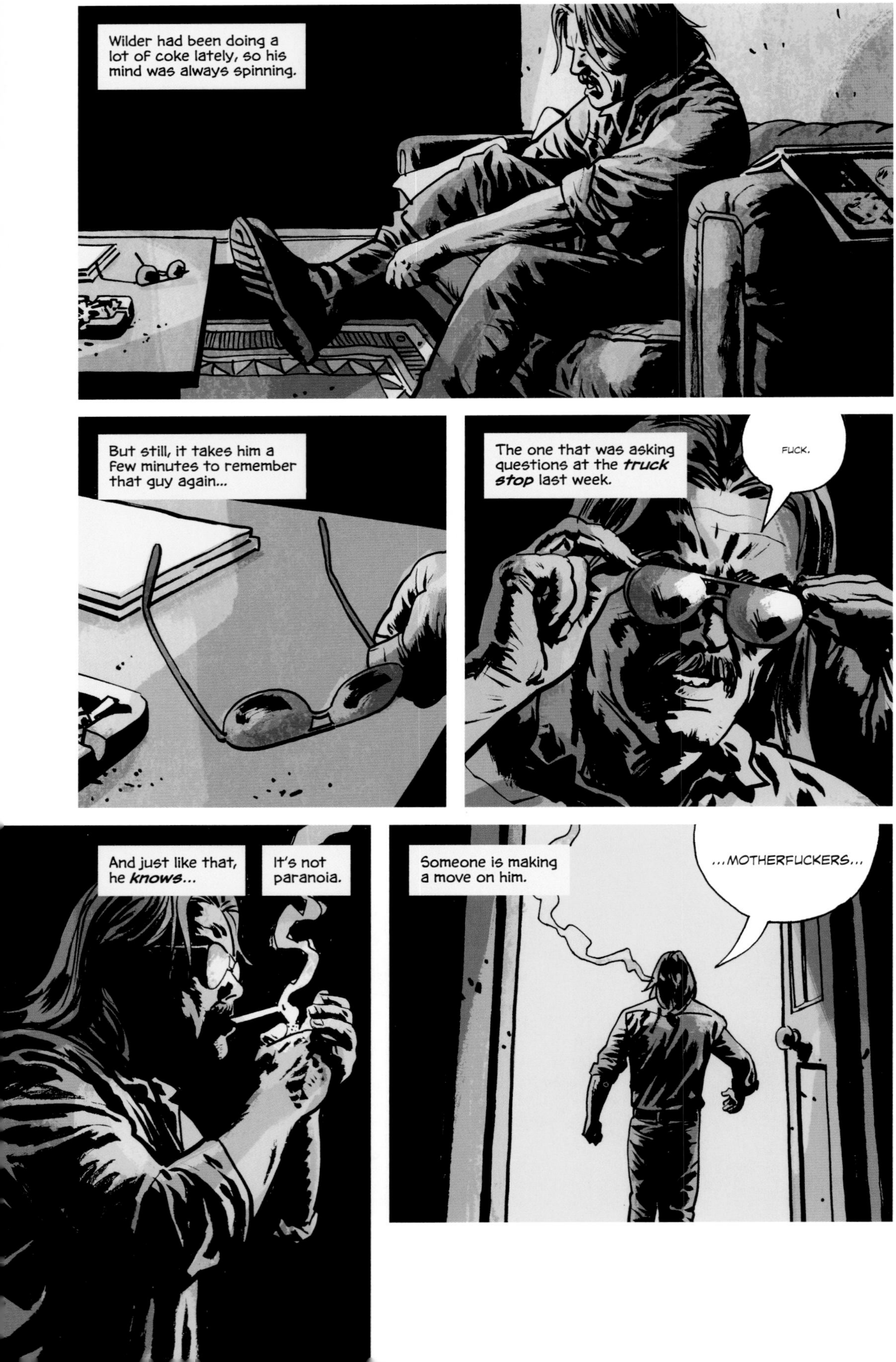
Wilder had been doing a lot of coke lately, so his mind was always spinning.
But still, it takes him a few minutes to remember that guy again...
The one that was asking questions at the *truck stop* last week.
FUCK.
And just like that, he *knows*...
It's not paranoia.
Someone is making a move on him.
...MOTHERFUCKERS...

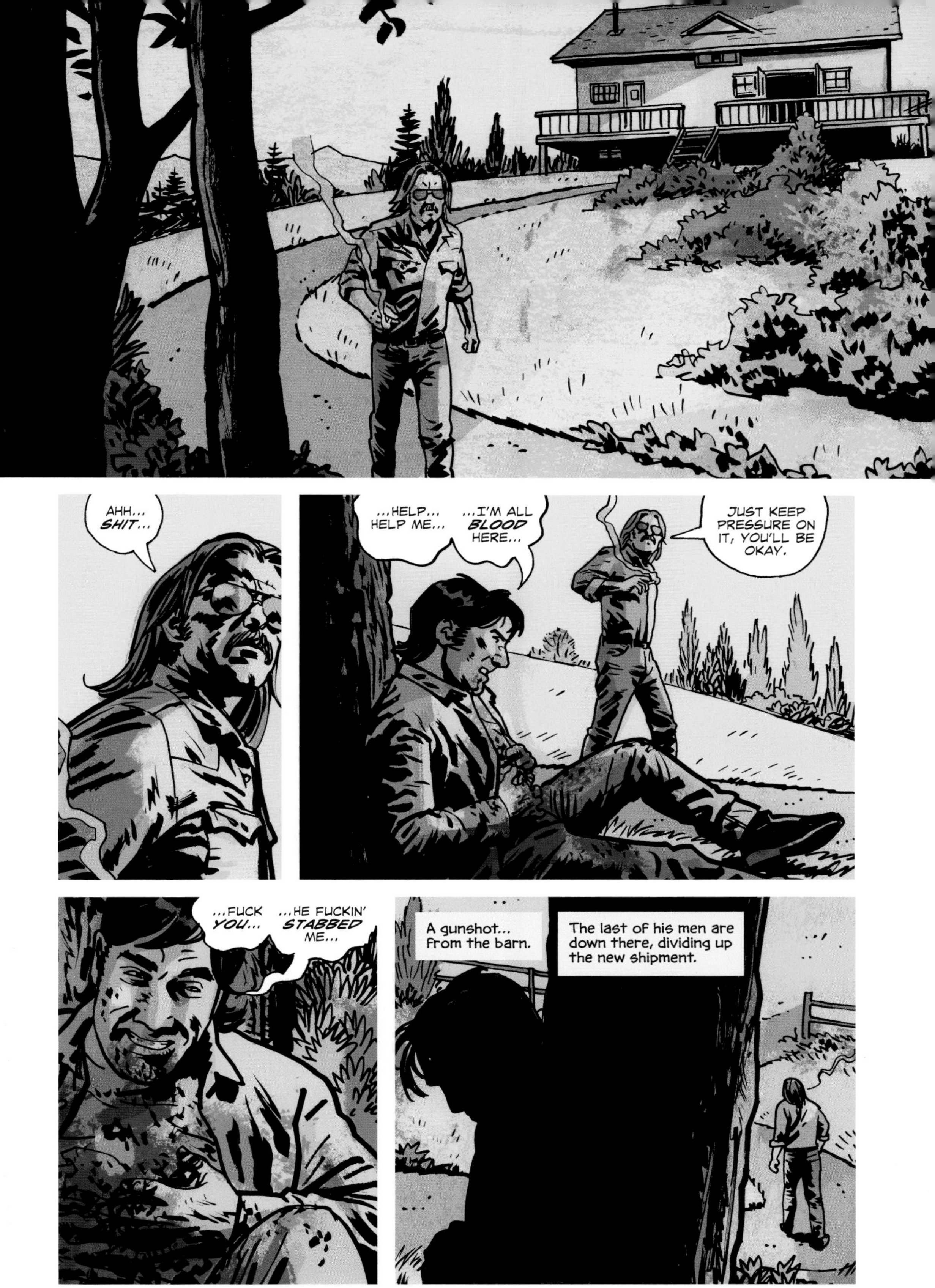

AHH... SHIT...
...HELP... HELP ME...
...I'M ALL BLOOD HERE...
JUST KEEP PRESSURE ON IT, YOU'LL BE OKAY.
...FUCK YOU...
...HE FUCKIN' STABBED ME...
A gunshot... from the barn.
The last of his men are down there, dividing up the new shipment.

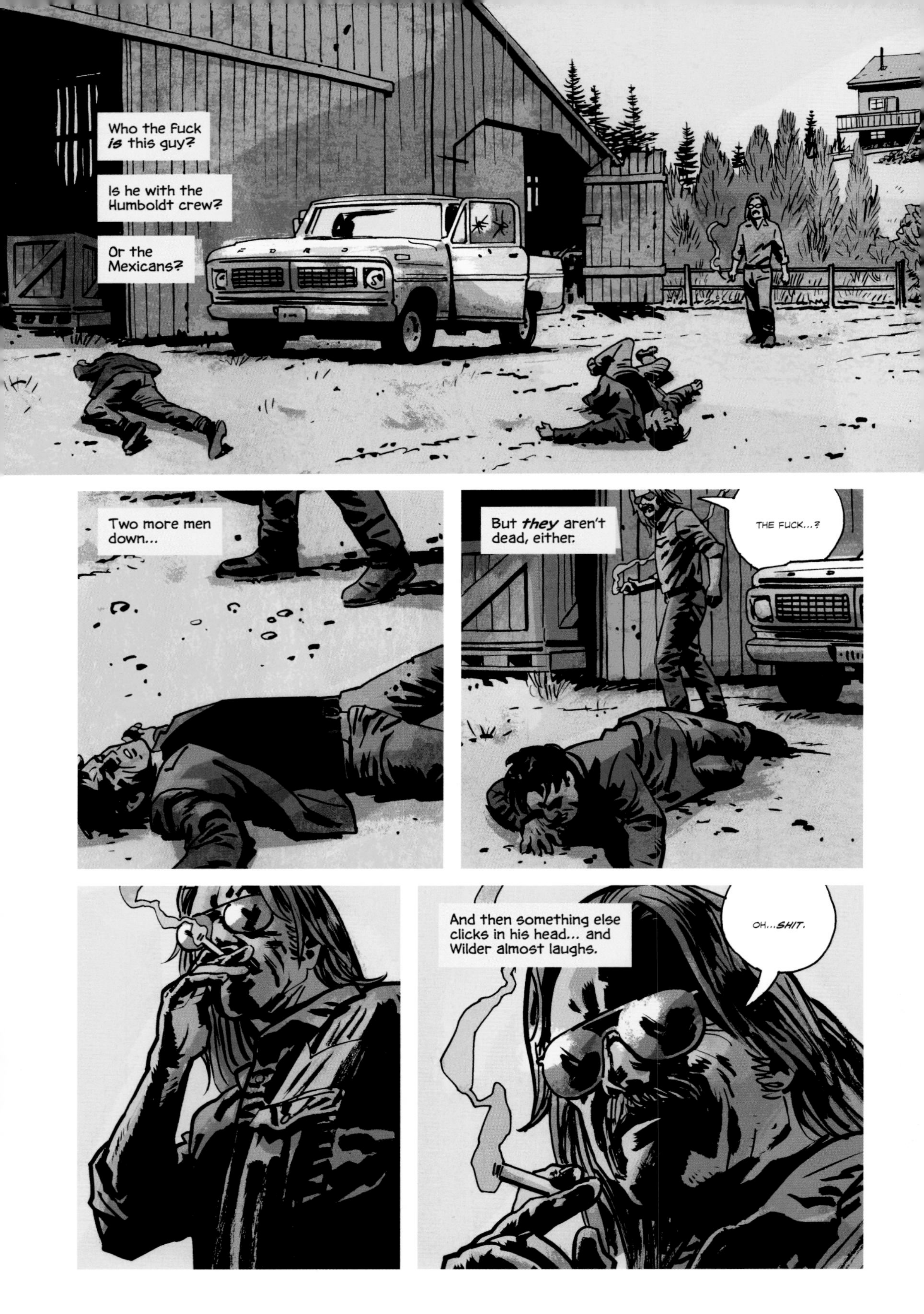
Who the fuck *is* this guy?
Is he with the Humboldt crew?
Or the Mexicans?
FORD
Two more men down...
But *they* aren't dead, either.
THE FUCK...?
And then something else clicks in his head... and Wilder almost laughs.
OH...*SHIT.*

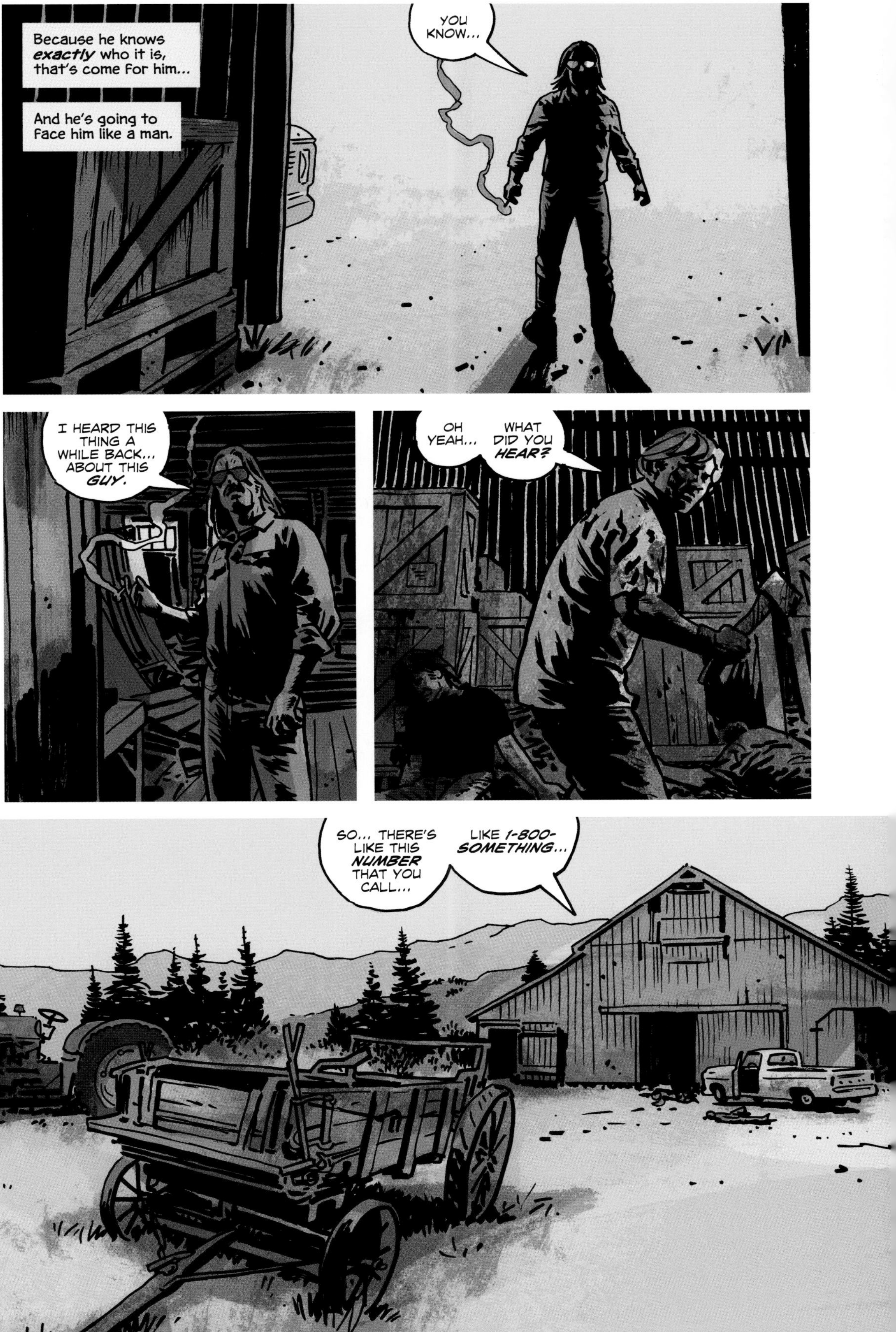
Because he knows *exactly* who it is, that's come for him...
And he's going to face him like a man.
YOU KNOW...
I HEARD THIS THING A WHILE BACK... ABOUT THIS *GUY*.
OH YEAH...
WHAT DID YOU *HEAR?*
SO... THERE'S LIKE THIS *NUMBER* THAT YOU CALL...
LIKE *1-800-SOMETHING*...

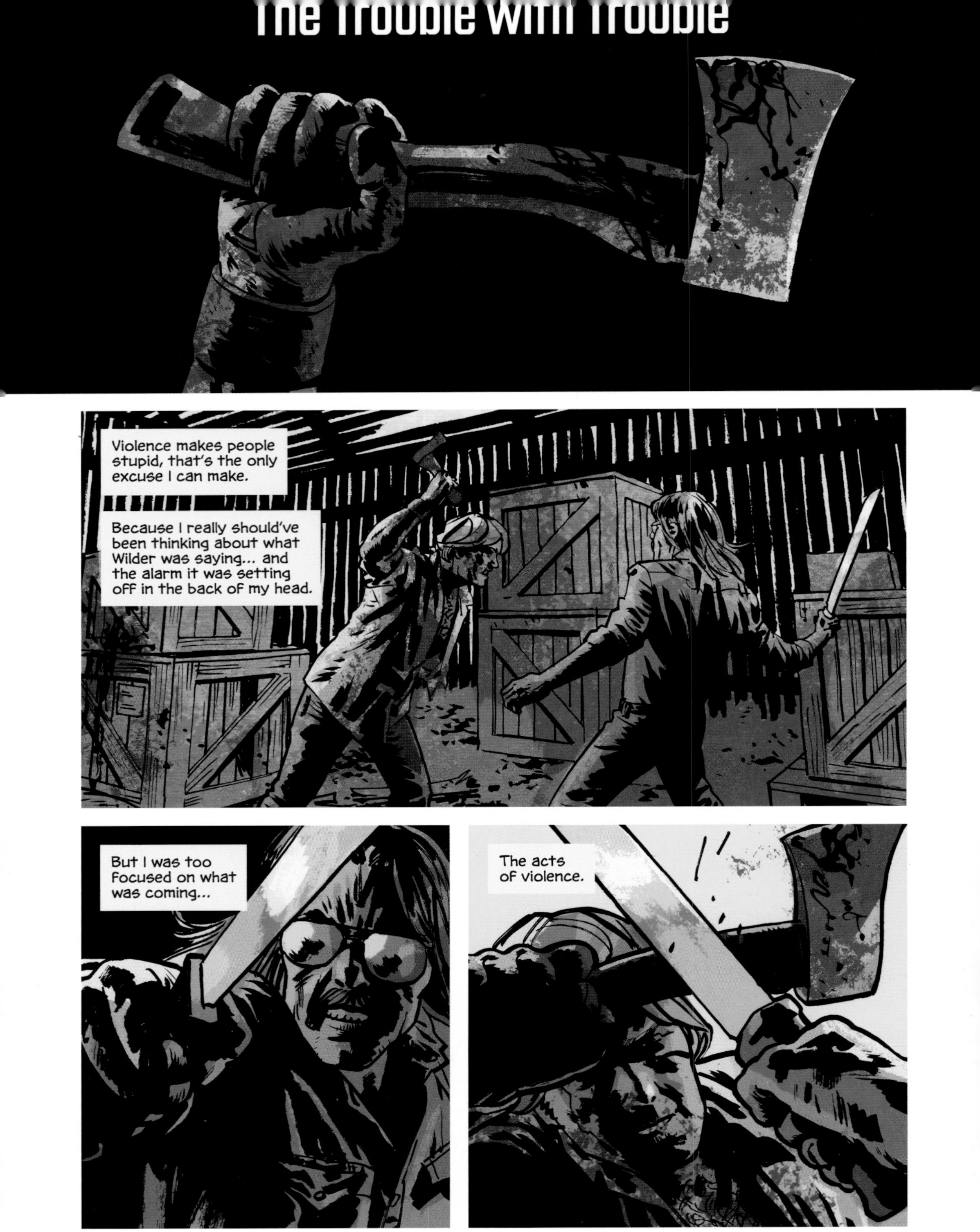
The Trouble with Trouble
Violence makes people stupid, that's the only excuse I can make.
Because I really should've been thinking about what Wilder was saying... and the alarm it was setting off in the back of my head.
But I was too focused on what was coming...
The acts of violence.

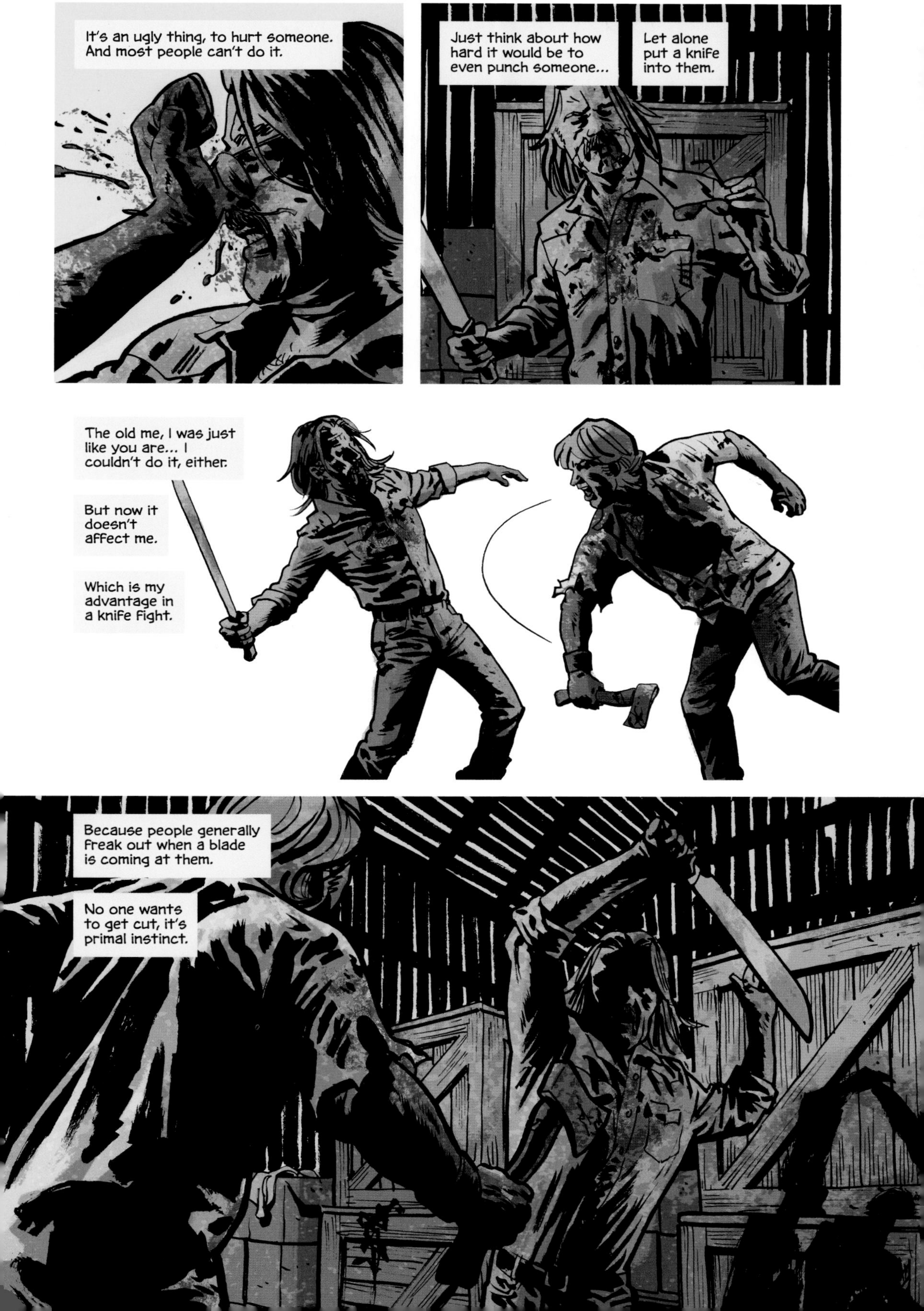
It's an ugly thing, to hurt someone. And most people can't do it.
Just think about how hard it would be to even punch someone...
Let alone put a knife into them.
The old me, I was just like you are... I couldn't do it, either.
But now it doesn't affect me.
Which is my advantage in a knife fight.
Because people generally freak out when a blade is coming at them.
No one wants to get cut, it's primal instinct.

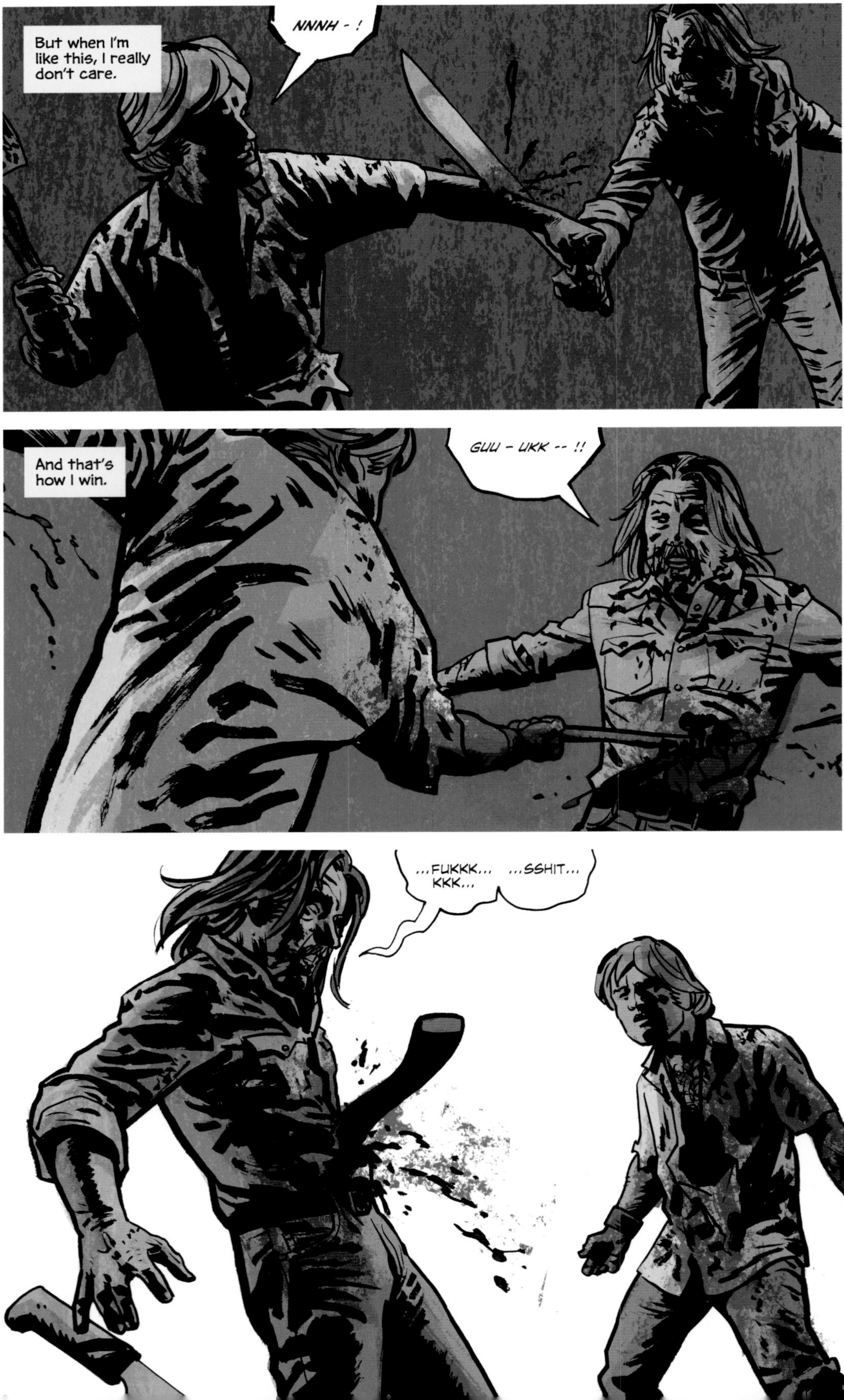
But when I'm like this, I really don't care.
NNNH - !
And that's how I win.
GUU - UKK -- !!
...FUKKK... KKK...
...SSHIT...

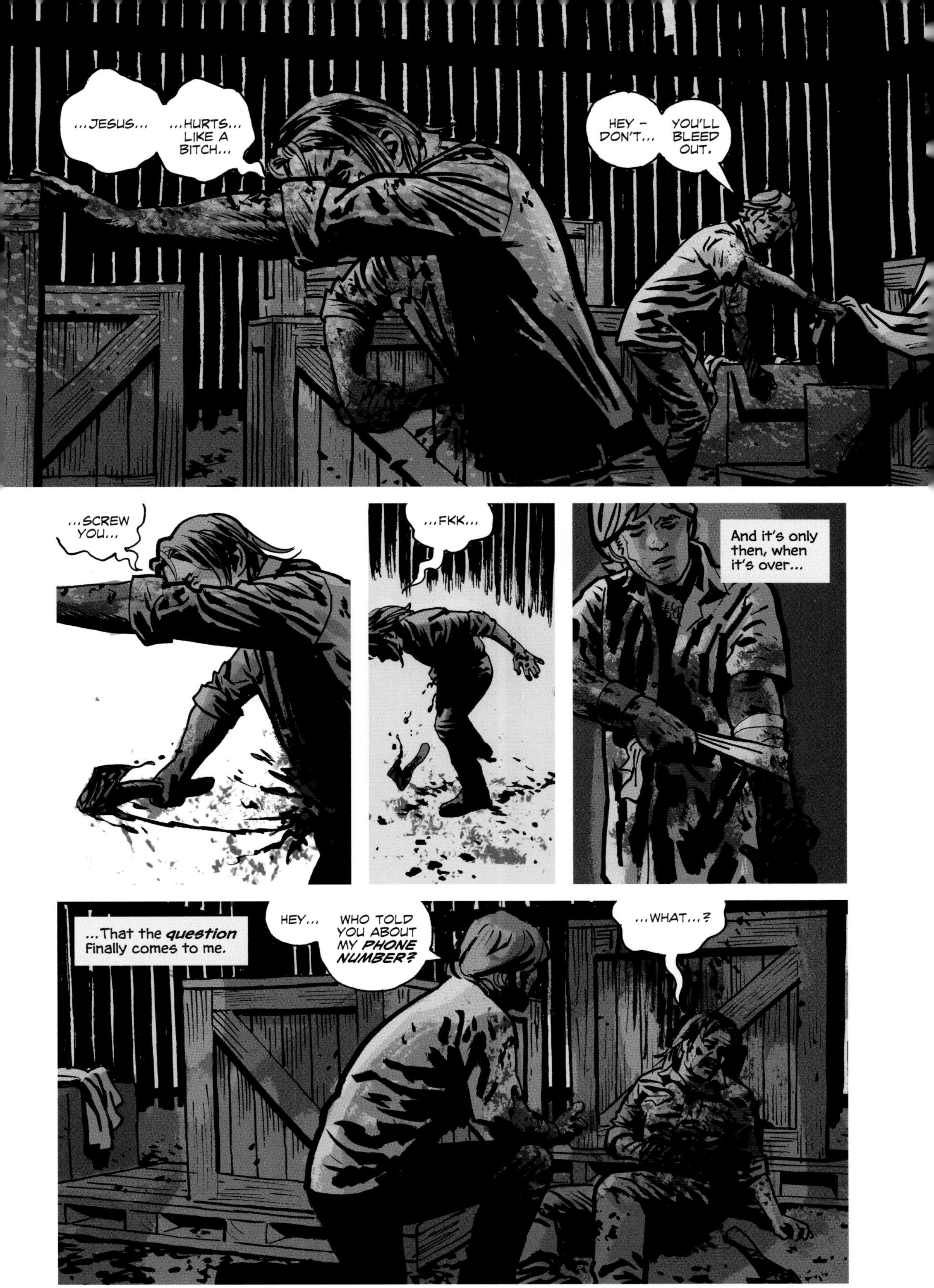
...JESUS...
...HURTS... LIKE A BITCH...
HEY - DON'T...
YOU'LL BLEED OUT.
...SCREW YOU...
...FKK...
And it's only then, when it's over...
...That the *question* finally comes to me.
HEY...
WHO TOLD YOU ABOUT MY *PHONE NUMBER?*
...WHAT...?

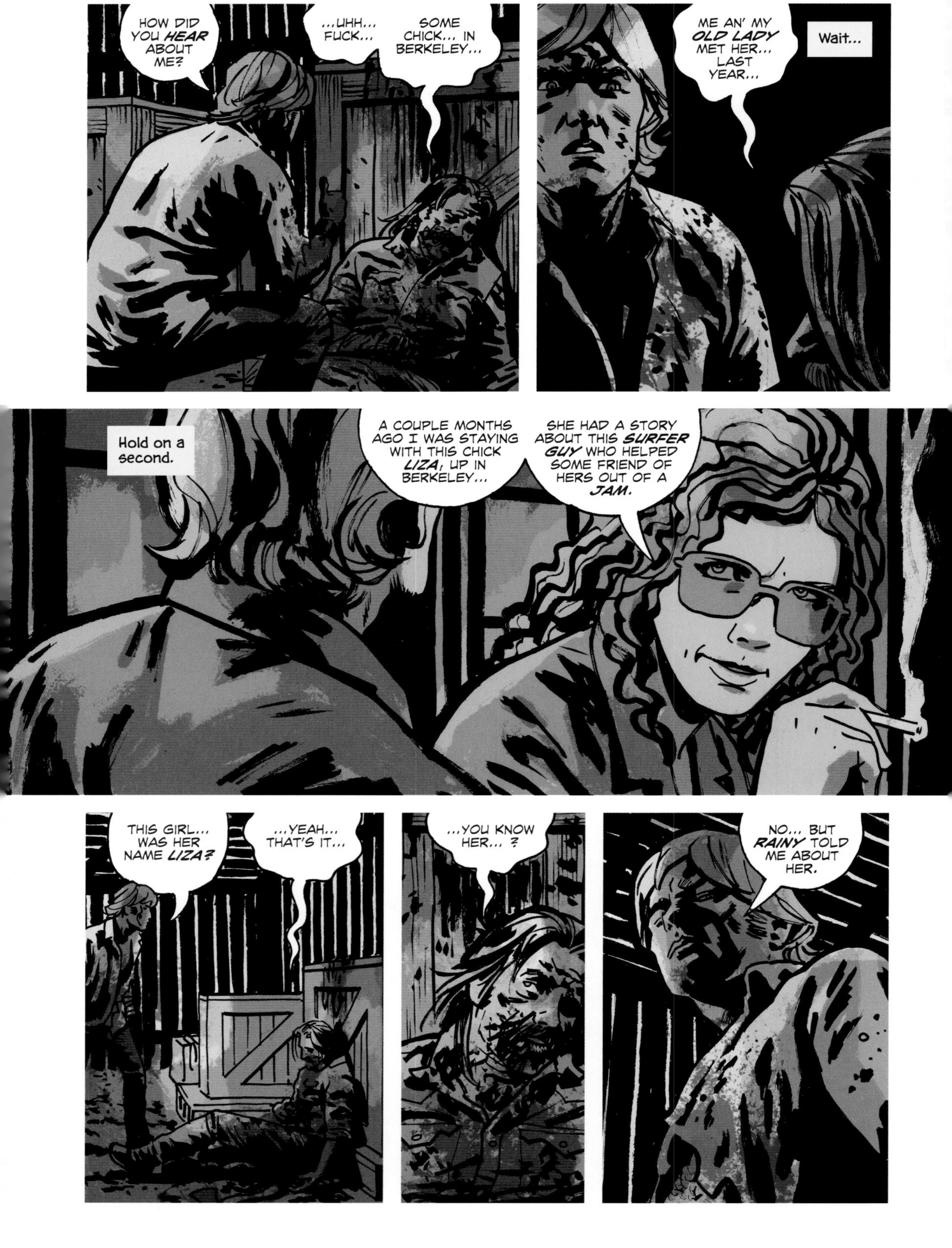
HOW DID YOU HEAR ABOUT ME?
...UHH... FUCK...
SOME CHICK... IN BERKELEY...
ME AN' MY OLD LADY MET HER... LAST YEAR...
Wait...
Hold on a second.
A COUPLE MONTHS AGO I WAS STAYING WITH THIS CHICK LIZA, UP IN BERKELEY...
SHE HAD A STORY ABOUT THIS SURFER GUY WHO HELPED SOME FRIEND OF HERS OUT OF A JAM.
THIS GIRL... WAS HER NAME LIZA?
...YEAH... THAT'S IT...
...YOU KNOW HER... ?
NO... BUT RAINY TOLD ME ABOUT HER.

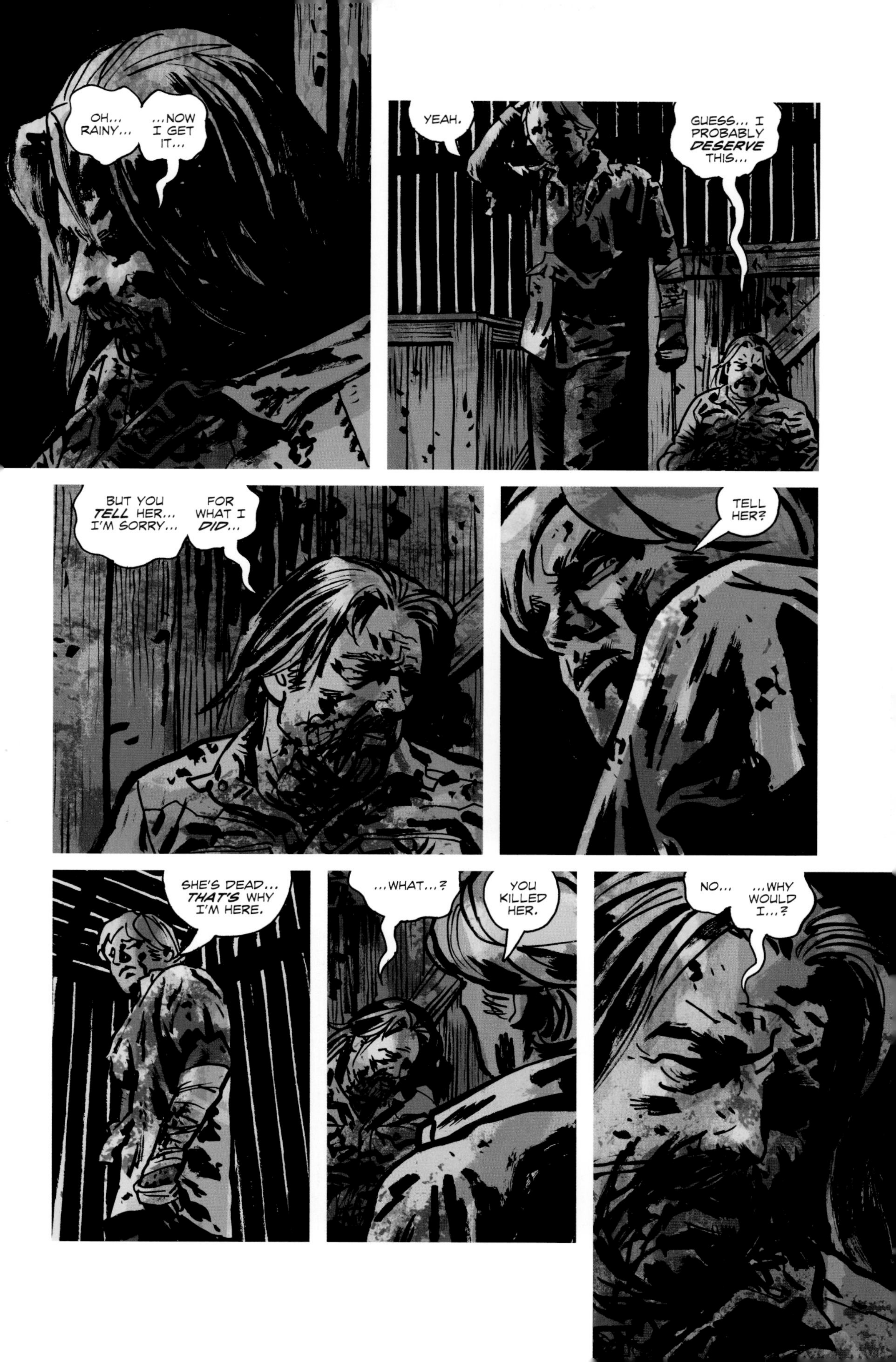
OH... RAINY...
...NOW I GET IT...
YEAH.
GUESS... I PROBABLY DESERVE THIS...
BUT YOU TELL HER... I'M SORRY...
FOR WHAT I DID...
TELL HER?
SHE'S DEAD... THAT'S WHY I'M HERE.
...WHAT...?
YOU KILLED HER.
NO...
...WHY WOULD I...?

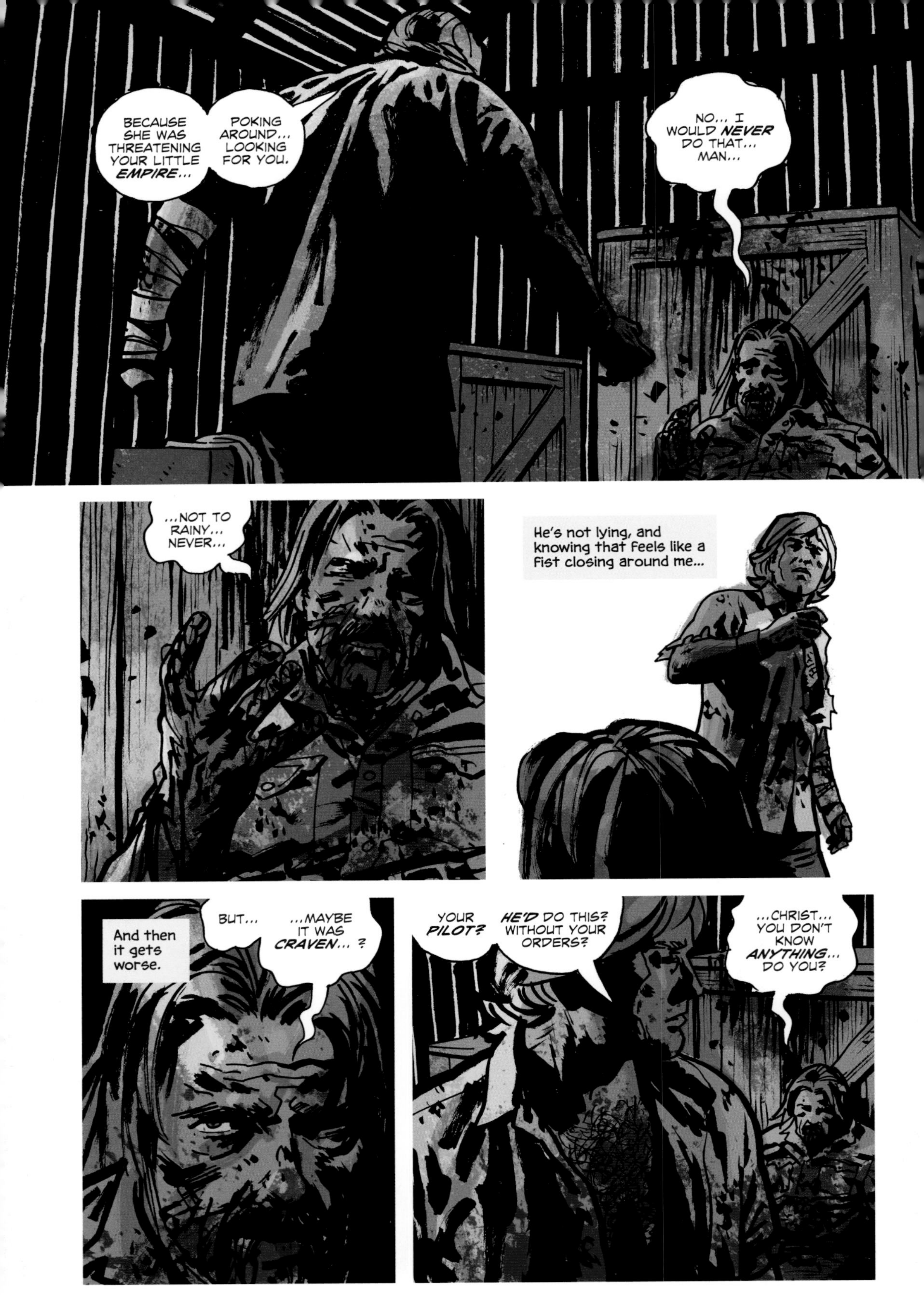
BECAUSE SHE WAS THREATENING YOUR LITTLE *EMPIRE*...
POKING AROUND... LOOKING FOR YOU.
NO... I WOULD *NEVER* DO THAT... MAN...
...NOT TO RAINY... NEVER...
He's not lying, and knowing that feels like a fist closing around me...
And then it gets worse.
BUT...
...MAYBE IT WAS *CRAVEN*... ?
YOUR *PILOT?*
HE'D DO THIS? WITHOUT YOUR ORDERS?
...CHRIST... YOU DON'T KNOW *ANYTHING*... DO YOU?

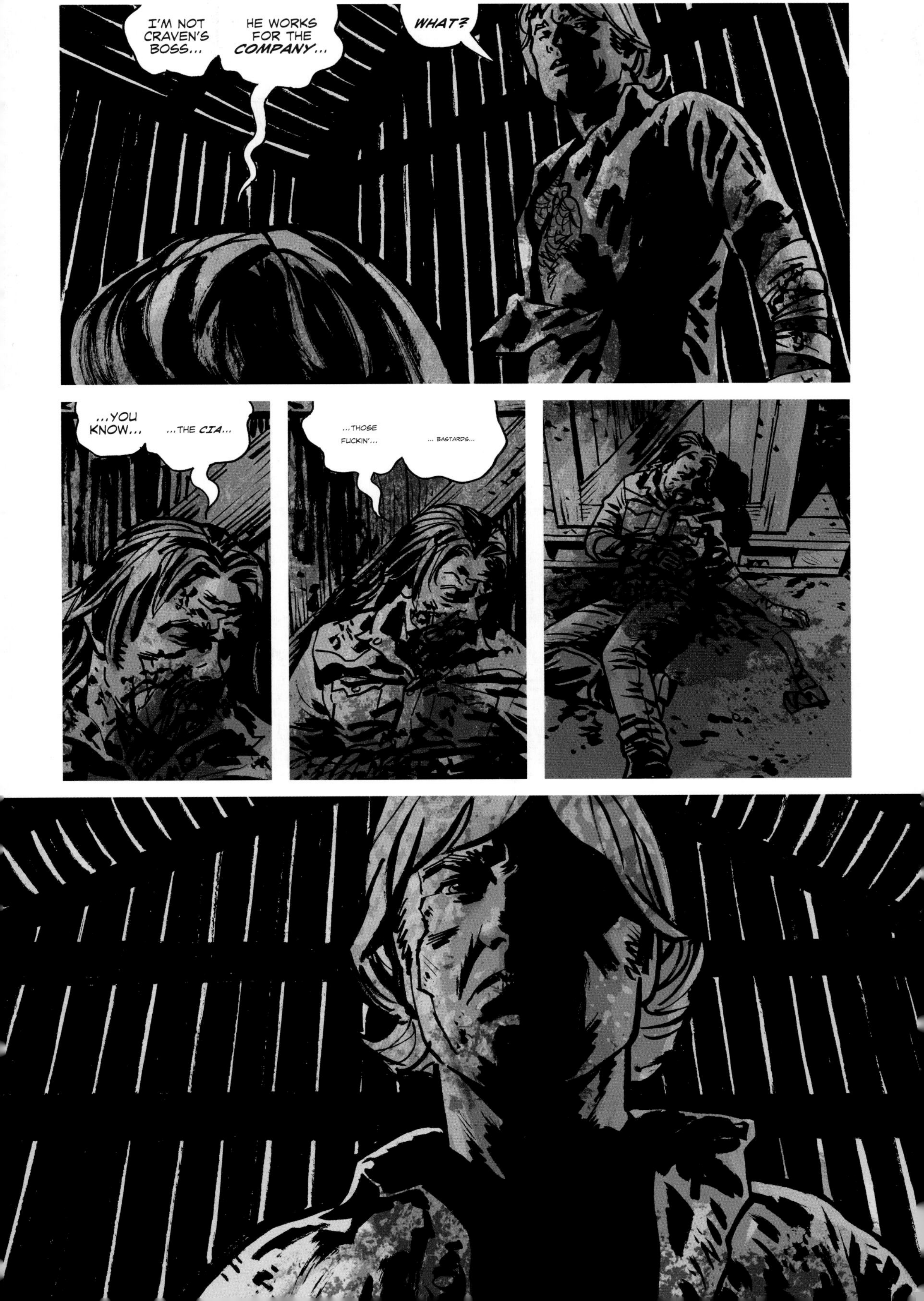
I'M NOT CRAVEN'S BOSS...
HE WORKS FOR THE COMPANY...
WHAT?
...YOU KNOW...
...THE CIA...
...THOSE FUCKIN'...
... BASTARDS...

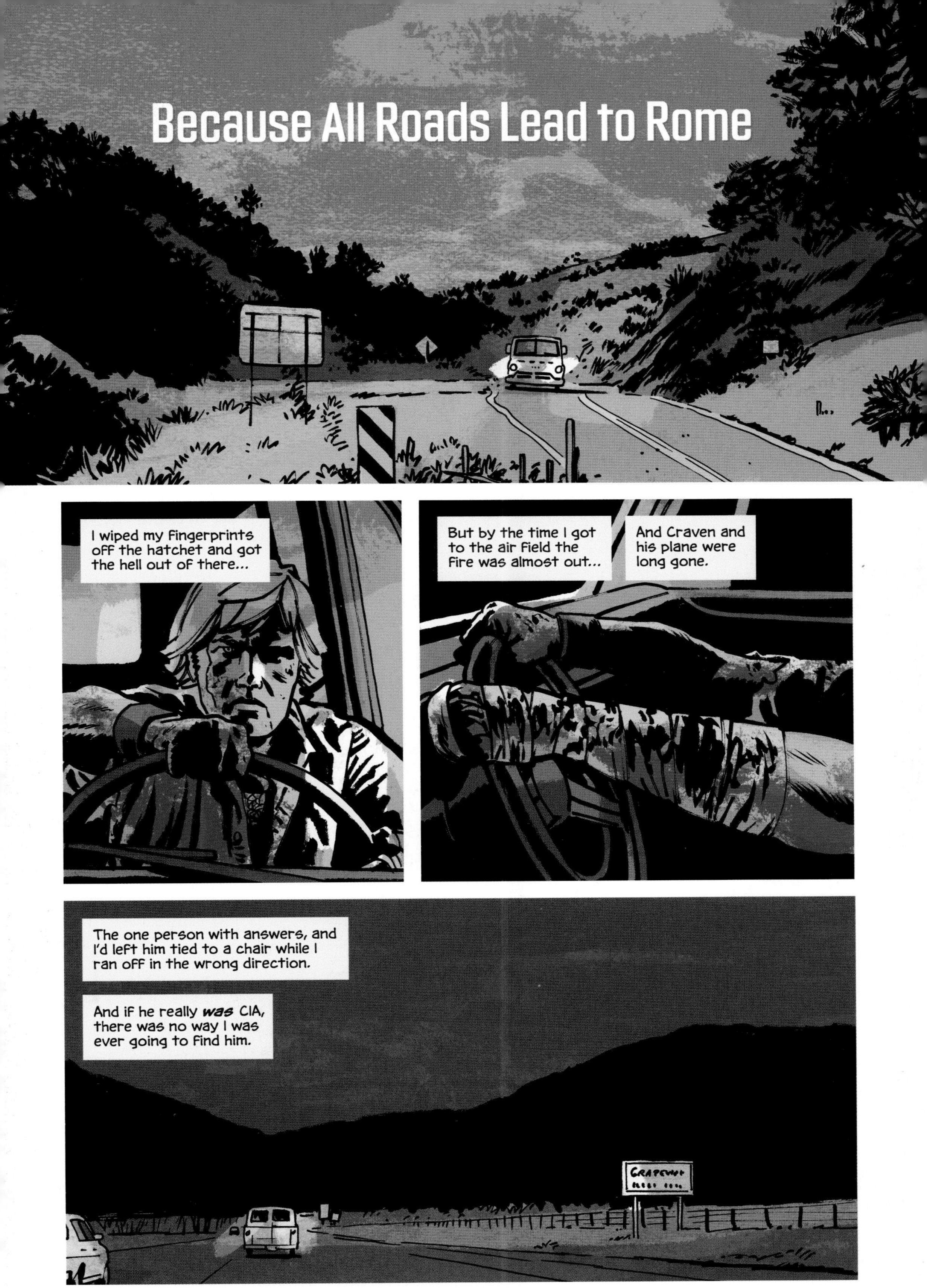
Because All Roads Lead to Rome
I wiped my fingerprints off the hatchet and got the hell out of there...
But by the time I got to the air field the fire was almost out...
And Craven and his plane were long gone.
The one person with answers, and I'd left him tied to a chair while I ran off in the wrong direction.
And if he really *was* CIA, there was no way I was ever going to find him.

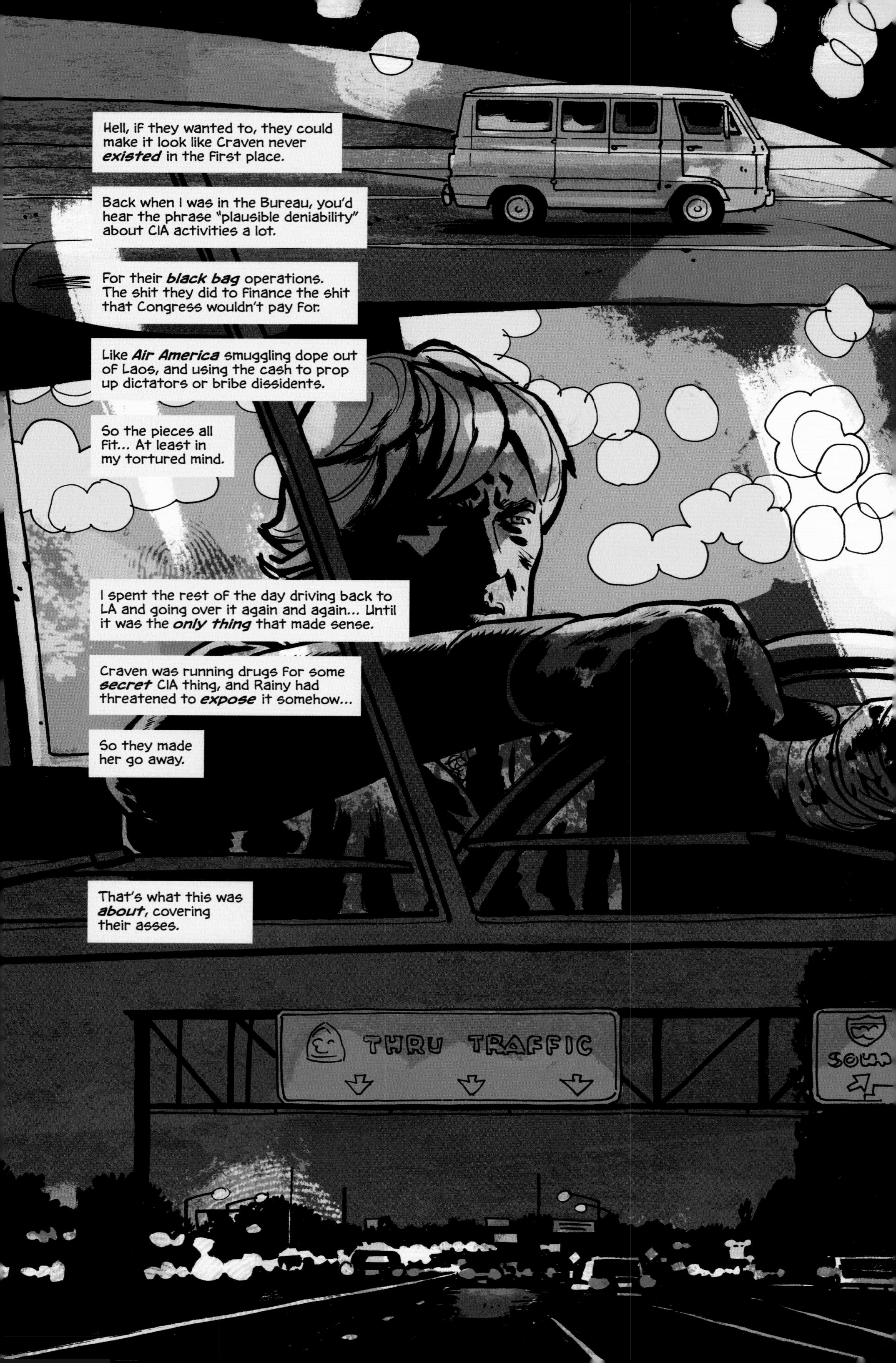
Hell, if they wanted to, they could make it look like Craven never *existed* in the first place.
Back when I was in the Bureau, you'd hear the phrase "plausible deniability" about CIA activities a lot.
For their *black bag* operations. The shit they did to finance the shit that Congress wouldn't pay for.
Like *Air America* smuggling dope out of Laos, and using the cash to prop up dictators or bribe dissidents.
So the pieces all fit... At least in my tortured mind.
I spent the rest of the day driving back to LA and going over it again and again... Until it was the *only thing* that made sense.
Craven was running drugs for some *secret* CIA thing, and Rainy had threatened to *expose* it somehow...
So they made her go away.
That's what this was *about*, covering their asses.
THRU TRAFFIC

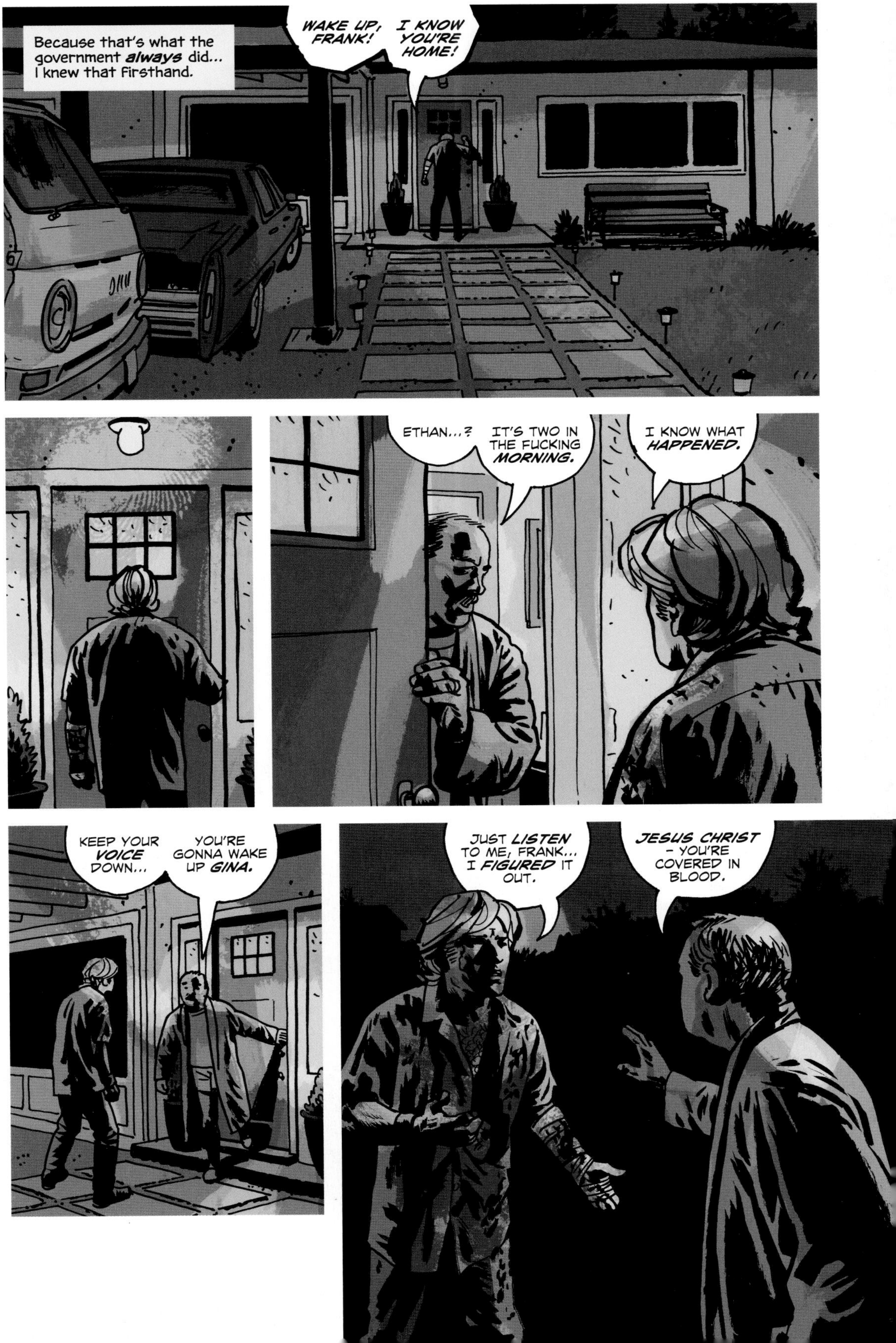
Because that's what the government *always* did... I knew that firsthand.
WAKE UP, FRANK!
I KNOW YOU'RE HOME!
ETHAN...?
IT'S TWO IN THE FUCKING *MORNING.*
I KNOW WHAT *HAPPENED.*
KEEP YOUR *VOICE* DOWN...
YOU'RE GONNA WAKE UP *GINA.*
JUST *LISTEN* TO ME, FRANK... I *FIGURED* IT OUT.
JESUS CHRIST – YOU'RE COVERED IN BLOOD.

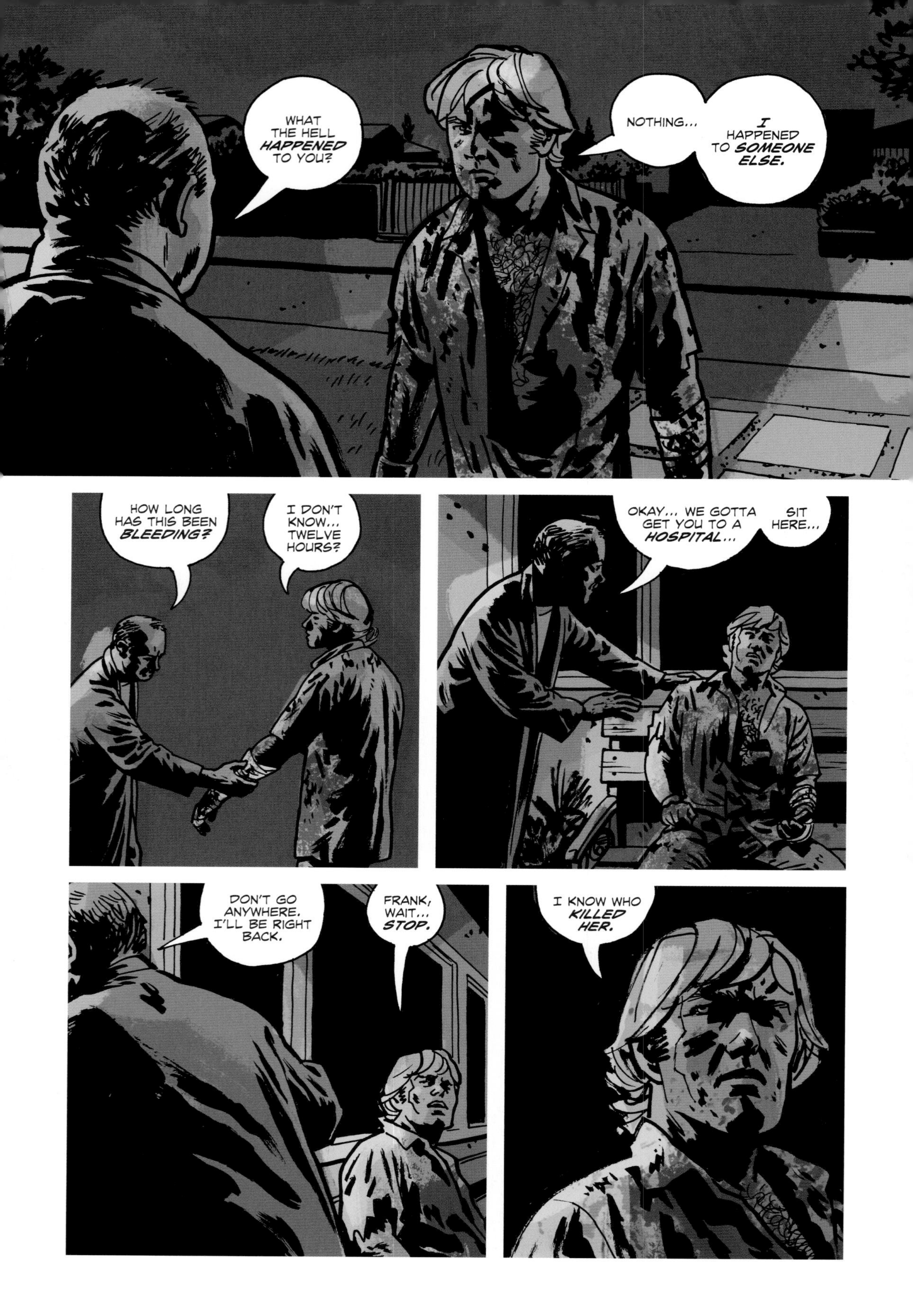
WHAT THE HELL HAPPENED TO YOU?
NOTHING...
I HAPPENED TO SOMEONE ELSE.
HOW LONG HAS THIS BEEN BLEEDING?
I DON'T KNOW... TWELVE HOURS?
OKAY... WE GOTTA GET YOU TO A HOSPITAL...
SIT HERE...
DON'T GO ANYWHERE. I'LL BE RIGHT BACK.
FRANK, WAIT... STOP.
I KNOW WHO KILLED HER.

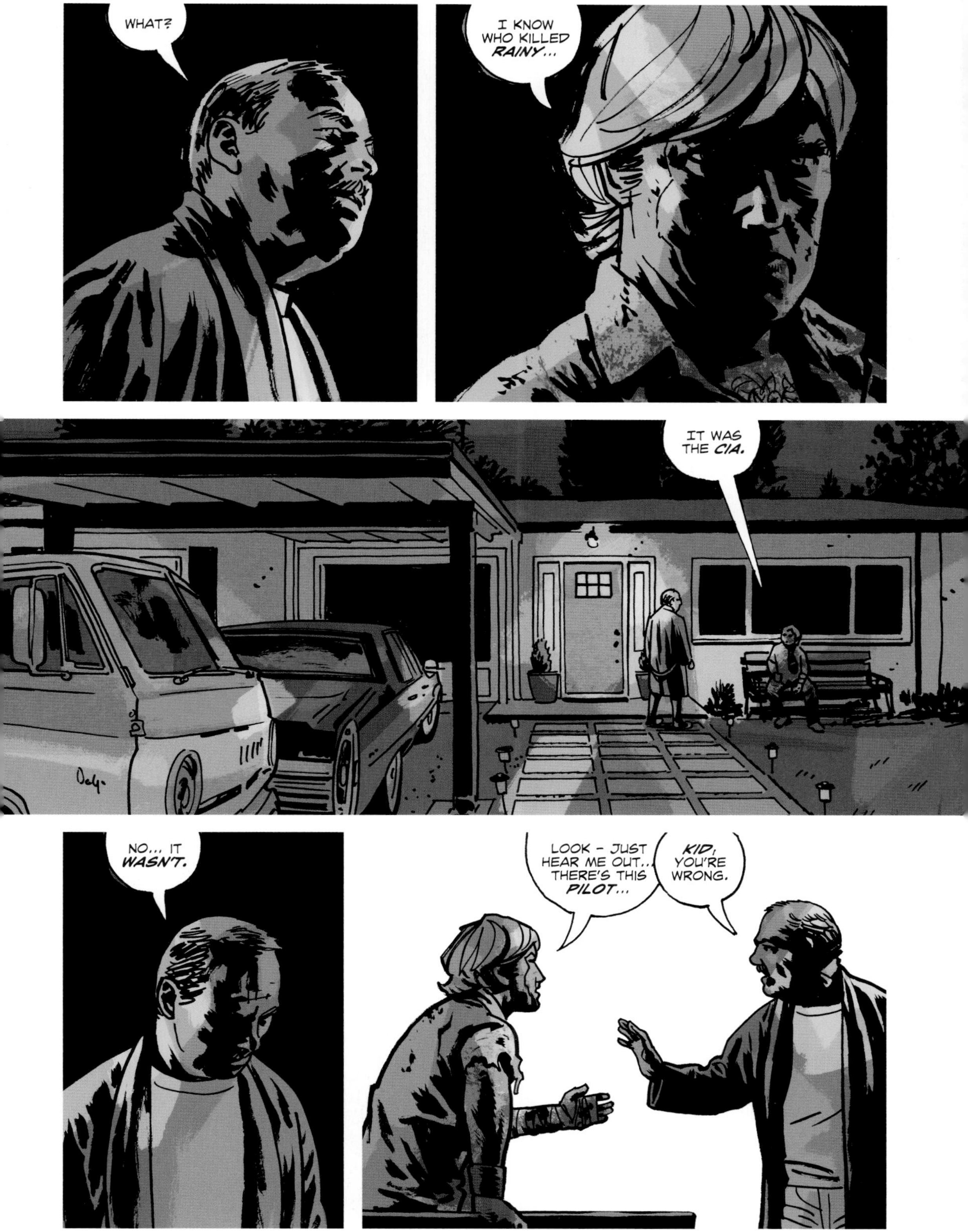
WHAT?
I KNOW WHO KILLED *RAINY*...
IT WAS THE *CIA.*
NO... IT *WASN'T.*
LOOK - JUST HEAR ME OUT... THERE'S THIS *PILOT*...
KID, YOU'RE WRONG.

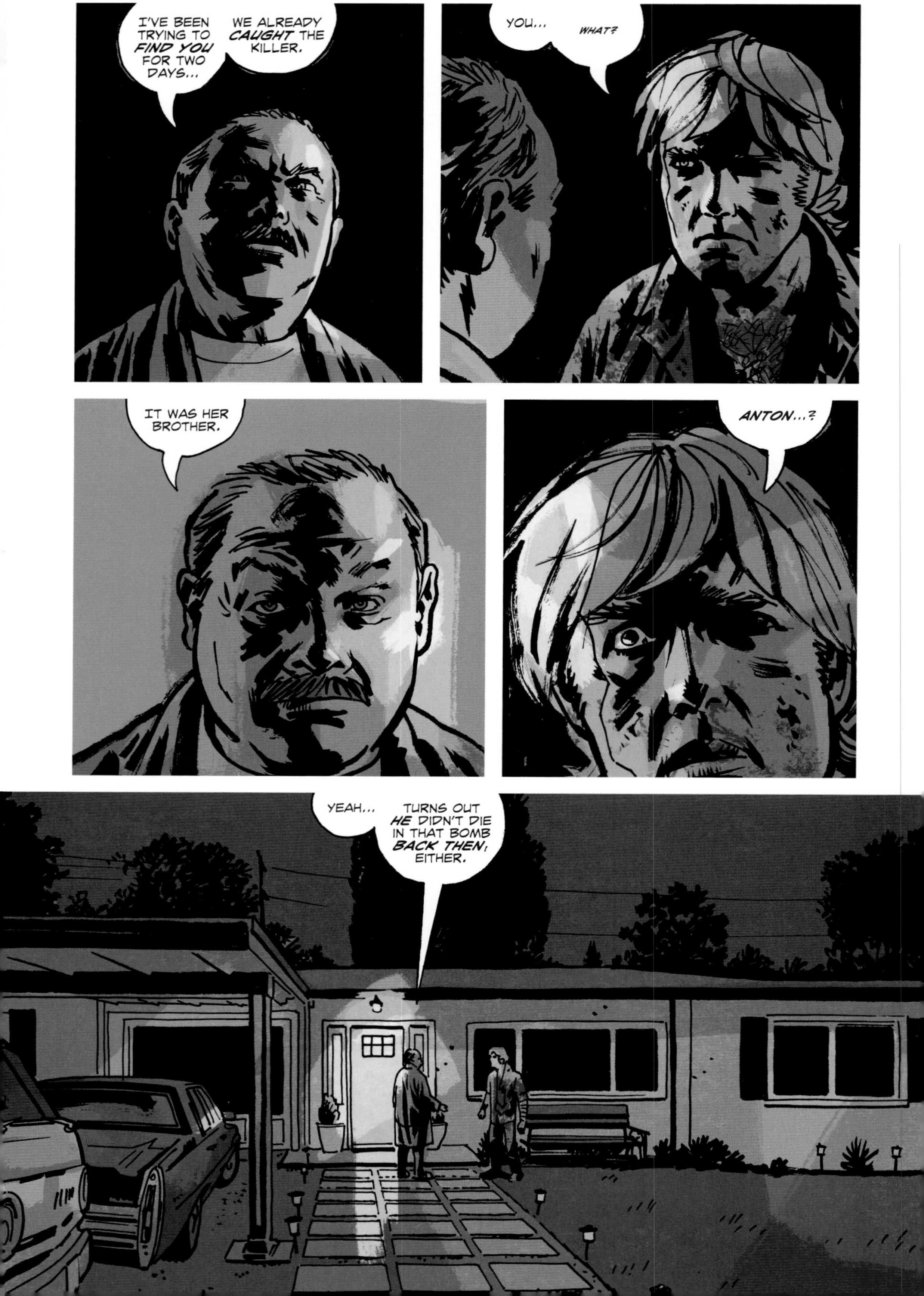

I'VE BEEN TRYING TO FIND YOU FOR TWO DAYS...
WE ALREADY CAUGHT THE KILLER.
YOU...
WHAT?
IT WAS HER BROTHER.
ANTON...?
YEAH...
TURNS OUT HE DIDN'T DIE IN THAT BOMB BACK THEN, EITHER.

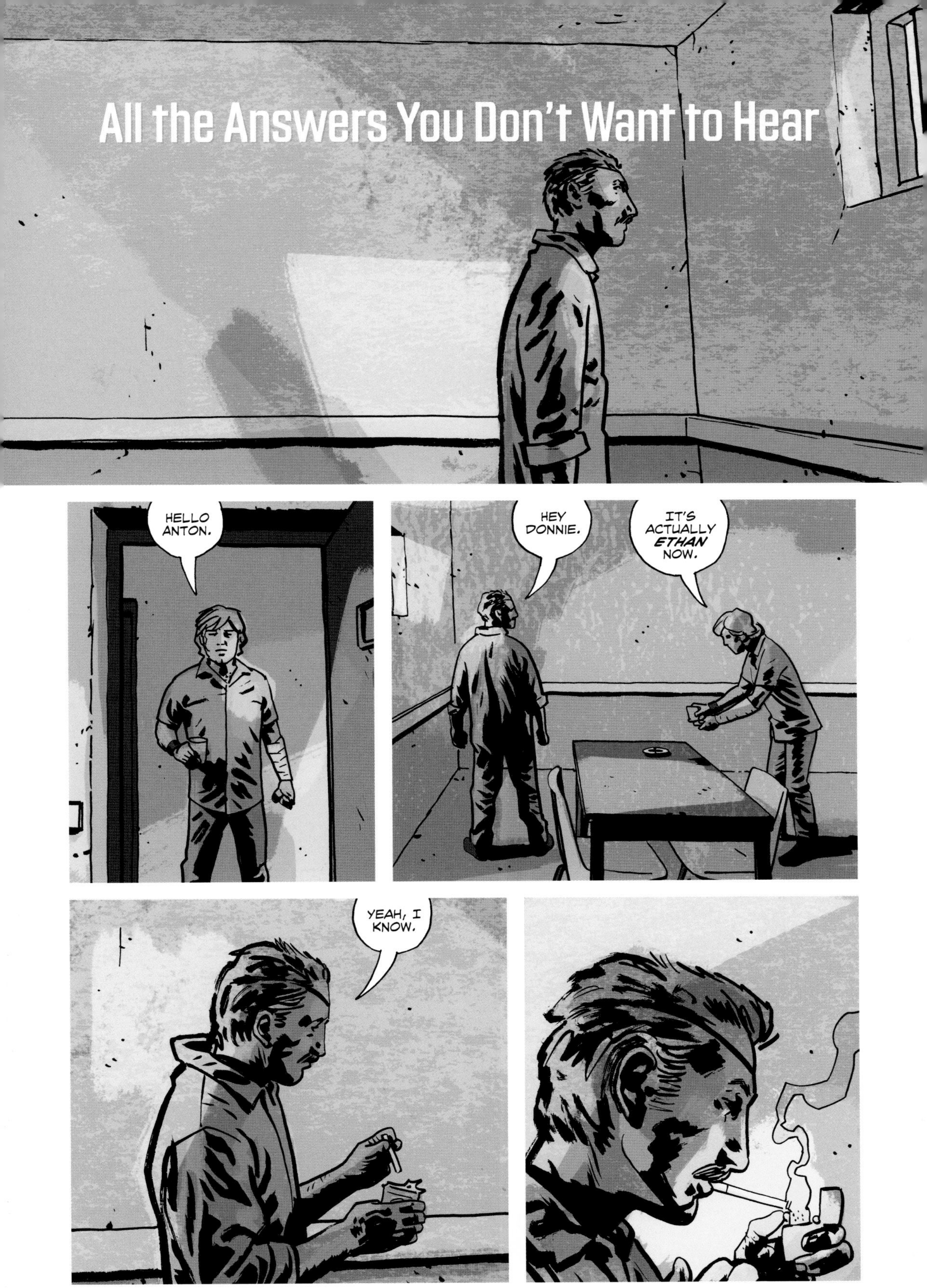

All the Answers You Don't Want to Hear
HELLO ANTON.
HEY DONNIE.
IT'S ACTUALLY *ETHAN* NOW.
YEAH, I KNOW.

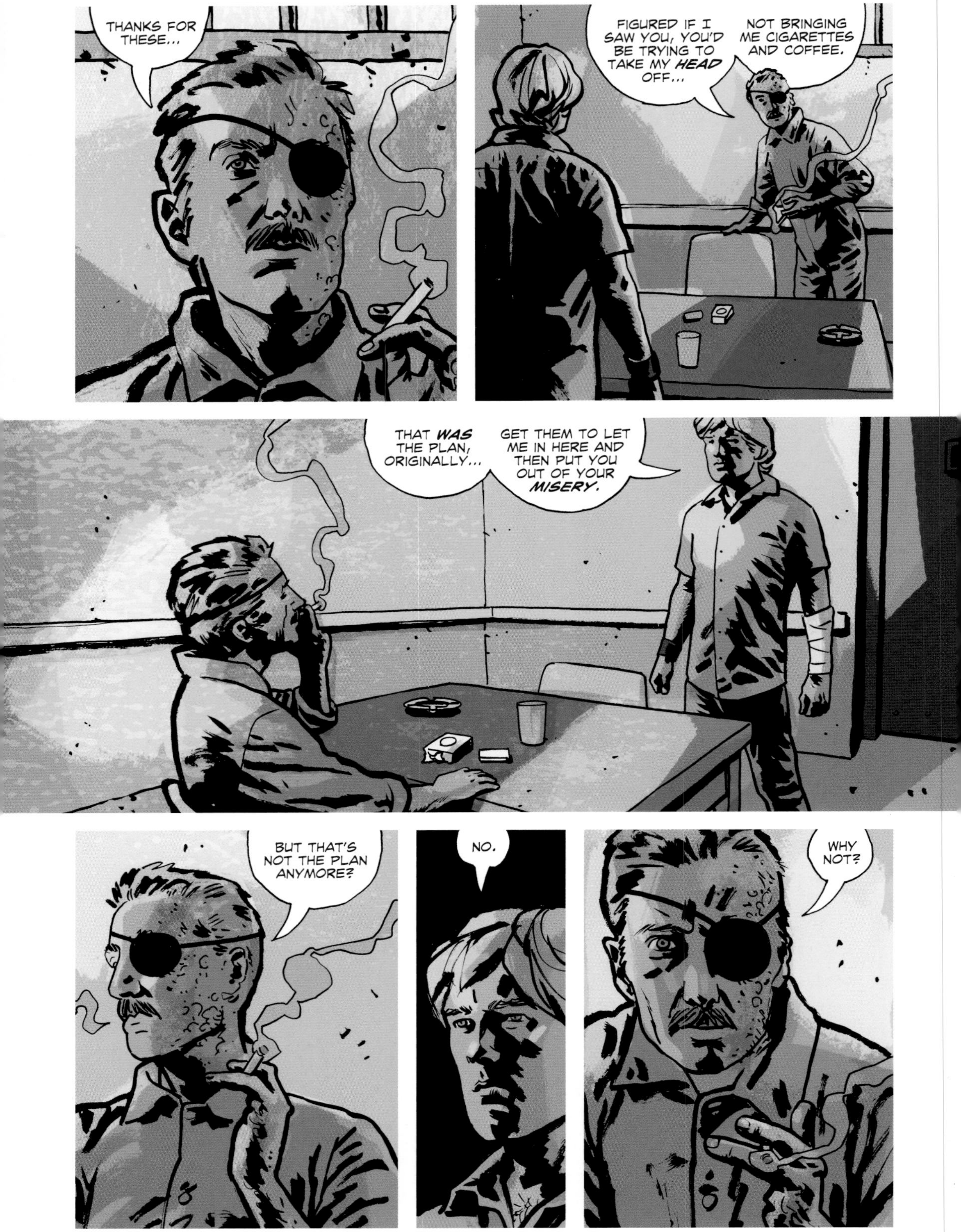
THANKS FOR THESE...
FIGURED IF I SAW YOU, YOU'D BE TRYING TO TAKE MY *HEAD* OFF...
NOT BRINGING ME CIGARETTES AND COFFEE.
THAT *WAS* THE PLAN, ORIGINALLY...
GET THEM TO LET ME IN HERE AND THEN PUT YOU OUT OF YOUR *MISERY.*
BUT THAT'S NOT THE PLAN ANYMORE?
NO.
WHY NOT?

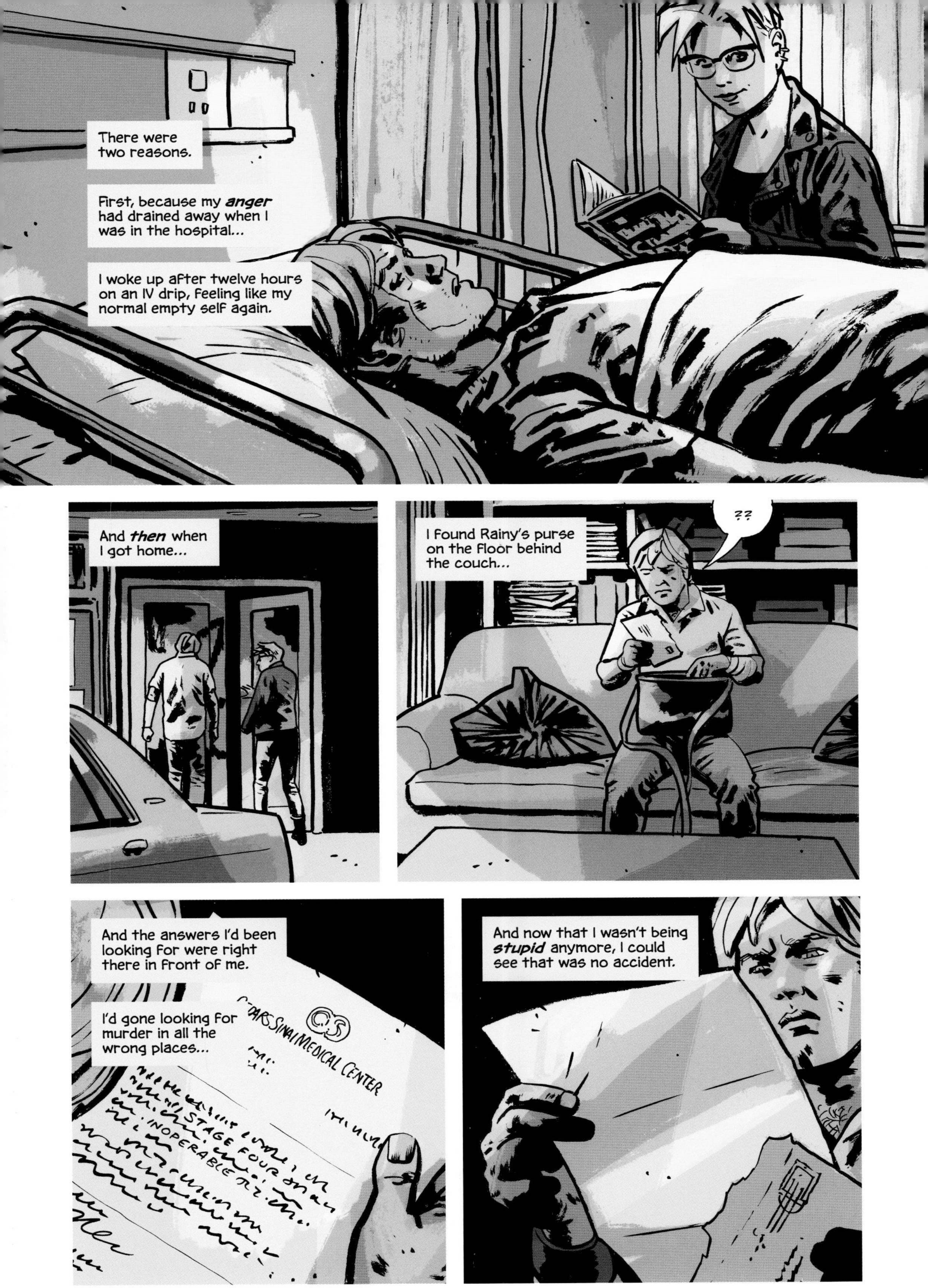
There were two reasons.
First, because my *anger* had drained away when I was in the hospital...
I woke up after twelve hours on an IV drip, feeling like my normal empty self again.
And *then* when I got home...
I found Rainy's purse on the floor behind the couch...
??
And the answers I'd been looking for were right there in front of me.
I'd gone looking for murder in all the wrong places...
SINAI MEDICAL CENTER
STAGE FOUR
INOPERABLE
And now that I wasn't being *stupid* anymore, I could see that was no accident.

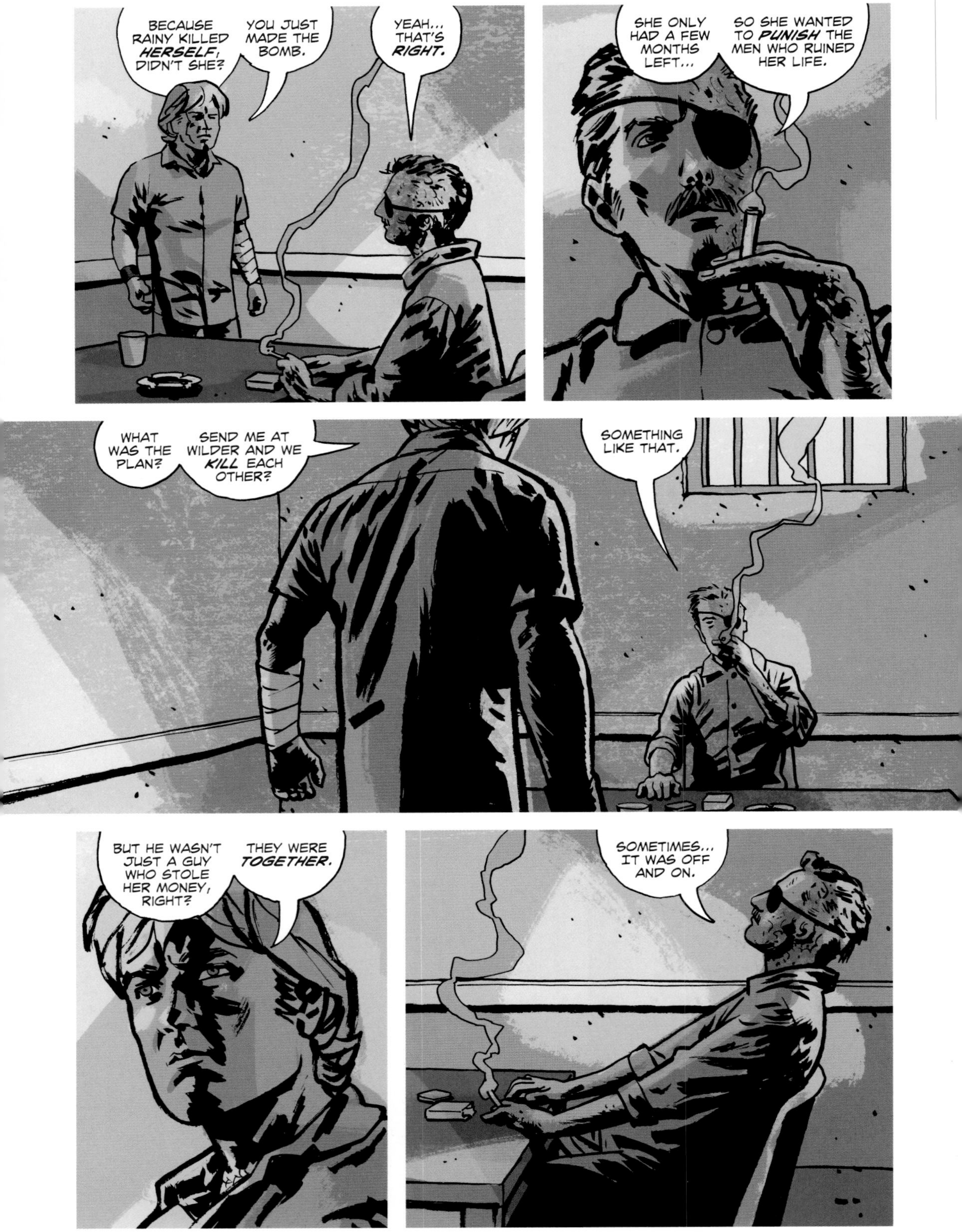
BECAUSE RAINY KILLED *HERSELF*, DIDN'T SHE?
YOU JUST MADE THE BOMB.
YEAH... THAT'S *RIGHT.*
SHE ONLY HAD A FEW MONTHS LEFT...
SO SHE WANTED TO *PUNISH* THE MEN WHO RUINED HER LIFE.
WHAT WAS THE PLAN?
SEND ME AT WILDER AND WE *KILL* EACH OTHER?
SOMETHING LIKE THAT.
BUT HE WASN'T JUST A GUY WHO STOLE HER MONEY, RIGHT?
THEY WERE *TOGETHER.*
SOMETIMES... IT WAS OFF AND ON.

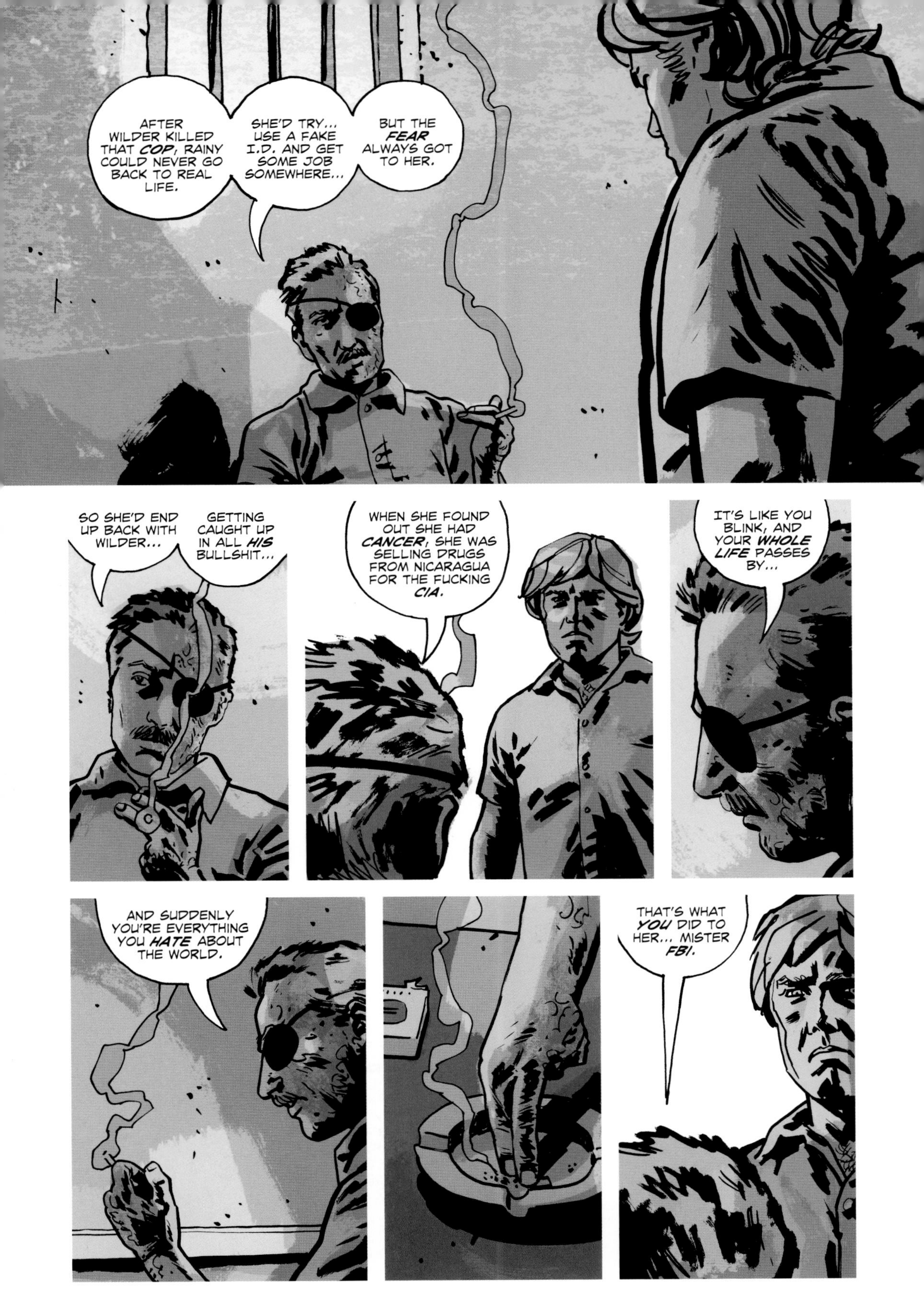
AFTER WILDER KILLED THAT *COP*, RAINY COULD NEVER GO BACK TO REAL LIFE.
SHE'D TRY... USE A FAKE I.D. AND GET SOME JOB SOMEWHERE...
BUT THE *FEAR* ALWAYS GOT TO HER.
SO SHE'D END UP BACK WITH WILDER...
GETTING CAUGHT UP IN ALL *HIS* BULLSHIT...
WHEN SHE FOUND OUT SHE HAD *CANCER*, SHE WAS SELLING DRUGS FROM NICARAGUA FOR THE FUCKING *CIA*.
IT'S LIKE YOU BLINK, AND YOUR *WHOLE LIFE* PASSES BY...
AND SUDDENLY YOU'RE EVERYTHING YOU *HATE* ABOUT THE WORLD.
THAT'S WHAT *YOU* DID TO HER... MISTER *FBI*.

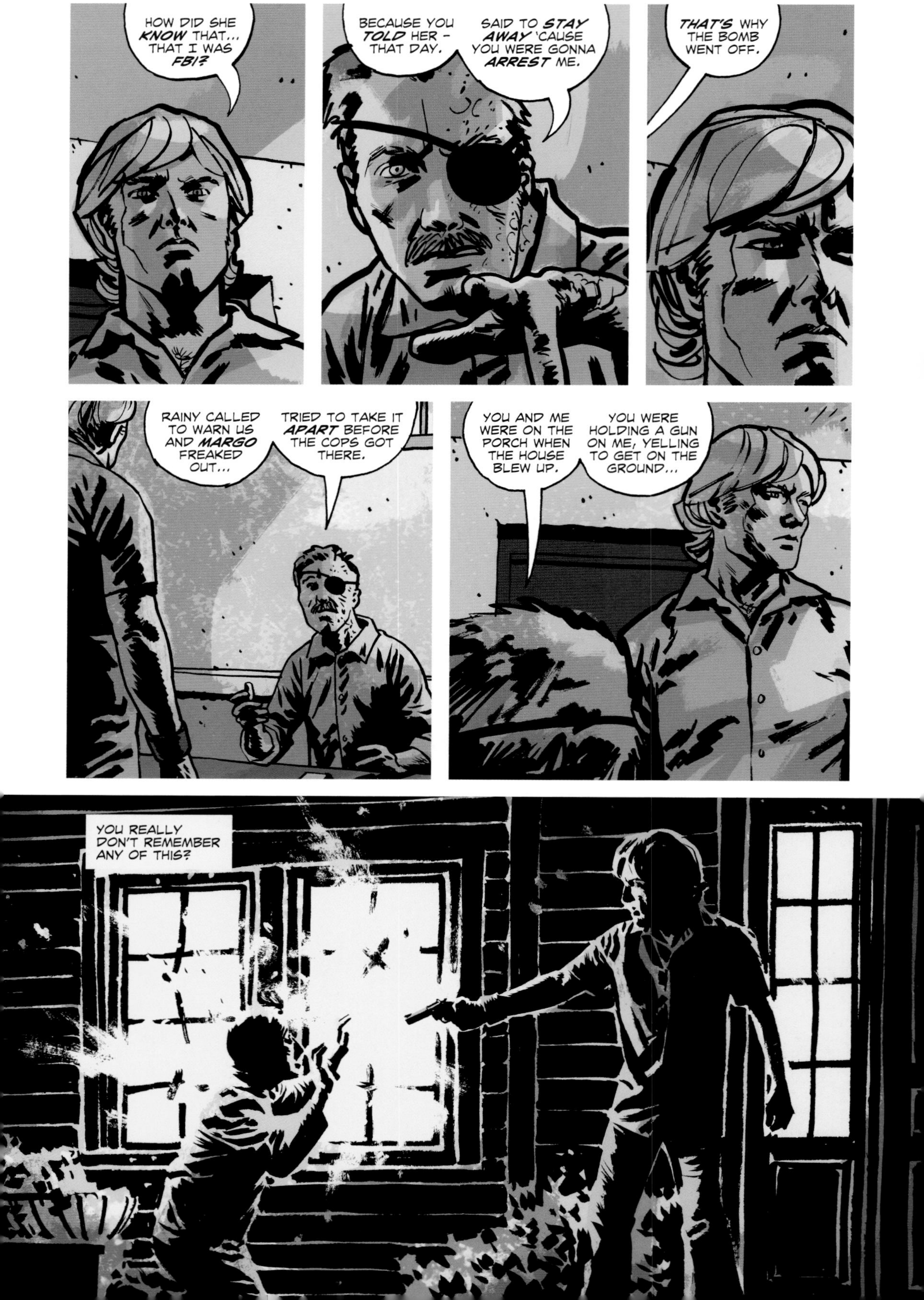

HOW DID SHE KNOW THAT... THAT I WAS FBI?
BECAUSE YOU TOLD HER - THAT DAY.
SAID TO STAY AWAY 'CAUSE YOU WERE GONNA ARREST ME.
THAT'S WHY THE BOMB WENT OFF.
RAINY CALLED TO WARN US AND MARGO FREAKED OUT...
TRIED TO TAKE IT APART BEFORE THE COPS GOT THERE.
YOU AND ME WERE ON THE PORCH WHEN THE HOUSE BLEW UP.
YOU WERE HOLDING A GUN ON ME, YELLING TO GET ON THE GROUND...
YOU REALLY DON'T REMEMBER ANY OF THIS?

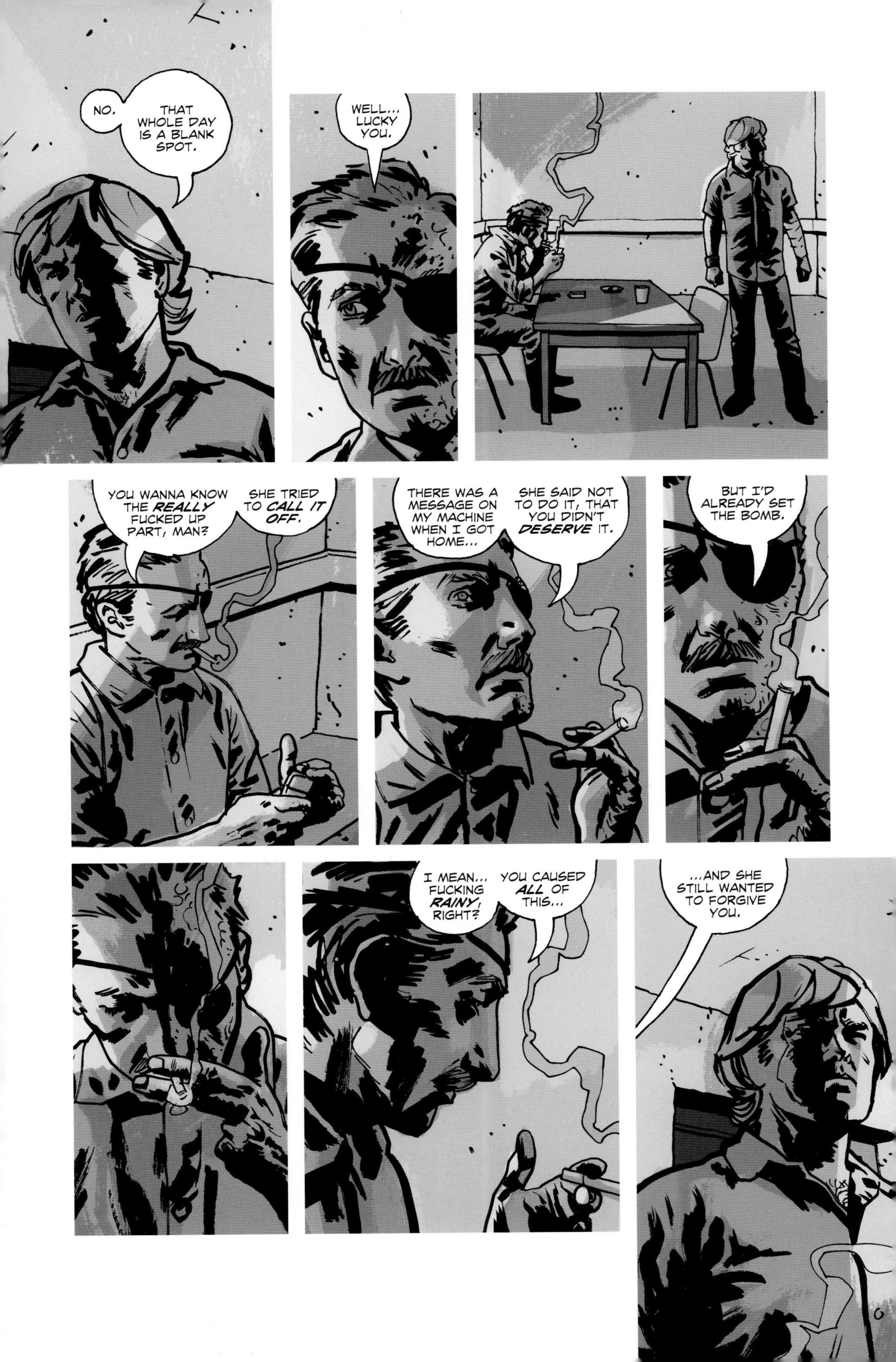
NO.
THAT WHOLE DAY IS A BLANK SPOT.
WELL... LUCKY YOU.
YOU WANNA KNOW THE REALLY FUCKED UP PART, MAN?
SHE TRIED TO CALL IT OFF.
THERE WAS A MESSAGE ON MY MACHINE WHEN I GOT HOME...
SHE SAID NOT TO DO IT, THAT YOU DIDN'T DESERVE IT.
BUT I'D ALREADY SET THE BOMB.
I MEAN... FUCKING RAINY, RIGHT?
YOU CAUSED ALL OF THIS...
...AND SHE STILL WANTED TO FORGIVE YOU.

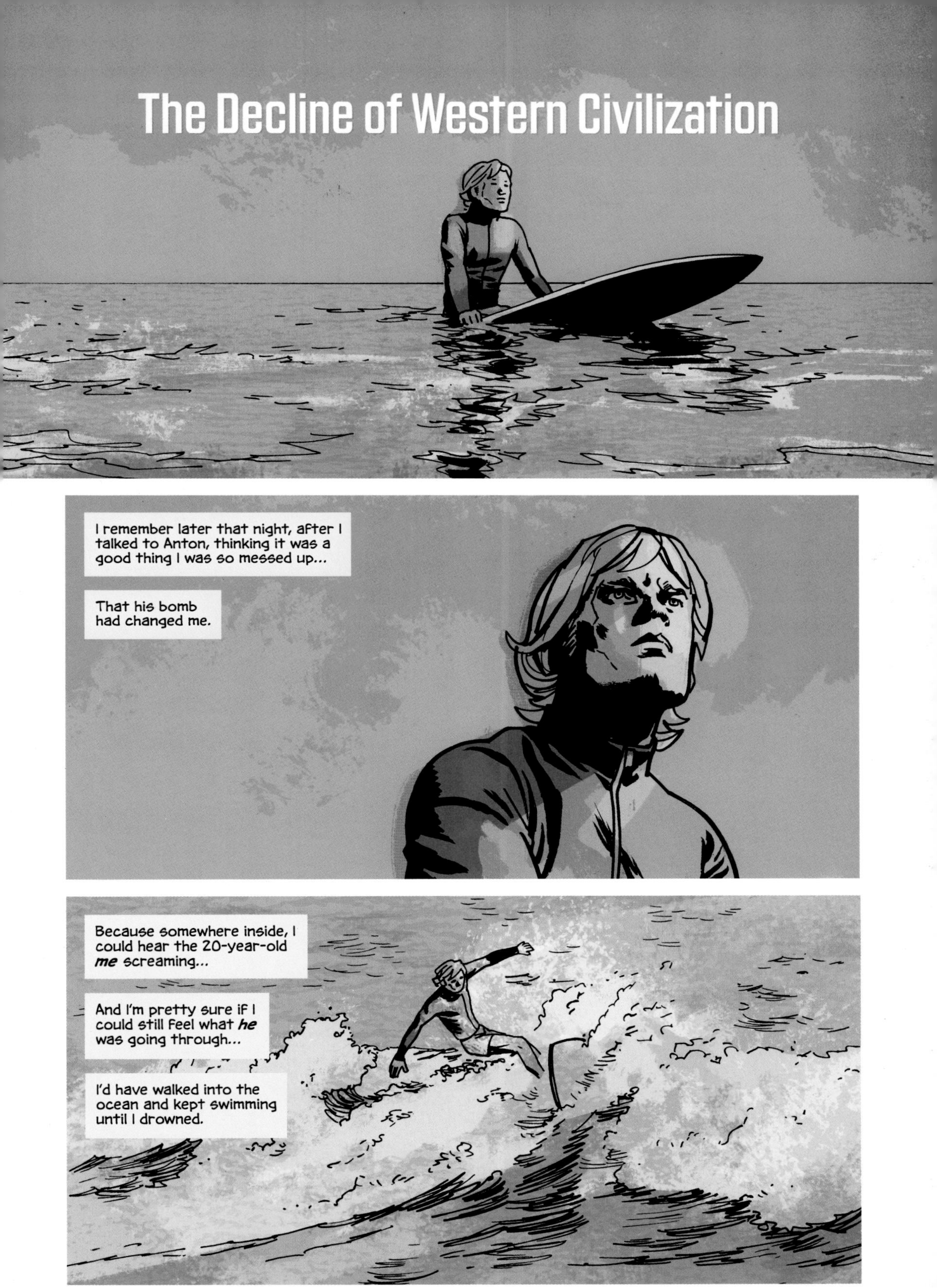
The Decline of Western Civilization
I remember later that night, after I talked to Anton, thinking it was a good thing I was so messed up...
That his bomb had changed me.
Because somewhere inside, I could hear the 20-year-old *me* screaming...
And I'm pretty sure if I could still feel what *he* was going through...
I'd have walked into the ocean and kept swimming until I drowned.

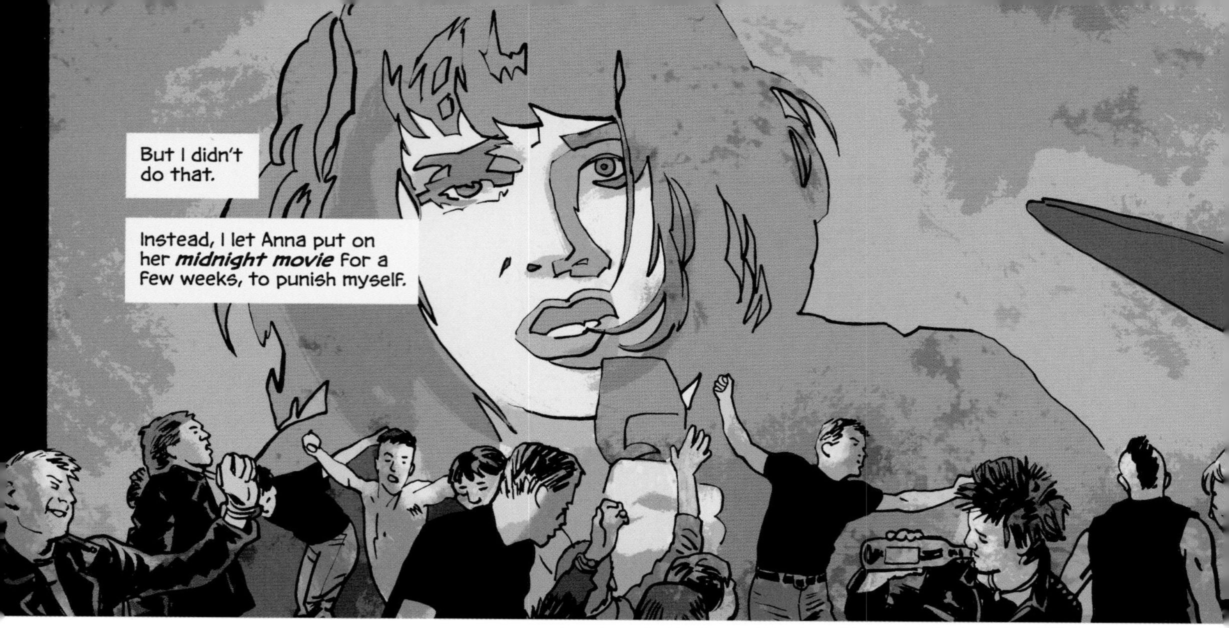
But I didn't do that.
Instead, I let Anna put on her ***midnight movie*** for a few weeks, to punish myself.

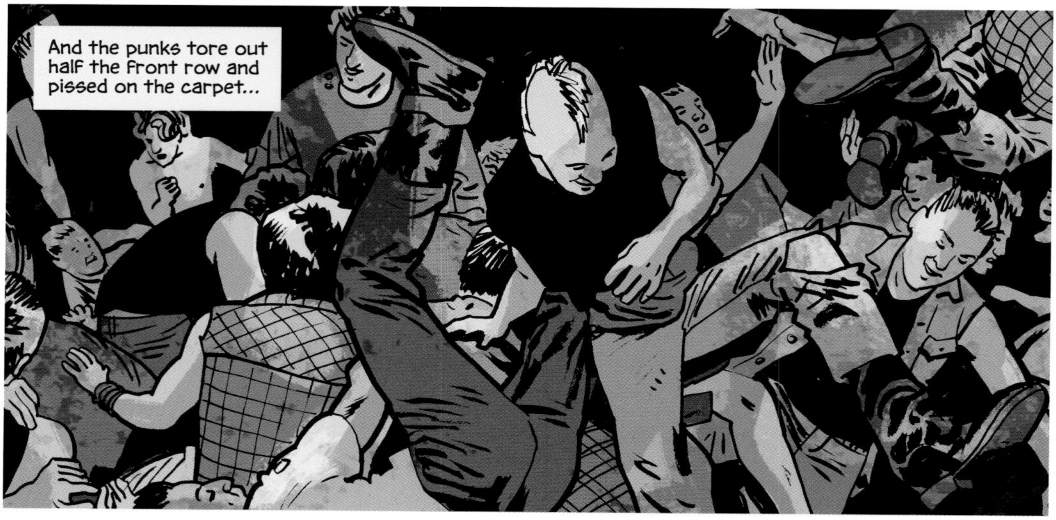
And the punks tore out half the front row and pissed on the carpet...

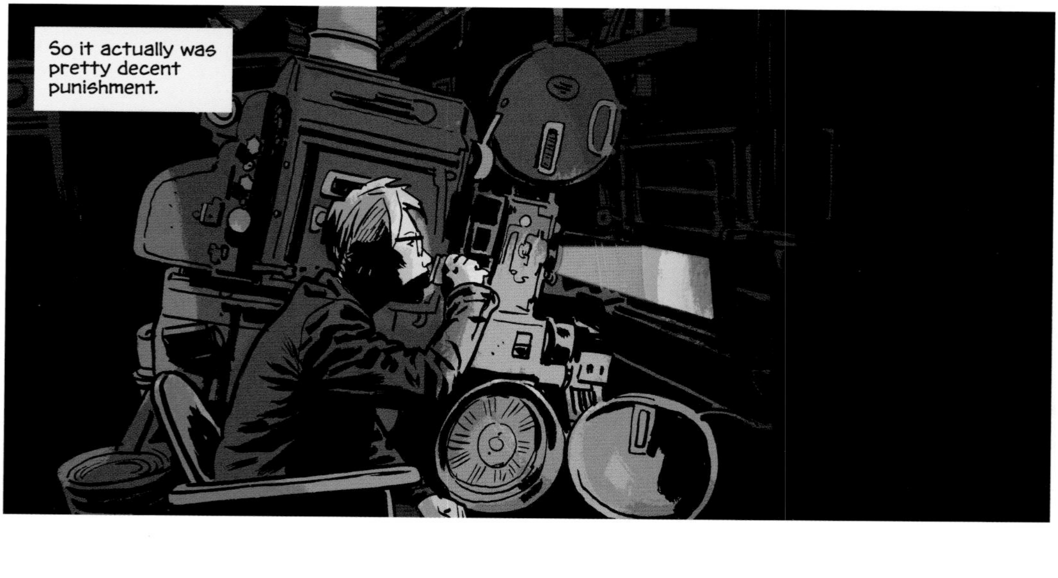
So it actually was pretty decent punishment.

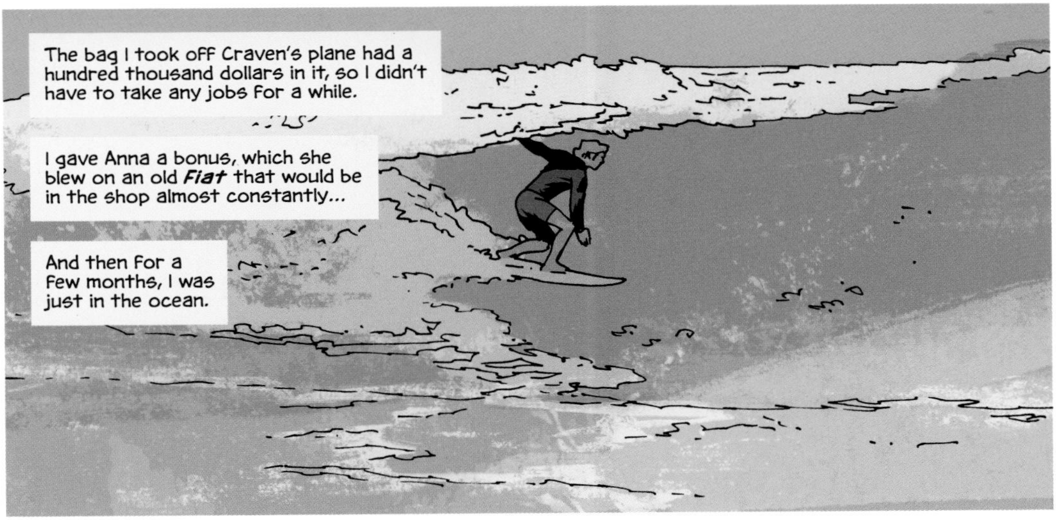
The bag I took off Craven's plane had a hundred thousand dollars in it, so I didn't have to take any jobs for a while.
I gave Anna a bonus, which she blew on an old *Fiat* that would be in the shop almost constantly...
And then for a few months, I was just in the ocean.

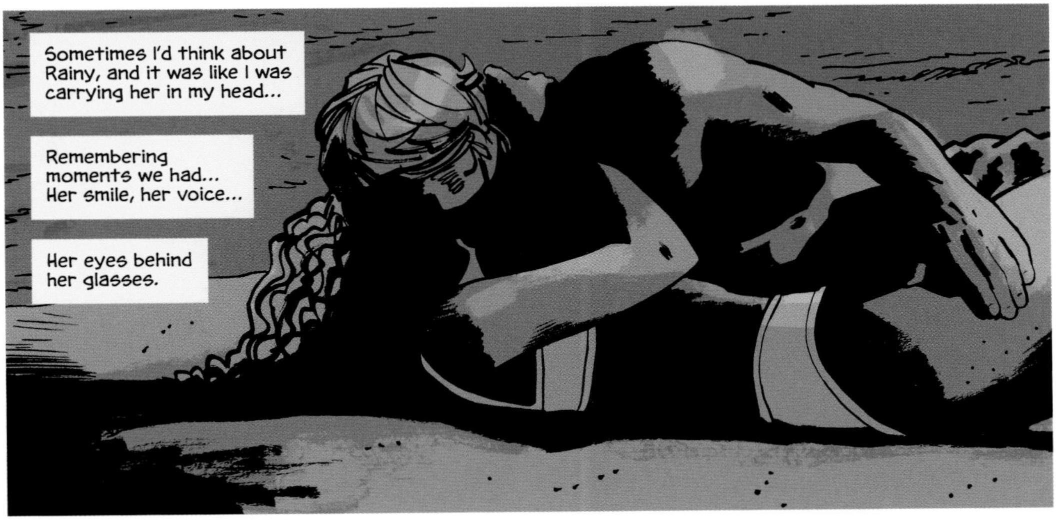
Sometimes I'd think about Rainy, and it was like I was carrying her in my head...
Remembering moments we had... Her smile, her voice...
Her eyes behind her glasses.

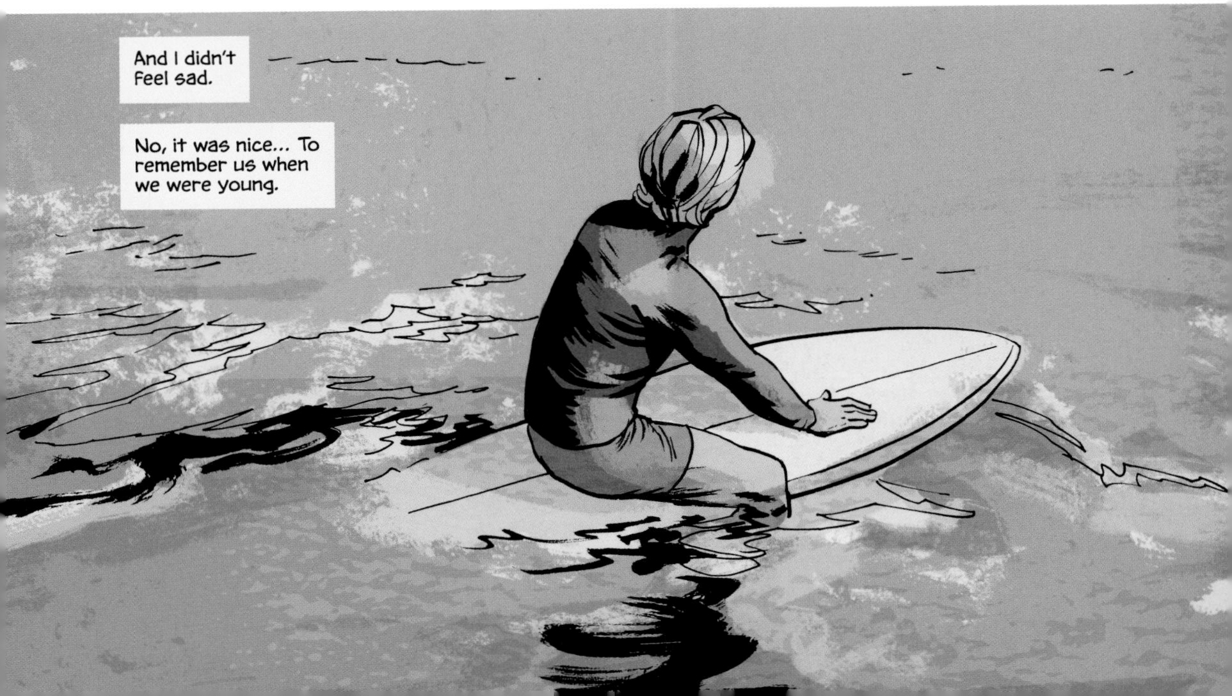
And I didn't feel sad.
No, it was nice... To remember us when we were young.

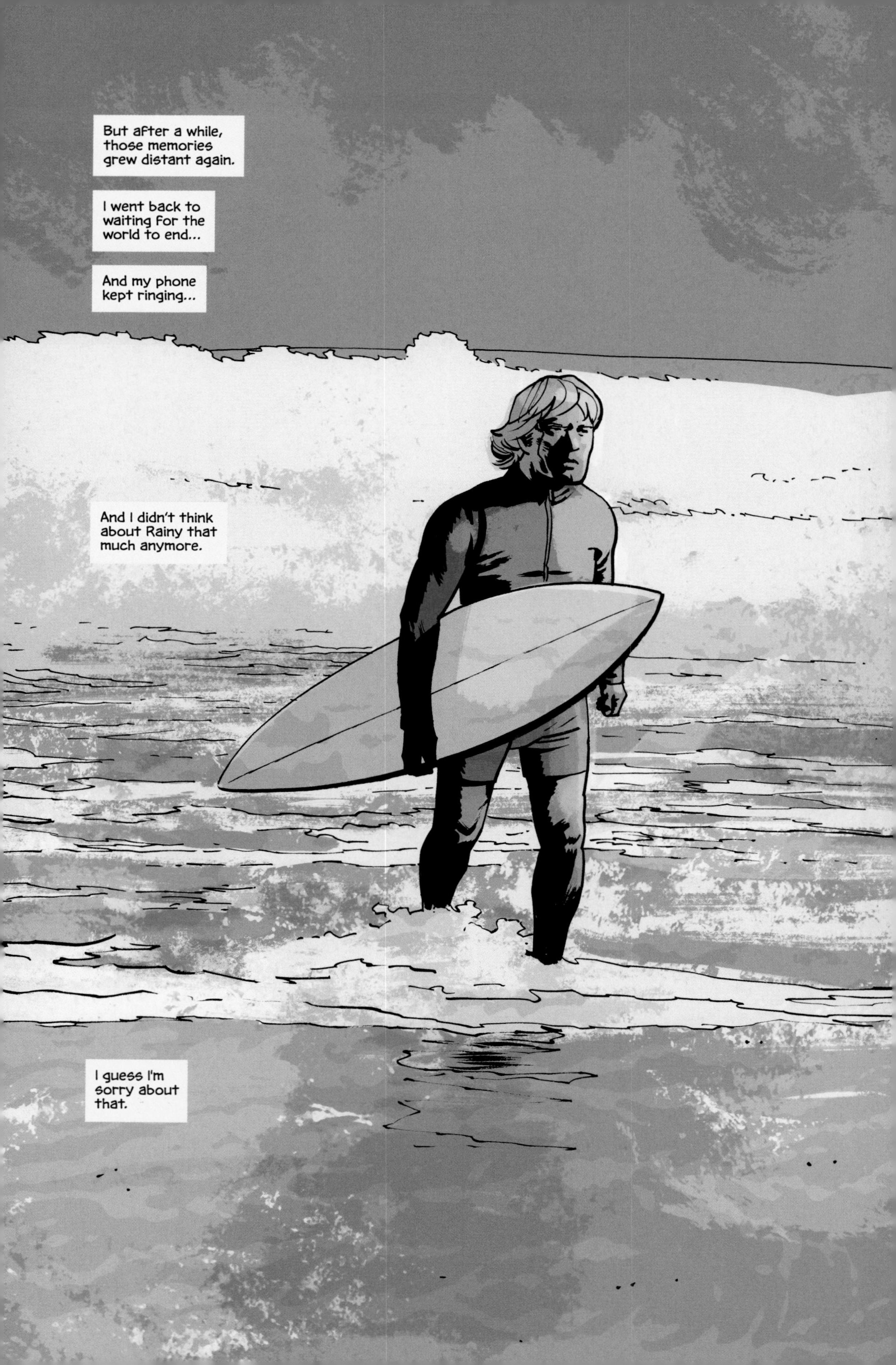
But after a while, those memories grew distant again.
I went back to waiting for the world to end...
And my phone kept ringing...
And I didn't think about Rainy that much anymore.
I guess I'm sorry about that.

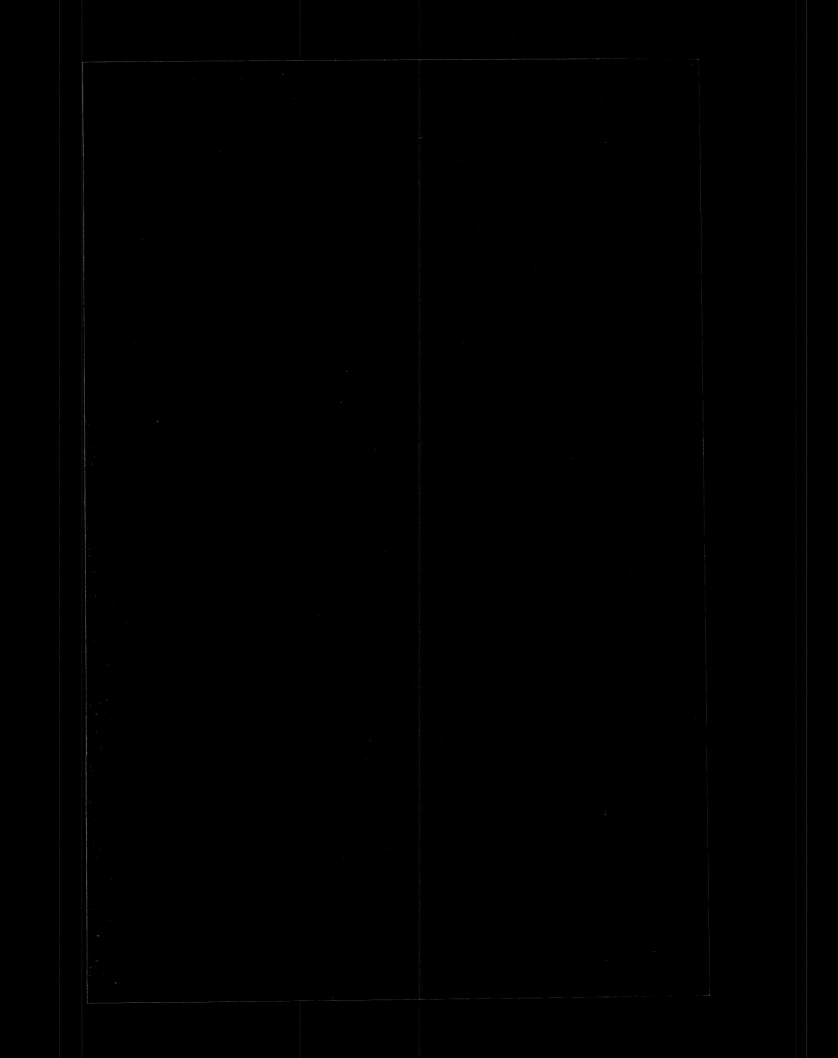

Afterword

When I was growing up, the walls of whatever home we lived in were always covered in bookcases. My dad was an avid reader and collector, and he was constantly reading three or four different books. And he wasn't a snob about it, he'd read Nabokov and Chandler or Ludlum one right after the other. As a kid, though, I was naturally drawn to the colorful images on the series pulp books that he read — the recurring adventures of detectives or roughnecks or spies. That's probably where the first seed of Ethan Reckless was planted, watching my dad lose himself in some thriller or mystery with a cool painted cover.

And for years I've wanted to do something along those lines in comics, our version of that kind of series paperback "hero" — especially after seeing how Darwyn Cooke had adapted Richard Stark's PARKER books into amazing graphic novels. I wished we could do something like that, a series of full-length pulp books, but it felt unfeasible. Until this point, other than two short novellas, all our work has been serialized first, and that was the treadmill we were on for close to twenty years. We put out 10 to 12 comics a year, and then collected them in trades and hardbacks, and that was how we did it. But then the pandemic hit, and the comics market was shut down for months, and that changed everything.

We'd been about to start something else, but stuck at home with the world falling apart, I found myself going back to some old favorite series detectives, and wanting to give that same kind of escape to our readers, too. To create an outsider with a sense of justice, who you root for and want to see what they get up to next. So one morning I just started filling up a notebook with character ideas and details... the Navy brat childhood (which was my childhood, too, but Ethan is much older than me), his COINTELPRO and Weather Underground days and how they ended, the early '80s Southern California setting, the abandoned movie theater/office ... and the 800 number. It all came together like I'd been secretly thinking of it my entire life. Ethan Reckless would be our take on a classic series character, but with a different edge, and using his point of view to look back at when the world made a little more sense, yet still felt like it was doomed.

I knew the only way to do this idea right was as graphic novels, and since I had a notebook full of more Ethan Reckless ideas, we decided to do something unheard of in US comics, and put out three of these books over the course of one year. Which hopefully will not kill either one of us, or Jake (less likely as he's much younger). But this was how paperback original characters used to launch, and I wanted to be sure our readers knew they wouldn't have to wait long, even though we're not on the shelves every month anymore.

So, I hope you enjoyed your first time out with Ethan Reckless. On the following pages, you'll find an ad for the next book, and several pages of art process for how Sean made this one look so amazing.

Ed Brubaker
October 2020

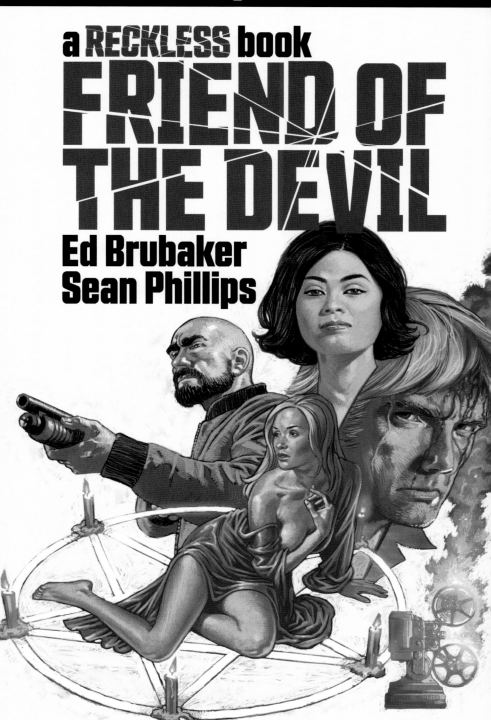

a RECKLESS book
FRIEND OF
THE DEVIL

Ed Brubaker
Sean Phillips

Process

PAGE TWO

1—Full tier – And now we meet the main villain of this book – Wilder. He's in his mid-to-late 30s, and looks tough. Like an ex-biker who's gone legit or something – he's an ex-hippie bomber who's been living on the run for a decade, robbing banks and smuggling drugs, and he's gone from true believer to totally corrupt murderer in his years on the run. He's wearing mirrored sunglasses, and has sort of longish hair, and a mustache that's very 1979. He's standing in a doorway to a back office room inside this building, holding a half-smoked cigarette, ready to hit it again. He's in a wide-collared shirt, with the sleeves rolled up. He's got some rings on his fingers. In general he looks like a mean and predatory man, showing no fear.

>WILDER: And if you got a good enough story, then there's this guy that shows

>up...

>WILDER: ...And he solves your problem for you.

2—Wilder inhales on the cigarette again, raising his brows.

>OFF: Is there a question in there?

3—Wilder exhales smoke, tilting his head a bit.

>WILDER: Yeah, there is.

>WILDER: You're the guy? From the phone number?

4—Then he inhales again.

>OFF: I guess so.

5—Full tier – We're sort of behind him Wilder as he stubs out his cigarette in an ashtray on a nearby work bench along the wall. Past him, we see a man in shadows in the background, with pallets of crates behind him. This is who Wilder is talking to.

>WILDER: You make a lot of money doing that?

>WILDER: Getting into shit that's none of your business?

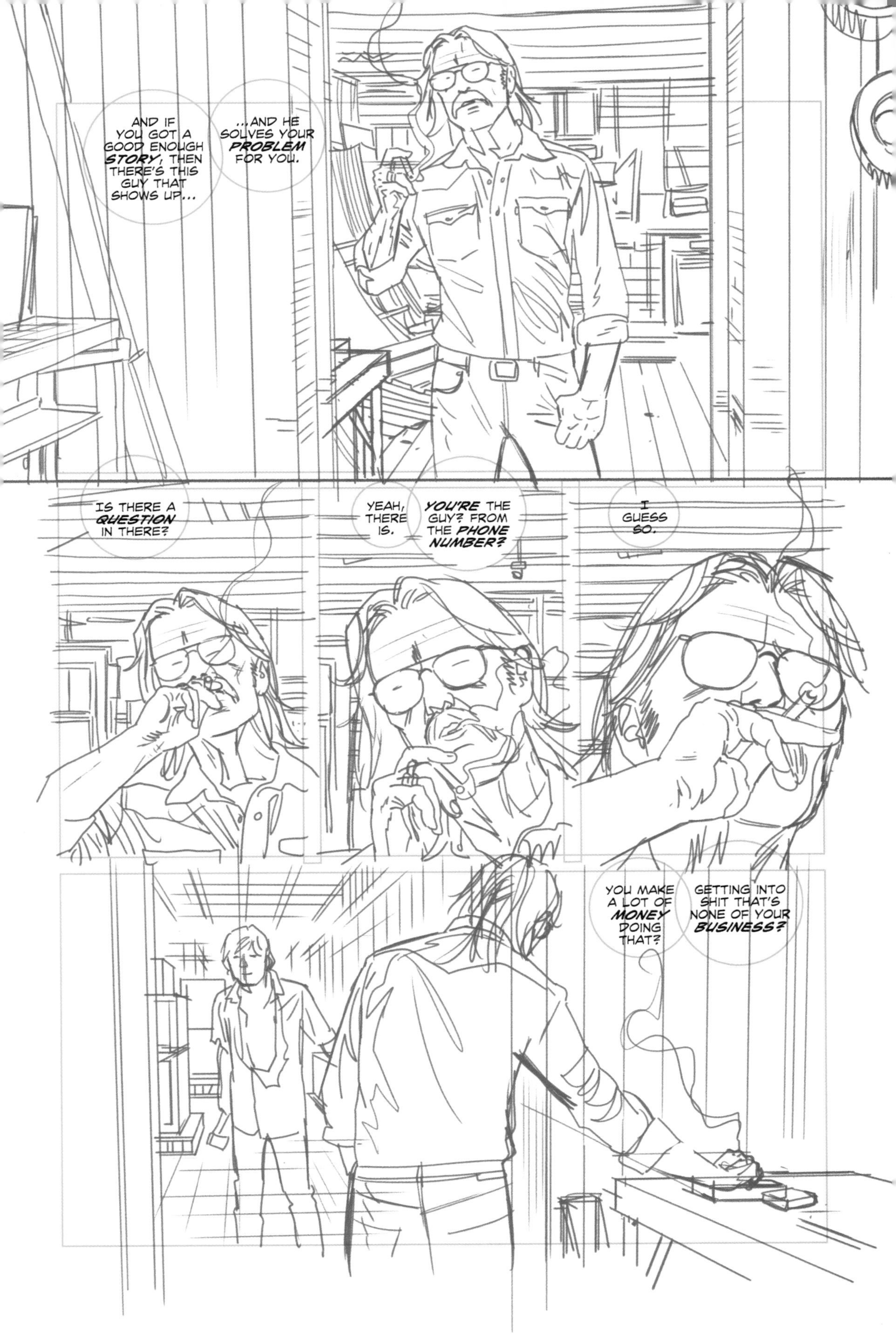
AND IF YOU GOT A GOOD ENOUGH STORY, THEN THERE'S THIS GUY THAT SHOWS UP...
...AND HE SOLVES YOUR PROBLEM FOR YOU.
IS THERE A QUESTION IN THERE?
YEAH, THERE IS.
YOU'RE THE GUY? FROM THE PHONE NUMBER?
I GUESS SO.
YOU MAKE A LOT OF MONEY DOING THAT?
GETTING INTO SHIT THAT'S NONE OF YOUR BUSINESS?

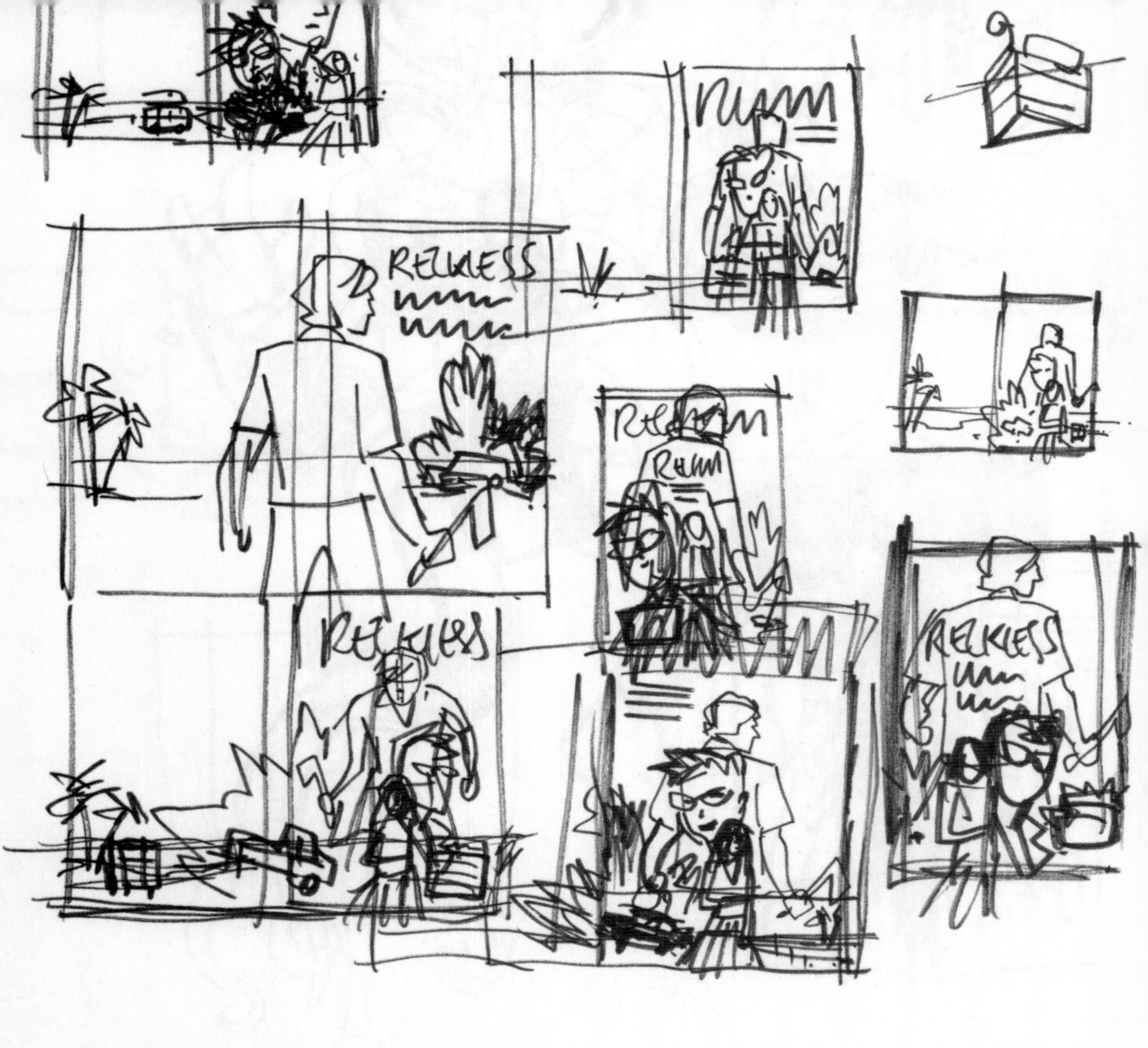
RECKLESS

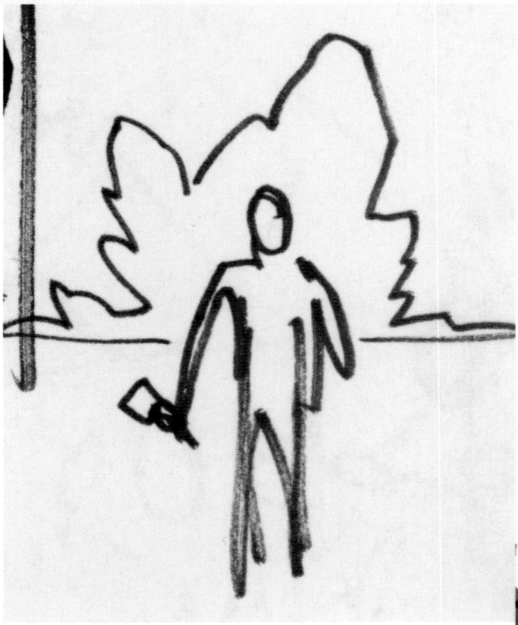

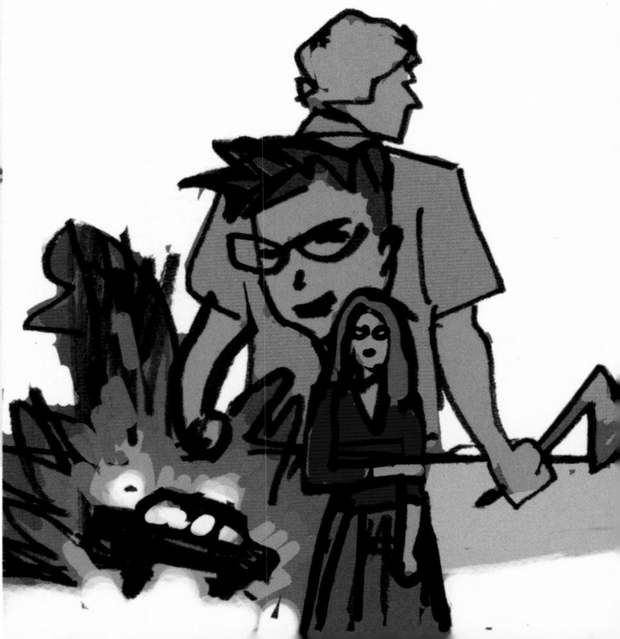

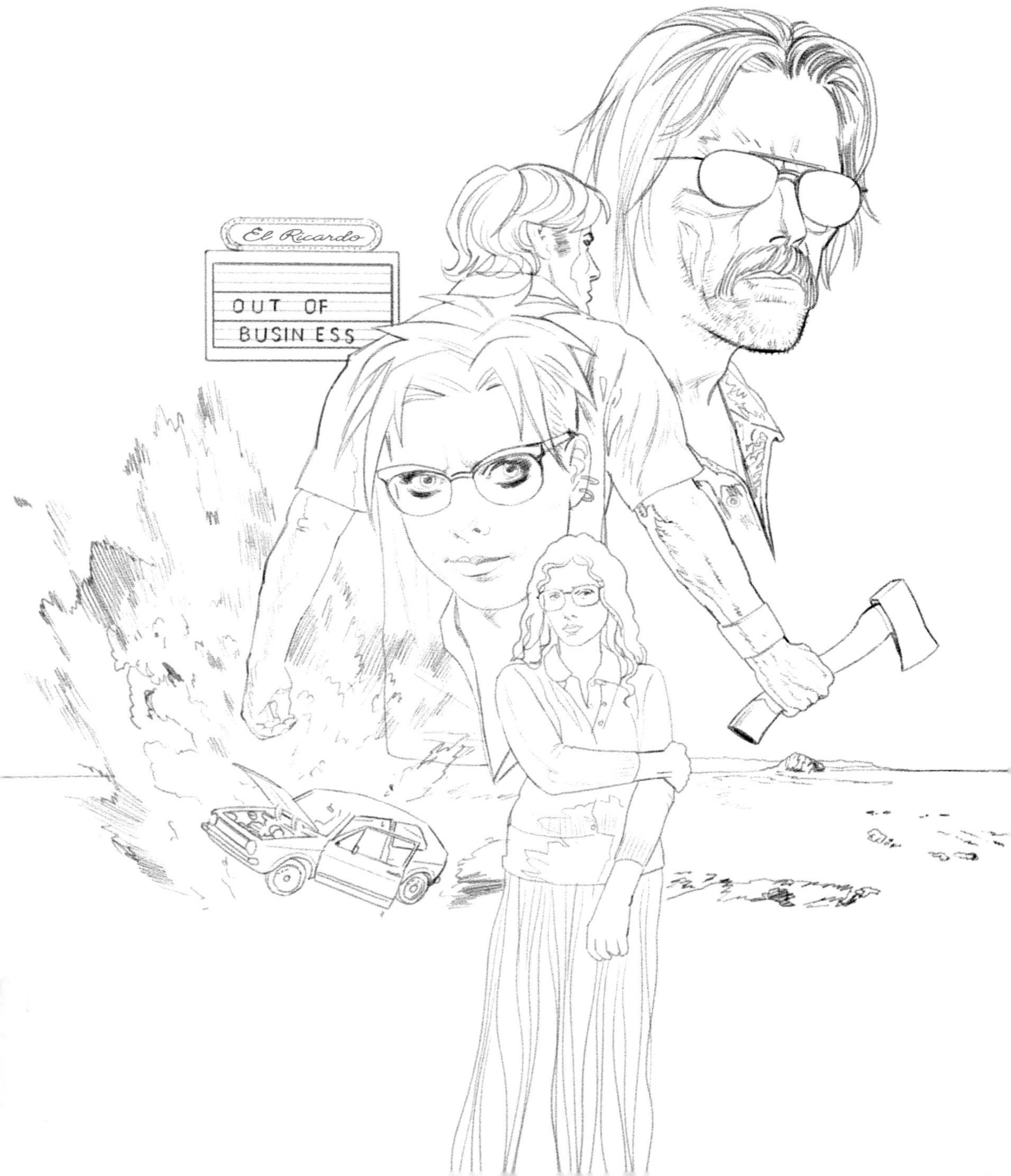
El Ricardo
OUT OF
BUSIN ESS

And Look For More From
Brubaker and Phillips

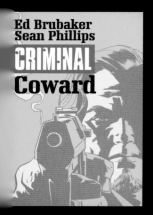

Ed Brubaker
Sean Phillips
CRIMINAL
Coward

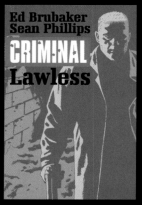

Ed Brubaker
Sean Phillips
CRIMINAL
Lawless

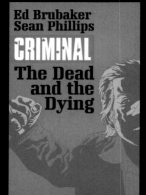

Ed Brubaker
Sean Phillips
CRIMINAL
**The Dead
and the
Dying**

Ed Brubaker
Sean Phillips
CRIMINAL
**Bad
Night**

ED BRUBAKER   SEAN PHILLIPS
FATALE
BOOK ONE
DEATH CHASES ME

ED BRUBAKER   SEAN PHILLIPS
FATALE
BOOK TWO
THE DEVIL'S BUSINESS

ED BRUBAKER   SEAN PHILLIPS
FATALE
BOOK THREE
WEST OF HELL

ED BRUBAKER   SEAN PHILLIPS
FATALE
BOOK FOUR
PRAY FOR RAIN

Volume One
**KILL or
be KILLED**
Ed Brubaker
Sean Phillips
Elizabeth Breitweiser

Volume Two
**KILL or
be KILLED**
Ed Brubaker
Sean Phillips
Elizabeth Breitweiser

Volume Three
**KILL or
be KILLED**
Ed Brubaker
Sean Phillips
Elizabeth Breitweiser

Volume Four
**KILL or
be KILLED**
Ed Brubaker
Sean Phillips
Elizabeth Breitweiser

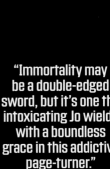
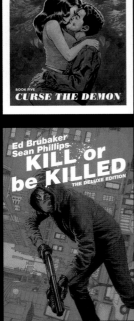

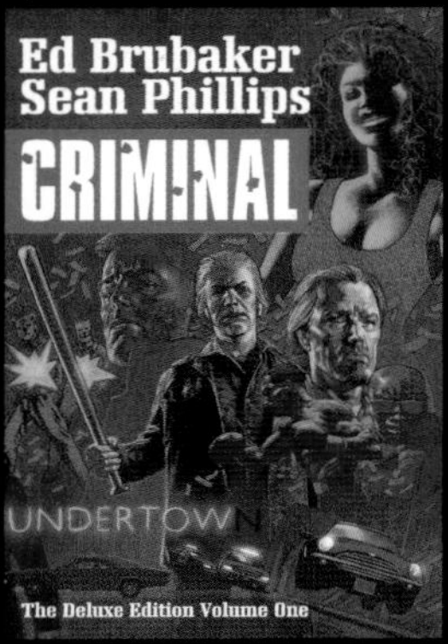
Ed Brubaker
Sean Phillips
CRIMINAL
UNDERTOWN
The Deluxe Edition Volume One

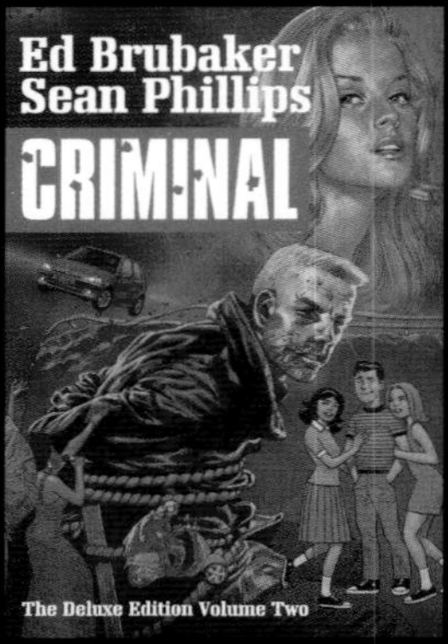
Ed Brubaker
Sean Phillips
CRIMINAL
The Deluxe Edition Volume Two

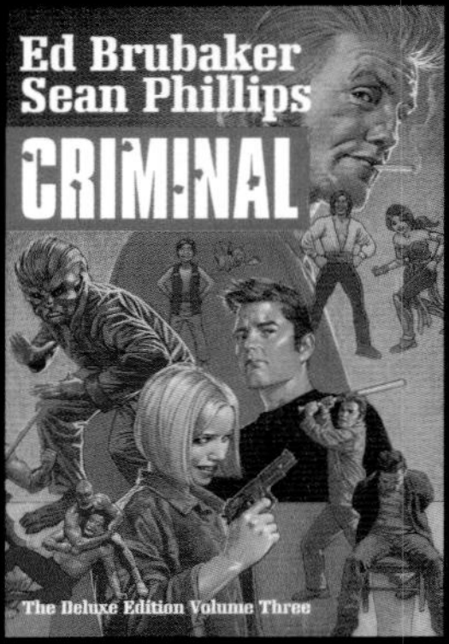
Ed Brubaker
Sean Phillips
CRIMINAL
The Deluxe Edition Volume Three

"Sean Phillips and Ed Brubaker represent the gold standard for comics noir - brutal, beautiful and best."

— Ian Rankin, author of the John Rebus novels

"The powerhouse creative team of Brubaker and Phillips combine elements of noir and coming-of-age stories in this psychologically and emotionally complex drama about desperate men and women daring to strive for better lives in a violent world where hope and love are dangerous liabilities."

— Library Journal

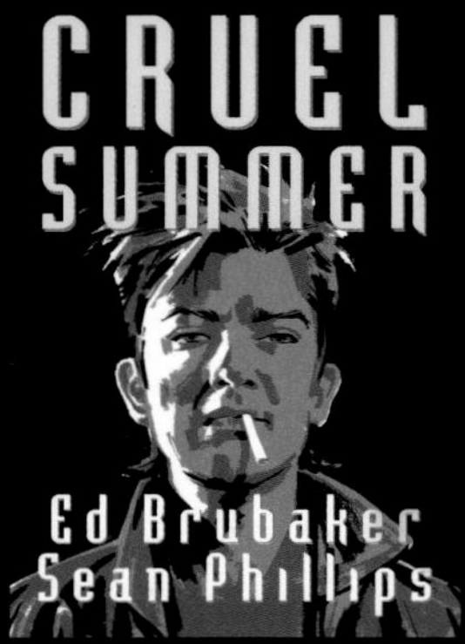
CRUEL
SUMMER
Ed Brubaker
Sean Phillips

Newsweek's Best Comic Books of 2018

Thrillist's Best Comics & Graphic Novels

Diamond Gem Award for Best Original Graphic Novel 2018

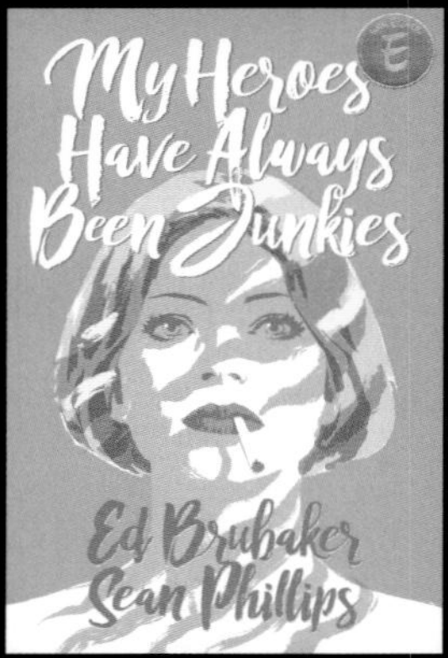
My Heroes Have Always Been Junkies
Ed Brubaker
Sean Phillips

Eisner Award Winner – Best Original Graphic Novel

Ringo Award Winner – Best Original Graphic Novel

"Far and away the best work yet from one of the best teams in the history of comics."

— Brian K. Vaughan (PAPER GIRLS, SAGA)

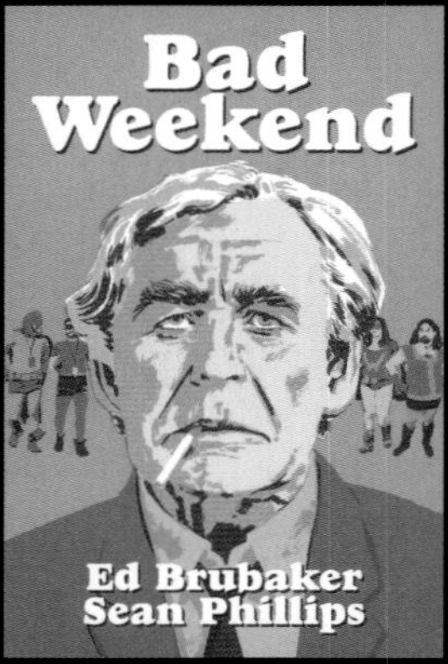
Bad
Weekend
Ed Brubaker
Sean Phillips

"Easily one of the best comics of the 21st century... a story that reflects the crooked soul of our times."

— Tom King (Mr Miracle, Sheriff of Babylon)

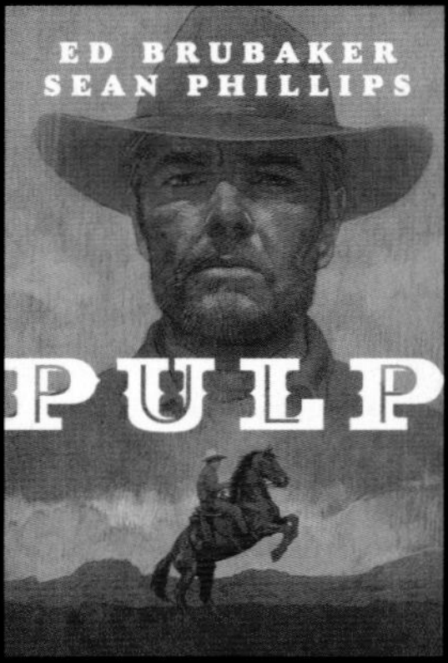
ED BRUBAKER
SEAN PHILLIPS
PULP

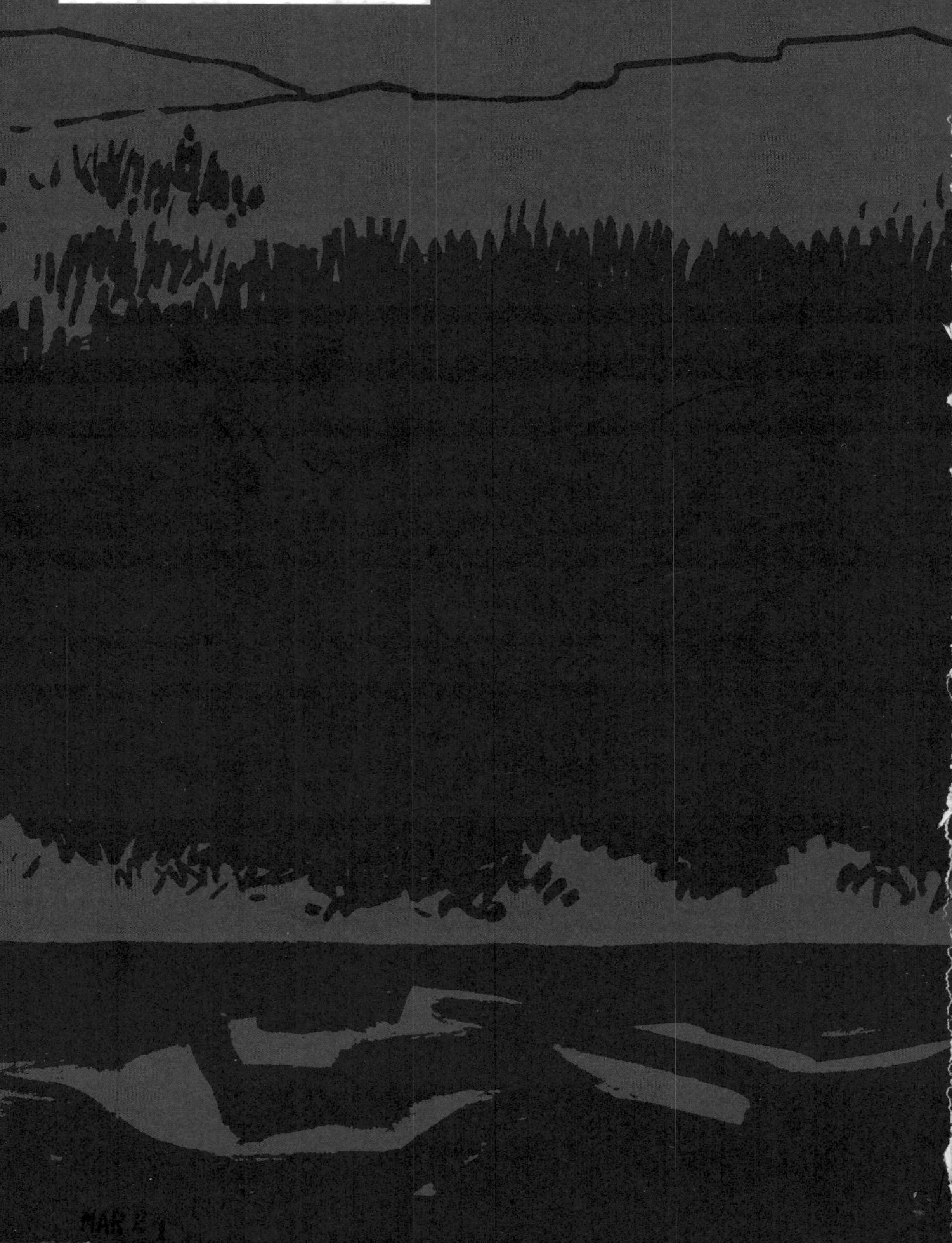